M.B. Vincent is a married couple. She writes romantic fiction; he writes songs and TV theme tunes. They've even written musicals together. They work at opposite ends of the house, and they meet in the middle to write about Jess Castle and Castle Kidbury, the West Country's goriest market town. When they're not making up books, tunes and mysteries, they head out in an open-top car and explore. They particularly like West Country market towns ...

M.B. VINCENT

Jess Castle
and the
EYEBALLS
of DEATH

SIMON &
SCHUSTER

London · New York · Sydney · Toronto · New Delhi

A CBS COMPANY

First published in Great Britain by Simon & Schuster UK Ltd, 2018
A CBS COMPANY

Copyright © Just Grand Partnership, 2018

The right of M.B. Vincent to be identified as author
of this work has been asserted in accordance with the
Copyright, Designs and Patents Act, 1988.

1 3 5 7 9 10 8 6 4 2

Simon & Schuster UK Ltd
1st Floor
222 Gray's Inn Road
London WC1X 8HB

Simon & Schuster Australia, Sydney
Simon & Schuster India, New Delhi

www.simonandschuster.co.uk
www.simonandschuster.com.au
www.simonandschuster.co.in

A CIP catalogue record for this book
is available from the British Library

Paperback ISBN: 978-1-4711-6823-9
eBook ISBN: 978-1-4711-6824-6
Audio ISBN: 978-1-4711-7697-5

Typeset in Sabon by M Rules
Printed and bound by CPI Group (UK) Ltd, Croydon, CR0 4YY

Simon & Schuster UK Ltd are committed to sourcing paper
that is made from wood grown in sustainable forests and support the Forest
Stewardship Council, the leading international forest certification organisation.
Our books displaying the FSC logo are printed on FSC certified paper.

For Niamh Strachan,
the wonderchild who's growing up
to be a wonderwoman

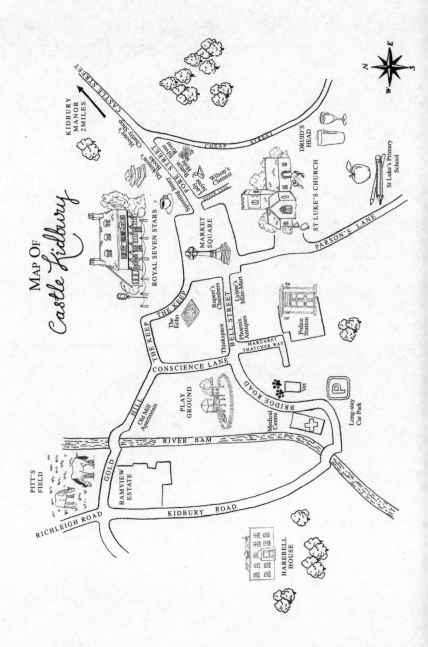

MAP OF
Castle Kidbury

From the *Kidbury Echo*, page 3:

'MARROW MAN' TRIUMPHS AGAIN

Local resident Keith Dike yet again took the top prize in the marrow section at the Castle Kidbury Show. Keith (pictured right with his mammoth gourd) puts his three-year winning streak down to his special compost. 'It's a closely guarded secret,' he said as he accepted the coveted Gold Rosette and a £10 gift voucher for Lynne's Minimart. Keith vowed to return next year, with an even bigger marrow.

GOLD HILL

Danny was walking his dog.

'Just walking my dog,' he murmured to himself. 'Just walking my dog.' He reached down to pat Jumble and she leapt at his fingers before darting away. 'Anybody asks, I'm just walking my dog.'

They trudged together up the slope. Gold Hill was the highest point above Castle Kidbury, but Danny didn't look down at the houses. He didn't notice the streetlamps flicker off as the new day broke. Something up ahead held his attention. Something familiar, that today looked different, and odd.

'Come on, Jumble.' Danny narrowed his slanted eyes at the scarecrow, troubled that its hat seemed to be missing. He didn't notice the aqua-blue Morris Traveller below, on the road that approached the hill.

The car's progress was slow on the empty stretch. To one side, caravans and tents gathered to disfigure the green and pleasant land. The car stopped at the traffic lights on the outskirts of the town proper, even though they shone green, inviting it in.

'No hat!' Danny's breathing was laboured. The scarecrow was a landmark, even though its function was obscure, with no crops to guard at the top of the hill. It was an unchanging feature of these 'walks' with Jumble. 'And no overcoat.'

Below, the old Morris avoided the town centre, beetling instead through the crescents and closes of a hinterland housing estate.

Now the dog was entranced by the scarecrow, when usually she barrelled past, nose to the ground. Jumble snuffled at the dark figure outlined against the brightening sky. She growled, her small stiff body trembling.

'Jumble?' Danny and his dog were best friends, apart, of course, from *her*, who wasn't exactly a best friend, but was something more, something special. He was tuned into her the way he was tuned into Jumble, and he'd never seen his dog maddened like this. As if bursting to tell him something, but unable to tear its eyes away from the scarecrow.

There was a smell. Of wrong things. Of things that had gone off. Danny could almost taste it. He was scared, but nobody had told his feet; they carried him towards the scarecrow.

The dot that was a car left the maze of the estate and had a wide road all to itself.

On the hill, Danny fell to his knees and wailed.

The scarecrow should have been a collection of sticks, its twiggy arms stuck through ancient sleeves, a trilby jammed on its weathered football face. Instead, it was solid and meaty. It was naked, streaked all over with jammy blood. It was a man, arms out, gory head down, nailed in place like that Jesus his nan was so keen on. But a Jesus frozen in an agonising scream.

Danny couldn't stop crying. He knew that somehow he'd be in terrible trouble over this.

The crucified man leant forward, pinioned by bony wrists and ankles. As if he was straining to be free, to walk down to Castle Kidbury and beg for help.

A breeze lifted his gummy hair. Blackish blood filled hollow eye sockets.

Danny turned and ran. He didn't look back in case the Jesus man had ripped his nailed wrists from the wood and stepped down to follow him, bloody feet slithering on the wet grass. Danny stumbled and fell. He got up. He shouted; afterwards, he couldn't remember which words.

Far below, out of earshot, the car had stopped at the top of a winding drive. Eventually the driver's door opened and a figure got out, to be swallowed by a grand house.

Chapter 1

THE PRODIGAL DAUGHTER

Sunday 15 May

Jess let herself into Harebell House, relieved that her key still worked. Chintz. Flagstones. The tick of an inherited Grandfather clock.

Sundays in small market towns have their own special atmosphere, of bells and hush and a sense of *waiting*. In Harebell House it always felt like Sunday.

'Dad?' she called. He was an early riser, and Jess imagined him padding about somewhere in the rambling house's innards. 'Dad?' Slightly louder. Her voice echoed in the flagstone hall.

A door opened and a creature roared in, a flash of wheat-coloured fur. Moose jumped up at Jess, deliriously happy as only a dog can be.

'Moose!' Jess matched his enthusiasm, glad of its uncomplicated simplicity. 'Oh Moosey Moose!' She put her arms around him and smiled as he barked.

A woman stepped through a glazed door, a hen sitting complacently in her arms. Her broad face was pinkish. She was blonde, but country blonde, not town blonde.

Jess took a step backwards, let Moose drop. 'Who the hell are you?' The woman wore slippers, she noticed. She was perfectly at home, whoever she was.

'No, my darling,' said the stranger, an Eastern European rhythm to her words. 'Who hell are *you*?'

'I'm Jess,' said Jess. She glared, unable to dial it down.

'Ah, the famous Jess . . .' The woman looked her up and down. 'I see what your father means.'

'Where *is* my father?'

'Jimmy's out, darling.' Perhaps she saw the tremor that ran through Jess at such familiarity with the forbidding Judge James Castle. 'Don't worry, I'm not your new step-mummy.' She laughed, shoulders shaking, chicken juddering. 'Come on. Cup of tea, isn't it?'

The kitchen was its timeless self. Scuffed wooden table of enormous size. Scarred units painted cream. A self-important Aga. But it was shipshape, cleaner than it had ever been. Worktops scoured. Chrome gleaming.

'Sit.' The order was peremptory. The chicken was dropped out through an open window. 'Kettle is just boiled.'

Jess sat, like an obedient pet, in her habitual dark, shapeless separates that disguised the ins and outs of her body. Baggy tee over baggy skirt over leggings. She noticed that her Doc Martens had trailed mud into the pristine kitchen and felt pleased.

The teapot was new; Jess thought of it as an inter-loper, then caught herself thinking that and despaired. The teapot was just a teapot.

She pulled off her all-seasons knit hat and freed her disordered dark-brown hair, the same colour as her eyes. She folded her arms brusquely, more like a toddler than a woman in her early thirties. 'So ... do I get to know who you are?'

'My name, my darling, is Bogna. Not spelt like the seaside place.' She laughed again, that hearty laugh. 'I am housekeeper. I look after beautiful house.'

'Dad never said.'

'His head is full of serious stuff.' *Stoof*. Bogna's accent was soothing, despite her workmanlike way of moving and dressing. Battered jeans. A man's aged shirt. Somewhere in her fifties, she was a little battered herself, but radiant with it. 'Some days I barely see him. He is not like retired man. Always out. Or in his study.' *Stoody*.

'Is he, you know, okay?'

'You'll find out, my darling.'

Looking about her, Jess registered an absence. 'Where's Miffy?'

'Dead,' said Bogna.

'What?' The cat had warmed Harebell House laps for a decade. 'Nobody said ...'

'You weren't here, isn't it?'

They drank tea in silence. The garden beyond the windows gradually brightened, its topiary taking shape.

Jess stood and opened a kitchen cupboard. Cleaning products stared back at her. 'Oh. Biscuits?'

9

Bogna tutted. 'Not allowed.'

'Not ...?'

'The Judge must not get fat.'

Jess narrowed her eyes. 'Where's the biscuit tin gone?'

Bogna shrugged; she knew nothing of the tin's long history, of the part it played in comforting a younger Jess when she sloped in from school. 'Recycled, I suppose.'

Jess remembered the form of the tin, its ridges, the metallic sound of it. She mourned it keenly for a moment before noises outside made both women lift their heads.

Stamping of feet. A bicycle being parked in the glassed utility room to the side of the kitchen. A clearing of a throat. The door opened, and His Honour Judge Castle QC entered, head down to remove a sperm-shaped helmet, saying, 'Twenty K, Bogna! Mostly uphill, to boot. Not bad at all.'

The Judge was all in black Lycra, his long, sexagenarian body sleek and, to Jess's eyes, inappropriately lithe. She mentally pixelated certain regions.

Bending to pull at the Velcro straps on his cycling shoes, the Judge said, 'Something's going on up by Gold Hill. Three police cars sped past me. Almost—' He straightened and saw Jess, who had half stood to greet him. 'Ah. I see.'

He left the room.

Bogna pulled in her chin. 'What's bitten *him* on bum?'

'I'll go to my room.' Jess picked up her rucksack. 'Unless that's been recycled?'

Harebell House was a labyrinth of genteel good taste. Tucked away down a short wallpapered hall off a landing, the room was exactly as it had been through Jess's teenage years. Striped walls. Louvred built-in wardrobe. Avocado sink. Ruffled blind.

The record player she'd refused to retire sat boxily on the floor. Propped against it, an LP. Elvis's chubby cheeks and killer smile. *GI Blues* was an album she'd almost worn out, despite its lack of cool. 'Wooden Heart' was the most worn of all the tracks.

She sat on the bed, then let herself lie back, giving into the feelings that crowded her. It was comforting to be in a room so familiar. It was also pathetic.

More pathetic than comforting, she thought. Jess was back in the place she least wanted to be.

The tape recorder in Interview Room One whirred, registering nothing but the slither of fabric as DS John Eden crossed his legs. He gazed at Danny, who kept his eyes on the floor.

Danny was clearly frightened at finding himself in Castle Kidbury police station. Slumped, plump thighs apart, his mouth hanging open, he hadn't said a word when DS Eden explained that he wasn't under caution. The Appropriate Adult – a permed woman whose face still bore the marks of her pillow – seemed satisfied that Danny understood what was going on, but Eden wasn't so sure.

'You know me, Danny,' he said, leaning forward. 'I gave a talk on personal safety at the Trust.' Danny worked part-time at a charitable trust over in Richleigh. 'You can talk to me.' DS Eden pushed a packet towards him. 'Come on. Say something before I eat all the Maltesers.'

Danny was locked into a private place, and DS Eden didn't blame him. The crimson mess hammered to the makeshift cross on the top of Gold Hill would give anybody nightmares, never mind a Vulnerable Adult like Danny.

'Nobody thinks you've done anything wrong.'

The weather on Danny's face changed slightly. His almond-shaped eyes, with their archetypal folded eyelids, flicked around the room.

Eden glanced again at the scant notes taken by the officer on the scene: *Witness heard wheezing in mist. Witness very distraught.*

'Your mum's very worried,' he said. 'As soon as she's got your brother and sister to school, she's coming here. We know you rang her when you found the ...' Eden faltered; he didn't want to say 'body', even though that's what the poor, slaughtered thing was. 'When you found the man on top of the hill. Your mum was fast asleep, like the rest of Castle Kidbury.'

Danny blinked. He sank lower in the chair. His Appropriate Adult yawned.

'Good thing you ran into Mr Else.' The farmer had been poking in bushes at the foot of the hill, cursing, searching for a strayed sheep; Castle Kidbury sheep had been meeting sticky ends of late. The boy had run, screeching like a banshee, out of the haze. 'You were very upset, weren't you?'

Silence.

'Danny, something puzzles me. It was early to be out and about. Why were you and Jumble up on the hill as the sun came up? Were you meeting somebody?' Eden rubbed the back of his neat head. His brownish hair, short as a schoolboy's, was so clean it squeaked. 'You know about the sheep, don't you? We all do.'

Appropriate Adult tutted and sighed. 'Poor creatures,' she murmured.

Noting that she hadn't voiced any sympathy for the man currently being zipped into a body bag, Eden went on. 'Everybody was very upset when the sheep were killed and left out for people to see. That was horrible. But this is different, don't you think? This is more serious, Danny. Do you get that? That it's serious?'

Danny looked directly at Eden for the first time. His teardrop eyes swam.

Eden felt the interview shift. He spoke more softly. 'If you saw anything, Danny, you can tell me. Nothing bad will happen to you.' He hesitated. 'I promise,' he said. '*Did* you see something? Somebody? Danny, do you know who did this?'

'I don't want her to get in trouble.' Danny's voice was tiny.

'Who, Danny?'

'She's special. She's a goddess. I swore I wouldn't tell.'

'Goddesses have names. What do you call her?'

Danny struggled. A tap at the door made him jump. Softly, too softly for the tape to pick it up, DS Eden muttered, 'Oh for fuck's sake,' before saying, 'Interview suspended at, let me see, zero six twenty-three.'

DC Karen Knott, a smudge of a woman with an *Only me!* air, put her head around the door. In a self-important whisper, she said, 'Thought you'd want to know, Sarge, we got a positive ID from the family. It *is* Keith Dike.'

'Poor sod.'

'He was probably off his head, as per usual. Easy pickings for some psycho.'

'Let's not use words like psycho, Knott. Not yet.'

'Sorry. Yeah.' Knott leant further into the room. She wore forgettable separates. 'All right, Danny? I've got your mum out here doing her nut.'

'I don't want to get her in trouble.' Danny sat up, angry now, and hit the table.

Forgetting to turn on the tape, Eden snatched his moment. 'We can't help you both if you don't tell us who she is, Danny.'

But Danny lapsed into silence, and was handed over to his distraught mother without another word passing his lips.

Creeping downstairs, Jess felt like a burglar. She didn't want to attract Bogna's attention. The housekeeper sang loudly in the kitchen, producing sound effects of general domestic clamour. Jess wondered where Bogna lived, then wondered if she lived in. Her brother had never thought to tell her about this development, but then, Stephen's world ended at the tip of Stephen's nose.

Stealing towards the study, Jess gathered herself on the parquet flooring. She was used to bearding her father in his den: it had always been Jess who sought out the Judge, never the other way around.

A hoarse bark from outside was all it took to sway her. Her father could wait. Harebell House was a place of many doors; she could escape into the garden without passing Bogna in the kitchen.

Hollyhocks. Catmint. All echoing the lavender and green of the wisteria that hung around the house like a frothy wig. Grasses whispered as she passed. The barking grew nearer. Moose must have cornered a squirrel. Jess didn't panic; the squirrels never came off worse. Moose's bark was, as the proverb promised, worse than his non-existent bite.

A gate she'd not walked through for years. Arched wrought-iron in a high wall. Jess pushed at it, and it spoke, like a sore throat.

The dog was in a sky-blue tiled rectangle carved into the ground. Jess joined him, taking the slope from what had been the shallow end. Sitting beside the dog – who was still insanely pleased to see her – she asked him rhetorically if he could remember the pool when it was full.

'It was such a laugh, Moose. I was in and out of it all day. But then Mum drained it and locked the gate, so that was that.' Her soft-hearted mother, crying as she turned the big key, just couldn't bear to see her children in the water after what had happened at a long-ago birthday party.

15

'Yes, Moose, Mum *was* lovely, wasn't she?' The golden retriever's coat was sun-warm against Jess's face.

Moose pawed her, a little whine escaping.

'What's that?' Jess cocked her head. 'You think I'm hiding, do you? You think I should just get on with it and face Dad?' Jess got up, wiped moss from her skirt. 'As usual, Moose, you're right.'

With Moose at her heels, Jess retraced her steps to the Judge's study door and barged in. 'Well, it goes without saying I'd find you in your man cave. Like you'd be anywhere else. I'm not impressed with this cycling nonsense by the way.'

Jess landed on a leather Chesterfield armchair. Its vast size made her feel small. Moose threw himself on the rug, one eye open. 'Sooo, thought I may as well pop in, see what's what in Sad Valley.'

'It's been a year, Jess.' The Judge was grave as he turned his chair to take her in across his broad, leather-topped desk. The deliberate way he moved and spoke told Jess she hadn't won; he wouldn't allow her to orchestrate this. 'A whole year.'

'The new job, you know ...' Jess shrugged, feeling her hair drop out of the half-hearted bun she'd wrangled at her dressing table mirror. 'It's been intense.'

'We haven't seen you since the funeral.'

'No, well ...' Jess had airbrushed that day from her memory banks. She galloped on to a burr that had been bothering her. 'I know you expected me for Christmas, but ...' Her shoulders dropped. 'I couldn't, Dad. I just couldn't.'

'I see.' The Judge nodded and pushed at the white hair that, according to the portrait over the mantelpiece, had once been a chocolate-brown quiff. '*We* all managed to do it. Stephen and Susannah and the children. Iris. Josh. But, no, not you. Not Jessica Castle.'

Her eyes filled as she looked past him. '*Jess*,' she corrected him, softly. She had slept through most of Christmas Day; woken on the sofa by the Queen's speech, she'd had hot chocolate in her hair. 'I couldn't bear to look at the empty place at the table.'

'So you made another one.'

'I'm sorry.' She meant it, but she wondered why it was always her who was sorry.

'I see.'

Jess speculated: what did her father see? As far as she could make out, he saw very little that he didn't want to. She shrank even smaller in the Chesterfield; this whole room conspired to hurtle her back to childhood.

'I assume from the earliness of the hour, from the dramatic nature of your arrival, the fact that it's mid-semester, that this isn't a casual social visit. What have you done now?'

'Does it have to be something I've done? What if I just wanted to see my own flesh and blood?'

'Very well. Tell me nothing has happened. Tell me everything is fine.' The Judge steepled his fingers beneath his chin, his stillness contrasting with his daughter's unease.

She paused. She gave in. 'Dad, that job just wasn't

me. The whole set-up.' Jess sketched something – even she didn't know what – in the air. 'I felt hemmed in.'

'Oh Jessica,' sighed the Judge. 'It wasn't *you*? What does that mean? Mum was so chuffed when you got that position. After everything that went on with you. And where are we now? May? Nine months later and it's over. You couldn't even last a year. You couldn't get out of bed and go to work in the morning like everybody else.'

'It wasn't about getting out of bed!'

'So it was your customary objection to being "normal".' The Judge made a noise Jess knew well. A cross between a tut and a snort. A snut, perhaps. 'If you'd stuck with your law degree instead of studying the ancient past perhaps you'd be able to deal with the present day. You were always drawn to ancient history. Perhaps if Harriet hadn't saddled you with that damn silly middle name ...'

For one terrible moment Jess thought he was going to go against Castle tradition and say the name out loud. But no. 'I hate the law,' said Jess, aware this was as blasphemous in the Judge's study as swearing in a cathedral. There was no need to drag her mother into this, let alone try to blame her. 'It was a mistake to go back to Cambridge. Too many ghosts.'

'For Christ's sake.' The Judge raised his voice. 'How many young women get an opportunity like that? It was handed to you on a plate. An old tutor puts in a good word and you waltz right into a lecturing post. But it's not *you*, you say. What does the faculty have to say about this? Max stuck his neck out for you; you mark my words, that chap must be furious.'

'I haven't exactly told Max.'

'Not *exactly*?'

'Jesus, Dad, we're not in your courtroom!' Jess stood up and planted her hands on his desk, leaning over for the full disclosure she'd known he'd tear out of her. 'I ran away, okay? That's what you want me to say, isn't it? Jess cocked up yet again.'

'When?'

Jess winced and shut her eyes. 'Last week.'

'You mean you literally ran away?'

'Yes.'

'Without telling anybody?'

'Yes.'

The Judge sat back. He regarded her evenly. 'And so you came home.'

'Yup,' said Jess. 'I came home.'

This bit was important.

As important as the crucifixion. It must be done carefully. There would be pictures in the news. Maybe the front page of the Kidbury Echo. *Everyone would see. He had to get this just right.*

Words could come out wrong. But not the box. The box was solid and good and straight. He passed his hand over it. The grain went with the symbols. The hinge was almost invisible.

The inside shone pleasingly in the dim light. Perhaps no one would ever know of the craftsmanship. Not once the box had been filled. The contents would overshadow the message.

Some messages, even if you shout them, remain a secret.

The box sat in his hand and was perfect.

The paper bag sat in a soggy red puddle. Pulling a face, he wiped around it with a rag. The bag split and he had to catch them before they hit the floor and rolled away.

That was funny. Like a cartoon. Humming, he tucked the goodies into their bespoke new home and closed the lid. Surely the gods would smile on him.

Chapter 2

PAN'S PEOPLE

Monday 16 May

The noise was a heavy boom, undercut with silvery chatter. Jess, eyes firmly shut, sensed the weight of the water above her head. She was in it, of it, her lungs were shrieking.

She sat up. The bed was dry. The room was as it should be. Padding downstairs in bare feet, doing up her shirt, Jess fled the dream. She thought it had gone; perhaps it had only been waiting in the bricks of Harebell House.

DS Eden agreed with the inspector that, yes, the red-tops would have a field day with something as newsworthy as a crucifixion. And yes, the local press would find out any minute because Castle Kidbury nick leaked like a sieve. Furthermore, he accepted the urgency of being seen to be doing something. And yes, results were necessary. And yes, young Danny Ruhrmund was refusing to cooperate, but that didn't mean—

Realising his superior had rung off, Eden slammed down the phone and barked for DC Knott. He planned to funnel the crap down through the pecking order, but when Knott's plain, keen face showed round the door, he said, 'Karen, how's your mum?' instead.

'A martyr to her legs as ever, Sarge.'

DC Knott lived with her mother, who was never quite well but never quite died either; the whole station was aware of her pitiful home life.

'Sorry to hear that. Come in, come in.'

The woman always lurked at doors, as if waiting for an invitation.

'Knott, did Danny say anything worth mentioning before him and his mum left?'

'Not a dicky bird.'

'Any ideas about who he meant when he said he didn't want to get "her" into trouble?'

'Nope, Sarge. I asked his mum, but she was more interested in getting him home.'

'Did you mention the cross to her?'

''Course not, Sarge.'

'Good.' Eden didn't quite believe her. 'Any word from Richleigh yet?' Keith Dike's remains had been taken to the better-equipped police station in the neighbouring, more populous town whose borders encroached on Castle Kidbury by way of meandering housing estates and business parks.

'The medical examiner, some bloke called, um,

something,' said Karen, flipping through a notepad, 'he's still working on the body, but he did say the eyes were removed before death.' She seemed thrilled by this news. 'Apparently you can tell because the blood—'

'Fine, good.' Eden held up a hand. Karen Knott was morbid. He was not. 'We need to pick up the ringleader of that crew on Pitt's Field. Pronto.' Eden didn't believe in hunches; he believed in solid police work. Yet there was something about the guy on Pitt's Field that set his copper's synapses snapping. It would be better than leaning on Danny, which was what his bosses were suggesting. 'What's he call himself again? Pan, or something stupid like that.'

'Yes, sir, Pan. You think those travellers might have something to do with Keith's death? Keith's missus came up with a list of people who had it in for him.'

'Everybody had it in for Keith. He was one of nature's gits. But I can't imagine anybody going to the bother of building a cross for him. This looks like some kind of ritual, Knott, not a bust-up between pissheads.' Eden almost said 'Pardon my French', but he remembered that the female officers prided themselves on immunity to bad language. 'I reckon it's those Pitt's Field weirdos who've been stringing up Else's sheep as part of some sort of ceremony, so let's get this Pan bloke in and ask him a few questions, eh?'

'In case they've, like, got more ambitious. Moved up from sheep to humans?'

It sounded stupid when she put it like that. It was a knack that Knott had.

The unwashed mob on Pitt's Field got on Eden's every nerve. The grime, the lack of order, the roll-ups, made him grind his teeth as he passed them on his way to the station each morning.

'They'd have the time on their hands to pull a stunt like this. Plus, if they're off their heads, they'd have the confidence.'

'But wouldn't they have to be, like, *animals*, Sarge?'

'Animals wouldn't do what we saw this morning, Knott.' He hesitated by the door, straightening his tie in the glass panel. 'How is it out there?' Eden nodded towards the outer office, where phones rang and conversation eddied. 'How are they taking it?'

'You know, Sarge. They're making jokes. But I heard DC Kennedy being sick in the loos.'

The sight of the body, so shocking in the banal landscape, had shaken Eden. He'd seen the professionals around him – the forensic team, the photographer – swallow hard, set their shoulders. Castle Kidbury just wasn't that sort of town. Results were needed. 'Go and pull in this Pan, Knott. But gently does it, okay? No fuss.'

'Lentils,' said Jess to herself, opening another cupboard. 'Lentils, lentils, and oh look! More fucking lentils.'

Nothing dented Jess's appetite – a trait her mother had commented on approvingly even while the older woman was on yet another cabbage-soup diet. Running away from a plum job for reasons she couldn't fully explain to herself or her father, driving through the

night, disappointing the Judge for the umpteenth time –
all of it made her long for a bowl of Coco Pops.

'Where's the normal food, Bogna?'

Bogna, her hands deep in water at the sink, laughed.
'My darling, I ban sugar in this house. We eat
healthy here.'

'You eat boring here.' Jess felt aggrieved; this was her
kitchen, in a way. 'Dad doesn't need to lose weight.' The
Judge was a paper clip. Thin, coiled, pointy edges. Her
mother's kitchen had been a production line of gigantic
roasts and steaming stews. Dumplings. Beef Wellingtons.

'Why not have some—'

'There is nothing,' said Jess, 'that I want in
this house.'

Composing a shopping list in her head – chocolate
milk/Hobnobs/cheese – helped Jess calm down.
Speeding wasn't easy in her aqua-blue Morris Traveller,
built in gentler times, but she put her foot down and
barrelled along the Kidbury Road towards Richleigh
and the Waitrose that had flowered on its ring road.

Windows rattling, clutch complaining, the car
pulled out to avoid a huddle of police cars on a verge.
Jess squinted into the field and saw a very un-Castle
Kidbury whirl of activity.

Uniformed officers were manhandling people in the
mud, slipping and sliding as they carted individuals
out through the barred gate. A van pulled up, spray-
ing muck, and the complaining, gesturing mob were
goaded through its back doors.

Jess passed the scene and made it two hundred yards before she squealed on the brakes and backed up.

'Hey!' she yelled, leaping out. 'What's going on?'

She was ignored; the officers had their hands full. The squatters of Pitt's Field would not give up their guru without a fight.

'Fascist pigs!' yelled a woman who'd cultivated dreadlocks despite being unquestionably Caucasian. 'Scum!'

Jess, her Doc Martens slithering in the wet dirt, pushed past the heaving tableau. There was a medieval feel to it, like Bosch's demons prodding sinners down to hell.

Scattered, dilapidated caravans. A yurt. A slag heap of bin bags. Fitful bonfires. Birdsong. Coppers swearing.

A barefoot toddler, her face crusted with dirt, smacked into Jess's shins.

'Whoa there.' Jess bent down to pick up the child, who acquiesced calmly and bent her head to Jess's shoulder. 'Who are you, then, eh?'

'She lives there.' A woman hurrying by in tattered harem pants pointed at the most vintage of all the caravans.

In the doorway of a lozenge-shaped trailer, its seams leaking rust, stood a tall, thin woman of Jess's age. They were dressed similarly – loose obfuscating layers – but she had a dirt tan that rendered her grey.

'Caroline Mansfield, you old tart!' Jess dodged through the scrum. 'What are you doing here?'

The last time Jess had seen her old school friend was at one of the weddings that spread like a virus through their social circle one bygone summer. Caroline had been wearing a fascinator and a linen suit; she'd smelt of Miss Dior.

'Welcome to modern Britain,' shouted Caroline. There were twigs in her hair. 'This is what it's come to.' She was too agitated to be surprised by Jess's materialisation. 'We're not hurting anybody. We just want to be left in peace. They want to cut Pan down because they know he sees through them.' She put out her arms for the child, shouting 'Bastards!' loudly over its blonde curls.

'Is she yours?' Jess could see something of Caroline in the little girl. 'She's so sweet.'

'Jess, this goes against nature.' Caroline bobbed on the step and the shabby caravan bobbed with her. Her eyes widened over Jess's head. 'Shit, guys! They've got Pan!'

Caroline took off on bare feet, foisting the child back onto Jess, who lurched behind as best she could.

More dark uniforms had arrived, bulky and well-fed alongside the raggedy bohemians.

'Who's Pan?' shouted Jess as a nucleus of unwashed civilians and pissed-off police officers clustered around a decrepit Winnebago.

'He's the reason,' said Caroline. 'He's the point of it all.'

'He looks like Russell Brand,' said Jess.

Tall, long-limbed, heavily bearded and with dark eyes that, even at this distance and in the midst of a scuffle, glittered, Pan let himself be taken, arms outstretched, by the police.

Jess was reminded of school assemblies at Easter; this Pan was a passive creature, his head lolling, just like the languid Jesus of church murals.

'We love you, Pan!' yelled Caroline as the thin blue line bundled him towards the gate.

An officer, red-haired and sweating, peeled off from Pan's escort to lift Caroline off her feet.

'No you fucking don't!' Jess, child in her arms, raised her boot, but before it could make contact she too was seized by a passing flatfoot and dumped in the back of the van. The doors closed, somebody slapped twice on its side and they were off.

Caroline crawled to Jess's side. She placed a gentle hand on hers. 'You're with us now. You're joined with the great Pan.'

'Shush, please,' shouted DC Knott.

The babble continued. The custody suite at the station seethed with infuriated ... *What are they?* wondered Jess, stuck among them, arms glued to her sides.

It was a fancy dress party, she decided. Not one real honest-to-God hippie in the place. Mostly young – nobody over thirty-five – and all in disintegrating clothes that hailed not from gap-year travels in Peru but from Gap. Very little West Country twang in the aggrieved shouting, but plenty of private-school vowels.

Something else united them – they were all women. The great Pan recruited only the fairer sex.

Jess elbowed her way to the duty desk, where Knott was still appealing vainly for silence. Time to disassociate herself from her companions and get back on the road to Waitrose.

Jess opened her mouth just as a besuited man appeared behind Knott and roared 'Quiet!'

That did the trick. Jess closed her mouth and the clamour around her died.

'My name,' said the man, 'is Detective Sergeant John Eden. I'm leading a major investigation into the death of a local man. All I want to do is ask Mister, er, Pan, a few questions. I have no idea what the rest of you are doing in my station.'

Jess caught his sideways look at the female officer, whose lips were pursed.

'But now that you are, and since you apparently assaulted police officers in the course of their duties, we need to take all your names – your *actual* names, please – and process you.'

The babble started up again. They knew their rights, these bourgeois gypsies, and they were vocal about them. Jess, who'd grown up among law manuals, didn't add to the noise. If she'd curbed her impulse to stick her nose in, she could be enjoying a nice Ginsters pasty right about now.

Somebody's eyes were upon her. Jess lifted her head to see the beleaguered female officer staring straight at her.

A word in Eden's ear and he, too, was looking at her. He didn't seem to like what he saw.

'*You*,' he said to Jess, 'are all I bloody need. Does the venerable Lordship know his daughter's out and about kicking coppers?'

Chapter 3

RUMPOLE TO THE RESCUE

Still Monday 16 May

DS Eden's cassette deck whirred pointlessly once again as Jess sat opposite him in the interview room. Arms folded. Resolutely silent.

'Come on. I know who you are. You're not one of those New-Age poseurs.' Eden tapped his pen on the table. 'Tell me what you were really doing at Pitt's Field.'

Jess's eyes flickered over the plate of chocolate digestives on the Formica between them.

'I've got Hobnobs, too.'

Jess refolded her arms. She wasn't to be broken so easily.

'Chocolate fingers?' Eden gave the slightest of smiles and leant in. 'Custard creams?'

'I was driving past, that's all.' Jess hesitated. 'Custard creams, please,' she added in a small voice.

Eden gestured to DC Knott, who stood leaning against the door. The officer left the room rolling her eyes.

'Go on, Jess. Give me more.'

'All right. I was driving along the Kidbury road and I saw your debacle.'

Eden straightened up. '*My* debacle?'

'*Your* debacle. So I thought I'd see what our fine boys in blue were up to.'

'And?'

'And ... your lot were hassling *that* lot and then I spotted somebody I was at school with, so I wanted to find out how come she was one of Pan's people, see what they're about.'

Eden sat back in his chair. 'What *are* they about?'

Knott returned with a plate of custard creams and slapped them huffily on the table.

Jess knew she had Eden's full attention. Cramming two biscuits into her mouth, she said thickly, 'Dunno.'

Eden slid the plate away from her.

'I really don't know!' she protested, bereft. 'I haven't seen Caroline in years. She's always been an airhead who jumped on any old bandwagon. If they're all like her, they're hardly a threat to national security.'

The door flew open. In strode a tall man in a pinstripe suit. He placed a leather briefcase squarely between them on the table.

'Thank you, DS Eden,' he intoned, like a Hugh Grant-a-gram. 'Would you and your colleague mind stepping out while I consult with my client?'

Jess pulled in her chin. 'What the fuck are you talking about?'

The man's equilibrium faltered. 'I'm your counsel, Ms Castle. Rupert Lawson.'

'Yes, I know *who* the fuck you are. I meant what are you doing here?' She turned to Eden. 'Am I under arrest?'

'Not unless you want to be.' Eden seemed to be enjoying the sitcom unfolding before him.

Rupert Lawson interjected, 'Detective Sergeant Eden, I should remind you that—'

'Oh shut up and sit down,' snapped Jess, as if the strapping lawyer was a naughty schoolboy.

Fazed, Rupert sat down heavily.

'Okay, here goes,' started Jess, 'in sixth form, Caroline dabbled in New-Age stuff. Crystals, chanting and whatnot.'

'So what?' said Karen, surprising Jess, who'd forgotten about her. 'It's the West Country.'

Eden nodded agreement. 'Nothing unusual in that round here.'

Wolfing another custard cream, Jess said, 'What I'm saying is, Caroline was searching for something, for the meaning of life.' She swallowed noisily. 'It's a cult.'

'How do you know that? Aren't they just hippies, travellers, whatever?'

'I don't *know* know, I just know.' Jess, wiping her mouth with a baggy sleeve, saw how Eden's eyes met Rupert's for a moment, as though the two men shared a thought. A thought that was unflattering to her.

'Look, they're not travellers. For one thing they're not rough enough. These are bored trust-fund kids. And that "Pan" idiot was spouting some sort of witchcraft lingo when he was carted off, but it was complete bollocks. It's not like he was quoting from Benjamin Ray's *Satan's War Against the Covenant* or something. Caroline was transfixed. He's using them. It's about control. It's pound-shop paganism.'

Eden put his hands behind his head. 'I see, Miss Castle. We're an expert on paganism, are we?'

Rupert puffed out his chest. 'Sergeant, my client is finished here and so—'

'Shut up, Rumpole.' Jess turned to Eden. 'Yeah, I am an expert, DS John Eden. PhD from Exeter. *Doctor* Jessica Castle to you.'

Cogs seemed to whirr within Eden as he stared at her. Impulsively, he opened the folder in front of him and splayed three or four photographs under Jess's nose.

'Christ!' Jess recoiled from the vivid images of blood and animal hair. Dead eyes with a slit instead of a pupil stared out at her. 'What's this?'

'Exactly. What is it?' demanded Eden. 'Satanism?'

'No, it's a sheep.' Ambushed, Jess felt no compunction to play nicely. 'A dead sheep, come to that.'

'What's happened to it? Is it a sacrifice of some sort? Are we dealing with Satanism here?'

Her curiosity kindled by his urgency, Jess took the question seriously. 'Everybody thinks *ooh, black magic* when an animal's throat is cut, but this isn't a sacrifice.' She tapped one of the images, a woolly cadaver spreadeagled on a bush. 'Look. Its throat's been cut but it hasn't been bled. Sacrifices are bled. Blood, DS Eden, is sacred.' She paused. 'This is somebody playing at sacrifices, somebody with no real knowledge of the rituals involved.'

Pulling out a drawing in thick pencil, Eden slid it towards her. 'And this symbol?'

Jess shook her head. 'Not one I've seen before.'

Rupert butted in. 'Lovely though it is to chat, my client doesn't have to—'

Both Jess and Eden ignored him, the policeman cutting across him to ask, 'Could it be religious? Pagan, maybe?'

Jess shook her head, certain of herself. 'Not any religion I've studied. *Possibly* Ancient Greek. Except it's not. I reckon it's made up. Pretendy sacrifice, pretendy symbol. Where'd you find this?'

Eden looked down at the images, then lifted his head and sighed, as if he'd come reluctantly to some sort of decision. 'It was carved into a body.'

Jess stared.

Eden spoke slowly. 'What do you know about crucifixions?'

Rupert slapped the table. 'Okay, time's up. This isn't an interview. Unless I'm missing something, my client's not under caution, so this little tête-à-tête is over,

Detective Sergeant.' He gestured for Jess to stand. He was brisk now, determined.

Eden sat back, blowing out his cheeks. 'Fair enough. You're free to go.' He eyed Jess. 'Don't disappear. I might be in touch again.'

'Ooh, can't wait,' said Jess.

Rupert, already at the door, held it open, but Jess lingered. She crossed to a map of Castle Kidbury on the wall and trailed her finger along Kidbury Road to where it met Gold Hill. 'This crucifixion—' she began.

'Nobody said there was a crucifixion,' said Eden.

'You kind of did,' smiled Jess. Her finger halted at the junction of Kidbury Road, Richleigh Road and Gold Hill. 'My dad said there was police activity on Gold Hill. If the crucifixion was on the hill, that makes it a double cross. A cross on a cross.'

Eden tucked the photographs back into the folder.

Rupert let out a sigh.

'That's very powerful. Crosses were hijacked by Christianity but they've always been a significant symbol. They represented joining, coming together, the combined energy of male and female. In maths, the cross has evolved into the character for addition.'

'And?' Eden wasn't really listening.

Knott growled under her breath.

'If this murderer is keen on symbolism, and it looks like he is, then the double cross points to Hecate.'

Knott perked up. 'Do you know where she lives? I can go pick her up this minute, sir.'

'She's a goddess,' said Jess.

35

Knott jumped.

Eden pretended not to notice, but Jess had. 'Am I on to something? Have goddesses been mentioned already? Hecate's a wild girl. Pre-Christian. Ancient Greek. Like all pagan deities, she's very human, imperfect, complex.'

Eden coughed, brushed down his shoulders. The interview was over for the second time. 'You talk about this Hecate in the present tense.'

'Well, it looks like she might have a hand in this.'

'I'll ask my people to pick up any Ancient Greek ladies they see on Castle Kidbury High Street.'

'They'll easily recognise her,' said Jess, finally giving into Rupert's impatience. 'She has three heads.'

Jess stared at the blurred hedgerow through the passenger window of Rupert's leather-upholstered Mercedes convertible. It was near silent. Nothing like a Morris Traveller, she thought. He'd 'done well', she supposed, since she'd last seen him. He'd done exactly what he'd been groomed to do. Following the rut his father and grandfather made from public school to university to the bar, just like her brother Stephen.

Rupert's success wasn't surprising. Even aged ten, in the throes of a childhood crush, Jess had seen something in Rupert. Something she liked.

Pity he turned out to have no imagination whatsoever.

'Well, Jess, you certainly have a knack for turning a drama into a crisis. First day home and you're in the slammer.'

Jess shifted in the luxury seat. 'Fuck you, Rumpole. Anyway, how come you appeared on your white charger?'

'Eden's no fool. Once he heard the Castle name, he called your brother.'

Jess's innards did a backflip. 'Terrific.' Another black mark to very obviously not discuss at Sunday lunch.

'Stephen's in court all day, so he called in a favour and here I am.'

'Whatever.'

Rupert's groomed eyebrows climbed a little. 'Oh no. Not at all. Stop with the thank yous. Please don't mention it. I like nothing better than a mouthy pro bono case before lunch.'

Lost in thought, Jess ignored the invitation to spar. Turning suddenly to Rupert, she said, 'A crucifixion. Here, of all places.'

'*If* there's been a crucifixion, it's none of your business. All that matters is that you were in a police interview and now you're not.' Rupert was immune to the excitement bubbling up in his passenger. 'Eden didn't confirm it.'

'Rumpole, don't you have blood in your veins? There's been an actual crucifixion right here in chocolate-box Castle Kidbury. You mark my words.'

Rupert smiled. 'Your father says that.'

DC Karen Knott was officious. 'Gentleman to see you, sir.'

The gentleman turned out to be Paul Chappell, who

was on first-name terms with both Eden and Knott. He was, Eden noted, looking unusually dapper.

'Is that the right word?' John Eden liked plain words, ones that did their job and went no further.

'I'd like to think so.' Paul Chappell's body was not a temple, but a testament to KFC. A divorcee, he ate at his desk at the *Kidbury Echo*, and it showed. He did a twirl to show off the grey suit. 'Haircut.' He pointed to his Weetabix wedge of frizzy hair. 'Got me teeth done.'

Suppressing a smile, Eden joked, 'Who's the lucky lady?' but it turned out that there *was* a lucky lady.

'Way out of my league. Sexy, educated, charming. This online dating is a godsend for men like me.' Paul wiped a damp strand of no-colour hair from his sweating forehead. 'You can woo them with words, see, before you take them out. I'm treating her to lunch at the Seven Stars tomorrow.'

'Pushing the boat out then?' said Eden. The Royal Seven Stars was a hundred metres from the door of the *Echo*.

'I got your press release about poor old Keith Dike. I've already interviewed his missus. She's in the dark about what happened to him, but I'm guessing it was murder, yes?'

'I can't comment, Paul. You know that.'

'When I say "guess", I mean I know it was murder. A little bird told me the method was ... unusual.'

'We'll brief you when we're ready.'

'Come on, John! A murder on my patch. Throw me a

bone. A chat with the widow isn't enough. I'm drowning in stolen bikes and parrots who can swear. This is actual news! A murder in Castle Kidbury at last.'

'I'm not as chipper about it as you are.'

'This,' said Paul, producing a carrier bag, 'is why I'm here. I believe it's pertinent to your enquiries.' The bag made a thump as it landed on Eden's desk. Paul was grave. 'I warn you, John. This is properly horrible.'

DS Eden pulled on thin plastic gloves and opened the bag carefully with his pen. 'How did you come by it?'

'It was left on the *Echo*'s step. I almost fell over it coming into work. All wrapped up in brown paper and addressed to me. I've kept the paper for your forensics boys.' Paul waved the precious evidence he'd rolled into a ball.

Eden frowned. 'A box.' It didn't look too horrible to him. In fact, it looked rather beautiful. He took it out and set it carefully on his blotting pad 'This is yew, I think.' Eden knew it was a fine wood, not some soft stuff from a builder's yard. 'Nice marquetry work.'

The lidded box, an elegant soft rectangle, was out of place in his practical office. Warm, handmade, it glowed. Eden said what he saw as he examined it.

'Inlaid depictions of trees along the top. Four of them. Each one different.' He had a sinking feeling. This new case was unfurling in a peculiar way. Already getting away from him. 'That one's a yew, I think. Is that a poplar?'

'Don't look at me,' said Paul. 'There's more stuff around the sides.'

'These are inlaid as well.' Symbols were set into the box so expertly that the effect was seamless. Eden wanted to feel them; the forensics guys would crucify *him* if he touched the evidence. Instead, he turned the blotter slowly. 'One vertical line on each side of the box, with dashes through them. Oh, and these two here, like the letter V on its side, they're mathematical.' He thought of Jess. 'The signs for "more than" and "less than".'

Symbols were even worse than fancy words; they misled, they lied.

'Bugger me if I know what any of it means.' Paul took a seat, his thighs lapping over the sides of the chair. 'It's what's inside that made me bring it here.'

Gingerly, Eden opened the lid. He gagged. He recovered. 'Eyes,' he said, needlessly.

The maker of the box had carved a pair of concave dents, just the right size for the eyes that sat in them. They looked in opposite directions. Trailing ribbons of gore were tucked neatly around the white orbs. They looked alarmed. As well they might. They looked fresh. They were, without doubt, the eyes only recently removed from Keith Dike.

Snapping the lid shut, Eden thanked Paul. 'You could have run with this on your front page, but you did the decent thing.'

'I *will* have to publish, though.' Paul sat forward. The office chair complained.

'Not yet. Please.' This week was only a day old and already like no other week Eden had lived through.

'Withholding this information could be vital. Nobody knows that the murderer removed the eyes. That might help us nail him.'

'I don't want to get in the way of justice. And I want to keep our relationship shipshape. So nothing yet. But as I've scratched your back, could you please tickle mine?'

The mental image was almost as bad as the eyes. 'How do you mean?'

'I won't publish yet. Scout's honour. But when the time's right give me the nod so I can be ready ahead of the big boys. 'Cos the nationals'll be sniffing around if my source is correct and poor old Keith Dike was crucified.'

That little bird needed strangling.

Eden owed Paul. Eden always balanced his books. He nodded once, barely. 'Nothing yet, Paul.' He held up a forefinger. 'You can print that somebody's helping with our enquiries. I'm sure you know it's that Pan bloke from Pitt's Field, but no names yet, okay? I'm letting him sweat a bit before I interview him. We found plenty of Mary Jane, so we have forty-eight hours to play with.'

'That's a deal.' Paul rubbed his hands gleefully. 'Next time we meet I'll have seduced my future wife. Wish me luck, John.'

DS Eden didn't hear. He was staring at the eyes and the eyes were staring back.

'John, those lines with the dashes through them, could they mean passage of time? You know, like prisoners mark off the days on cell walls.'

'Possibly.' Eden would come to no conclusions in front of a journalist.

'Maybe this box is telling you when the next murder is.'

'The next one?' Eden gaped at Paul. 'Isn't one enough?'

The Mercedes glided to a hushed stop alongside Jess's Morris Traveller.

'You still have that old heap.'

'Yes, I do. I love her.'

'It must be older than both of us put together.'

'Since you ask, she was born in 1970.' Jess undid her seat belt.

'How do you keep it running?'

'My mate takes care of it.'

'He must be a whizz with a spanner, this mate.'

Jess opened the passenger door. 'He's a she, actually. Catch you later.' She slipped out briskly, making for her car without a glance behind her.

Rupert shook his head and rubbed his eyes, as if recovering from something. He put the Merc into reverse, turning to check his blind spot.

A knock on the window, and Jess was there.

Rupert jumped.

The window hummed down. 'Yes?'

Jess smiled. A real smile, giving up her dimples.

'Thanks, Rumpole,' she said.

Chapter 4

THE EYES HAVE IT

Tuesday 17 May

A smudged face close to Jess's own. Colourful, like a clown's.

The face rippled. Disappeared into the depths of the water.

Jess gasped for breath. She was sinking.

She was awake.

Jess opened her eyes, still quivering. The room took shape, at first unfamiliar, then all too familiar. She wasn't drowning, she was home.

Bogna put on her glasses and read aloud from her iPad. She read slowly. Inching along the lines. A chicken strutted beneath the table. Moose seemed uninterested.

"*'The murder of local man, Keith Dike, 58, of Abbotts Avenue, has appalled Castle Kidbury residents. DS John Eden remains tight-lipped about*

43

details, stating only that an individual is helping the police with their enquiries.'" Bogna slapped down the tablet. 'That means he did it!' Bogna was triumphant. 'I heard,' she said, looking left and right, as if a spy might lurk by the Aga, 'that this poor Keith was hanged.'

Shelling peas at the table, Jess shook her head. 'Nope,' she said. She'd almost finished her chore. She would have liked to shell peas all day. It was a time-less task, something women had done for hundreds of years. Something she'd done with her mother. She looked up to see Bogna tie an apron round her waist. 'Where'd you get that?'

'This?' Bogna looked down at the candy-striped pin-afore. 'Hanging up, my darling, in pantry.'

'I made it.' Jess remembered the sewing teacher, her dried-up apricot face. 'For my mother.'

Suddenly still, Bogna looked down at the apron. 'Ah, well, she can't use it now, can she?' All a-bustle once again, she began to weigh flour.

Jess wandered out to the front of the house. She hated wandering; she was a strider by nature. She was not needed in this house. Bogna had everything under control, and her father was invisible. He haunted his own home.

The wisteria was still. Harebell House was a paint-ing of itself. An image of Englishness. Of dysfunction, which is how Jess had come to think of her heritage.

A fierce longing overtook her – a cigarette would make it all so much better. A sense memory claimed her. She felt the cigarette between her fingers. On her lips. She felt the hit of the smoke.

Jess staggered, back in the present. Smoking was a sly lover, always ready to beguile. Her heart sank. She knew without looking in her suitcase that her nicotine patches were in a drawer back in Cambridge.

Her Doc Martens carried her out of Harebell House. The well-worn path to 'town', or what passed for it. As a teenager, she had stomped this journey daily. Nothing much had changed. Castle Kidbury was set in aspic.

Kidbury Road.

The bridge.

The long-stay car park.

The medical centre.

The vet's.

And then the long turn into the main thoroughfare.

A time machine had malfunctioned and deposited Jess right back where she started. She caught sight of herself in a tea shop window; she had certainly changed, even if the town hadn't.

Cobbles, so beloved by tourists, were hazardously slick after the morning's rain. Jess braced herself for the parade of 'old faces' that would come thick and fast. Cambridge was Gotham City compared to this backwater; she'd rather liked the anonymity.

Approaching the square, Jess ticked off the familiar shopfronts. Phoenix Antiques. Dalby's Butchers. Lynne's Minimart. Then onto Fore Street and there, untouched, was Dickinson's Books. Lady Jayne still purveyed horrific mother-of-the-bride outfits. The Buttonhole was new; a florist's.

Coming out of the newsagents, a boy – no, a

man – almost ran into her. The lack of an apology was obviously due more to shyness than bad manners. He raced off, head down, but not before Jess had clocked his freckled face. She strained for his name. *Neil*. She recalled a to-do when his grandmother died. The Judge had been part of a council effort to move his granddad to a home and Neil to adult safekeeping, even though Neil had been old enough to live alone. Neil had refused. *Good for you!* Jess was in the mood to applaud people who stood up to her dad.

She turned back, almost colliding again, but this time with a comfortably engineered woman in her sixties.

'Jess, love, hello.'

Think. The name appeared. 'Sheila,' said Jess. 'Hi.' Sheila had done Harriet's nails in hospital. Towards the end.

And ... there it was. The head tilt. The puppy eyes. The sympathy which landed on Jess's skin like acid.

'I do think of your mum often.'

Sheila was a kind woman, full to the brim with feeling. But Jess couldn't bear her just now.

'Yes, that's, um, nice, but, you know ...' Jess backed away.

'I do know.' Sheila watched Jess as she turned. 'I do, love.'

The Bread Basket was gone. This was a shock. Jess had subsisted on their egg and cress baguettes during her GCSEs. In its space was The Spinning Jenny. It was cafe-like, which was all Jess required of cafes.

The war memorial on the square. The old pump which

featured in many day-tripper photographs. Coming around the side of it was a woman too groomed for Castle Kidbury on a Tuesday. 'Goodness me, it's Jess.'

She had a Julie Andrews quality. A purity. A clean beauty.

'Helena,' said Jess. She realised it was her turn to do the head tilt. The puppy eyes. She snapped out of it. Such displays of sympathy were more for the giver than the receiver. 'You look well.'

The compliment was ignored. Helena's smile was genuine, but she was in a hurry, she said. How lovely to see her, she said. She walked on in 'for-best' court shoes.

It was a relief that Helena was too busy to stop. It would have meant a detour to a part of the past that Jess, for all her interest in ancient history, preferred to avoid.

The chemist's was gone. It was now a gift shop, in a town that already met all Jess's needs for novelty doorstops and scented candles. She remembered the old-fashioned Wilson's Pharmacy and turned once again.

Wilson's was down a narrow slit of road. Talc in the window. A toiletries bag. A toothbrush.

A bell above the door announced her entry.

'Good afternoon.'

He was tall and a little heavy. Hair glossy black and as old-fashioned as the shop. Eyes dark and warm, with eyeliner provided by Mother Nature. *Middle Eastern*, thought Jess. 'Good afternoon.' She relished the for-mality. Chemists *should* be formal; they deal with the sticky bits. The rude bits. The oozing bits. She approved of his white coat, his tie.

Jess browsed the toothpaste and the make-up and the American Tan tights. She felt him watch her, benignly.

'Is there anything specific you need?' His accent was quaint. Educated.

'Actually, yes. Do you stock nicotine patches?'

'Giving up, yes?' The chemist shook his head. 'You have my deepest sympathy.'

'You've done it?'

'I've never dared.' He had turned away, was leaning down to a broad white-lipped drawer. 'I'm completely hooked and I accept it. But these,' he tapped the box in his hand, 'are good, I hear. Back home, everybody smokes.'

'I stopped ten years ago.'

'And you're still wearing these? You shouldn't.'

Loath to admit she was now addicted to the remedy for her addiction, Jess asked, 'So where's "back home"?' Jess had read his name on his lapel badge. Kuzbari.

'I am from Syria.'

Syria, to Jess, meant war. Bombed-out streets the colour of hay. Children's bodies lined up in rows after a gas attack. She almost said she was sorry to hear that. Instead, she said, 'You're a long way from home.'

He seemed to weigh that up. 'Yes.' Mr Kuzbari put the patches in a small paper bag. 'You see Syria on the news, I expect.' He accepted her nod with a nod of his own. 'They don't show the pomegranates. The dates. The wonderful mahshi my wife makes.'

The mention of food had Jess standing an inch taller.

'Oh yes. You take a zucchini – very fresh – and stuff

it with tender ground lamb and rice and nuts.' His natural pout deepened. 'There's nothing like it.'

'Certainly not in Castle Kidbury,' agreed Jess. 'Although Greggs do an excellent pasty.'

'Ah, Greggs!' Mr Kuzbari laughed. 'The height of British cuisine.'

'Does your wife cook . . .'

'Mahshi,' offered the pharmacist gently.

'Yes. Mahshi. Does she cook it here?'

'Yes. But it's not quite the same.' Mr Kuzbari shrugged. 'Many things are not the same.'

Jess paid up. She didn't want to leave. She liked the air of gentle learning around this man. The previous chemist had spectacles on a chain and Jess had never forgotten his expression when she came in for the morning-after pill.

The Royal Seven Stars was still there. Jess felt nostalgia curl about her. She hoped against hope it would still have red velour seating, still have the bulky hotel reception desk on the left and the dark wooden public bar to the right.

It did.

Same desk. New receptionist. Jess remembered her as a kid, but now Carli had gel nails and fake lashes. Her heart was real. 'All right, you!' she yelled when she saw Jess.

'Is that how you welcome guests at this establishment?'

'What?' Carli was an irony-free zone.

'No, I mean, oh nothing. Hi Carli.'

'You're back then,' said Carli.

'I am,' agreed Jess.

'That's nice.'

'Is it?' Jess corrected herself; no joking with Carli. 'Yes, it is. It's nice. Is Eddie about?'

'Yeah, somewhere. I like your hair,' said Carli as she picked up the buzzing phone and said 'GoodmorningRoyalSevenStarsHotelHowMayIHelp?' She put her hand over the receiver and hissed at Jess. 'Scary about Keith Dike! I heard he was beheaded.'

Eddie was in the dimmest recess of the bar, ticking things off a list. When he saw Jess, he smiled and rocked back on his heels. Short. Stocky. A yeoman. Eddie looked like the copper he had once been. 'What do we have here?' Broad Manchester out of place among the clotted cream.

Jess felt at home around Eddie. No airs and graces with him. 'It's been ages,' she said, before he had a chance to do so.

'Nah, feels like yesterday. You back for good then?' Eddie threw in a wry look, as if scoffing at the very suggestion.

'Just visiting. Making sure you haven't changed the decor.'

'Plush red seats, patterned carpet and horse brasses are what people expect from a coaching inn and that is what they'll bloody well get as long as I'm behind the bar.' Eddie leant on the counter. 'This murder ... has your dad got any ideas?'

'If he did, he wouldn't tell *me*, Eddie.' Jess vaguely

remembered Keith Dike. 'Was Keith the one whose trousers fell down every night at five to eleven?'

'You could set your watch by Keith's trousers. Colourful bloke. And horrible, to be fair. But why anybody would want to kill him ...'

'Maybe it's a serial killer.'

'Yeah, you get loads of them in market towns,' smiled Eddie. 'Fancy a drink?'

'Just a lemonade. Proper R. White's mind, not that cloudy nonsense. And crisps ... chicken flavour.' Her mouth watered. Lovely, bad-for-you crisps.

The door of the gents' delivered a small shabby man to the bar. He was talking to himself, mid-conversation. Coughing. Patting his pockets. Like a collection of ferrets, his body fidgeted beneath a filthy overcoat. He saw Jess and his eyes widened as if he'd seen an apparition. 'Jessica Castle? What brings you hither?'

Jess dodged the outstretched arms, parleyed them into a handshake. This close, Squeezers smelt like a hamster cage. 'What are you up to, Squeezers?' She liked him. He was peculiar. Among the tidy houses and tended gardens of Castle Kidbury, this made him precious to Jess.

'I can't say.' Squeezers looked both ways in the empty bar. 'Something big. Another job for Beefy Dave.'

Jess looked to Eddie for clarification; if a leaf stirred in the town, Eddie knew about it.

Eddie shrugged. 'Never met the guy. But if I ever get my hands on him ...' He whispered, 'He runs Squeezers ragged, the bastard.'

'Either of you need any marbles?' Squeezers was urgent, furtive. 'Nice tidy consignment, I've got.' Squeezers made himself jump with the disclosure and an asthma inhaler fell from his complicated clothes. He picked it up, sucked greedily on it and leant on a polished table. 'I've got to run,' he wheezed.

At his feet a hairy item stirred. Darling was a dog, or as near as dammit. Thin as a lurcher, nervous as a greyhound, her eloquent brown eyes stared out of a coat of many colours, all of them best described as 'meh'.

'I've an appointment at the cop shop.'

'What've you been up to now, cock?' Eddie shook his head, schoolmarmish.

'Nothing. It's to do with this murder, I think.'

'You what?' Eddie laughed. 'You, Squeezers? Come off it.'

'That Detective Sergeant wants to talk to me.' Squeezer's rabbit-bright eyes narrowed. 'I don't like the cop shop much,' he said quietly.

'I'll come with you,' said Jess.

Eddie's eyebrows lifted.

'I'm not letting Eden push him around, Eddie.'

Eden sat on one side of the banal table, Squeezers and Jess on the other. She'd turned up with him, declaring him to be a Vulnerable Adult and herself to be his Appropriate Adult. Ever keen for a simple life, Eden had allowed it, and now they waited for the inevitable cups of tea from the inevitable DC Knott.

'So, helping Squeezers is the only reason you're

here, Jess?' asked Knott as she sugared and milked and was mother. 'You're not here, for example, to nose around?'

'Just doing my civic duty, Karen. Any of those custard creams left?'

Wishing Jess and Knott had mute buttons, Eden began. 'Thank you, Squeezers, for coming in. The reason I wanted to see you—'

'Why *do* you want to see him?' asked Jess.

Eden carried on as if she hadn't interrupted. 'Is because I remember you suffering with asthma. Is that correct?'

'It's not a crime,' said Jess, 'to have asthma.'

'I might have asthma.' Squeezers had refused to take off his coat and now he withdrew into it. 'Then again, I might not.' His eyes flickered here, there, all over. He looked at his tea but lacked the courage to reach for it. 'I hate cop shops,' he murmured.

'Am I right in thinking you use an inhaler?'

'I did *not* nick it!' Squeezers was adamant. 'From the chemist's, on Saturday. *That* is a lie!'

'Squeezers,' sighed Eden, 'don't give me *more* work to do. Just a yes or no, all right?'

'You've called him in to make up numbers, haven't you?' Jess leant back. Cockiness set at eleven. 'You have to look like you're doing something, so you drag in the village idiot for questioning.'

'Ooh, is he here?' asked Squeezers, looking round for this village idiot.

'Squeezers!' DS Eden slapped the table.

'Yessir!' yelled Squeezers. 'I do have asthma and I do have an inhaler.'

'Right. Good. You were wheezing on your way in, weren't you?'

Jess put her head to one side. 'Was Keith Dike wheezed to death?'

'Squeezers, do you *really* need an Appropriate Adult for this little chat?'

'S'pose not.' Squeezers was genial.

Jess kicked him. Quite hard.

'Then again,' said Squeezers, shooting her a sore look, 'I quite like having an app ... appro ... approprial dultitude, so ...'

'You're stuck with me, sergeant,' said Jess.

Knott leant over Eden's shoulder. He ducked out of her way as she said, 'I like you for this, Squeezers, I really do.'

'I like you too, Miss DC Knott,' said Squeezers.

'Knott, could you ...' Eden sat up straight again as his DC withdrew. 'Squeezers, we've asked you in because the first person on the scene heard wheezing as he approached, and so we're touching base with everybody who has compromised breathing.'

'Of course there was wheezing,' said Jess. 'You don't nail a bloke to a cross without wheezing.'

'We have to start somewhere, Jess,' said Eden evenly. 'Squeezers, I'd like to know your whereabouts from approximately eleven p.m. on Saturday evening to five a.m. Sunday morning.'

'That's easy.' Squeezers looked at the ceiling.

Presumably he'd riffled through a mental Rolodex. 'The Druid's Head. There was a lock-in. I slept under a table and woke up at opening time.'

Eden craned his neck to look at Karen. 'Knott, check that with the Druid's Head.'

'Keep an eye on him, Sarge,' said Karen as she backed out of the room.

They sat in silence and waited for DC Knott to do her thing.

The phone on the desk buzzed. 'Yes? Okay. Thanks, Knott.' Eden put down the receiver with some relief. 'Squeezers, you're free to go.' He showed him to the door. 'Your alibi checks out. Stay out of trouble, okay?'

Squeezers bowed. A discreet fart sounded. 'I would be loath to lower your opinion of me, sir.'

Eden watched Squeezers make his way, head held high, through the station. 'I'm not sure he could. The cheek of it!' He gasped. 'He's swiped a packet of biros from DC Carver's desk.'

The phone buzzed again. 'Jess, hang on one second.' Eden jogged back to the table. He winced when the caller identified themselves. 'Yes, guv. I'm just—' He motioned for Jess to wait outside.

She did just that. With her ear cocked.

'Uh-huh ... um ... I ...' Eden seemed to be waiting for the wall of sound on the other end of the line to cease. 'With all due respect, sir ...' He paused, listening. 'Yes, I hate that phrase too, to be honest, but, guv, I don't see Danny as having the strength necessary to erect a cross and then haul a body onto it, never mind kill the victim in the first place.' Another pause. Shot through with tension. 'Yes. I do hear you. I'll talk to him again.'

A smash, the kind of smash a phone makes when jammed back onto its mount.

'You were listening.' Eden wasn't asking. He was telling.

Jess put her head around the door. 'They're leaning on you to lean on Danny.'

'My nephew has Down's,' said Eden. He was pulling on his jacket with unnecessary force. 'No way does he have the muscle tone for a caper like this.' He closed his eyes. Opened them again. 'I don't want to generalise, but it's vanishingly rare for a man with Down's syndrome to commit violent crime.'

Jess remembered Danny from her babysitting career. 'Danny's one of the good guys.'

'Any more thoughts about that symbol I showed you?'

'The one on Keith's body? Plenty. None of them helpful. I can tell you what it isn't. It's not Greek. It's not Roman. Certainly not Ogham, or Futhark. It's most probably made up. It doesn't really signify anything much.'

'If it meant something,' said DS Eden, 'that would help.'

Knott was back. Bristling. She looked from her boss to Jess and back again as if she'd caught them doing something illicit. 'You still here, Dr Castle? What *is* your relationship to Squeezers?'

'We're lovers,' said Jess.

Eden passed his hand over his face.

Chapter 5

THE HIGH MASTER PIG-WIZARD

Wednesday 18 May

Kidbury Road.
The bridge.
The long-stay car park.
The medical centre.
The vet's.
And then the long turn into the main thoroughfare, where the gabled buildings leaning over the pavement regularly gave American coach parties orgasms.

One or two new faces might render Castle Kidbury bearable. Jess needed enough time here to sort out the mess she'd made of Cambridge. Not, she scowled, because her father demanded it – never that! – but because the shame had arrived and Jess wasn't loving it one bit.

A waft of bacon lured her away from the window of Dickinson's Books. *Later*, she thought. Culture could wait. She pushed at the door of The Spinning Jenny.

Bacon and eggs ordered, she sat by the window.

'Hello again!' Rupert made it from door to Jess's table in one manoeuvre. 'Checking out the new joints in town?'

'Just the new bacon and egg joints.' Jess pushed her hair into her face, adjusting to the presence of her brunch companion.

'Excellent plan.' Rupert turned to the short woman slicing cake behind the counter. 'A latte, thanks Meera.'

'To go?' asked Meera. An Indian curl to her words.

'To stay.' He turned to Jess. 'I hope.'

Jess nodded. It was a very nonchalant nod.

Rupert sat, dwarfing the dainty chair, navy coat puddling on the tiled floor. 'Have you ladies met? Meera, this is Jessica. Meera and Moyra took over this place a couple of years ago.'

'Nice to meet you, Meera. I'm Jess, as opposed to Jessica.'

'I've heard about you, actually.' Meera sauntered over with Rupert's drink.

'Really?' Jess did her damnedest to look as if that didn't bother her.

Evidently she didn't try hard enough. Meera smiled, amused, one hand on the back of Rupert's chair.

'You're a bit of a gypsy, they say.'

Jess allowed herself to feel flattered. There were worse reputations to have. And she'd deserve them.

As Meera returned to her cakes, Rupert asked, 'Still hot on the trail of Castle Kidbury's Satanist cult?'

'You can laugh,' said Jess, as Rupert did just that.

'But I'm intrigued. I mean, someone's trying to make the murder look like ancient rites, when it's just gobbledygook.'

'So this PhD of yours—'

'This PhD of mine?' It was a rebuke.

'Sorry. Didn't mean to trivialise it. Your PhD ... does it make you an authority on these things?'

'My area's history, with an emphasis on paganism. Mostly Britain and Ireland, but with bits of Scandinavia thrown in for the hell of it. Plus, of course, you can't ignore the Greeks. But my specialism is from when the Romans left Britain till the Tudors. Roughly. In a nutshell.'

'Impressive stuff. I'd just say one thing ...'

'Do tell me, Rumpole, what's this one thing you would say?'

'DS Eden. Good man. Fine detective. But he does things by the book.'

'So?'

'He relies on procedure, evidence, science. He's not your old-school police, like Eddie was. No hunches. No gut feelings. He likes experts.'

Jess wondered where this was going as bacon, eggs and tea arrived on the table.

'What I'm saying,' continued Rupert, 'is be careful. Be mindful of Eden drawing you into a potentially disturbing case. It would be worth being a little circumspect.'

'So, I need to be careful, mindful and circumspect?' Jess did wide-eyed very well.

'A little wary.'

'Careful. Mindful. Circumspect. And now wary as well. Should I write this down?'

Rupert stirred his latte. 'Just a thought.'

'Sorry, Rumpole.' The fried egg and Rupert's deflation softened Jess a little. 'All my life, men in suits have told me where I'm going wrong. My grandpa, dad, brother. You all sort of sound the same to me. Pinstriped background noise. I tend to ignore it.'

'Whereas you're a better, different cliché. The headstrong lass who hides her privilege and drives an old banger around the countryside.' Rupert sounded defensive. A little hurt.

Which made Jess feel bad. *This*, she thought vehemently, *this is why I don't do men*. 'I might be exposed to yet more potentially disturbing stuff later. I've been asked to sit in on Pan's police interview.'

Rupert's eyebrows conveyed his surprise.

No need for Jess to admit that she'd practically begged until Eden conceded that, yes, her expertise might be useful, and she could listen in from another room.

'I'm saying nothing.' Rupert mimed pulling a zip across his mouth. A glance at his watch. 'Bugger. I'd better dash. Got court papers coming.' He stood as neatly as he'd seated himself. 'So enjoy the bacon and eggs. And ...'

'And?' Jess looked at him squarely. This talent of Rupert's to make her smile was irritating.

'Perhaps I'll see you. Around. Around and about, that is.'

'Perhaps.' Jess forked another slice of breakfast. 'Perhaps not.'

'So mysterious and elusive,' whispered Rupert as he left. 'With a mouthful of bacon.'

Eden was communing with his tape machine again.

'Interview with suspect known as "Pan" commencing at 13.23 on Wednesday the eighteenth of May at Castle Kidbury station with me, Detective Sergeant Eden, present and Dr Jessica Castle observing via video link.' Eden sat back, gaze fixed on the bearded figure opposite.

Pan smirked down at the table is if he read a joke there.

'I'll start by asking why you refused legal counsel. You know it's your right.'

Pan shrugged. Eyes down. Amused. Fidgeting.

'Fair enough. Let's get on with it. Do you suffer from asthma?'

Pan shimmied provocatively. 'Asthma, man.' His head wobbled. 'Asthma.'

'A respiratory problem, then.' Eden spoke deliberately. 'Do you experience trouble breathing?'

'Yeah, well, we all have trouble breathing, don't we? Who can breathe when the air is toxic?'

'Not that toxic in the West Country, surely.'

'I mean pigs sharing the same air as me. Pigs poison the air.'

Eden's nod said he knew how this was going to play out. 'You don't like pigs then? We are, I assume, talking about the police force?'

Pan shrugged. He had a repertoire of tics.

'Let's see if I can help you with that. Give you something to really dislike me for. What's wrong with your breathing, Pan? Because you do wheeze. Snore too, according to my custody officer. Is it weed? Meth? Crack?'

Pan gave a slow shake of his head. Eternally amused.

Eden stood up to riffle through a stack of files. He sat heavily. 'What's this?' He stabbed a finger at the drawing. The circle with the zigzag through it. The lopsided cross on top of it.

Pan sat upright. 'Where'd you get this?'

'What is it?'

Pan slumped. 'You don't recognise it? Man, it's everywhere. It's the "Omen of the Coming of the High Master Pig-Wizard, He Who Will Suck Life from the Bones of Men and End All Days".'

Eden gawped.

Pan cackled. 'Or something. Who knows? It looks like a very special squiggle. Well done, Mr Pig.'

Eden stared. '*You* may think this is funny. I'm deadly serious. You're here because of all the drugs we found lying around at Pitt's Field, but if you want to get back to your lady friends you'll have to answer my questions.'

'I don't do drugs. I get what I need from nature. From the cosmos. A natural high. *Super*-natural.'

This excursion into transcendental territory delivered Eden a cue. 'How do you feel about sheep, Pan?'

Now Pan was engaged. He grinned and pulled his

chair so he was locked against the table. 'I like 'em. They're mild. Sheepies go with the flow.'

'You like them enough to steal them from farmers?'

'Maybe I do.'

'You like sheep enough to sacrifice them?'

Pan threw back his head and crowed with laughter. 'Why not? Sounds like a laugh.'

'Is it a laugh to slit their throats and leave them pinned to barbed wire by the road?'

Pan pursed his lips. Gave his signature shrug.

'Anything else you like killing? Do you sacrifice anything else? Other animals. Pigs maybe. Or humans. Does that constitute a laugh too?'

'Naughty naughty.' Pan was lucid now, shifting his tone abruptly. His voice still had its sing-song mock-nutcase tone, but he locked eyes with the detective sergeant. 'I know where this is heading. There's talk, you know? People saying there's a crazy man tearing people's guts out, ripping their limbs off. Setting the blood free!' Pan chuckled. 'You know something? I get it. I get where the magic killer dude is at. I feel what *he* feels, because I know the devil, Mr John Eden. Just like your man does. I commune with the souls of the dead. I worship the goddess, yeah. But you have a problem.' Pan shook his head. 'Just because you want it to be me, don't mean it *is* me.' Pan shoved the table an inch, disturbing Eden's mug of coffee. 'You saying such things does not please me.'

Eden sensed a stalemate. He shifted down a gear. 'If you don't do it yourself, do you get your women to do it? Perhaps you seduce them into murder. Sending girls out into the night to "set the blood free".'

Pan bleated his crazy laugh again. 'Like I said, Piggy Wiggy, that sounds good. I like the Pan you're describing. The thing is, my son, you haven't got diddly shit on me. Maybe I'm into the sheep thing. Then again, maybe I'm not. I've got some big respect for whoever it is you're after for the human sacrifice. But I didn't do it. All you've got is a handful of spliffs. You know they're for personal use. So give me an on-the-spot fine and send me on my way. The Durham pigs don't even target recreational users anymore.'

'You're not in Durham anymore, Toto.' Eden noticed that Pan didn't get the *Wizard of Oz* reference. 'You're on my patch, and the reason we've been able to hold you is the presence of crack paraphernalia on your field.'

'Not my field,' said Pan, quick as a whip.

'We found taped-up plastic bottles with straws stuck into their sides. Lighters everywhere.'

'One man's *paraphernalia* is another man's trash. You found nothing like that in my van. And that's why ...' Pan performed a drum roll with his nicotine-stained fingers. 'You have to let me go.'

'He's a total arsehole,' said Jess, hot on Eden's heels to his office.

'I'd hoped for input of a more professional nature.' Eden sat at his desk with an audible sigh of relief.

The desk, thought Jess, reflected his mind. It was neat. Organised. Something he could control when the rest of the world refused to cooperate. No framed photographs, she noticed. A computer. A proper pen. A stack of files that had been fastidiously tidied; Jess knew how files could take over your life if you didn't show them who's boss.

'Knott!'

Eden's shout made Jess jump.

'My professional input,' began Jess. She tried to look casual, as if she sat in on police interviews every other day, while inwardly reeling from the fact that Castle Kidbury nick – that blank building in the business park at the end of Margaret Thatcher Way – really did have a video link set up for the interview rooms. She'd assumed that was the stuff of television producers' fantasies. 'Pan's not specific when he talks about ritual or sacrifice. He uses colourful language but doesn't name any deity except Satan, who's like the *Elvis* of black magic; everybody knows about Satan.' She paused. 'Although he did mention the undead . . .'

'He mentioned a goddess. Could be your . . .' Eden tapped a key and looked at the computer screen. 'Hecate.'

'Hmm.' Jess faced the fact that Pan had said something solid; a cold wind disturbed her excitement at being a legit police consultant. 'Hecate, among her many other jobs, looks after the undead. The vengeful souls. He does spout a lot of random bullshit, though. Perhaps he just got lucky.' She realised Eden was looking at her. Hard.

'You don't want it to be him.'

'No. Yes. I mean,' Jess pinned down the feeling, 'I suppose I just don't want to think I've met a sadistic killer.'

That look again. Appraising. 'This isn't a hobby, Jess. This is police work. It's not pretty.' He shouted again – '*Knott!*' – just as Karen appeared in the doorway.

'All right, all right,' she said, mock-shirtily. It turned to genuine shirtiness when she saw Jess.

'Did you ...' Eden gestured at the package in her hand. 'That urgent thing I asked you to do?'

'What? Oh yes, boss. I put a tenner in the whip-round for Hemmings' retirement on your behalf.'

Eden's eyelids fluttered. 'And?' He held out his hand.

'And?' Karen looked confused. 'Um, and they'll probably get him a tankard with his name on, or maybe a—'

'I meant, may I have the urgent item in your hand, Knott.'

'Sorry, sir, what am I like?' giggled Karen. With great reverence, she handed Eden the rectangular cardboard box. 'It's been thoroughly gone over, sir. You can touch it as much as you like. They've cleaned it up. They took out the—'

'Thank you, Knott.'

Karen smiled and carried on. '—disembodied eyes.'

'Eyes?' said Jess. 'Did she say eyes?'

Karen slipped out.

'It's an art,' said Eden. 'That knack Knott has for saying exactly the wrong thing. Forget the eyes for a minute, Jess.'

'Bit of an ask, but okay.'

'And just talk to me about this.' Eden set down the

carved box. It glowed warmly in the frigid practicality of his office.

'Wow.' Jess bent down. She trailed a finger over the inlays. The lines. The dark trees. She looked up at Eden. Her tone was accusing. 'How come you didn't show me this earlier? It's slap bang in my area. This could be the killer talking directly to us!'

'Hang on a minute.' Eden fixed on her. 'You're not police. I don't have to stick every last piece of evidence under your nose just because you've got a GCSE in old stones. There's a reason we don't disclose details to the public. And you *are* the public, Jess.' He seemed to hear himself, and softened slightly. 'Besides, perhaps these images are just doodles.'

'Are the Palaeolithic cave paintings in Lascaux doodles? Are the ancient murals in the Valley of the Kings doodles? Every time man daubs a mark on a surface, he's communicating. Your signature is a symbol. That!' Jess, revving up, pointed at the portrait of the Queen on the wall of Eden's office. 'She's covered in symbols. Her crown. Her sash. Her orb. They all scream one thing: power.' She folded her arms. 'With her symbols, Her Majesty Queen Elizabeth II is warning you not to fuck with her.'

'I get it,' said Eden. Level. Contained. 'Symbols aren't doodles.'

With respect, with something like awe, Jess took up the casket. It was ten centimetres by eight, about five centimetres high. A basic rectangle with a lid that fitted whisper-tight. Smooth to the touch. The inlays were flush with the polished gingernut yew. 'This is pains-takingly done.' She lifted the lid carefully. She tried to ignore the blackish tidemark left by blood. 'These craters? Are they where the eyes sat?'

'Yes. Those lines and dashes, Jess, are they just made up?' asked Eden.

'They're a language.' Jess felt a vibration in the room. A green shoot of excitement. 'It's Ogham.' The hollow beat of old drums sounded in her ears.

'Do you . . .' Eden sounded as if he was afraid to ask. 'Can you read Ogham?'

'I can.' Jess felt power tingle in her fingers as she care-fully replaced the lid and turned the box over and over. She had purpose. *I'm useful.* 'The trees are talking to us, too.' She stroked the four of them in turn. 'This is an ash. This is poplar. Yew. Rowan.'

'And it's made of yew, too. Could that be significant?'

'Very possibly.'

'Yew trees grow in churchyards.'

'They're associated with death, but that's a Christian thing. Christians,' said Jess, 'generally ruin everything when they get involved. Your druid knew how to have a good time. To the ancient people, the yew was as much about life as it was about death. Rebirth. Yew leaves were laid on graves to remind the dead that death was just a pause before the afterlife.'

'He's mocking his victims,' said Eden.

'Hmm. Or is he promising them eternal life?'

Knott had stolen back in. 'Whichever it is, he's got a bloody cheek.'

Jess ignored her. She was deep in her own world, the equivalent of Eden's desk; it was where she felt secure. Where she was always right. 'Yew's toxic, of course. The ash suggests wisdom. Protection. Poplars are about vision. Sages use it to *see*. To see beyond what's around us.'

Karen shuddered. Took a step closer to Eden.

'The rowan is also about protection, but it's connected to clarity. To showing the way.' Jess felt her breathing quicken. 'This box is trying to tell us something.'

Eden's breathing hadn't quickened. 'The funny lines around the sides. Is Ogham an alphabet?'

'In a way. A much more instinctive, less rigid way.' Jess loved Ogham the way some people love people. 'See these strokes across a central perpendicular line? They refer to the first letters of trees. It's an alphabet based on trees, if you can imagine such a thing. It's pure,' she said, almost to herself, as those Celtic mists curled about her.

Knott cut through the mist. 'Beardy-weirdy codswallop.'

Eden stared at his constable as if wondering what he'd done in a past life to deserve her. 'Knott,' he said. 'Leave us for a while, would you?'

'She did *not* like that,' said Jess, as Knott closed the door behind her with a little too much energy. 'Our murderer's familiar with Ogham. And in Ogham, the yew is very sacred.' A thought pounced; Jess blazed. A piece had fallen into place. 'The yew is also a reminder that this life is all illusion. This box has a secret. But if it's *telling* us it has a secret . . .'

69

'It might also give us the tools to solve it.'

Jess sniffed the casket, sending Eden's eyebrows up into his Lego hair. 'Shamans used to get high on the resin from yew trees. Gave them visions.'

'Unless you have a vision of the name and address of the killer, that's not much use to me.'

'You don't have to believe in magic for it to work. Look, I'm an academic. I'm all about the facts, but whoever crafted this box has knowledge of the old ways, and they mean a lot to him.'

'The box is our way into his head.'

'Exactly.' Jess hesitated before picking up the box again. She felt the responsibility keenly. 'There's one letter on each side of the box. This tells me where to start.' She pointed to the 'more than' symbol.

'So *that* tells you where to stop.' Eden indicated the 'less than' symbol.

'Yessir.' Jess turned the receptacle in her hand, interpreting as she went. She concentrated. She was rusty. 'E,' she said. 'Y. Another E. And . . .' She squinted, remembering.

'S,' said Jess and Eden in unison.

'Eyes.' Eden snorted.

'Our man is literal *and* sarcastic.' Jess enunciated what was in the air. 'Very Pan.'

'Yet this is sensitive work.' Eden caressed the box. Then pulled his hand away.

Jess understood its allure. It was a sensuous little thing, despite its dark purpose. Perhaps because of it.

'Nothing here about your three-headed goddess?' Eden seemed to want a 'yes'.

70

He got a 'no'. 'Hecate is associated closely with the yew tree. Death. The underworld. That's all Hecate's brief. Bulls slaughtered in her name were garlanded with yew, and yew trees were planted in circles to protect centres of natural energy. We came along and built our churches on those energy spots. Plus Hecate helps her worshippers with potions, some of them good, some of them deadly. Yew's a big ingredient when cooking with Hecate.'

'All very interesting, but not sure where it gets us.' Eden took the box suddenly, dropped it back into its cardboard case. 'Don't discuss this with anybody, Jess. These symbols don't leave this room.'

'Got it, no leaky-weakies.'

'If that happened I'd have no option but to remove you from the investigation.'

Jess pulled on her jacket. 'You mean I'm *on* the investigation?'

'I suppose,' said Eden, disassociating, looking at his computer screen, 'I do.'

Chapter 6

AN AFFAIR OF THE HEART

Thursday 19 May

The dream chased Jess out of bed earlier than she would have liked. So early that she witnessed the Judge on his way out of the front door with his bicycle.

Lycra, she thought, *should be a restricted product for the over-sixties.*

'See you,' she said. The phrase served a double purpose. Polite enough to build a bridge, casual enough to irk him. She leant on the polished oak console that had stood in the hallway since before she was even an idea. The arrangement of inherited this and that on top of it hadn't changed. A pink snuffbox. A brass tray where keys and buttons were thrown. 'Where's the fox?' Jess frowned.

Out on the porch, the Judge didn't look back. 'Do you mean Mum's fox?'

'You hated it,' remembered Jess. She hadn't much

liked the porcelain animal herself. Pert. Sarky. Bright orange. 'Mum loved it.'

'She did.' The Judge swung a leg over his bike and was away.

Even that one small rebellion couldn't be allowed. Harriet had made acquiescing to her husband an art form, but she'd hung onto that fox. The Judge had muttered about it every evening when he came in. Harriet had countered that it made her smile. It had kept its place on the oak table.

Now it was purged. The Judge sure had an eye for detail.

'Moose?' She trailed through the kitchen, through the back door and out into the sun-filled garden. Jimbo, the Castles' gardener since forever, took pride in his work; the lawn glowed, spilling out towards the old orchard.

She heard Moose. A distant, restrained 'uff' rather than his usual out-and-out 'arf'. Jess followed the sound to the narrow passage that ran beside the defunct pool. Moose capered leadenly along it. Jess smiled, an artless wide grin that transformed her wan face. Beyond this dark, green passage was a glorious grotto of roses. Her mum had loved her rose garden as though it were a discreet lover. She talked to it and believed it talked back. The roses knew Harriet. And Jimbo would have kept it just so. Radiant and generous.

Jess reached the end of the passage. Her head swam as if she'd been struck. 'What the fucking hell is this?'

'Hello, my darling.' Bogna's blonde head appeared

from behind a thick patch of rhubarb. There was mud on the end of her nose. 'Welcome to my allotment!'

Jess's eyes welled. She was livid, impotent in the face of desolation. 'What have you done, Bogna? What have you done?'

Bogna approached her, reached out, but Jess wasn't having it.

'Oh no. You might get your hands on the garden, but you *don't* get your hands on me. This was Mum's rose garden. She loved this place more than anything and you come here . . .' Jess began to splutter. 'You have come here and you've stolen the kitchen, you've stolen her apron, you've thrown away lovely *special* things and now you kill what she loved most. Get the fuck out. I don't care what "the Judge" says, get out of my house and keep going till you drop dead!'

Bogna gently took her hands. She pulled her to her, pushing through the angry resistance. She held Jess tight as the tears came. 'It is all right, my *kochana*. There, there. It's all all right, isn't it.'

Bogna's arms melted Jess's fury into shame. She was an overgrown child. Running away from college. Screaming at Polish women. 'It's not all right, Bogna,' she whimpered. 'It's all wrong.'

'Let's sit in the kitchen,' said Bogna, releasing Jess from her somewhat firm embrace.

The kitchen was always cooler than the rest of the house. It was where she and Stephen had played in the unbearable heat of childhood summers.

74

Bogna brought a teapot – the new, upstart teapot – to the table.

Jess sipped silently. She was chastened by Bogna's generosity.

Bogna began. 'Jimmy is ... *your father* is unwell.'

'Unwell?' Jess's mind emptied. 'When you say unwell, Bogna, what does that mean?'

'It is his heart.'

Jess's face crumpled. 'Oh God. Fuck, fuck, fuck.' Remorse flooded into the empty spaces of Jess's brain. 'Why didn't somebody call me? What is it, when did—'

'Just before Christmas. Heart attack, *kochana*. He was lifting boxes of your mother's clothes and he falls down. Just like that.' Bogna clapped her hands. Jess jumped. 'The doctors at hospital tell him it is arctic stasis. Or attic stavros, something like that. He has pills now and he feels better.' She smiled. 'Can I tell you why I do these things you do not like?'

Jess nodded.

'I did not know your mother, of course, but I see she was loved by everyone. Especially by your father.'

Jess snorted.

'No, my darling, it is very true. I came here to keep things a bit tidy just. I soon saw that Jimmy was living without reason he used to have for living. So when he was ill, I thought, well, that's it, it's up to me to keep him well. I am not trying to be wife, *kochana*. I don't want nuffing from him. Only for Jimmy to get better. To want to live. So I make an allotment, you see! To grow him

75

healthy things to eat. To make his heart well. And, yes, Jimbo took away Mum's roses.' Bogna offered her hands from across the table. 'Jess, your mother is gone. But your father is here. Let's make sure that he *stays* here.'

Kidbury Road.

The bridge.

The long-stay car park.

The medical centre.

The vet's.

And then the long turn into the main thoroughfare. A right. A left. A cut-through.

The house Jess was looking for was on the end of a row of hobbit cottages, the one spacious modern house on the street.

'Jess?' It was Eden, emerging from a twee wooden porch.

'Do you live here?' The house didn't suit him. 'Jesus, do you both live here?' she said, as Karen Knott followed him down the path.

'We're going door to door,' said Karen.

'Like on the telly,' said Jess.

'Just like that.' Eden was thin-lipped.

'Bit beneath a detective sergeant, surely?' Jess savoured his repressed sigh.

'The boss requested more manpower. Didn't you, sir?' asked Karen, as if her superior officer was a dim but well-loved pet. 'No go, so he's out here, doing his bit.'

'Nice,' said Jess. She meant it. 'Getting your hands dirty.'

'Where are you off to?' asked Eden.

'Don't let us hold you up,' said Karen.

'I'm on my way to ...' Jess lifted her arm to point, then dropped it. Best if she didn't say. 'Why don't I help you?' Jess had no intention of following Rupert's advice; why break the habit of a lifetime? Besides, he was wrong about Eden; the man didn't drag her into anything disturbing, he kept her at arm's length. 'In case signs and symbols come up.'

'Most irregular,' snapped Karen.

Jess was already halfway up the next path. She raised the brass knocker. An elderly lady in standard-issue knitted cardigan opened the door.

'Good morning.' Eden held his police badge aloft. 'I'm DS Eden from Castle Kidbury station and I wondered if you had time for a few questions.'

The lady peered at his badge.

Knott said, 'It's Mrs Holyoake, isn't it?' She leant against the door jamb. 'I remember you from the Neighbourhood Watch meetings. How's your budgie? Still bald?'

'What we'd like to know, Mrs Holyoake,' interjected Eden, 'is whether you knew the late Keith Dike.'

Mrs Holyoake put her hand to her throat. 'Dreadful business. I heard he was eaten by circus animals.'

Jess converted her giggle into a complicated cough.

Eden glowered at Jess. 'Could you tell us how you knew Mr Dike, and if you know of anyone who might have had a quarrel with him?'

'Keith Dike put my family through hell.' Mrs

Holyoake twisted a tissue in her arthritic hands.

'Go on,' said Eden. He was alert, like Moose when he heard the fridge door open.

'My husband bought a carburettor for a Robin Reliant off him a while back. Paid him cash. Keith only goes and gives him a carburettor for a Ford Escort.' Mrs Holyoake pulled in her chin, her tale of despair finished. 'Ooh, my hubby was livid.'

'Would it be possible,' said Eden, 'to talk to your husband?'

'Dead, dear. Since 1983.'

Four more houses. Four more swirly hall carpets. Four more tales of Keith Dike's lack of civic duty.

'We're learning nothing new about Keith,' said Eden as they convened by the big house on the end. 'It's all *he painted my shed the wrong colour* or *his whippet crapped on my dahlias.* Nobody liked the sour old bastard, but nobody would kill him, either. People were even good enough to take him home from the pub when his trousers fell down.'

Knott closed her eyes in virginal horror. 'He was a dirty filthy pervert, Sarge.'

'Keith was not,' snapped Eden, 'a pervert. He was a mardy pisshead whose trousers didn't fit. Honestly, Knott, sometimes ...'

There was a clatter at the modern house as two figures bustled out.

'Danny!' called Eden, hand raised in greeting.

'Jess!' Danny's face erupted into a smile.

'Is this where you were headed?' Knott, who caught

on to very little, managed to catch on to this. 'To interview a suspect on your own?'

'He's not a suspect, he's an old friend.' Jess was rumbled. Part-rumbled; she'd been looking forward to seeing Danny.

Hugs. Danny was big on hugging.

'Danny has something to say.' Danny's mother was mithered. Coat askew. 'Tell him, Daniel. Tell Mr Eden what you told me.'

Danny's good cheer evaporated. Head down, teeth gritted, he said, 'I was going to meet Tallulah.' He turned to Jess. 'I'm not a sneak. She said I could give her name.'

'He. Has. A. Girlfriend.' Danny's mother was appalled. A tired woman, she was doing her best not to be angry. 'She's, you know, like him. He knows that's not on.'

'Is she nice, Danny?' asked Jess.

'She's a goddess,' said Danny.

Eden and Jess very carefully didn't look at each other as they said their goodbyes.

'Right, that's Barton Street done.' Eden scratched a line through a page of his notebook and turned to DC Knott. 'Where next?'

'Technically, it should be Parson's Hill, sir, but we did diverge from the itinerary at—'

'Just name a road, Knott!'

DC Knott's plain little gob, the face of a parlourmaid in a BBC period drama, fell. 'In that case, Parson's Hill, sir.' To Jess, she said, 'You don't have to come'.

Jess wondered if Eden knew that his DC was in love

with him. 'Do you have a boyfriend, Karen?' she asked as they toiled up Parson's Hill.

'I'm married to the job, like the boss,' said Karen. She seemed proud of this.

Eden muttered, 'I wouldn't say I'm married to the job.'

'At least, sir,' said Karen, 'the job won't treat you like a right bitch and bleed you dry of your last penny, eh.' She shook her head, remembering. 'Mrs Eden was a right bitch.'

Eden stopped dead, about to say something, but thought better of it. 'Let's stick to the matter in hand, Knott.'

'*He's lonely*,' mouthed Karen, pulling a sad face.

'Nah,' said Jess. 'He's in his element.' She saw something raw on Eden's face. She let him walk ahead.

Two more streets. Many gossipy anecdotes. Nothing, as Eden said, 'of any real use'.

'If Keith was unpopular, but not so unpopular that somebody would kill him, it's a motive problem,' said Jess as they approached the car park on Cheap Street. 'A murder occurred, but there's no reason for it.' Jess slipped into the tone she used for lectures. 'It's like archaeology. When you find something from the past but you're not sure what it is, you place it in various contexts to give you possible answers. You try to establish what it is you *do* have, so you have a better idea of what you *don't* have. You slowly build a picture until you're closer to the truth. Being a detective is a bit like being an archaeologist.'

'Except somebody's dead.' Eden was sharp. 'And whoever killed him is still at large. So, no, it's not like archaeology and we're not putting together a broken jug on *Time Team*.'

'Understood.' Jess had shown her hand; she needed to ease off, insert herself into the drama more subtly. Eden mustn't know how badly she needed this case while she licked her wounds in Castle Kidbury. 'Any chance of a lift?'

She winced as Eden's face hardened.

Apparently there wasn't.

Chapter 7

IF I'D KNOWN YOU WERE COMING
I'D HAVE BAKED A CAKE

Friday 20 May

In her bed, Jess drowned over and over. It was hard to discern the true nature of sounds through the distorting water. Were they screams or laughs?

A chunk of broken glass drifted by. Too close. She panicked. She scrabbled away. She woke up.

It was late. Even by her standards. By Harebell House standards, it was criminal. The old floorboards were cold beneath Jess's bare feet as she stood outside her bedroom and listened. This house always had something to say.

This morning it echoed her dream. Running water. She heard humming. A gentle whining. She crept instinctively up the narrow stairs to the attic bathroom, where she found her father wrestling with a soapy Moose.

'Ah. Jessica. Good. You can help.'

Jess knew the drill. She secured Moose by the collar as her father scooped the reluctant hound out of the bath and onto the mat. Fickle old Moose hated both getting into the bath and out of it.

'You had that watery dream again.'

Jess felt spied on. 'How the hell do you know that?'

'The noises from your room.' The Judge worked around any need for eye contact by concentrating on the wriggling golden retriever. 'Whimpers. You used to have that dream when you were small. Your mother gave you the creeps when she shut off our pool so dramatically.'

Could he have forgotten? Only an ogre of self-absorption could forget such a day. 'Dad, seriously, it wasn't our pool that gave me the creeps.'

Childhood memories are out of whack.

Adults so tall.

Their behaviour seen only opaquely.

The seven-year-old Jess who'd dangled her legs in the water at a birthday pool party had misunderstood the parallel grown-up world around the noisy indoor lagoon.

The adults were dry. Dressed up. The kids were sopping wet.

Something held the day as if in a pair of scissors. A sharp edge hovered over the bunting.

Beneath the chlorine was a vaporous smell the adult Jess would recognise as wet paint.

The dad of the house – she hadn't known his name;

seven-year-olds don't clock the names of their friends' fathers – kept saying stuff in a funny tone. Bitey. Funny but horrid. As if he was saying two things at once but one of the meanings was covered up. She remembered him taking Harriet by the hand when they arrived – oh Mum! So slim and so pretty and without a line on her face in this troubled home movie – and pointing to a plaque.

Decorative, out of place, it was a pretty carving of a lady. 'See that, Mrs C,' the dad had said. '*That's* the only thing in the whole place I was allowed to choose, even though muggins here paid for everything.'

Jess had looked around for Muggins.

Close up, the dad smelt peculiar. Like the glass of wood-coloured water her own dad sometimes poured himself after a day in court, just before he locked himself away in his study.

The memory was not only tilted, it was stained. Jess refused to examine it too closely in case she saw her own guilty face reflected in the scissor-cut water.

'Jessica!' The Judge's voice brought her back to the moment. 'Towel!'

Jess knelt and took Moose's collar again as her father towelled the dog's coat, before releasing him to shake the remaining water from his fur with a forty-kilogram shudder.

'I have a vague plan to convert one of the barns just to deal with this,' said the Judge. 'Running hot water. Walk-in tub. Industrial hairdryer. As it stands, the bathroom needs a wash after this bugger has one.'

Jess just looked at him. 'Dad.'

The Judge looked back. He was very still.

'Why didn't you tell me? I'd have come back at Christmas if I'd known.'

The Judge reanimated. 'First of all, it wasn't that big a deal. I was packing boxes in the loft. And then I was in a room at the hospital. Simple as that. Didn't feel a thing, actually. None of that left arm, crushing chest pain stuff they go on about.'

Jess shook her head. 'You make it sound like a sneeze.'

'Well exactly. It came, it went.'

'Dad,' pleaded Jess. Her voice cracked a little on the simple word.

His hands planted themselves in his pockets. 'Now look. We've all had plenty to deal with. There was my bloody retirement. Your mother.'

'Everyone knew except me.'

'I didn't want to bother you with it, Jess. You were still getting over Mum. And you ... Well, it's done now. There we are.' The Judge drained the bath, fiddling with the plug. He was hapless at anything domestic.

'So what *is* the problem with your heart? Bogna said something about arctic stasis.'

'Not quite.' The Judge smiled. 'Aortic stenosis. Quite common in men my age. Easily dealt with.'

'Oh, that's all right then.' Jess was arch. 'So if I google "aortic stenosis" that's what it'll say? Easily dealt with?'

The Judge threw the sponge into the empty bath. 'Maybe not in so many words.'

Jess rubbed her forehead. 'For fuck's sake, Dad.'

Her father glared his courtroom glare. The one he'd used for sentencing wife beaters to three years in jail and for reprimanding ten-year-old Jess. The Anglo-Saxon, Norse and Celtic nonsense was bad enough, but he abhorred bad language.

Especially, Jess knew, from a *woman*.

'Sorry. But, Dad, heart attacks kill people.'

'Yes, yes, I know, but it wasn't a big one. I'm still here. Fit as a flea. I keep myself busy, I have a routine, look after the dog. Keeps my mind off ... things. Bogna's a marvel. Got me on a good, proper diet.'

'Yeah, I know about *that*.'

'And I'm doing twenty K on the bike every morning.'

'Dad!' snapped Jess. 'You sound like one of *those* people.'

'Which people?'

'The ones who say "twenty K".'

The Judge shook with a silent laugh. 'Listen to me, Jessica. It's treatable. I'm on medication, I'm taking exercise, and there's a procedure I might be eligible for. Quite common for men my age. Easily dealt with.'

Easily dealt with, thought Jess. Just the way her father liked it.

Tallulah, Eden found as he chatted to her in the interview room, was self-possessed. She answered his questions with aplomb.

Yes, she'd been up on the hill. No, she hadn't seen Danny. He was a bit late and she'd told him before not to keep her waiting. She'd hurried away when a taller man came up through the mist. She worried it was her father, that she and her Romeo had been found out. The man wheezed. Was dragging something.

Then Tallulah had questions for Eden.

'Is anything going to happen to Danny? He's a really good person. We're engaged.'

DS Eden liked Tallulah a lot. He liked the haughty way she refused DC Knott's offer of squash, and her certainty that she would marry Danny. He sent her home in a police car. He recalled the beleaguered love on Danny's mother's face.

There were a lot of loose ends in policing.

'There's nothing to read in this house,' said Jess to her father as they cleared away after a home-made, frugal (i.e. no seconds) lunch.

'Harebell House is *full* of books.' The Judge put the plates in the sink. Left a mug on its side. An intelligent man, he had never brought his brain to bear on washing up. As he walked away, he said, 'You do love a good moan, Jessica.'

He was right on both counts. Most rooms had a smattering of books, perched lazily on tables like guests at a so-so party. The large drawing room, with windows to the front and back, was lined with built-in shelves, all of them packed with books.

'Law books,' scoffed Jess. She trailed her finger along the spines. Biographies of Prime Ministers. Victorian novels. Around the bow window that framed the lawn in small squares of green, she found Ms Georgette Heyer and Ms Barbara Cartland.

Her mother's books were stories of romance. Of ladies in muslin and velvet, dropping gloves in front of their beaux. They exuded a femininity that Jess had never aspired to. No heroine in those pages wore what Harriet used to call 'bovver boots'. Nor did they go all the way on the first date.

Jess tried to remember her last first date.

Kidbury Road.

The bridge.

The long-stay car park.

The medical centre.

The vet's.

And then the long turn into the main thoroughfare. Dickinson's bookshop smelt of old paper, dust and the proprietor's cat. Shakespeare sat on a cushion by the cash register, judging customers and letting out the occasional sarcastically timed fart.

Jess tickled Shakespeare under his chin. The cat struck out a vindictive paw. 'How old are you by now?' she asked it, and was surprised when it answered.

'Almost fourteen.'

The voice was Graham's. He bobbed up from beneath the counter. Glasses on top of his head. A moustache as dated as the rest of him. Jess had long suspected Graham Dickinson wore tweed Y-fronts. There were no niceties. No *good to see you, when did you get back?* He loathed being interrupted while he read his way through his stock. With a book open in one hand, he added only, 'Yes?'

'I want a book.' Only when she'd said it did Jess realise how obvious this sounded. She allowed Graham a regal roll of his eyes. 'Fiction. Modern. No slushy stuff. Blockbuster, maybe.'

'Right-hand shelves by the window, third row up.' Flipping his glasses down onto his nose, Graham returned to Tolstoy.

'I liked the Beeb adaptation of *War and Peace*.' Jess enjoyed his tut. She waited a beat before asking, 'Is the book as good?'

Graham put down Tolstoy and covered Shakespeare's ears. 'You always were a cheeky madam,' he said; his version of *welcome home*. 'Go to the *Da Vinci Code* section where you belong, young lady, and leave me in the company of the greats.'

None of the books offered the right kind of escapism. There were too many guns, too much talk of 'gutwrenching suspense' on the covers. Jess wanted something outside her own experience, but nothing apocalyptic. She wasn't in the right frame of mind to read about the planet being invaded by hyper-intelligent wasps.

The Pagan/Occult/Superstition shelves were still by the cubbyhole which housed Graham's kettle. She'd campaigned for him to separate 'Pagan' from its bedfellows, but he'd stood firm. She'd been a loyal customer, passing Wilson's, where her school friends were spending their pocket money on lip gloss, in order to purchase Buckland's *Complete Book of Witchcraft*, or *Gods and*

Myths of Northern Europe by Ellis Davidson. She'd been a strange kid, by her own reckoning.

Wandering back to the fiction section, Jess was considering why she needed so desperately to escape into a make-believe world – perhaps the Judge was right and her middle name had predetermined her obsession with myth – when the bell over the door tinkled.

Rupert. Suddenly very *there* in his uniform of pin-stripe suit and well-cut overcoat. Not looking her way, he browsed the shelves. He frowned, leaning in to read titles. He felt his chin. He made a little *hmm* noise. He was a useless actor.

Jess cleared her throat. When Rupert twirled round, she put up her hands and said, 'Gosh! What a surprise!'

'Jess,' said Rupert, as if she was the very last woman he expected to see in Dickinson's Books. 'Hi. Just looking for something to read. I love this place.'

'Who are you?' asked Graham querulously.

'Oh *you*,' said Rupert.

'I mean it, who are you?' Graham was not a team player. 'Have you come to make a purchase or to waste my time?'

'Bit of both,' said Rupert. He grabbed the nearest volume. Small, red, 'foxed', as booksellers say, it looked old. 'I'll take this.'

'Eighty-nine pounds, please.'

Shakespeare looked smug as Rupert recovered his poise and took out his wallet. 'Are you, um, sure?' he asked weakly.

'Quite sure. Eighty-nine pounds is the book's market

value.' Graham spoke to Jess as he laboriously processed Rupert's credit card. 'And you? Are you buying or using my establishment as a bus shelter?'

'I'm still browsing.' Jess privately thought that the average bus shelter was cleaner than Graham's shop, and involved less cat.

By her side, Rupert stared at the rows of spines. 'Still in town, then?'

'For the time being.'

'Don't you have a job to go to? I recall Stephen saying something about Cambridge.'

'Christ, my brother *does* listen occasionally. Yeah, I have a position at Cambridge, but it's kind of messed-up.'

'Was it you who messed it up?'

'Actually,' said Jess, with mock pride that made Rupert laugh, 'I did.'

'So you're looking for another job?'

'Not exactly. I'm mulling over my options.' Jess studied the shelves as if they held the meaning of life. 'Heard anything more about the murder?'

From the counter, Graham interrupted. 'The murder? A calamity! I keep Shakespeare in at night now.'

'Very wise,' said Rupert, with the merest of side-eyes at Jess.

'I heard the killer drained the body and stuffed it with straw.' Graham shivered happily.

Rupert lowered his voice, to exclude Graham. 'This messed-up position at Cambridge – you're a lecturer?'

'I'm not sure.' If a tree falls in the forest, does it make

a noise? Similarly, if a lecturer has no students to lecture, is she just flapping her chops? 'I'm taking some time out.' She groaned. 'That sounds wanky. Next thing, I'll be finding myself. Truth is, since you insist on knowing, I'm in limbo.'

'No, you're in Castle Kidbury.'

Graham butted in. 'The town's named after her, you know.'

Jess pushed her hand over her red face. 'Graham, please don't—'

Graham came out from behind the counter to say, pedantically, 'It's a common misconception that Castle Kidbury is named after a castle, but look around you, dear boy. There *is* no castle. There's always been a Lord Castle at Kidbury Manor. You and I, we're mere serfs.'

Rupert bowed, with a dandyish flourish.

'If you ever do that again,' said Jess, 'I'll kill you. You'll know all this, Rupert, from Stephen.'

'Yeah, 'course I do. Your brother's very proud of his posh connections. Just think,' said Rupert, 'you could have been Lady Jessica.'

'That amuses you?' pouted Jess.

'Frankly, yes.'

Unlike Stephen, Jess was grateful that her father's side of the family had lost the manor and gone into law. She made for the door. 'Thanks, Graham,' she called.

'Next time,' he snapped, 'buy something.'

Rupert was quickly at her side as she meandered along the pavement.

'Don't you have somewhere to be? Hoodlums to defend?'

'Hoodlum-free day today.' Rupert sauntered, matching her pace. His dark fringe swished over one blue eye. 'Apart from our murder, Castle Kidbury's a pretty crime-free place.'

The window of Lady Jayne sported a static tableau of mannequins in pastel dress and coat combos. As if one of the dummies had come to life, a woman in man-made separates rushed out, colliding with Jess and Rupert.

'For heaven's sake—' All was forgiven when Patricia Smalls recognised Jess. 'Look who it is! I heard you were back.' She air-kissed the younger woman. Patricia crackled with energy. Even a friendly greeting felt like a drone attack. 'Did you know I'm mayor now? I am. Can you imagine?'

Jess really couldn't. Patricia Smalls was a family legend. The Judge had once driven the wrong way down a one-way street to avoid her. She was everywhere at once. If you spotted her coming out of the florist's and ducked into the gift shop, you might very well come up against her by the fridge magnets. 'Congratulations.'

'It's nothing, really. Although I did beat Marjorie Beals. Which was nice.' Patricia looked from Jess to Rupert, then back to Jess again. 'Aha,' she said. Her pencilled eyebrows waggled like mating caterpillars. She brought her face close to Jess's. Jess could see every pore in her sizeable nose. 'He's a catch, dear. His people have a chalet in the Norfolk Broads.'

'You're kidding!' gasped Jess.

Patricia Smalls seemed to consider the possibility that she was being mocked. Deciding against it, she reconfigured her mobile, slightly orange face, to convey 'polite distress'. 'Isn't this murder business shocking? I mean, Mr Dike was nobody's idea of a good citizen, but to pull him apart and sew him back together in the wrong order!'

The rumours had taken on a life of their own. 'I'm sure DS Eden will keep us all safe,' said Jess.

'As mayor, I'm in constant contact with him. I think of you all as my children.' Patricia had something green on one of her prominent front teeth. 'I'm sure all the nastiness will be tidied away before our summer day trippers start turning up.' She looked around her, breathed in deeply. 'Ah! Is there anything more lovely than an English market town in May?'

Jess breathed in, too. 'Mmm. The sweet smell of roses and blood.'

Suddenly hawkish, Patricia asked, 'Is your father at home?'

'I think so.'

'How is he?' The mayor put her head to one side, as if asking after a poorly hamster. 'Bearing up?'

'Yup.' Jess had no desire to share her father's state of mind with this busybody.

'I'll drop in. Cheer him up. He needs a lady's touch.' She was off, careering like Road Runner in her size-eleven sandals down Castle Kidbury's high street.

'She's . . .' Rupert found himself unable to adequately describe Patricia Smalls.

'Isn't she just?' Jess put her head on one side too. 'How are *you*, Rupert? Bearing up?'

'I'll be better after a cream tea.'

Bogna was kneading dough when Jess, full of clotted cream, got home. 'Your father has bone to pick.' She slapped Jess's hand away from a cooling loaf. 'You told Patricia Smalls he was in.'

'Mea culpa.' Jess went to open the fridge but thought better of it. 'Where's Moose?'

'Sitting with your visitor in conservatory.'

Intrigued, wary, Jess made her way to the Edwardian orangery that sprouted from the back of the house. She peered through the old glass. Among the palms and the dated rattan furniture, a woman bent over Moose. They seemed to be dancing.

'Mary!' Jess raced in. She stopped short of her friend. Mary didn't like sentiment. Wasn't at home to Mr Soppy. 'It's so brilliant to see you.'

'Is it?' Mary didn't mirror Jess's enthusiasm. 'I had to track you down. You could have called. As far as your housemates knew, you're a missing person.'

'Yeah.' Jess exhaled. She kept coming up hard against this brick wall of consequences. 'I was about to call. I've been kind of ... It's difficult.'

'*Everything's* difficult, you eejit.' Mary, 'Dublin' written through her like a stick of rock, couldn't stay angry. No milk-white Colleen, she was mixed race, with hair that bobbed in corkscrews around a droll and foxy face. Sturdily built, she wore combat trousers and a vest. No bra ever troubled Mary's frontage.

'Are you staying?' Jess was hopeful.

'If you'll have me.' Mary took up Moose's paws again. 'Come here, you sexy hunk of dog. I love you. Yes I do! You're so handsome.'

This habit of talking to Moose as if he was human made Jess uncomfortable. 'Get a room, why don't you.'

'She's just jealous.' Mary kissed Moose and let him down. She stretched, yawned. 'I need a kip. You and me are out on the lash tonight.'

'The lash? There is no lash,' said Jess. 'Castle Kidbury is lash-less.'

'These provincial places are the worst of all.' Mary seemed confident of her facts. 'You told me yourself you spent your teen years smoking dope and snogging petty criminals behind the town hall.' She threw herself down on lumpily upholstered rattan. 'Heard you had a murder.'

'Yeah. Really grisly one.'

'Anyone you know?' Mary seemed half-hopeful.

'The town git.' Jess had been so caught up in the puzzle of the murder, its mystery, that the man at the centre had been reduced to a caricature. 'Keith Dike, I mean.' She'd been shallow; a cardinal sin in her personal theology. 'It wasn't personal. I think we've got a maniac on our hands. The police think differently.'

'Jaysus. If you're not safe in a chocolate-box English town, where *are* you safe?'

'Safety's an illusion.'

'Bit deep for the time of the day.' Mary studied Jess. 'You look tired.'

'Thanks.'

'I really was worried, you know. You taking off like that.'

There were few personnel in Mary's life; no sign of the stereotypical vast Catholic clan. Jess was important to Mary. That set off a glow in Jess's chest and she said, 'I'll try to explain. After you've napped.'

'Are you going back?' Mary was mistress of the direct question.

'I don't know.' Jess held up a forefinger. 'No more questions, because I have no answers yet.'

'I know a "Keep Out" sign when I see one.' Mary jumped to her feet. 'Right. Show me where I can lay me head for a bit. I need to be rested for the gig tonight.'

'Gig?'

'Baldur.' When Jess looked blank, Mary said, 'According to the leaflet, they're *the* local band.'

'Baldur's a Norse god.'

'He's also a shit-sounding pub band, I'm glad to say.'

'Son of Odin,' said Jess. This was her safe place; the past. 'He had an evil, blind twin. He represents beauty, light, innocence. Oh, and rebirth.' That was an attractive word.

'They're playing at the Druid's Head. Which one's that?'

'You know there's always a nice pub and a not-so-nice pub?'

97

Mary looked delighted. 'It's the not-so-nice pub! Feckin' excellent.'

Jess knew she was disappointing her friend with her lack of ardour, but 'out on the lash' with Mary meant watching her drink the bar dry as she homed in on the evening's sexual target. Mary could teach the Norse gods a thing or two about debauchery.

'Oh, come on, Castle. I've got to get you out of this mausoleum. This house was different when your ma was alive. All those Sunday lunches and parties, and, Jaysus, do you remember that treasure hunt she organised? Pure gas, that woman.' Mary picked up her bag, put her arm through Jess's. 'We're going out tonight whether you want to or not. Even you with your tin ear can enjoy some live music.'

'Oi!' Jess was insulted. 'I don't have a tin ear. I love music. You know how special Elvis is to me.'

'Really? You even manage to ruin the King by preferring the bloody movie songs. "Wooden Heart", my arse.'

It was decided. They would be painting Castle Kidbury red.

Appropriately enough, the colour of blood.

Chapter 8

BALDUR AT THE DRUID'S HEAD

Still Friday 20 May

To step into the Druid's Head was to step into the kingdom of the fruit machine, of bikers skilfully weaving through students with unwieldy drink orders. The chatter was loud. The music was loud. The air smelt of cider and there were far too many tattoos.

Jess hated it.

'Good, we're here before the band go on.' Mary had to holler over the din. 'What do you want?'

'A Coke.'

Like a Navy SEAL off to neutralise the enemy, Mary cut through the sea of bodies. When she reached the bar, she turned, arms aloft. 'Woo hoo!' she shouted.

To Jess's dismay, everyone in the place spontaneously echoed the gesture. 'Woo hoo!' they howled. Mary had staged a coup; she was now Queen of the Druid's Head.

The last time Jess had trod this sticky carpet it had

been to drink underage, necking snakebite and smoking rollies. One or two of those pallid delinquents might be in the crowd.

No. Even allowing for the passage of time, none of the faces were familiar. Humiliatingly, they were mostly younger. By at least five years.

Except for one woman, hovering by the stage. A fall of black hair. Thin. Bending to look up into the faces of the band members engrossed with knotted cables and guitar amps.

Jess ransacked her memory banks. Surly self-consciousness. A little-girl awkwardness. The name landed. Theresa. Theresa something.

'Who,' said Mary, emerging from the scrum, 'is that guy there?'

Jess turned to peer in the direction of Mary's nod and saw a second familiar face. 'Him?' she winced.

'Yes, *him*. Sex on a feckin' stick.' Mary took in Jess's expression. 'Is he an ex?'

'Definitely not. All the girls fancied Gavin.' Jess had been inoculated against his charm. She cursed him for the wavy hair and the eyelashes – visible even at this distance – that caught Mary's eye. 'Let's not, eh? Not him. Anybody else in the whole stupid pub but him, Mary, please.'

'What's he like?'

'Shallow. Big-headed. Thick.'

'Sounds promising.' Mary marched away to initiate first contact.

Gavin leant over an amp. Ripped jeans. Sleeveless

tee. Mary stood so close behind him that it was practically assault.

'Hey. Love your jeans.'

All six foot three of Gavin turned to look down at her. 'Hiii,' he drawled in the daft mid-Atlantic accent Jess remembered. 'You Irish? Cool.'

We're off, thought Jess. Chief among Mary's talents – she was a taekwondo master who could fix cars and speak Italian – was her ability to pick any man she chose and sleep with him. Generally, these gents were discarded afterwards without ceremony. Both approachable and enigmatic, Mary never revealed where she'd honed her various skills.

She was a creature of her own design.

'Yeah, I'm from Dublin.' Mary's hand was on Gavin's arm.

Gavin *believed* himself to be a creature of his own design, but with his just-so dishevelled hair and his artfully torn jeans, he was a mishmash of obvious pop-grunge idols, with a good measure of trite mysticism thrown in. *Baldur indeed!* After only ten minutes in the Druid's Head, Jess was almost out of scoff.

'Love your accent.' One of Gavin's fingers snaked through the loop of Mary's belt. 'You gonna hang for the gig?'

'I came from Dublin just to hear you play.'

Jess choked on her Coke, but Gavin didn't glance at her. 'Cool,' he repeated, confused. Even Baldur's family members hadn't heard of Baldur.

'Cool,' parroted Mary.

This mirroring was part of the routine.

'See you after maybe?' Gavin's nonchalance didn't convince.

'No feckin' maybe about it,' smirked Mary.

No way, thought Jess. *Not in Harebell House*. Not under her dad's roof. Not with *Gavin*. She had to get in the lovebirds' way without revealing the reason for her aversion.

'What's going on?' Theresa inserted herself squarely between Gavin and Mary. She had the bone-white skin and tendency to spots that Jess remembered from the days when the girls from Kidbury Girls Upper School (Jess's tribe) and the girls from Richleigh High (Theresa's tribe) had squared off by the market cross.

'Hi, T.' Gavin had the air of a marked man. 'I was just explaining to these ladies—'

'Are you a fan?' asked Mary. She knew a territorial skirmish when she saw one; she liked to get stuck in.

Fleetingly, Jess felt sorry for Theresa. The woman had no idea what she was dealing with.

'I'm a superfan,' said Theresa. Her lips disappeared as she pursed them together. Her eyes, Jess noticed, were huge. There was a lurking beauty in Theresa, papered over with attitude. 'Aren't I, Gav?'

'She is,' agreed Gavin. Meek.

'Me too,' said Mary. 'Sure, who wouldn't be a fan of these fellas?' She slipped a hand into the back pocket of Gavin's jeans.

He froze.

'Gavin,' said Theresa deliberately. 'You're off women, remember? You're dedicating yourself to the music.'

'Now *that* would be a shame.' Mary must have squeezed, as Gavin gave an involuntary yip. 'Listen, love.' She addressed Theresa. 'Are you Mrs Gavin? 'Cos if so I'll back off.' She withdrew her hand.

Gavin grabbed her wrist. 'No. It's cool.' He turned to Theresa. Swallowed hard. 'T, you're my number-one fan, yeah? What would I do without you, right?'

The self-serving compliment turned Theresa's ghostly skin pink. 'I'll still be here when *she's* gone, Gav.'

He kissed her on the cheek.

A *dismissal*, thought Jess, who found it hard to watch. And then she was drawn in.

'You.' Theresa had turned her slightly protruding dark eyes on Jess. 'What brings you back here? Thought you were too good for us.'

'Turns out I'm not,' laughed Jess. She felt Gavin take her in for the first time; she was accustomed to being invisible in Mary's high-octane shimmer. *Don't say hello to me.*

She needn't have worried. Gavin's manners had got tangled up in his libido.

A thought occurred to Jess. 'Theresa, way back when, didn't your mum used to ...' The sentence ran out of steam.

'Clean for Gavin's mum, yes.' Theresa lifted her chin. 'Guess what, Judge's daughter, some people don't inherit huge houses and they have to go out and work for a living.'

'I wasn't making a point, Theresa. Just reminiscing.'

'Yeah. Right.' Theresa backed away through the crowd. 'Until later, Gavin.'

'Don't worry,' said Gavin. 'Theresa's cool.'

The all-purpose adjective. Jess looked around. Embarrassed that she'd come on like Lady Bracknell. Bored. Keen to exit Gavin's orbit. She stumbled when a man her own height barged past. 'Watch it!' she said, aware that behind her, Mary and Gavin were eating each other's faces.

'Can I, like, get by?' He wore glasses. Those clunky black ones that were once NHS standard issue but now bestowed trendiness on the wearer. 'I'm with the band.'

'Good for you.' Jess tried to manoeuvre herself out of the way. 'What do you play? Oboe? Flugelhorn?'

'Ha ha,' said Glasses. He looked properly at Jess. 'I designed the logo.'

'You clever old thing.'

'Fucking provinces,' he said under his breath as he shouldered his way bar-wards.

'Nice to meet you too!' called Jess.

A beery cheer went up. Gavin leapt casually onto the makeshift stage. Athletic, beautiful, full of grace. Stupid.

'Gav-*in*!' shrieked Mary. 'Woo hoo!' She nudged Jess. Hard. 'Find yourself a fella, you, before it heals over.'

Baldur's set was pretty much as Jess had imagined.

Self-penned miserabilist sixth-form stuff prettified by Gavin's surprisingly pleasant voice. He was 'screaming inside', according to the lyrics, and 'singing out the pain'. None of them made any sense. The bulge in his jeans as he dedicated 'Hell Beneath Hot Water' to 'the Irish girl' was visible from the back of the pub.

Theresa sat, rapt, throughout. Worshipping. She knew he'd come back to her; Jess could see that. A groupie has to learn to share.

'He's a genius.' Mary pogoed on the spot.

'He's a prat.' Jess was a still point in the chaos.

'You're right. Sexy though.'

'You were very efficient tonight, Mary.'

'You know me. I zero in. Identify target. Aim. Shoot.'

'There'll be no shooting at Harebell House, understood?' Jess was hoarse. 'My dad doesn't need shenanigans under his roof.'

'Shenanigans!' Mary laughed and necked her beer. 'Fair enough. Shame though. Gavin's ripe. Ooh, here comes another fine piece of machinery.'

Jess turned. 'Rumpole! Where's your pinstripes?'

'I don't wear them *all* the time.'

'Actual jeans.' Jess was next door to approving. 'And a rugby shirt. But of course.'

'Introduce me, introduce me.' Mary zeroed in for the second time that night. She liked to have back-up plans.

'*This* is not for you, Mary. *This* is Rupert.'

Rupert took Mary's hand and kissed it.

He's pissed, thought Jess. Just a little. Looser. A bit daft. 'Rupert's a barrister.'

'Ooh, posh,' said Mary. 'D'you have a wig?'

'Ignore her. What brings you to this hellhole?' The band had finished, but Jess still had to shout over a DJ. 'Surely Handel's more your thing.'

'I'm not your brother, you know.' Rupert looked insulted. 'I love it here! The atmosphere, the music—'

'Hey, Rupert mate, how's it going?' Gavin was back, glueing himself to Mary.

'Love the new tunes.' Rupert added a mumbled, self-conscious 'dude'.

'Cool,' nodded Gavin. He turned. His name had been peremptorily called.

'That moody bird again,' said Mary.

'Theresa flogs our CDs in the interval. I should help.' Gavin peeled himself regretfully from Mary's curves.

'Gavin! Come on!' Theresa's hands were on her hips.

'They're ten quid if anybody wants one.' Before he bounded away, he said to Mary, 'You can have one free, gorgeous.'

'When he says free ...' said Jess, 'I think you might have to do various sexual things in order to actually get a CD.'

'Happy to!' Mary stole another beer from a passing tray. 'That Rupert's a sexy biscuit,' she whispered into Jess's hair.

'Shut *up*.' The last thing Jess wanted was Rupert hearing Mary's nonsense. He was disattending. Bobbing out of time to 'Smack My Bitch Up'.

'Keep your hair on. I'm just saying. He's well up for it. Just take him somewhere for ten minutes and—'

'Please. No advice. Not from you, Mata Hari.'

Mary hooted and began to weave her way back to Gavin.

Rupert tuned back in. 'Sexy biscuit, am I?'

'Rupert, that's just Mary, don't—'

Rupert cut her off with a wave of his bottle. 'God, yes, understood.' He hovered, irresolute, then turned and danced his way back into the melee.

Jess watched him. Decided that he was not born to boogie. She squirrelled her way to the back of the room to wait for Mary. It was stale, air-locked. Here, on the fringes, were the older people, the shyer people. She recognised a face or two.

Sarah somebody. Jess racked her brain. The woman sucked on her drink like a baby with its bottle. She looked younger than when Jess had left town; a nip, a tuck, a lift and hey presto! Sarah had a frozen face. Sarah Wilkinson. That was it.

A sulky guy in front of her turned and bulldozed his way out of the pub, letting in some scented spring air. He was the son of a neighbour. Jess had thrown back his football many times. She doubted if he played anymore; he reeked of whisky.

A young guy inched past her, close enough to tread on her toes. 'Ouch, Neil,' she said gently.

He looked perturbed. Neil had never understood teasing.

'I'm Jess. Do you remember?'

'I remember you. You all right?' Eyes on the floor. He had always been shy. 'Band's shit.'

'You look well.' A lie. Neil looked like the runt he was.

'You too,' said Neil automatically. 'I have to, um, I'm dying for a wee,' he said, and was gone.

All things must pass. Suffering. Civilisations. Even Baldur gigs.

With post-gig ringing in her ears, Jess welcomed the cool of the pub car park. She hung back as Mary packed up the drummer's kit.

'Youse have a van?' she yelled over her shoulder, like the seasoned roadie she very possibly was. 'Let's get going.'

Jess sidled over. 'Look, tonight, give me a break and just come home.'

Mary thought for a moment. She dropped the cases. 'Done. Let's go.'

Capitalising on Mary's unusual cooperation, Jess hurried her out to the street.

Theresa tailed. 'He's mine, you know,' she shouted. The tone was perfectly judged to start a car-park scuffle. 'I love him. You're nothing to him.'

'Why are you fighting with me?' Mary was incredulous. Claws sheathed. Jess knew she wouldn't use her weapons on this wretched girl. 'Have a go at Gavin.'

'We're not conventional.' Theresa came nearer. She was, it would seem, up for a fight. 'We don't need to prove anything. I share him. Even with the likes of you. Because he always comes back.'

'Theresa,' said Jess. 'Enough, okay?' She put her arm through Mary's and they started along the pavement.

'You've still got a fat arse, Jess Castle!' shouted Theresa.

'A simple goodnight would suffice!' shouted Mary.

Footsteps behind them. Rupert bounding along. 'You two sneaking off?' He blocked their way. He was wobbly. As if on the deck of a boat. 'The night is young!'

Jess ignored him. Like a thrown brick, a realisation had landed. 'The symbol! That's it! Mary! Quick! Where's that flyer you had? For the gig?'

Bemused, Mary produced a crumpled scrap from her combats.

Stabbing the photocopied flyer with her finger, Jess squeaked, 'Where's his number?' She rummaged and found a business card. 'Come on, come *on*.' She paced back and forth in the pale circle of a streetlight, mobile in hand, calling and recalling. Rupert, swaying, was forgotten. 'Shit! I'll have to nab him first thing.'

'Who're you calling?' Mary was manoeuvring Rupert towards Jess. It wasn't easy. He was keen, but out of touch with his feet.

'Eden.' Jess was too distracted to notice the manoeuvring.

Rupert opened his mouth, thought better of it, then said it anyway. 'I hope it's not about that pagan psychopath thing.'

'What if it is?' Jess was wired.

Mary nudged Rupert. A wee shove. Like a stage mother.

'Jess. Um. I was wondering . . .'

Jess looked suspiciously at Mary, then back to Rupert. 'Go on.'

'Is there someone … that is to say, do you have a … are you seeing …'

Jess folded her arms. 'Yes, Rupert, I'm seeing a guy. A few guys actually. Odin. And Frigg. Then there's Thor, Canute, Niall of the Nine Hostages.'

'I see, right.' Rupert backed away, as if unsure what had just happened.

'Not forgetting Zeus, of course. But that's purely for sex. He likes to dress as a swan.'

Rupert looked as if he was thinking very hard and getting nowhere.

'Come on, Mary.' Jess grabbed her hand.

A few yards down Cheap Street, Jess stopped and turned.

'Rumpole?'

'Yeah?' Rupert was wary.

'The answer to your question is no. I'm not seeing anybody.'

'Good,' said Rupert. 'I mean, not good. Not bad. Doesn't really matter, so, obviously, just, you know—'

'Goodnight Rupert,' yelled Mary. 'You hopeless feck.'

He must stay calm. Think simple thoughts.

Yes, it had all gone wrong, but that wasn't his fault.

Invoke the goddess. But but but! Deities don't give answers. They give you hints. He had to trust the dead, though. They knew best.

Chapter 9

Love Me To Death

Saturday 21 May

Jess was electrified.

Up before the sun. Pacing the rag rug in her room. The constant reiteration of Eden's mobile ringing out in her ear gave her a headache.

She pulled on some clothes. If everything you own is black, you're coordinated without trying. She tried Eden again. Straight to voicemail.

Purpose hit her like adrenaline. Today would not unfold haphazardly like all the other days since Cambridge.

Beyond her bedroom window the green outskirts of Castle Kidbury were stock-still. Jess knew there was scurrying life in the hedges. Small mammals already halfway through their working day. She had to join them. She'd been asleep too long.

The *rat-a-tat-tat* of her boots on the stairs. The quiet

kitchen. The jars and the pots and the utensils, all asleep. As was Moose. He woke immediately, staggered to his feet. Hopeful.

'Sorry Moosie, not now.'

The bite of boot on gravel. Her car waiting. Jess smiled at the defiantly old-fashioned silhouette. The driver's seat was uncomfortable, but her behind was accustomed to it. 'Start,' she begged, turning the key in the ignition. 'Please.'

A bang on the window. Jess rolled it down and Mary inserted her wild-haired head. 'Wait for me.'

Mary speed-shuffled to the passenger side in unlaced trainers.

She didn't even ask where Jess was going. Mary was an excellent partner in crime. *I should be more Mary*, thought Jess.

Or not. She noticed what Mary was wearing. 'Are they ... they are! My dad's pyjamas!'

Mary waggled her arms, hands invisible in the long striped sleeves. 'Found 'em folded and ironed in the kitchen.'

The car showed willing. It flew along the Kidbury road, into the budding day.

The desk sergeant didn't look up from his paperwork. He pencilled a word here and there. 'Sorry, love,' he repeated.

'It's urgent.' Jess wished Mary had waited in the car. The pyjamas lacked gravitas. 'I have information.'

'Tell me, love, and I'll pass it on.'

She wasn't his love and she didn't want him to pass it on. She wanted to be in the thick of it. An ignoble thought, but there you go.

The one fact the genial, unhelpful officer would confirm was that Eden was on duty. 'Like the rest of us. Not much kip last night.'

Mary stretched. Her yawn was operatic. 'Know how you feel.'

DC Karen Knott bustled out from what Jess thought of as backstage. Without noticing Jess – her demeanour suggested she was too important to take in mere civilians – she called over her shoulder, 'Tell the boss I'm on my way to the crime scene. If anybody wants me, I'll be at St Agatha's.'

'Will do.' The desk sergeant rolled his eyes. He waved his pencil at Jess. 'Go on then. Off you trot to St Agatha's.'

Bless you, Karen, thought Jess, following the busy busy busy little woman through the revolving door.

'Crime scene?' Mary fizzed and popped and danced alongside her. 'A murder? An actual murder!'

'Don't,' said Jess, 'do that when we get there.'

St Agatha's was on the Richleigh road, on the edge of town. Its architectural style could be defined as Ugly Modern Catholic.

Very different to Castle Kidbury's charmingly rustic Church of England chapel, it was a concrete wigwam. Sharp edges. Angles. A groovy mosaic – now hopelessly dated – of a Picassoesque St Agatha was embedded over wide double doors.

St Agatha's martyrdom had been extra grisly, even by the standards of such events; her breasts were cleaved off with a sword. Jess hitched her bra strap as she parked the Morris Traveller.

'This is my lot, isn't it?' said Mary, peering through the windscreen. 'Catholics. Bells and smells.'

'It's different inside. Not so space-age. Nice and gloomy.' Jess recalled the Masses she'd been frog-marched to as a schoolgirl, in the interests of inter-faith unity. There'd been an enormous crucifix behind the altar. She could still see the life-size Jesus. His eyes had rolled to the back of his head. His side dripped blood. His loincloth barely covered what her mother would call his 'essentials'. To a child, it seemed more like a slasher film than a place of worship.

'How're you going to get past all those bods?' asked Mary.

'Wing it.' Jess slammed the car door behind her and marched to the gate of the church. At this early hour, only a few local rubberneckers were on this side of the black and yellow tape that wrapped the church like a gift.

Danny was among them, on tiptoe. He caught Jess's eye.

'What's going on?' he called.

'Why are you here, Dan?' Jess made her way over.

His mother rushed up. 'We have to get in.' She was petulant. 'Danny and me, we're doing the flowers for my sister's girl's wedding. The police won't tell me anything.'

115

'It's another murder,' said Danny.

'Let's hope not,' said Jess.

On the far side of the gate was an organised melee. Like worker ants, various professionals streamed in and out of the church. A man in a crinkly paper suit leant against a tombstone. Reflective tabards and an air of conviction.

Jess yearned to be on that side of the gate.

'Morning,' she said to the scrawny officer barring her way. There was power in his spotty face, the thin arms sticking out of his Daz-white shirt. The power to admit Jess or keep her out.

She flashed her library card, snapping its leather folder shut as he bent to examine it. 'Professor Jessica Castle. Cambridge University. John Eden's expecting me.' She raised her eyebrows. Used her best student-scaring expression.

'I dunno, I better ...' The young policeman looked vaguely around, searching for a higher authority.

One appeared. In a strikingly cut brown cashmere coat, Mary approached the gate, put her hand on it, and said, 'I have that data you wanted, ma'am.'

They were through, in a flurry of power dressing and oestrogen.

'Quick. Quick.' Jess daren't look back. High on their success, they bundled into the darkness of the church. The daylight shut off cleanly. They waited for their eyes to adjust.

The sense of industry was more intense inside St Agatha's. Silent, determined people beetled through the pews. The hum of learned consultation. The occasional blaze of a camera flash. Yellow cards with black numbers on them lined the aisle.

As Jess looked up, the noise they made receded. The rushing in her ears was all she could hear.

It took shape in the darkness. The crucifix she remembered, caught by a shaft of red light from the stained glass that studded the angled ceiling. On the cross, a body. This Jesus was in jeans. Laid over the figure of Christ. A blasphemous spooning.

No shoes. A chest invisible beneath a vest of blood. Long muscled arms slung over the Redeemer's outstretched ones. The wrists were lashed to the cross with rope. More rope secured his neck so that the face stared out at the busy congregation. The body, slightly on the slant, was a dark, dripping silhouette.

Jess swayed. She smelt the peculiar sweet tang of blood. Iron-rich. Wet.

So many times she'd read about sacrifices. The Viking blood offerings, known as Blot. Wicker men burning with real men trapped inside. Here was actual death. The real thing. So much blood, yet her own seemed to have deserted her legs.

Beside her, Mary sank to her knees. She vomited.

Heads turned.

'Get her out of here!' shouted somebody behind a protective white mask.

Mary's words echoed in the sacred wigwam. 'I did it! I did it!'

Jess tugged at Mary, who'd coiled into herself. 'Shut up!' she begged. 'Mary, stop it!'

One of the figures running their way was Eden. When he saw Jess, he slowed. He turned, saying, 'I've got this. Get back to what you were doing.' He stood over the two women. 'Explain. Now.'

'I shagged him to death!' keened Mary, her hand reaching out to the figure on the cross.

The desecrated face was Gavin's.

Jess closed her lips against a flood of bile. His eyes were two bloody cavities. His hair was a bouffant of gore. Still, he was recognisably Gavin.

She almost knelt in front of him. She understood in a new way the power of those sacrifices she'd studied. A body without a soul was a human's worst nightmare.

Gavin was at last the superstar he'd dreamt of being.

'Help me get her on her feet.' Eden was thin-lipped. He put his hands under Mary's armpits.

Jess had never seen Mary cry before.

A woman in blue environmental overalls left her sketch pad on a pew and rustled over. 'Do you need a hand? What's the matter with—' She blinked beneath her elasticated hood. 'That's my coat!'

Impatiently, Mary tore off the chocolate-coloured cashmere she'd swiped through a car window. She seemed more angry than ashamed at being outed as a thief.

The woman staggered back as Mary thrust the coat at her. 'It's covered with ... *eeurgh.*'

'We'll sort it out later, Linda.' Eden staggered with Mary to a side door.

Beyond it was a mossy passage, more of a slit, between an ancient, high wall and the concrete church. Jess could see sunlight warming up gravestones, but the alley was damp and chill.

'I killed him.'

'Will you stop saying that, Mary,' snapped Jess. 'Don't listen to her, please.'

'I'm not taking her seriously.' Eden handed Mary a proper handkerchief. She blew her nose and calmed down a little. 'This is the work of a serial killer.'

'God.' Jess wrapped her arms around herself. 'In Castle Kidbury?'

'Postcodes aren't murder-proof.' Eden pressed his hand through his immovably short hair. 'Two deaths. Two crucifixions. I have to face facts.'

'We all do.' The wind was knocked out of Jess. She'd never before had use for the expression *shit just got real*, but it certainly did the trick here.

'A serial killer means chaos.' Eden was talking half to Jess, half to himself. 'Police work, dogged detection, doesn't cut it. I'm trained to search for motive, but serial killers do it for Looney Tune reasons.'

'"Next door's dog told me to do it,"' suggested Jess. She'd read about the Son of Sam murder spree in 1970s New York. 'Let me help.' Gavin's death was a game changer. The off-stage demise of a layabout drunkard was one thing, but Jess had seen Gavin alive just hours ago. They had history. However hard she tried to pretend otherwise. 'I have new information.' As Eden looked at her expectantly, Jess turned to Mary. 'I can't concentrate with you carrying on. You *didn't* shag Gavin, remember? I didn't let you.'

Eden looked puzzled. Impatient. Knackered.

'I *did* sleep with him.' Mary met Jess's eye defiantly through her tears. 'We cooked it up between us. He got the band to drop him off outside your place. I'd told him which window to climb up to.'

'You said you were tired. You wanted to go straight to bed.' Jess assimilated the story.

'Half true.' Mary blew her nose again.

Eden winced at his hanky's ordeal.

'I let him in. He had a bottle of Jack Daniels on him. We were quiet. I knew you'd come over all spinster aunt if you heard us.'

Jess looked at Mary. Just looked. She'd get her later, for saying that. Or try to; Mary was un-gettable.

Eden took out his notebook. 'What time,' he asked, 'did Gavin Blake leave you?'

'It was *quite* a night, I can tell you.' Mary stopped sniffling. 'He's got amazing—'

'Spare me.' Eden closed his eyes.

'Well, we snoozed for a bit and then, you know, *again*.' Mary couldn't entirely spare her audience, it would seem. 'He went out through the window about, ooh, one a.m. Yeah. One o'clock. I remember looking at me watch.'

'Was he planning to walk home?'

'Yeah.'

'You didn't hear a vehicle?'

'Nothing. Sorry.'

'You've been very helpful.' Eden turned to Jess. 'You said you have fresh intel?'

'I've been trying to get hold of you since last night.'

'I'm a little busy.' Either Eden was brilliant at dead-panning or he felt this needed saying.

Jess produced the band's flyer. 'There's your symbol.'

'This is the band that poor bloke sang with?'

'Yes. Baldur. Their logo was carved onto Keith Dike's torso. That's why I didn't recognise it. It was made up to promote the band.'

'Right.' Eden frowned. He flicked back a couple of pages in his notepad. 'Look, this is what the killer cut into Gavin. A line of symbols, this time.'

'Is this another band, Jess? Or is there deeper significance? They're not Christian, are they?'

'No. They don't "feel" Norse, either. They're very simple.' The shapes set off no pagan drumbeat in Jess's head. 'It's round the corner of my mind. I can feel what it is, but ... Listen, I'm tired. I'll look into it.'

'Good. Thanks.' Eden and Jess regarded each other for a moment.

'You look worn out,' she said.

'I'm fine.' Eden rolled his neck. 'I just hope forensics can give us something.'

'DNA.' Jess had watched *CSI* enough times to feel confident she'd said the right thing.

'Trouble is, there'll be too much of the stuff. There was Mass in this church yesterday evening and it hasn't been cleaned. The lab will be knee-deep in old-lady DNA.' He sighed. He looked older. 'Can you really help, Jess? I need to catch whoever's doing this.'

'Yes.' The puzzle was diverting. It kept her from wandering up and down the cul-de-sac of her thoughts. That was only part of it; she was zealous about the investigation now.

A murderer had targeted her home town. A life had been extinguished up on a hill, another in church. *I can help.*

It would be penance, of a sort.

Chapter 10

THE MASKS OF BABYLON

Still Saturday 21 May

DS Eden's blue Ford Focus possessed neither the charm of Jess's Morris Traveller nor the taupe luxe of Rupert's Mercedes. It was, as Eden himself might have said, 'a perfectly good car'.

'You needn't be concerned about your friend,' said Eden. 'Ms Spillane's not implicated. Apart from anything, she wasn't in town for Keith Dike's murder. She mentioned something to Knott about a girl with black hair.'

Jess nodded. 'Theresa. Theresa, um, Peake.'

'I know her. Difficult woman.'

'You could say that. Obsessed with Gavin.' Jess glanced at Eden. 'I can hear you thinking it; obsessed enough to kill him?'

'More likely to kill Mary, surely? This isn't a crime of passion, Jess. Unless you believe Theresa was also madly in love with Keith Dike.'

'You should talk to her anyway.'

'I'm the detective sergeant in charge of the investigation, Jess. Of course I'll talk to her. It may just turn up something. For now, let's focus on our friend Pan. He seems a good place to start.'

'Do you think he's the killer?'

'I won't have an opinion until I have all the information. Pan's not on the level, I know that much. And he annoys the hell out of me. But I don't have a hunch about him. I don't have hunches full stop.'

'Really?' Jess was taken aback that a copper could be so non-judgemental. 'Not like Columbo then?'

'No, Jess, not like Columbo.'

Jess watched Eden as he drove along Kidbury Road at precisely sixty miles per hour. He should, by rights, have been an uninspiring character; everything about him was standard. Ford Focus. Department-store suit. Five foot ten and a half with man-shaped hair. He looked about forty, but then he probably always had. Despite his ordinariness, there was something about him she appreciated. Eden was *good*. He was careful. And he kept his temper; a talent she envied. It dawned on Jess, as they slowed at Pitt's Field, that she admired him.

Which didn't mean she agreed with him. When you're tracking a serial killer, hunches are all you've got.

Three battered caravans and a tent sat in the middle of the field, the surrounding grass flattened. Bonfires had been lit and left. Camping chairs faced this way and that. Rags were strewn around the place. It was deathly quiet.

Eden gave the handbrake a precise tug. 'When we get in there, I want to you to be observant. Any signs, any artefacts, I want to know about them. We need to be quiet. Catch him off guard. Got it?'

Jess got it.

They picked their way over to the caravans. As they drew closer, Jess could see a slight rocking motion to the largest one. Eden stopped and pressed his finger to his lips. In a split second, he'd yanked the door open and boarded the vehicle.

'This is the police. Stay exactly where you are.'

A mattress took up most of the van. Bodies darted under the sheets like mice. Only Pan sat up. Chest hairy. Expression lairy.

'Look who's dropped in,' he said.

Naked, arms out in a cruciform pose that held echoes for Jess, Pan was beatified by a beam of sunlight that slanted in through a tear in the roof. He lounged, resplendent, as if he were covered with silks and velvets rather than a jumble of nylon sheets and stained sleeping bags. The smell of sex had seeped into the soft furnishings.

'Climb in, son.' Pan's smile was odious. 'It's naughty times in Babylon!'

'Babylon?' Jess was crisp. 'Do you even know where Babylon was?'

When Pan turned his eyes to her, they glittered. 'It's in my bed, *kochana*.'

Jess wished later she hadn't let her mouth drop open. His evil code was easy to read: *I know things I shouldn't know.* As if Pan had bugged the safe kitchen in Harebell House. As if he'd scooped the word out of her brain. 'Babylon was in modern-day Iraq,' she said, clambering back to the dry land of certain fact.

'Wherever it is, you're welcome to it,' barked Eden. He pointed to a fuzzy print of an old woodcut sello-taped above the mattress. 'What's the meaning behind that? The smutty picture?'

'How dare you?' laughed Pan. 'That is sacred cop-ulation between the ancients. I bet Dr Jessica Castle knows all about it. Now, Mr Pig, there's some long words coming, so I'll go slow for you. *Hieros gamos.*'

Both men looked at Jess.

'*Hieros gamos,*' she said, 'is sex elevated by ritual. The female, or goddess, or Mother Nature if you like, bestows qualities of leadership on a mortal male, via the energy of sex.'

'Kind of Carry On up the Ancient Gods,' said Pan. 'Proper kinky and a lot of fun. Innit, ladies?' He moved his legs and the bedding quaked happily.

'Stop giggling!' said Eden. 'You seem to have many goddesses, Pan.'

'Nah. These are handmaidens.' Pan looked at Jess. Intense. A look she assumed he'd used on Caroline. 'Not many actual goddesses around, but you do come across them now and then.'

'What are all these?' Eden pointed with his pen to a row of painted masks mounted along the caravan wall.

'They're our ceremonial masks. The masks of Babylon.' Pan squinted round Eden at Jess. 'Do you like them, my darling? We wear them in the pursuit of absolute pleasure.'

'Not really into dodgy papier mâché. They'd look more at home in a primary school.'

'Ah. Spirited.' Pan smiled approvingly. 'We like spirited. You, my sweet, are welcome to join us. But you,' he turned sharply to Eden, 'will need a warrant, my old cock, if you want to linger longer.'

Eden took out his notebook. 'Tell you what, I'll show you a warrant when you show me proof of ownership of this vehicle.'

Pan was unnervingly still until his shoulders gave way and he let out a howling guffaw. 'Clever boy. Actually, I keep that in storage along with my other documentation. It would be reasonable, would it not, to grant me a day or two to retrieve it?'

Eden was grave. 'Where were you last night?'

'That'd be telling.'

'I expect you to do just that. Now.'

Stalemate.

A face emerged from under the sheet. 'He was here,' cheeped Caroline. Mascara made sooty tracks down her cheeks. Her pupils were pinheads.

Jess's insides froze. Eden was right. This wasn't like archaeology. It was sordid.

'You were here with him?' asked Eden, pointing at Pan.

Caroline nodded, pulling a sleeping bag up to her nose.

'All of you?'

127

'Yes,' came a unison reply from under the covers.

'We were enacting the ceremony of Babylon,' said Pan.

'What time did this ceremony start?' Eden was dour.

'Sundown.' Pan lifted his arms as if to embrace the spiritual wonder of such a time.

Caroline said, 'About a quarter to nine.'

'And when did it finish?'

Pan's smile was wolfish. 'It's still going.' Bodies rippled beneath the covers. 'Ooh,' sighed Pan, eyes closed, lascivious. 'Just ask 'em. I was here all night. All. Night.'

'Fine,' Eden replied, snapping his notepad shut. 'I'm not finished with you, Pan.'

'Ooh, is that a promise, sir mister policeman sir?'

Jess and Eden sat for several silent minutes in the parked Ford Focus. He had pulled a sandwich out of a bag. He didn't eat it. He just stared at the ramshackle caravans sinking into the mud.

Jess needed a shower. She'd been a student; she was no stranger to grotty living. But she'd never witnessed anything as low as this. It would be sweet to punish Pan for what he was doing to Caroline.

Eden drummed his fingers on the steering wheel. 'Who knows if those women are telling the truth? He's probably trained them to vouch for him. But if they say they were with him last night, I have to accept it.'

'Poor Caroline,' sighed Jess. 'She's got a kid. They're vulnerable.' An idea struck her. 'What if he's violent towards them?' she asked. 'You could get him for that at least. How about you let me talk to Caroline? Maybe I could get her to admit that he hurts them, then you bring him in.'

Before Jess had even finished, Eden was resolutely shaking his head. 'He's got them in his thrall. Even if this Caroline did say something, she'd retract it afterwards. In any event, I couldn't let you talk to her without my being present.'

'I could wear a wire.' Jess rather fancied wearing a wire.

'Those masks. Of Babylon.' It evidently cost Eden to quote Pan. 'What did you make of them?'

'Masks are profound,' said Jess. At ease. In her comfort zone. 'We have a fascination with them. We've been wearing them for about nine thousand years. Masks disguise, entertain, protect. They transform men into gods.' She looked over at Pan's pleasure palace, its wheels missing, bin bags taped over the windows. 'Pan's masks are craft-shop nothings.' She took the sandwich from him. Death made her hungry. Like everything else.

Eden looked at his sandwich. Mourning it. 'Yet he did know about *hieros gamos*.'

'People, and by people I mean blokes, often cherry-pick paganism for the rude bits. Doesn't mean he has real knowledge.'

'He clearly has a criminal history of some sort. Clued up about his rights. He can play the system.' Eden started the car. 'I need to do some digging.'

'Do you really think it's him? Would Pan crucify people?'

Eden looked at her. 'No hunches, Jess, remember?'

'Not like Columbo.' She took a last look at the campsite.

Eden drove like a seasoned cabbie. Neat turns. Appropriate speed. As they neared the police station – he asked Jess *not* to refer to it as the cop shop – they passed a fleet of bulky vehicles at the Bell Street junction.

'Shit. Here we go.'

'Sky News,' read Jess, as a white van stood idle at the lights, a satellite dish on its roof. 'BBC.' A silver trailer the size of a horsebox tailgated its uppity rival.

'We won't be able to move for reporters.' Eden's anger manifested in a slight tightening of his fingers on the steering wheel. 'They'll sensationalise everything. Get in my way.'

Jess sank in her seat. Castle Kidbury was her secret, her haven. Tonight it would be reduced to a telegenic rectangle on screens all over the country. 'They might help.'

'The media have their own agenda. They'll nickname this idiot, giving him publicity.'

The leviathans dwarfed the cars around them. Made the shops look even more twee. The twenty-first century had planted a metallic paw on Castle Kidbury. Jess had pressed a pause button on the town when she left home; by coming back she'd hit play. This was a fantasy, of course; life had gone on without her. People had aged. The library had closed down. Her father had fallen ill.

'The sooner we solve these murders the sooner we can shoo away Sky News.' She sensed rather than saw the small lift of Eden's eyebrows at that 'we'.

'This kind of scrutiny means the top brass getting nervous about the optics.'

'And in English?'

'I could be taken off the case if I don't close it quickly. I need to stay. I take the responsibility of Castle Kidbury's safety more seriously than some media-savvy blow-in. I'm local, that matters. I have far more chance of catching this individual.'

'You can say bastard. I won't faint.'

'I can't afford emotion, Jess.'

His need to stay on the case, however, was entirely emotional. Jess believed his zeal; there was nothing careerist about Eden. *I'm not cynical about him.* For somebody who'd been cynical about Noddy in her high chair, this was an accolade.

'I saw somebody at Gavin's gig you should pull in.' She hoped that was the right expression. 'Pushy sod. Boasted that he designed the Baldur logo. The one on Keith's body.'

'Name?'

'Too busy disliking him to ask.'

The speakerphone butted in.

'*Guv,*' said Knott. '*I'm at Theresa Peake's abode. Can you hear me?*'

'Go ahead, Knott.'

'*I broke the news of the death gently to her.*'

I bet you did, thought Jess.

'*And she's taken it very badly. Hysterical. Can you hear me, sir?*'

'Knott, this is the latest technology. I can hear you.'

'*She's under sedation, sir. Doc says we can talk to her later today or tomorrow morning at the latest.*'

Jess found a packet of crisps in the glovebox.

'*Ms Peake's very shocked, sir. Reckons she loved this Gavin Blake. Is that ... was that a crisp crunching? Is that woman with you?*'

Despite being dismayed that she could be identified by the sound of cheap snacks, Jess rather liked being 'that woman'.

'Knott, get a couple of the team onto checking out all owners of vans large enough to carry a crucifix.' Eden turned to Jess. 'Keith's cross was jointed in the middle. Our man's inventive.'

'*Will do, sir.*'

'Have Paul Chappell at the *Echo* on standby. If our killer's MO remains constant, he should expect a box to turn up at some point. I want it the minute it arrives.'

'*I'll make that clear, sir. Can you h—*'

Eden severed the connection. 'Five days.' He followed a minivan through a narrow turn. 'Since the last murder.'

'Does it mean anything?'

'Everything means something.'

'True.' Echoes sounded in Jess's head now that she'd recovered from the day's gory start. 'Did you see that enormous yew tree in the churchyard? St Agatha's is famous, well, famous locally, for that yew.'

'And Hecate's connected with the yew.'

He does listen. 'It's a stretch, but maybe draping Gavin over Jesus on the cross is a reclamation of the church for the old ways.'

'Bring me facts, Jess.' He seemed to relent when she was silent. 'Listen, you're my way into this guy's head. Keep doing what you're doing. It's valuable.'

'What am I, though? Do I get a title? Ooh, am I a consultant?'

'If you like.'

Bit of a lukewarm response, thought Jess. 'Don't I get something with the title? Like an identity card? A badge. How about a siren for my Morris Traveller?'

'Don't push it,' said Eden.

At the window table of The Spinning Jenny, Jess trotted through her messages.

Many from Mary:

> I'm at the police station their tea is shite

> I've told da copz everything five times over!!!!!

> I'm at harebell house boggie has put me to bed with soup i love boggie!!!!

One from the faculty head at Cambridge, which she deleted without opening.

One from her father:

> Much as I like Mary I would appreciate some
> notice regarding visitors.

It was tempting to reply to the Judge with advice regarding removal of the stick up his arse, but Jess talked herself down from that ledge. It was his house, after all. He had a right to be consulted.

> Sorry Dad.

Ogham was less dense than communications between the Castles.

Through the window, a power-suited woman with a microphone accosted passers by outside Lady Jayne. A burly man with a shoulder-mounted camera filmed Mr Kuzbari shaking his head, dodging away. A woman laden with carrier bags ignored the reporter. Patricia Smalls crossed the road in order to casually saunter past. Jess saw the feigned surprise when they spoke to her. *I hope you've got all day, Sky News lady.*

Jess snatched up her phone. Were she and Rupert at the asking-each-other-out-for-coffee stage? Would he take it all wrong? What did all wrong mean anyway? Should she text him? Before she'd thought it through she'd already sent a message.

> Free for a coffee at Spinning J? In need of
> legal advice.

A white lie. Everybody knew they didn't count.

At the counter, Squeezers doffed an imaginary cap at Jess. He turned back to Meera, cupping a filthy hand to a filthy ear. 'Eh, lovey, what's that? No credit?' He looked incredulous in his decrepit trench coat. Darling, who was at his feet despite the 'Guide Dogs Only' sign, whimpered. 'I'm a man of my word.'

'You're a man of many words and I'm not interested in any of them.' Meera turned her back.

From the hinterland of the kitchen, Moyra appeared. Tall, thin, with a dish mop of peroxide hair, she backed up her partner. 'No cash no coffee, Squeezers.'

'Here, I'll buy him a coffee.' Jess knew she was being had. It didn't matter.

'Shame to have coffee without a nice sausage sandwich to go with it.' Squeezers batted his eyelashes.

'Go on, then.'

'Thank you, dear lady.'

'Squeezers, do *not* kiss my hand.' Jess cringed in her chair as he approached, crouching, subservient. 'Tell me something. How many times have the police called you in for one of their little chats recently? Say, in the last month.'

'This month, hmm, about five times.' Squeezers picked his nose. 'May's been a bit of a slow one.'

'That's outrageous, you see that, right?'

'Outrageous, yes,' said Squeezers mildly. 'Thank you again. You have facilitated an important business meeting with my associate over there.'

A man waved from the corner table, tucking away

his copy of the *Sun*. Ryan, half man half rat, was Castle Kidbury's premier creep. Mean-faced, smelling of cigarettes, he had somehow won the heart of Carli from the Royal Seven Stars.

Wondering what kind of business these associates had to discuss, Jess earwigged. She caught only snatches of baffling conversation. 'Washing machine.' 'Risking my life.' Then Ryan banged the table. 'I want to meet Beefy Dave or the deal's off!'

Beefy Dave. Squeezers' shadowy puppet master, the one who pulled the strings of all Squeezers' pathetic crimes.

She realised that Moyra was talking to her, and agreed that, yes, these murders were terrible and what were the police doing about it and, no, she didn't feel safe walking around her own town.

Ping!

There in five.

He was there in four. 'You know me so well,' said Rupert, taking up the latte Jess had waiting for him. 'What's the legal problem?'

'Oh, that,' said Jess. 'I can't really talk about it.'

Rupert's bottom paused an inch above his chair. 'So why am I here?'

'Because it's sunny and you can't work *every* day and there's coffee and I've run out of reasons.'

Rupert smiled to himself. Sat down.

'I mean, I *could* ask for your input about the serial killer case I'm *consulting on*.' Jess wondered how smug she looked. Very, probably. 'But the details are classi-fied, so . . .'

'Didn't we agree you weren't going to get involved?' Rupert's face morphed from playful to grave.

'*We* didn't agree anything.'

'This guy's dangerous. You could end up being a target.'

'Don't be silly.' Jess hadn't thought of that. *Was* it silly? Or was Rupert making a valid point that most adults would have thought of?

'Your brother'll kill me if I stand by and let you get yourself nailed to a cross.'

'Yeah, that's the main reason I don't want to be cru-cified. Because my brother would be piqued.'

The door opened and Eddie flew in. Out of breath. 'Emergency at my pub,' he gasped, leaning over the counter, red in the face. 'We've run out of green teabags.'

'Oh Eddie.' Moyra flicked him with a tea towel. 'You had me worried. Thought there'd been another murder.'

'No, Moyra, love. I reckon he'll lie low for a while. He might skulk off, start again in some other part of the country.' He spoke with the authority of an ex-copper. 'The problem is once it starts to escalate. They can't hold back. If there's a third murder, there'll be a fourth hot on its heels, believe me.'

'DS Eden will catch him before that,' said Jess from her seat.

Eddie wheeled round. 'Eden?' He paused. As if he had plenty more to say but wasn't sure whether he should. 'Solid detective,' he said eventually. 'Good lad.'

'Yeah,' said Rupert. 'He's a good lad. All right, Eddie?'

Jess wondered at the abrupt change in Rupert's accent; he'd hurtled downmarket. Oh dear God, he was being blokey. For Eddie.

'All right, Rupes,' said Eddie. He accepted the green teabags from Meera. 'Cheers, love. We've got reporters in at the Seven Stars. They're looking for quinoa and vegetarian options and whatnot. I knew you two lesbians would have this sort of healthy nonsense in.'

Meera rolled her eyes. Moyra shook her head. 'We don't have green teabags because we're lesbians, Eddie,' she said. 'We have them because we're a tea shop.'

'Yeah, yeah.' Eddie thanked them, offered to pay, was refused, said he'd return the favour. 'Give me best to your dad, Jess,' he said with a wink as he left.

Colliding with Eddie, Danny and his mother came in with a flurry of 'Oops' and 'No you first' and 'Thank you'.

'Isn't it marvellous news?' Danny's mum spotted Jess and squealed at her. 'The murder! It means Danny's exonerated.'

Danny, at the counter, taking a scholarly interest in the iced buns, wasn't celebrating.

'I rang Mr Eden first thing and told him that Danny was in all night and I know that because now I sleep on the landing outside his bedroom door.'

'That must be hard.' *For both of you*, added Jess

silently, watching Danny's back as he prevaricated between pink or white icing.

'I have to keep him away from *her*.'

Meera silenced the cafe with a squeaked, 'Turn it up! Turn it up!'

Squeezers raised a grimy hand to the television fixed to the wall. Darling stole half his sandwich and bore it off beneath a table.

'It's Eden!' Meera clapped as if she was at the circus.

'Shush! Listen,' said Moyra.

'—*all we can to find this dangerous criminal. In the meantime, I have no further comment except to urge local people to be vigilant. Stay safe and report anything suspicious. Thank you.*'

'Is that it?' Meera seemed deflated as the doll-sized Eden on the screen turned and walked back into police headquarters in an outbreak of camera flashes.

'His hair looks nice,' said Moyra.

'They've got nothing.' Squeezers was vehement. He coughed and the entire postcode flinched.

Karen Knott was on the screen now; Jess could count the blackheads on her HD nose. '*That's all!*' she shrieked. '*Get away! No questions! Off! Go on! Off!*'

'Somebody,' murmured Rupert, 'didn't attend her police PR training module.'

'I reckon,' said Moyra, 'the murderer's somebody we've all known for years.'

Squeezers was still coughing. He was almost on his knees. 'I didn't do it, missus,' he spluttered.

'The only thing you crucify is your health.' Moyra

was pleased with this. 'His health!' she repeated to Rupert as she brought the bill.

Engrossed in thoughts of the bloody present and the ancient past, Jess let him pay without a tussle. She came to when he said, 'Jess?'

'Sorry. I was away with the fairies.' She stood up.

He loomed over her. 'I suppose this is our table now.'

'Is it?' Her smile was lopsided. 'I suppose it is, yeah.'

Chapter 11

HAPPY FAMILIES

Sunday 22 May

The water was like air around her.

She struggled, but the movement drilled her deeper down into the dark.

Her eyes stung.

She heard a shout. Clear, despite the water. 'It's all your fault.'

She opened her mouth and death rushed in.

Jess sat up in bed. Not dead. Not drowned.

But. The word nagged at her until she remembered.

But it was Sunday. Which meant lunch with the family.

She burrowed under the covers like a mole.

Harriet Castle hadn't insisted on much, but she'd always laid the table correctly. A formation of knives and forks either side of Wedgwood plates. The wedding-present candelabra. Two squat silver rose bowls of flowers from the garden. Best tablecloth. Linen napkins. Water carafes. A great-uncle's cruet set.

Jess and the Judge stood back. They'd done it as well as could be expected without Harriet overseeing them.

'Back in Cambridge,' said Jess, 'I used paper plates.'

'No doubt,' said the Judge.

They'd been press-ganged by Bogna, who'd said, 'I don't know how to bloody lay posh table.'

Dad never helped Mum, thought Jess. Not even when there were twenty to dinner, as there frequently were. Jess wondered if Harriet had ever asked for help. Then she wondered if she herself had ever helped, and stopped wondering.

Jess felt odd. Her hair was clean. She was in a fresh set of black bits and bobs. She'd applied lipstick. Formality set her teeth on edge; the Judge thrived on it. He was mixing gin and tonics – 'Whoppers!' – in jacket and slacks. An inevitable cravat.

Bogna also looked uncomfortable in a stretchy dress that she kept tugging at as she dashed to and from the kitchen. This was, she told Jess, the first time she'd ever sat down at the table with Jimmy's visitors. She didn't seem happy about it.

The gravel announced a car. Jess had a question before Sunday lunch proper kicked off.

'Dad, did you ever have a psycho in your courtroom?'

'Yes. Not always in the dock.'

Jess laughed the way he did. A small chuckle, confined to the throat. The merest lift of the shoulders.

The Judge nodded at the portrait over the fire, of a grand old gent at a leather-topped desk. Stick-thin. Solemn. 'Your great-great-grandfather once put away a man called Herbert Bullen. Killed four wives in succession. Not a shred of remorse. *He* was a psychopath. No empathy. Grandiose bugger. Squandered the money he made from his crimes and, at the end, didn't give a fig for his own life.'

'Grandiose. No empathy. No remorse. Sounds like Pan.'

'From Pitt's Field?'

'He's the only real suspect in the cross murders.'

'Or the Rustic Ripper, as the red-tops are calling him.' The Judge wrinkled his long nose. 'Not the tabloids' finest hour.'

'Trouble is, Pan has an alibi. Even it is from a gaggle of airheaded groupies.'

The Judge set down the last plate. Stroked his chin. 'Ah. So Eden can't hang on to him.'

They both cocked an ear to the noises on the drive. Little feet running. Weary adults shouting, 'Don't! Stop it! Leave that!'

'Stephen and the family,' said the Judge.

Jess applauded his attempt at enthusiasm. 'Forensics haven't turned up anything helpful.'

When the Judge turned stern, he looked just like the man over the mantelpiece. Apart from the wing collar. 'How the hell do you know about forensics? How implicated *are* you, Jessica?'

'I'm a consultant.' Jess had imagined announcing it

proudly to her father. It came out like a confession of wrongdoing.

'I sincerely hope you're not laying a trail of bread-crumbs to the door of Harebell House for this murderer to follow.'

'If I get crucified I'll make sure I do it off the premises.'

'Sis!' Stephen was in the room. Two small children, crazed like gremlins, had preceded his entry. His wife brought up the rear.

His hair was giving up, Jess noticed. Retreating back over his head. He'd put on weight. Tall. Wide. Rugby shoulders. Stephen was in off-duty gear of ironed jeans and a cricket jumper.

He punched her on the arm. No hugs: they weren't *French*, for God's sake.

'Hear you've been a naughty girl,' he said satirically.

'Hear you've been a really boringly good boy,' said Jess.

'Darling! Have you lost weight?' Susannah wrapped herself around Jess. A cloud of perfume. The rustle of yummy-mummy separates. 'You look amazing! That colour's brilliant on you.'

It's just black, Jess wanted to say. Instead, she said 'Thank you' and kissed her sister-in-law's cheeks and made approving comments about Susannah's hair/body fat/trousers. It was impossible to dislike Susannah. Yes, she was depressingly upbeat about every last little thing, but the woman *meant* it.

'Sorry we're late.' They weren't; Susannah had a

compulsion to apologise. 'We had to take a detour around the television crews camping out on the square. They were filming Squeezers playing the spoons.'

'Stolen spoons, probably,' said the Judge.

A woman, an old woman, entered quietly. She had cheekbones you could slice bread with. A twinkle in her eye that might kill.

'I didn't know you were coming!' Jess almost knocked over her diminutive great-aunt Iris with her embrace.

Strictly speaking, Iris wasn't an aunt. Generations ago, the Castle family tree had split into two distinct clans. Iris married into the branch that hung onto the noble rank, while Jess's forebears went into the law. Great-aunt, they all agreed, was a far nicer title than the more precise umpteenth cousin twice removed. Iris *felt* like a great-aunt. That was what mattered.

'Stephen brought me.' Iris Castle was crisp; Jess read the subtext. A five-minute car journey with little Baydrian and Ann could put years on a person.

'You'll be needing one of Dad's whoppers, then.'

Taking Iris's arm, Jess squired her great-aunt across the drawing room. Other people had sitting rooms; Jess would have preferred a sitting room. This was most definitely a drawing room.

Iris was a beauty. The sort that doesn't date. She was slender, but not arthritically so; red blood still pumped around her aged veins. White hair no particular way, yet sensational. She sat on a plump armchair and the others gathered naturally around as if this was her party.

'Baydrian. *Baydrian!*' Susannah had a hundred and one ways to say her six-year-old son's name. This was the way she said it when he took down books from shelves and chucked them over his shoulder.

Baydrian's sister watched silently.

One day, thought Jess with some satisfaction, *Ann will end Baydrian.*

'They do not look same,' said Bogna, 'for twins.'

'IVF,' said Susannah. 'We couldn't ... well, *I* couldn't ... so, they're not identical.'

Iris saved them all from another canter through Susannah's fallopian tubes by asking, 'Who's this striking young lady?'

Mary had joined them. Her nod to the occasion was a floor-length taffeta skirt she'd found in a wardrobe. Irritatingly, she looked great in it.

As Mary was introduced, and they all 'bottoms up'-ed, the Judge said, 'I invited young Rupert Lawson.'

To him, everyone was young.

'Why?' Jess wondered why she was so dismayed. 'You hardly know him.'

'Rising star, apparently. Good friend of Stephen's. Used to come to the house when you were kids.'

'I do know that, Dad.' Jess was a sulky teen, right down to the pout.

'It was Mary's idea.' The Judge raised his glass to her; Mary won everybody over. 'We could do with a fresh face at the table.'

'I worry about beef.' With Soviet sadness, Bogna looked longingly in the direction of the kitchen.

'Mum did *amazing* roasts.' Jess had a sudden, ferocious longing for Harriet's gravy.

'Bogna knocks up a fine Sunday lunch, too,' said the Judge.

'Stupid British tradition,' said Bogna.

A lull in the conversation opened up into a chasm they were all forced to stand around. Stephen did the decent thing.

'No Josh today, Aunty?'

'He's so sorry to miss you all.' Iris's grandson was a no-show at most family events; she didn't even try to sound sincere. Jess's mother used to say that Josh was behind the door when manners were handed out. *I should know*, thought Jess, *I was with him*. 'He's caught up on the estate.'

'Bamview council estate?' asked Bogna. 'On Richleigh Road?'

'Sadly no,' said Iris. She looked Bogna up and down. Liked what she saw. '*Our* estate. Kidbury Manor.'

'Stately home?' Bogna evidently didn't know her Castle lore. 'Wowee,' she intoned gravely.

'We weren't supposed to inherit,' said Iris. She held out her hand to Jess, who took it, standing by her chair. Iris had always done this at family do's when Jess was small. 'My late husband was the second brother. The one who usually gets to do his own thing. Then his older brother died, poor chap, and as there were no children, Seb and I had to come back from Kenya and take over the damn manor house.'

'The damn manor house,' interrupted the Judge,

'is a listed building of great historical importance with a medieval porch and a chapel which was consecrated in 1790.'

'The chapel roof leaks.' Iris was brisk. 'The porch is collapsing. You wouldn't believe how much it costs to restore a medieval fresco. The manor's a money pit. We should bulldoze it and build council houses. Why on earth should an old dame like me get to keep two hundred acres to herself? Just because I have a title? I never wanted to be Lady Kidbury.'

'I hate the house being open to the public.' The Judge stood in front of the empty grate, legs apart.

'Would you care to see my heating bills? Josh had no option.' Iris handed him her glass. 'Top-up, please, James.'

That was another of Iris's gifts – she could hoover up a glass of gin without seeming to once bring it to her lips.

Susannah jumped up. 'The present!' She rooted in one of the several holdalls she lugged everywhere.

'For me?' shrieked Baydrian.

'No,' snapped Stephen.

'Not all presents are for you, darling,' said Susannah, carefully calm. She stage-whispered to the adults, 'He has ADHD. Or . . .' Elbow-deep in a holdall, she turned to her husband. 'Was it PTSD?'

'PMS?' offered Stephen.

Mary stifled her snigger. Jess felt Iris squeeze her hand. They knew that the absurdly named Baydrian had no complicated condition. He was just a little shit.

'Here it is!' Triumphant, Susannah pulled out a

squashed gift bag. 'James. For you. To say thank you for having us.'

'There's no need.' The Judge meant it. Gifts made him uneasy, and Susannah brought gifts each time she visited. The bag bore the logo of Castle Kidbury's most overpriced gewgaw shop; a hotly contested title. 'How lovely,' said the Judge, peering in at the contents. 'What, um ...?'

'It's an incense burner.' Susannah was mildly crestfallen. She took the item out of the Judge's hands and began to assemble it on the coffee table. 'This goes here, then you stick this here ...'

'All that to make the house smell?' Mary was unimpressed.

'Incense ...' said the Judge uncertainly.

'I chose Magical Woodland,' said Susannah.

He'd rather have Wet Dog, thought Jess. She relinquished Iris's hand to answer the doorbell.

On the step, Rupert bore flowers and a bottle.

'Am I late? I know your dad's big on timekeeping.'

'Is there stuff in your hair?' Jess peered up at him. He was very tall; sometimes she forgot that. The frisson she experienced when she remembered was of no matter. 'Are those Converses new?' She pointed at the trendy but too-clean shoes.

'I agree,' said Rupert. 'Polite hellos *are* overrated.'

Mary barrelled out of the drawing room. She grabbed Rupert by the arm. 'Save us!' She dragged him towards the conservatory. 'Save us, for feck's sake, Rupes, from polite conversation and demon children.'

Tomato plants stood triffid-like along the conservatory windowsills. It was sultry, the gentle May sunshine magnified by the profusion of glass.

Ever alert for a game, Moose jumped onto Rupert's lap. The dog thought he was still a pup; Jess could hardly see her guest, and enjoyed his confusion about whether or not it would be the correct etiquette to shove his host's golden retriever onto the floor.

'So, anyways, let me tell youse about me interview with your man, Eden,' said Mary. She lit up a cigarette and blew the smoke expertly out of the side of her mouth, towards an open pane.

'She was in pyjamas the whole time,' interrupted Jess.

'Nothing surprises me about you two,' said Rupert, peering round Moose's shaggy head.

'Eden goes, was this Gavin kinky, like?' Mary hooted, head thrown back. 'Poor sod. I felt sorry for him. He had to ask me all about the sex, you know?'

'I bet you told him,' said Jess.

'He asked if Gavin was into Satanism. I goes, no, but he was bang into blowjobs.'

'Lovely.' Jess shared a look with Rupert. She realised she hadn't wanted Rupert to come to lunch because as long as he was outside Harebell House he was *hers*. Jess had never liked sharing. Doner kebabs. Toothbrushes. People.

Mary went on. 'Eden was like, who did Gavin speak to at the gig. I told them about Theresa. Gavin told me she was a superfan. She writes a fanzine. Not much in it about the songs but plenty about Gavin's arse.' Mary looked into the middle distance. 'Which is understandable,' she said, in a dreamy voice.

'You know that saying "don't speak ill of the dead"?' said Jess. 'May I extend it to "don't speak hornily of the dead"?'

'Jesus, yeah. I keep forgetting he's dead.' Mary crossed herself. A committed atheist, sometimes the Irish in her won. 'Poor Gavin. Such a thick.'

Rupert raised his eyebrows, shook his head. Jess knew him well enough by now to know he was relishing this.

'I think,' said Jess, 'that the Baldur logo on Keith's body is a red herring. The murderer's carving random images on the corpses.' She described them. Triangles. Circles. Crosses. All the usual elements of ancient lore but in an unconventional order. They teased and nudged; *You do recognise us if you dig deep enough*, they said.

Rupert tried to flatten Moose. The dog did not cooperate. 'Is it after they're dead? Or does the killer cut into them while they're still alive?'

'Jaysus!' Mary shuddered. 'Listen to Cheerful Charlie.'

A gong sounded.

Moose jumped off Rupert's lap.

'Are you kidding me? said Mary. 'An actual feckin' *gong*?'

Jess did jazz hands. 'Lunchtime!'

All was correct. It was a still life of an English Sunday. The Judge stood at the head of the table. He held aloft a carving knife. The family sat around drooling. Even the children were mesmerised by the smell of gravy.

The doorbell rang.

The Judge put down his knife. 'Who in blazes can that be?' It's a serious matter to get between an Englishman and his beef. 'Get the door, Stephen. Send them away.'

Everybody stared at the joint of beef as Stephen hurried out.

'I do hope I'm not interrupting? Is James in?' The foghorn of Patricia Smalls carried from the hall. The armour-plated mayoress saw Stephen off easily. 'Why, look at you all!' Patricia breezed into the dining room holding a cut-glass bowl. 'I do love a family gathering.'

She never gives up, marvelled Jess. Patricia had pursued her father for years, not bothering to hide her amorous agenda from Harriet.

'Ah. Yes. Patricia.' The guest was the one person for whom the Judge's authority carried no weight whatso-ever. 'Why ... don't you ... Bogna?'

Bogna waited just long enough for her resistance to register. 'I'll get a chair then, isn't it?'

'Fabulous, dear. And put this in the fridge.' Patricia thrust the bowl into Bogna's arms.

'The famous Smalls trifle,' said Iris, with even more irony than she normally employed, as the room awaited the mayor's next pronouncement. Because there always was a next pronouncement.

'Don't mind me, James.' Patricia planted herself in Bogna's seat. She waved a napkin at him. 'Carve, do, go ahead.' She turned to the others. 'I'm here to tell you all about ThinkSpace.'

'What's the think space?' Mary flicked a pea at Baydrian.

'ThinkSpace, dear. One word, no definite article. It's a new concept for the community. Somewhere to contemplate and create. People are saying it's one of my best ideas.'

Nobody was saying that; Jess would put money on it. 'Sounds fascinating. How does the think space work?' She eyed Rupert slyly, inviting him to join the fun.

'One word,' said Rupert. 'No definite article.'

Iris began to pass around the roast potatoes. 'One takes it one goes there and there's space and one thinks?'

'Well, yes, but it's so much more than that. If I'm right, which I am, this venture will be transformative for Castle Kidbury.' Patricia sipped from Bogna's wine glass and winced. 'James! Surely you can offer us a better red than this?'

'I made wine.' Bogna stood over the incomer with a chair, but Patricia didn't budge. 'Don't move, darling.' *Darlink*. 'I'll sit beside you, isn't it.' She slammed down the chair, forcing Patricia to scooch along.

A discreet turf war began between the two women. 'It's a hub,' said Patricia as she withstood Bogna's elbows and accepted a plate of beautifully cooked beef from the Judge. 'A place for the community to cross-fertilise and share innovation.'

Susannah's sudden shout of 'Ann! Knickers *on*, darling!' went ignored by the family, who were accustomed to such outbursts.

'ThinkSpace ...' Stephen looked like Moose trying to work out how the fridge door worked. 'ThinkSpace? Sorry. No. Don't get it.'

'Darling Stephen,' said Iris, in her well-modulated tones, 'there's very little to get.' She winked at Jess.

'Where is the thinking space?' Jess was all apologetic innocence as Patricia corrected her.

'One word, no definite article. The library. The *old* library as we call it now.'

Jess growled and bent over her food. The library had been her shelter from both the rain and other people. Patricia, she knew, hadn't lifted a mayoral finger to save it from closure. Now, it seemed, the red-brick listed building was her personal hobbyhorse.

'James, I'm assuming you'll be my escort to the grand opening. Good, good,' she said as the Judge lifted a shocked face from the joint. 'We have a celebrity to do the honours.'

'A Kardashian?' asked Mary.

'A royal?' asked Jess.

'A weatherman,' said Patricia. 'Shane Harper.'

Blank looks all round.

'Shane Harper!' Patricia bristled at such ignorance. 'Of TV South West fame. Celebrated forecaster, highly influential.'

'I know him!' Susannah beamed. She liked to shed light. 'He does the weekends.'

'Is he a ride?' enquired Mary. 'I've never shagged a weatherman before.'

Patricia turned her laser to Mary. 'Have we met?' She liked to pigeonhole. 'You're Irish, aren't you? *And* half-caste.'

Looking wonderingly at her reflection in a spoon, Mary said, 'Jaysus, so I am!'

'What do you do?'

'You mean, for a job, like? I run a rage room.'

More blank looks.

'I hire out a big room where people come and freak out about their appalling lives. The walls are padded. The floors are wipe-clean. They can even smash things up if they go for the Platinum Package.'

'People pay you to break your furniture?' Iris was amused. A touch horrified.

'Basically. They get it all out their systems. Sometimes I go in at the end of the day and have a good auld scream meself.'

'There's a basis for this in ancient Celtic dance rituals,' said Jess. 'Sacrifices were a means of surrendering anger in an effort to appease gods.'

'She's off!' Stephen held up his fork. 'Everything has a basis in ancient times for sis. Or should I call you—'

'No you shouldn't.' Jess cut him off before he could shout the hated middle name.

Susannah put her hand on Mary's. 'Do you provide a rage room service for children? It could be just what Baydrian needs. Gifted children get *so* frustrated. Don't you, my little darling?'

Under the table, Baydrian was too busy drawing willies on Rupert's Converses to answer.

The men were on the terrace. The women were dotted around the sofas in the drawing room.

'This is so bloody old-school,' grumbled Jess. She was full of crumble. There'd been an accident and Patricia Smalls's famous trifle had gone all over the kitchen floor. Bogna blamed Moose. Moose kept schtum. Patricia Smalls had pronounced Bogna's crumble 'a little tart'. 'The menfolk smoking and talking about big important man things, and the little women in here talking about needlework.'

'I *love* needlework,' said Susannah from the rug, where she was attempting to minimise Baydrian's effect.

'When do we ever talk about needlework?' Iris's eyes, which changed colour with the time of day, were in their mauve mode. 'It's rather refreshing not to listen to them witter on.'

'Stephen *does* like his Formula One,' said Jess wearily. She waited for Susannah to defend her husband. Nothing happened. 'You okay?'

'Me? Yes. Fine. Why?' Susannah prided herself on being fine 24/7.

'Bloody Jimmy,' said Bogna darkly, 'better not be bloody smoking.' She had taken off her shoes and was rubbing her feet.

'James seems sunny,' said Patricia from Harriet's armchair. Jess had to sit on her hands to keep herself

156

from dragging the usurper out of it. 'I do hope he's getting over Harriet at last.'

'She was his wife, Patricia,' said Iris. 'Not a cold.'

'I didn't mean any disrespect.' Patricia stared at Bogna's stockinged feet as if they were dead fish. 'I'm just glad to see him in good spirits.'

'Pity Mum never got to see that side of him,' said Jess. She was sunk deep into the pink and gold cushions.

'Forgive me, child,' said Iris, 'but you know next to nothing about your parents' marriage. Children don't understand the secret language, and nor should they. James and Harriet's intimate life was not without good spirits and laughter.'

Jess harrumphed. Iris rarely corrected her. 'Dad was always moany when I was growing up.'

'To suggest that your mother was a little woman tiptoeing around your father does Harriet a disservice.'

'S'pose.'

'Annoying, isn't it,' said Mary, 'when people are right?' She held her hand up for Iris to high-five.

'No, child, I don't do that,' said Iris.

'Fair enough, Iris!' Mary threw a cushion at Jess. 'I like your aunty.'

Bogna stood. 'Too much sitting around, isn't it.' She crept out to the hall without her shoes. Within moments, the women heard her shout. 'Jimmy! Naughty boy! Put down cigar!'

The men were herded back, sheepishly, by the grim Polish sheepdog.

'The Judge was only holding my cigar for me,' said Rupert.

'Don't be an arsehole, Rupert,' said Jess. 'Dad had a heart attack a few months ago. You lot shouldn't be egging him on.'

Stephen sat on the arm of the sofa. 'Hey, Jess, I've been telling the guys about Buemi's Grand Prix smash back in 2010.'

'Don't you recognise me, Stephen?' Jess was at her most arch. Which was very arch indeed. 'We grew up together. Have I *ever* been interested in posh boys driving their flashy cars round and round and round?'

'Typical Jess,' beamed Stephen. He had never taken his little sister seriously enough for her sharpness to cut him. He flashed a look at his father. The Judge had banned all talk of the Rustic Ripper over the beef. 'I hear you're a sleuth these days.' He laughed. And laughed.

'Not a sleuth, no,' said Jess, when Stephen had finished and wiped his eyes. 'But I *am* acting as a consultant for DS Eden. Dad doesn't like it, obviously.'

Stephen gave a dismissive wave. 'Never mind the pater. Give us the goss, Jess. Do you get to see crime scene photographs?'

'I attended a crime scene.' Jess couldn't resist.

'No!' Stephen was excited. Much more excited than he'd been at the twins' birth.

'Enough, I think, on this topic,' interjected the Judge.

'She's heading back to the law, Dad,' laughed Stephen. 'Slowly but surely. Via murder.'

'I bloody well am not.'

Iris was gathering her handbag, preparing to stand. 'I have every confidence that our Jess will unmask this Rustic Ripper.'

'Don't encourage her, Iris,' said the Judge.

'Why ever not? Here she is using all that expensive learning on a subject the dear girl adores, doing something important for her community. Damn sight better than standing in court in a silly wig.'

Before Jess could thank her great-aunt, Ann pushed Baydrian's face into the pot pourri. Baydrian and his mother traded screams.

Iris stood. 'I'm tired. Take me home, Stephen.' Iris, who never pleaded old age, exploited its perks. 'I dread to think what Josh has got up to at the manor while I was out. Probably decided on a new car park, or bought more tat for the giftey shoppy.' She insisted on pronouncing it that way ever since Josh had put up the sign reading 'This way to the Gifte Shoppe'.

Stephen, primed since birth to obey old ladies he was related to, obliged. He separated the children and dragged them from the room like sacks of millet.

'Thank you, Bogna, it was gorgeous,' cooed Susannah as her husband returned and strong-armed her to the door; her goodbyes were of the James Brown variety, and could take hours. 'Thank you for a lovely lunch in your lovely house, lovely father-in-law!'

Patricia was the first to fill the welcome silence. 'Now, James. Perhaps you could drop me home. I do so love to see a man at the wheel. Particularly,' she licked her dry lips, 'a man such as your good self.'

Bogna began to clear away cups and saucers. 'Time for Jimmy's nap. Doctor's orders.'

The Judge looked like he could kiss Bogna. 'I'd so love to drive you, Patricia, but what can I do?' He placed a hand on his chest.

'Rupert can give you a lift.' Jess didn't have to look at Rupert to see how that went down.

'How, um, kind.' Patricia didn't look grateful. 'Although I can stay for a while if—'

'I fetch bowl.' Bogna was already halfway to the kitchen.

Jess and Rupert watched from the Merc as Patricia let herself in to a wisteria-coated cottage.

'Were we cruel about ThinkSpace?' asked Rupert as he drove off with a toot of the horn.

'Fuck, yeah.' Jess was breezy. 'Smalls deserves it. She stepped on Mum to get to Dad.' *Harriet had just . . . taken it,* thought Jess. The dead, their stories complete, appear in bright detail.

'Quid pro quo.'

The bonhomie faltered without Patricia to unite them. Jess didn't really know this man. 'Any interesting cases at the moment?'

'Disputes mostly.'

Castle Kidbury's hinterland flew by. Jess's mind filled with triangles and crosses and squares and dots and dashes.

'There's even more press in town now.' Rupert kept the conversation in the air. 'CNN are here, for some reason.'

'Eden won't be happy.'

'You could go on telly, Jess. Be a talking head. A commentator. You'd be good at that.'

'Nah. I'd hate it.' Would she though? Jess preened slightly at Rupert's suggestion.

The silence reasserted itself until they were back at Harebell House. 'Thanks, Rumpole.'

'An absolute pleasure.'

She searched him for signs of sarcasm. There were none. She repaid him in kind. 'Castle Sunday lunches are usually torture. Having you there made it . . .'

Rupert looked expectant.

'. . . bearable.'

'You and your extravagant compliments,' said Rupert, before lingering to watch Jess dash across the drive in her bovver boots.

Chapter 12

KNOWN ONLY BY GODS

Monday 23 May

In the uncompromising strip light, Theresa looked poorly. Her eyeliner was black, indelible, layer upon layer. It couldn't disguise the purple swathes beneath her eyes or the bloodshot residue of tears. She gnawed at her nails as Eden took his seat beside Karen.

'I don't want to talk to you lot,' said Theresa. 'You can't help me now. He's gone.' She pursed her lips together. One tear escaped despite her attempt at self-control. 'Gavin's gone.'

Eden wondered when he could get back to normal police work. Car theft. Domestic disturbances. The occasional nice little arson. 'Perhaps you can help *us*, Ms Peake. I know this is a hard time for you, but there's just a few questions and you can go. What was your relationship to Gavin Blake?'

Knott added, 'Were you having sexual relations together?' Eden's black look skated over her head.

'What's it got to do with you?' Theresa was snarly in her grief.

But then, thought Jess, intent on the video link in the next room, *Theresa is snarly full stop.*

'We're trying to build a picture of Gavin's life.'

'His life was his band. I was part of that. I was their superfan.'

Christ, she's so proud of that fact, thought Jess.

'They wrote from the heart.' Theresa was overcome again. She rallied. 'I could hear Gavin's soul in his lyrics.'

Heart. Soul. Why not gallbladder?

'Were you friends? Close friends?'

'I knew him intimately. Better than any other human.'

Knott reactivated. 'So you were having sexual relations together?'

'Let me do this,' said Eden from the side of his mouth. 'Were you Gavin's girlfriend?'

'That means nothing. I was his soulmate.'

'And so I'll ask again,' said Knott. 'Were you having sexual re—'

'Knott, why don't you go and check up on the CCTV sweep?'

'Sarge, I—'

'Just do it.'

'Yes, sir.' Knott left the room with an air of meek defiance.

'Did Gavin have an interest in Satanism?'

163

'He was pure.'

'Yes, I'm sure he was, but—'

'He needed me.'

'That's good, but could you tell me a little about the people at the gig on the night of Friday the twentieth?'

'We needed nobody else. I saw only Gavin. He saw only me.'

'I understand the man who designed Baldur's logo was there. The boys in Gavin's band didn't know about him. You know Gavin so well, I'm sure you can tell me his name.'

'Why didn't you tell me first about Gavin's murder? Why did you go all round the band? They weren't as important to him as I was.'

Jess put her head in her hands. In Theresa's delusions she saw the common or garden bullshit women sell themselves when a man just isn't into them. She stood up.

'A name would help, Theresa.'

'I'm not a suspect.' Theresa gnawed at her nails. 'I can just leave. You can't make me talk to you.'

Eden blamed television. Everyone knew their rights these days.

The interview room door opened. Jess backed in carrying a tray. 'Here you go, Sarge. The coffee you wanted, the cake, and one for me. Couldn't let you have all the fun!' She sat down heavily before Eden could protest. 'Have some lemon drizzle, Theresa. I bet you haven't eaten.'

The conflict was plain on Theresa's face. The cake

reminded her she was hungry. Jess reminded her that she hated Jess. 'I'll stay a bit longer,' she mumbled and reached out bitten fingers for the sponge.

'Deep down, Gavin really loved you, Theresa. I could tell.'

Theresa chewed.

'Men don't know their own minds, do they? You were the best thing that ever happened to him, and if only he'd lived he would have realised it.'

Eden bowed his head. Jess kept him in her peripheral vision; although he seemed willing to let her burble on, he could shut her down at any moment.

'Why you being nice?' spat Theresa.

'Because, woman to woman, I know how you feel.'

Theresa digested that, along with the sugar icing. 'Do you think these twats can catch the killer?'

'I have every faith,' said Jess, 'in these twats.'

'Unthank,' said Theresa. 'That's the designer's name. Luis Unthank.'

Eden scribbled on his notepad.

'I didn't like him,' said Jess.

'He thinks he's the cheese and he's only the wrapper,' said Theresa. 'Flirts like a single man but he's married. He drives up from London and stays overnight for Gavin's gigs, and always comes onto me. Asked me back to his room at the EasySleep Inn after the pub. I wasn't having any of it.' Jess knew, without any doubt, that Theresa had slept with Luis Unthank.

'Him and Gavin were at art college together. Before Gav got thrown out. They didn't understand his genius.'

Eden sighed.

'Tell you who else I don't like,' said Jess. 'That Pan bloke.'

'Oh God, *him*.' Theresa wiped her nose, sat up straight. 'Always at our gigs.'

Jess felt Eden twitch.

'He loved Gavin, he did. Following him around. Gav avoided him. Said he gave him the creeps. He came onto me too. But, you know, I—'

'Wasn't having any of it,' said Jess, certain that Theresa had slept with Pan as well.

'Can I go now?' The brief window of cooperation slammed shut. 'And you tell your mate Mary that Gavin was laughing at her behind her back.'

Jess held her gaze. Read all the pain and all the hatred in Theresa's eyes. She could have countered it, could have said that Theresa was frightened that Gavin laughed at *her*, but she didn't. 'Take care, Theresa,' she said.

'Fuck you,' said Theresa.

Eden's office was significantly less tidy than it had been a week ago. Paper had taken over. Red Bull cans and styrofoam cups fought for a toehold in the mess. His whiteboard was criss-crossed by multicoloured spaghetti.

'Don't do that again,' he said as Jess fished a packet of Monster Munch from somewhere on her person and sat down.

'What? Interrupt? But I got her talking. Admit it.'

He didn't. 'I whistled up her record. Stolen shopping trolleys. Writing rude words on walls. Theresa's a sad girl not a bad girl, I think. This Gavin Blake took advantage, by the sounds of things. If Theresa had any violent previous I might like her for killing Gavin because he was, erm, intimate with your friend.'

'Believe me, she'd kill Mary, not Gavin, if she was going to kill anyone. Women are funny like that. Any links between Gavin and Keith Dike?'

'Not a dicky bird. Gavin was too self-absorbed to be hated like Keith was. Plus, there was that matter in his childhood . . . if anything, people felt sorry for him.'

Jess moved quickly on. The tragedy, she told herself, was irrelevant; Eden needn't know about her part in it. 'Can I be there when you talk to Luis Unthank?'

'No.' Eden sifted through the paperwork on his desk. 'Knott!' he yelled.

'While I've got you,' said Jess, licking Monster Munch dust from her fingers. 'Why don't you lay off Squeezers. Twenty interviews in four months? It's Beefy Dave you should be hassling, not poor old Squeezers.'

'Let's stick to the important stuff.'

'Guv?' Karen inserted the top half of her boyish body into the office. Beyond her, the incident room was as noisy as a nightclub. The manpower had materialised, just like that, as soon as the media mob arrived. The quiet provincial police station was groaning at the seams.

'Send somebody to EasySleep on the edge of town and see if they have a Mr Luis Unthank still registered there. Bring him in so I can rule him out.'

An officer hollered across the incident room. 'Who's got victim one's next of kin details?'

'You!' Eden strode to the door and yanked it wide open, shouting over Karen's head. 'As long as you're working in my nick you'll call the victims by their names.' He held the door, turned to Jess. 'And *you*, out you go. Do *not* interrupt my interview again.'

'Brownie's honour,' said Jess, nipping past him.

If Eden had whistled up Jess's record, he would have discovered that she was kicked out of the Brownies.

Fore Street was banal after the adrenaline of the interview room.

Jess shop-crawled, listening in on conversations. Murder was the topic *du jour*; each Castle Kidbury-ite had their theory. The more Jess discovered about the crucifixions, the less certain she was of any theory. The crimes were jumbled. Complex. Gritty. Like people.

Down Dunch Lane, just off Fore Street, Wilson's Pharmacy was dim. While her eyes adjusted, and the ranks of painkillers and corn treatments took shape, Mr Kuzbari emerged from the back room in a pristine white shirt. He wiped his mouth.

'Forgive me.' His voice was musical. 'I was just having a snack, Jess.'

He remembered her name. She was pleased.

'Welcome back. I hope you're well.' His politeness was ornate. Un-British. 'How can I help you?'

'I need ...' She looked around. Jess didn't need

anything. Not anything she could buy. 'More nicotine patches, please.'

'So soon? You're not abusing them, I hope. The side effects can be nasty.'

'I lost the last packet,' lied Jess. She'd been drawn to the shop by the knowledge that she'd find Kuzbari there. He was both foreign and familiar.

Satisfied with this fib. He handed her a small box. Took her money. Gave her change.

When she lingered, he said, 'May I offer you some tea?'

Jess grinned.

A round brass tray. A swan-necked metal pot. Two squat, tulip-shaped glasses. The tea was a pale gold. Jess had two attempts at pronouncing it properly.

'Zhourat,' repeated Kuzbari, amused.

'It tastes of flowers.'

'There's damask rose in there. Camomile. And, let me see ... lemon verbena. It's calming. Good for the digestion.'

'A wonder drink, no less.' Jess sipped. She was ready to believe in it. As credulous of its properties as Theresa was of Gavin's genius. 'Delicious.' She imagined the zhourat flowing through her veins like honey.

'I find I'm now addicted to the British cuppa,' said Kuzbari. 'At first, I turned up my nose. Milk and sugar?' He pulled a face, suave features contorted. 'Now I appreciate it. Especially when it rains.'

'This country runs on tea. We won two world wars

169

with it.' Jess remembered this man had fled conflict. 'I didn't mean to trivialise ...'

Kuzbari absolved her with a wave of his hand. 'Please don't worry. I'm glad you think of war as something from the distant past. I only wish I, too, believed battles could be won with tea. I struggle to believe what has happened to my country. It's like a bad dream. Yet I never wake up.'

Jess had the luxury of waking from her own nightmares. 'Do you think you'll ever go back to Syria?'

'I have nothing to go back to. My house is in ruins. My street is rubble. My work is ...' He seemed to shake himself. 'You didn't come here for a tale of woe, Jess.'

'I did. I mean, I want to know,' said Jess. 'Do you have children? God, I'm nosey.' She blew out her cheeks. 'Ignore me.'

'In Syria we're a nation of, what d'you call them, nosey parkers. It's good manners to ask questions. So I'm happy to tell you that, yes, my wife and I have three sons and one perfect daughter.'

Jess was afraid to ask. 'Are they ... safe?'

'They're in Peckham.' *Peck. Ham.* 'Perfectly safe.'

'Why aren't you with them?'

'Malva's studying for her medical degree in London. There was no work for me there. I came here for this job.'

'On your own?'

'On my own. I'm not accustomed to it, Jess. At home, there were people in and out of the house all day. Grandmothers snoring in the shade. Babies crawling under my feet.' It was hard to tell if Kuzbari's dark eyes were wet. 'Noise. Music. Talk.' He lit up. 'The Syrian national pastime is conversation.'

'You miss it.'

'I do.' Kuzbari didn't elaborate. After a long moment, he said, 'If we could have stayed, we would have done so. The bombing was too intense. I lost too many friends. It was when my brother—' He halted. 'There was great sadness. The little ones deserve to live without fear.'

Jess thought of Malva, raising four children in Peck Ham, all of them traumatised.

'British men!' said Kuzbari. Brighter. Upbeat. 'They are so . . .' He pulled his arms around his torso, pulled in his chin. 'In Syria we greet each other properly. We kiss on the cheek. We are *warm*.'

Jess noticed a studio portrait, framed in flamboyant gilt, on the wall alongside Kuzbari's diplomas. 'Your family?' She went closer. 'Your wife's *lovely*.'

'She is.'

The children had gappy teeth. The girl's hair stuck up. Kuzbari was almost unrecognisable. He beamed at the back of his little clan, in a pale suit, his face fresh. This was evidently a 'before' picture. Before the war.

'Who's this lady? I love her outfit.'

'My mother.'

The only one to cover her head, Kuzbari's mother wore an embroidered scarf over a voluminous black dress. 'She's more traditional?'

'Very much so. We are Muslim, you see. I don't eat

171

pork, or drink alcohol, but Malva and I are modern people. Not my *yuma*. She's traditional.'

'What does she make of London?'

'She's in Damascus.' Kuzbari tidied the glasses onto the tray. 'I left her behind,' he said.

Jess couldn't think of a thing to say.

'She's eighty. She lives with my cousin.'

'Is she safe?'

Kuzbari looked as if he pitied Jess. 'Nobody's safe in Damascus.'

'Why not bring her over?'

Later, recalling the conversation, Jess admired Kuzbari's restraint in not saying, 'Ooh! Wish I'd thought of that!' He simply said, 'That is now my life's work.'

'I wish I could help.'

'When I look out of my window and see how most people live. How much they have. How little they appreciate it. How they squander their lives . . .'

'Must make you angry.'

He didn't agree. He didn't disagree.

The bell above the door announced another customer.

'Ah, Mr Eden. I have your prescription just here.' Kuzbari disappeared behind a partition wall.

Eden jumped when he saw Jess. He glanced neurotically at the partition, behind which Kuzbari could be heard shuffling paper bags. 'You,' he said.

'Me,' agreed Jess. 'What prescription is this, then?'

'Nothing,' said Eden. He said it too fast. When Kuzbari brought out a package, he practically snatched it from him.

'Tea?' asked Kuzbari.

'Um, no.' Eden seemed confused by the offer.

Gesturing at the bag, Jess whispered, 'Piles?'

Eden closed his eyes.

'Warts?'

'Jess—' said Eden, as if in pain.

'Viagra?'

Kuzbari shuffled diabetes leaflets by the till. His mouth was disobeying him, zigzagging with amusement.

'You're not *pregnant*, are you, Eden?'

'Have you finished, Castle?' As Eden paid, he juggled his phone, thumbing open an image. 'What do you make of this? It's another, um, *present* from our mutual friend.'

'Another ...?' Aware of Kuzbari's eyes upon them, Jess merely raised her eyebrows.

'Yes.'

Jess took Eden's phone into a corner. Beside the washbags. By the talc and bath salts. She scrolled.

'It's not like the first box.' Eden stood behind her. Incongruous among the scents of lavender and rose. He was a creature of the office. 'It's plain.' He lowered his voice, even though Kuzbari had retreated to his anteroom.

The footed box was square. A high-gloss black lacquer. The interior was rough, pale, with the shadow stain of blood. Jess swallowed. It was Gavin's blood. 'There *is* one very important symbol on this box. But it's not in any of these photographs.'

'Then how do you know it's there?' Eden looked sceptical. Or, more sceptical than usual.

'It's a very special marking. The sign of a fearsome giant in Greek mythology. He had a hundred eyes.'

Eden nodded, encouraging her. Jess could almost hear his brain speed up.

'The giant's main task was to kill the half woman half snake, Echidna.'

'Don't tell me he crucified her?'

'Sorry, nope. He killed her while she was sleeping.'

'What was his name?'

'I'm glad you asked me that.' Jess couldn't keep this up. 'Argos.'

'Hmm,' said Eden, thoughtfully, before his eyes turned to slits. 'You mean—'

'I mean this is a child's jewellery box from Argos. Fourteen ninety-nine. I bought one for my niece's birthday last year. She hated it.'

'Stick to the subject.' Eden was cold.

'It should have a pink silk interior, with a revolving ballerina. That's been ripped out to make room for the eyes, I suppose.'

'Was Argos really a Greek myth?'

'Yeah. So was Nike. The gods are everywhere. Every time you eat a Mars bar you're paying tribute to the Roman god of war. Amazon was a mythical tribe of warrior women. There are probably Trojan condoms for sale in here. All those bunk-ups round the back of the Druid's Head commemorate Paris stealing Helen away from Menelaus.'

Eden gazed down at the tiny picture on his screen. Concentrating ferociously. 'It could mean something. Argos. A hundred eyes, you say?'

'Argos is Greek, though, and Ogham is Celtic. The inlays on that first box were so meticulous. I find it hard to believe our man would cross-reference like this with a cheap high-street piece.'

'Perhaps this murder was hurried.' Eden blinked, as if facing a hard truth. 'Perhaps he's speeding up. Which means he'll get more brutal.'

'You've been reading up on serial killers.' Jess had done the same. 'Unless he's a copycat.'

'How would he know about the eyes? And the box? And before you say it, I don't like Paul Chappell for this. He doesn't fit the profile.'

'Does the killer *have* to fit a profile?'

'Yes he does.' Eden didn't seem to like Jess's tone. 'Remember: no hunches. No left-field light-bulb moments.'

Jess nodded. She needed to be part of his team. Castle Kidbury was menaced by something far worse than the many-eyed Argos. But she did have her hunches. And she trusted them.

Chapter 13

PLEADING THE FIFTH

Tuesday 24 May

The Morris Traveller was a proper car that made proper car noises. The clutch hiccupped. The gearstick retched. The hypochondriac engine moaned. Jess had bought it from a scrap dealer for £400. She'd *saved* it. There had been barely time to fall in love with it before it broke down outside Exeter St David's station in torrential rain. A total stranger knocked at her window to help, and got the Traveller up and running in the blink of an eye. And thus began the ballad of Jess and Mary.

'You sure you won't come back to Exeter with me?' asked Mary now, from the passenger seat. She sat awkwardly. The upholstery was past its best.

'I'm not up to the wild nightlife of Exeter.' In truth, there was little about the place that was wild. Unless you happened to be out with Mary Spillane, who could locate the wildness in a morgue. 'I'll hang around here for a bit, keep an eye on Dad.'

'And Rupert.'

'And Eden needs me on the investigation.' Jess would not take the Rupert bait.

'You need the investigation, you mean.' Mary trampled her friend's delusions. 'I don't want to be around the murders anymore. It was exciting until it got personal. The whole thing with Gavin spooked me right out.'

'Not surprised. It's not every day your one-night stand ends up on a slab.'

'Please come.' Mary put her hands together in supplication. 'G'wan, Jess. A couple of nights away from tea shops and crucifixions. Bogna's doing a grand job with your da, and a break will help you make your mind up about Rupert.'

On certain topics, Mary could not be kept at bay. 'Go ahead, Mary. Say your piece.'

Mary was silent for a moment, as if exercising restraint. Then she blurted, 'Why not shag him and get it over with? All sorted. Done and dusted. Sure, you'll both be the better for it.'

'You make the act of love sound like popping a zit. Why will I be *better for it*? I don't want to *shag* Rupert. I don't want to shag anyone. I'm jobless and homeless, and to top all that, my dad's not well.'

'Rupe's a nice fella and you've not had much luck on that front.'

Jess lifted her nose. 'Haven't I?'

'No.' Mary was emphatic. 'You haven't. There was that professor one you were shagging, sorry, *seeing* in Cambridge years back. What was his name, now?'

'Max,' sighed Jess.

'And then that artist guy from Totnes who thought you were a witch and wanted us to wrestle in mud so he could paint us. After him was the one we called Lovely Pete, who turned out to be Lovely Married Pete.'

'You have a point, but Rupert's not the answer. Can we change the subject?'

'Only after I point out the poor eejit has a thing the size of Belgium for you. You don't need a PhD in goblins to figure that out.'

Richleigh's one-way system always lowered Jess's mood. Castle Kidbury liked to pretend Richleigh didn't exist. They weren't above using it, though, for its unsightly amenities.

The exception to the West Country's bond with mysticism, Richleigh's gods were the giants of retail. Endless parks of home improvement stores, supermarkets and bargain furniture outlets. *And yet*, thought Jess, *it doesn't have the common decency to muster up a proper kebab shop.*

The station was on the far side of town. Jess found a parking spot and walked Mary to the platform.

'Look,' started Mary, 'I know you hate being told. But it's going to be okay. Your dad'll be fine. He's got Bogna *and* you. Castle Kidbury's your home. It's where you're from, Jess. You might enjoy it if you'd only stop painting yourself into corners.'

178

The suggestion made Jess bridle.

'Stop overthinking. So you don't want to ride the arse off of Rupert; make a mate of him instead. Use Bogna. The woman's a loony, but I'd have her in a trench with me.'

Jess nodded. She would miss Mary's tough love. Not so tough, really, and very loving. A tear made its wet way down her cheek.

'Don't start that.' Mary wiped it away. 'You have family; I have no one. Try liking them a bit.'

They regarded each other. They both liked what they saw.

The Exeter train pulled in.

'Do you have everything?' asked Jess.

'If by everything, you mean this, then yes.' Mary held up a carrier bag. She travelled light. She'd arrived in combats and was leaving in jeans and a pilfered shirt. 'Gotta go, babe, and ingratiate meself with the guard. For feck's sake get yourself a hobby that isn't moping or murder, yeah?'

She took off. No goodbyes, not ever. A word with the train personnel, and Mary bounced into First Class.

Alongside the station minicab HQ was a florist. Leaning over the blooms in buckets was Danny. He was frowning.

'Buying flowers, you old romantic?' Jess punched him gently on the arm.

'I want a big bunch,' said Danny. 'But they're so dear.'

'Are they for a girl?'

'They're for … me.'

Jess accepted the fib. 'How's Tallulah?'

'We broke up.'

'Oh shit. Sorry.' Jess felt like a heel. 'That's rough, Danny.'

'Not because we don't love each other. Because my mum says it's for the best. She likes me to stay in now. I gave up my job.' He stared at a few coins in his plump hand.

'Which flowers would you buy if you could choose any of them?'

'Them.' Danny was certain.

Jess gulped. He'd pointed to a bouquet worthy of Maria Callas. 'Have them on me, Danny.'

He was grateful. He told her he'd pay her back. She said a kiss on her cheek would settle the debt. His lips were soft.

As Danny waited for the extravaganza to be wrapped, Jess's phone pinged.

Dinner Wednesday?

She waved to Danny.

Why not. I'll book somewhere. Pick me up at 8.

Rupert's reply appeared immediately.

Yessir!

Obeying the 20 mph limit along Fore Street, Jess saw a figure enter Dickinson's Books. She counted to ten to overcome the temptation to stop the car.

She stopped the car.

'Not you again,' said Graham. 'Buying something this time, one hopes.'

'Just browsing.' Jess gave the counter a wide berth; Shakespeare had another one of his intermittent gum infections.

There were books on the floor. Books on chairs. Books in boxes. Towards the back of the shop, in the Fine Art section, was her quarry. He wore long shorts and flip-flops. Jess did not look at his feet. Men's feet in flip-flops were one of her most cherished pet hates.

'Oh hey,' she said.

Luis Unthank was wary. 'Sorry. Do we ...?'

'I saw you at the gig. *That* gig. I'm an old friend of Gavin's.'

'Right. Heavy shit, yeah?' Unthank went back to browsing.

'You're Luis, right?'

'*Lu.*' He sounded aggrieved. As if everybody in the world knew he was Lu. As if Luis was an insult.

'Didn't you create their logo?'

'You a reporter or something?'

'No. But I'm into design. I love the Baldur artwork.'

He warmed up. Slightly. Took her in properly. 'It was a sweet little project.' He took down an immense book on Weimar culture. As he turned the pages, he said, 'I do a lot of branding. Hotel chains. Banks. So poor old Gavin's little band was a doddle.'

'It's an interesting symbol.'

'Thank you.' He accepted the compliment as his due.

'Did you research Baldur?'

Unthank looked at her sharply. 'What did you say your name was? You didn't, did you?' He took the book to the cash register. 'Can you do me a deal, mate?' he said to Graham, who was nobody's mate. 'It's a bit battered.'

'The price,' said Graham, 'is the price.'

As Unthank waited for his change, he set down a pile of business cards on the counter. 'In case a customer needs some branding or marketing help. Give 'em my card. We're all indies now. We can help each other out.'

Graham brought the card right up to his eyes. 'What's an imageer?'

'I'm a wizard of the narrative. A reputation saver.'

'If you say so.'

'See you, mate. And sort your cat out.'

When Jess pocketed a card and followed him out onto the cobbles, Unthank slowed down. 'This book is worth twice what that idiot asked for it.'

'Well done you,' said Jess. Silently, she added, *you utter plank*. 'Are you working on something now?'

'Branding for a car. It's German, so I'm digging into Bauhaus, expressionism. Nobody will appreciate it.'

Jess had read somewhere that psychopaths were bitter. Or at least she thought she had. She scurried after Unthank, in the opposite direction to her car. He walked inhospitably fast and it crossed her mind that he might think she fancied him. 'It's so cool,' she said, 'to talk to somebody who comprehends the importance of symbols.'

'They're everywhere, aren't they?' Unthank lit a cigarette. Didn't ask Jess if she wanted one.

'You utilise them, I guess, to sell.'

'To sell, yeah. Seduce. Persuade.' He took a long drag. 'Bully if necessary.'

'They have power,' said Jess. 'I respect symbols.'

'Funny way of putting it. Why respect them? Why not just interpret and *use* them to get what you want?'

'Because they border on the magical. Symbols speak subliminally to people. The swastika didn't just *happen*.'

'Woah.' Unthank ridiculed her with his feigned surprise. 'How'd we get to Hitler so quickly? Not all symbols are heavy. The sign outside my window at the EasySleep Inn is a classic of its sort and hasn't changed for twenty years. Nobody started a world war over it.'

She'd met his like before. Mocking. Sneery. Jess pretended to like him. 'How long are you around for?'

'Why?'

'Just thought, um ...' Jess pushed herself to say it. 'You might fancy a drink.' She went red. Red didn't suit her.

Unthank stopped. Held up his left hand. 'Married, love. New baby.' He looked as if he pitied her, and Jess wanted to take his oversized art book and shove it, with gusto, up his fundament.

They were by the market cross. Unthank leant against it. 'Now, *here's* a symbol and a half.' He seemed ready to talk now he had humiliated her. 'You see one of these crosses in every village square. But what are people actually seeing?'

Jess saw a tall, sturdy cross of mellow stone. It was pitted and warm, and every November it sprouted wreaths. 'They're seeing a reminder of the men who gave their lives for the rest of us. It says "remember me".'

'"Gave their lives" is a sugar-coated way of saying they died a miserable death in battle. The cross has something real to say, but it uses the voice we all have deep inside us. The non-verbal one. The primeval one. Yet everybody passes it while they do their shopping and walk their doggies, ignoring the fact that this cross evokes blood and bullets and death. Anyway. Nice talking to you.' Unthank saluted her facetiously. 'Might see you at the funeral.' He looked down his nose. 'You'll be there, of course. You being such a good friend of Gavin's.'

Jess let him disappear from view before she turned to hurry back to her car. Unthank had left her feeling an inch high.

By way of an antidote, Tallulah bounced across the square. Flowers in her arms, the sun in her hair, she was as high as a girl in a 1980s tampon advert.

Hoping the spring in her step was contagious, Jess hailed Tallulah. Asked about the flowers.

'From my fiancé.' Tallulah held them out for Jess to sniff. 'He's the nicest person I know and we're going to

184

have three kids. Maybe a chihuahua. Not sure about the chihuahua.'

'His mum doesn't approve, yeah?'

'How do you know?' Tallulah's face was an illustration of surprise.

'If you want my advice, keep going. When you find a nice person, hang on to them. In the end, nobody can argue with love.'

'Exactly.' Tallulah turned away.

A voice behind Jess said, 'You shouldn't poke your nose in. Could be dangerous to encourage them.'

'Hi Karen.' Jess turned. 'I'm not poking anything in. I'm *interested*. There are rules to this kind of thing.' Jess made up these rules on the spot. 'If you interfere in the right spirit, if you do it with love, it's allowed.'

Karen wasn't listening. Her rabbity nose twitched. 'There he goes!' She darted past Jess. There was a scuffle between her pristine jacket and a scabby raincoat. 'Gotcha!'

Squeezers' hands were behind his back as Karen frogmarched him across the square.

'Explain this, Karen!' Jess scuttled along behind them.

'His alibi collapsed.' Karen bent Squeezers into a waiting car, blue and yellow chequered. Through the window, she told him, 'There *was* a lock-in at the Druid's Head the night Keith Dike died, but nobody remembers seeing you there.'

The car drove away. Jess hit the side of it with the palm of her hand as it passed her. From inside, she heard Squeezers shout, 'I'll plead the fifth!'

Chapter 14

IT BEGINS AT HOME

Still Tuesday 24 May

The market square was quiet again after the clamour of Squeezers' arrest.

At a loss without Mary, Jess was tempted to chase off to Margaret Thatcher Way and wangle her way into the interview room with Squeezers. She set her shoulders against that idea. Better to wait for the call to come.

Jess turned in a circle. An axe had fallen on her routines.

No lectures to prepare. No student emails to answer about forgotten deadlines or lost work.

No need to visit the library and lose herself in research.

No despairing over her inability to compete with the lure of the mobile phones in her students' bags.

No elation when they laugh at her jokes, when they concentrate so hard that it's like an engine running.

No moment of pure connection.

A visit to Lynne's Minimart was in order.

Crunchies. Quavers. *Soleros*. Lynne's was a treasure trove for the greedy. Jess bit into her Curly Wurly, enjoying the way it resisted her, as she meandered along Fore Street.

The window of the charity shop was eclectic. The same battered mannequin that had stood there since biblical times wore a Primark kaftan. A beret sat on a disembodied polystyrene head, its expression felt-tipped in. A filthy soft toy with no eyes added a topical touch.

A selection of handwritten notes were sellotaped to the door.

DO NOT ASK FOR CHANGE FOR THE CAR PARK.

PUSHCHAIRS ARE DISCOURAGED
FOR OBVIOUS REASONS.

NO DOGS ALLOWED NOT EVEN GUIDE DOGS
WHO ARE STILL DOGS AFTER ALL.

A new one had been added, not yet faded by the sun.

DON'T ASK WE DON'T KNOW ANYTHING
ABOUT THE MURDERS.

The bell above the door jangled.

Volunteering her time would be a spring clean for

Jess's soul. As the Judge liked to point out, the Castles had a long history of public service; he meant brigadiers and MPs, but they who only stand and wait in Owl Sanctuary charity shops also serve.

Richard came out from the back room on oiled slip-ons. 'Oh,' he said.

'Ah,' said Doug, appearing behind him.

Of un-guessable age, they had run the shop and shared the flat above it for ever.

'Hello chaps.' Jess loved them. Jess was terrified of them. 'I'm here to volunteer.'

Doug was tall. Gothically white and thin. Held his nose very high.

Richard had to look up at Jess. His bog-brush hair had been apricot when Jess was at school, but now it was silver. He wore a neckerchief at all times. 'Hang on,' he said, gesturing at her with the arm of his television-set-sized reading glasses. 'You Harriet's girl?'

'Yes.' It made a change to be Harriet's and not the Judge's. Harriet had left a light footprint in comparison to her husband. Except, it would seem, in the charity shop.

Richard and Doug exchanged awestruck looks.

'Harriet was a goddess,' whispered Richard.

'A marvel. She could actually work the till.' Doug laid his pale hand on his pale brow. 'We shall not see her like again.'

'Castle Kidbury isn't the same without her.'

Jess couldn't agree more. But that was not a conversation she wanted to have there and then. 'Could you do with a hand?' She looked around. The shop had deteriorated since Harriet Castle had brought her Mary Poppins touch to bear on it.

From her mother's tales, Jess knew that keeping the shop clean, rotating the stock and selling the stock weren't the men's strong points. They were better at scandal and tea drinking and bitterly debating the relative merits of Sondheim and Lloyd Webber. Their true calling was their dictatorship of the Castle Kidbury Am Dram Society.

'We'll consider a trial period.' There was fake tan on Richard's paisley shirt collar. 'When can you start?'

'Now?'

'She's easy, Richard,' said Doug.

'She is, Doug,' said Richard. 'Jess, if you're half the woman your mother was you'll do just fine.'

'She's not though,' said Doug. 'I can tell.' He showed Jess the limited ropes. 'Till. Stockroom.' He pointed out landmarks with a plastic *Star Wars* lightsaber. 'Powder room. Kettle. Record player.' He sniffed. 'Not that we'll put you in charge of that until you've proved yourself worthy.'

'Is that *Evita*?' The record was scratchy.

'It is.' Richard beamed. 'I won the toss this morning. It's *Aspects of Love* next.'

'What would you like me to do?' Jess looked around her at the chaos of homewares and toys and books.

Doug put his hands to his head. 'Here's me forgetting we have a customer in the changing room! Go round and collect all the black stuff you can find. Gents or ladies, doesn't matter. Bring it over and hand it through the curtain.'

The rails were disorganised. There was no rail just for black clothes; the very rail Jess would gravitate to. She whisked through garments hanging limply on hangers of all sorts. Some needed a wash. Others needed a decent burial. The latent Harriet inside Jess arose: she would knock this place into shape.

Under her hand a yellow swimsuit.

Jess drew back as if it burnt her hand.

She didn't like the colour yellow. She couldn't countenance a daffodil. A yellow swimsuit was tailor-made to disturb her.

It wasn't just yellow swimsuits. It was swimming pools. It was women named Becky. Standing by the circular rail, Jess was back in her dream.

The lifeguard, so much taller than her little self, had evaporated. One minute there, the next gone.

The lady's movements were too broad. Her laughter too ready. Eyes rimmed with sparkling green, like mineral deposits around the bloodshot whites, came close to Jess's.

An atmosphere. Like ants all over her.

'Chop chop!' shouted Doug. 'The customer's waiting.'

Hurriedly, Jess thought *black, black, black*.

The dream was encroaching on her waking hours. She would examine why, how, later. For now, the customer was waiting and Jess was grateful to the customer for giving her purpose, and a reason not to examine the dream.

She knocked on the plywood side of the jerry-built changing room. In her arms were ruffled blouses, tight slip dresses, trousers, vests, shirts. 'Hello in there!'

A pale arm pulled her into the cubicle. Pan was naked from the waist up.

'Hello, sweet thing.'

He was very close. Jess pressed herself against the wall. She didn't leave. Later she'd wonder why not.

'Dr Jessica Castle. We haven't seen each other since you were in my boudoir. I was not decent, as I recall.'

Jess swallowed. This was exactly what Rupert meant by putting herself at risk. 'I . . .'

Pan took the clothes out of her arms. Removed the only barrier between them. 'Allow me.' He placed them carefully on a stool. He leant even closer. His breath was warm and musky sweet. 'D'you like this?' He fingered a pewter crucifix against his fluorescently pale chest. 'Just your thing, isn't it? The meeting of the ancient world with Christianity. Where epochs collide.'

'Nothing about you is my *thing*,' said Jess. 'That's a piece of tat jewellery. A knock-off, like you.'

'Oh come now,' Pan's lips were almost on Jess's cheek. 'Aren't we all God's creatures?'

Jess was frozen. A mongoose to Pan's snake. Time to be bold. 'Do you always talk such bollocks?'

Pan let out a sigh of genuine disappointment. 'Are you always so frigid?'

'Always.'

He laughed. It sounded almost natural. He inched backwards. An inner switch had been flicked. Pan's eyes now were just dark; the sexual glitter conserved for other, more responsive mongooses. 'You like to think you're special, Jess.'

'Pot. Kettle. Et cetera.'

'I see through you. Like you're made of crystal.'

Instinct told her *run*. Her spirit of adventure told her not to waste this chance. Jess was in the heart of the action. Next to Pan was, for good or ill, an exciting place to be.

'You're a little girl. You need protecting. Why doesn't your big important daddy look after you?'

'I'm a grown woman.' Jess felt her heart beating in her throat. 'My family is none of your business. You know a lot for somebody who never leaves his caravan.'

'You come on so street-smart. But you're made of the same stuff as your manor-house relatives. Should've seen that Josh's face when I led my little family into the edges of his fiefdom.'

He knew so much about her. Jess was no believer in mystical powers. The truth was worse; Pan had been snooping. She was out of her depth.

'I shan't take any of your wares today.' Pan pulled a tattered velvet jacket over his skinny shoulders. 'Nice to see you helping out here. Doing your bit for the less fortunate. Which, let's face it, for a Castle is just about everybody.'

Pan bent suddenly towards her. His mouth against her ear. 'You should pay me a little visit.' He was quieter now. His voice a feather. Stroking. Tickling. 'We have fun at Pitt's Field. Show Daddy what for. Stick two pretty fingers up at all those ancestors.' His eyes travelled around her face. 'So white. Exquisite, really.' He described Jess's cheek with his finger. 'You and your copper boyfriend aren't going to find anything on me.'

Jess was suffocating. As if this was her dream and the claustrophobic changing room had filled up with water. 'Did you kill Keith Dike?'

He pressed his finger onto her lips. 'Yes.' His eyes bore into hers. 'Oh, hang on, I meant no.' When Pan laughed, his eye teeth were pointed. 'Didn't kill the singer boy neither.'

Jess stood her ground. Didn't lift her hand to push away his. That would be admitting he bothered her.

Pan regained his full height. 'I thought maybe I had a little fancy for you. Turns out you're nothing. Poor little rich girl. Bored of you already, darlin'.' He pulled a comically sad face. 'This is you.' Ground his knuckles into his eyes. '*Boohoo. It's all gone wrong for me. Whatever shall I do?*'

Jess breathed in as he pushed past her out into the shop.

'Be seeing you, gentlemen,' he said. 'Pleasure as always.'

The scrape of fork on plate. Soft thud of glass on coaster. Jess and her father broke bread together. Jess's mobile was on her lap. Just in case Eden called. Her father maintained a strict no-phones-at-the-table rule.

'Bogna does a cracking shepherd's pie.' The Judge sat back.

'She does.' It was what angels would taste like. If you minced them.

'Bit hot on the old portion control, though.' The Judge rubbed his stomach. 'I heard you were in Mum's shop today.'

'How d'you know that?'

'Castle Kidbury jungle drums.'

'I volunteered. One morning and afternoon a week. Reminds me of Mum.' She decided against telling him about her brush with Pan. 'She used to bring all sorts of tat home. Like that fox that's gone missing. You never really liked it.'

'Always hated it. Reminded me of a red-haired fellow I was in chambers with.'

'Mum loved it, though.'

'Mum had funny ideas sometimes.'

The scrape of fork on plate.

Chapter 15

An Offering On Kidbury Henge

Wednesday 25 May

'Morning!' Jess sauntered into DS Eden's office.

'Morning.' Eden's mind was elsewhere. Perhaps on the untidy stack of files he was filleting. He looked up. 'Hang on, how did—'

'I'm on the case, aren't I?' grinned Jess. The truth was that the vast influx of worker bees into Margaret Thatcher Way had reduced the efficiency of the gatekeeper. 'I brought you these.' She dropped a box of doughnuts on Eden's desk. 'Brain food.' He hadn't called. Not for the first time, she was styling it out in the face of a man's indifference. 'Thought I might give you a hand.'

Eden lifted the lid of the box with a pen. As if the doughnuts might be dusted for prints. 'You mean you thought you could nose around.'

'Can't it be both?' Jess helped herself to a wheeled

chair that almost ran away with her. 'What's the latest on Squeezers?' Her mouth was already full of sugar strands. For the moment, she would hold her encounter with Pan in her back pocket. To be whipped out when Eden lost patience.

'Oh, *Squeezers*.' Eden shook his head, picking out a chocolate ring. 'Knott's got it into her head he's Castle Kidbury's very own Dr Crippen. Unfortunately for him he ticks some of our boxes on this case, so I can't ignore him.' He waved his doughnut. 'These are good. Waitrose?'

'Greggs.'

'An eyewitness put Darling, Squeezers' dog, if you can call it that, on Kidbury Road early on the morning of Gavin Blake's murder.'

'Squeezers would never let Darling wander about alone. That dog's his world.'

'Knott reasoned that he might if he was busy killing Gavin. We found the body of a dog in a hedgerow. Mown down.' Eden put down his doughnut. Amidst the carnage, he found time to mourn a whippet. 'As Darling is alive and well, Squeezers isn't incriminated.'

'Time you stopped picking on Squeezers. You lot behave as if he's implicated in every crime in Castle Kidbury.'

'He is.'

'Yet Beefy Dave never gets pulled in. Smells like corruption to *moi*.' Jess didn't dare look at Eden as she floated that thought.

There was a moment of charged silence. 'If you want

to carry on with your precarious role as *unofficial* con-sultant, I suggest you stop blundering about in those Doc Martens of yours. Concentrate, Jess. We have a killer to catch.' The anger in his voice was all the more sobering for its understatement. 'Squeezers is now released into the community having wasted police time and stunk up a custody cell. We had a whip-round for Darling, and he promised to buy her a collar. Now, do you want me to bring you up to date or do you want to turn my nick into Watergate?'

'Up to date please.' Jess was exaggeratedly humble.

'We've looked at Keith and Gavin from every angle. Very little commonality. Gavin drove Keith home once after a trousers-down incident. Keith was once arrested for peeing on the Blakes' garden wall.'

'Did Gavin still live at home?'

'Yeah. With his mum and dad. That big house by the Cheap Street crossroads.' Eden gave her a look. 'Why? You look perturbed.'

'No reason.' How could they, thought Jess, still live there? In the house where it all happened. Where Becky died in her little yellow swimsuit. Some people, she concluded, are dense like concrete.

'Any luck with the symbols?'

Eden looked hopeful. A blind man searching for something to hang on to. She disappointed him. 'What worries me is why one set of symbols is Ogham and the other something so obscure I don't recognise them.'

'The killer keeping us on our toes?'

'So if there's another murder there'll be another set of

symbols?' Jess rebuked herself when she saw how Eden shuddered at her casual mention of a third death. 'The Ogham around the side of the box is so literal – E. Y. E. S. The four trees are another thing altogether. If I distil what the ash and the poplar and the yew and the rowan stand for, to their essence, I end up with this.' She pulled a pad towards her. Ignored Eden's tut at such casual procurement of his stationery. She wrote four words in capitals.

WISDOM. VISION. AFTERLIFE. CLARITY.

'They sound so benign.' Eden was thoughtful. 'Apart from afterlife.'

'Which isn't necessarily spooky. We all die. Pagans were more accepting of mortality. They didn't fend it off with wonder drugs and plastic surgery. It helps, I guess, if you believe your soul carries on after death.'

A clatter at the door and Karen Knott was among them. 'Sir, your handler's here.'

'I'll be there in a minute, Knott.'

'Don't keep him,' said the DC to Jess. 'This is important.'

'Handler?' Jess saw an opportunity to provoke. She liked those. 'What bits of you does he handle?'

Karen answered for her boss. 'It's his Media Presentation Consultant. Guv's on telly now.' She stood a little taller. 'He's got to look his best.'

'It's more to do with efficient dissemination of infor-mation,' said Eden, hard on her heels. 'Although they do seem obsessed with my hair.' He passed a nervous hand over his neat head. 'And my tie.'

'You look lovely in that spotty one,' said Karen. She turned to Jess, collaborative for once. 'His wife used to buy him *horrible* ties. Didn't she, guv? Tartan ones. Some with Disney characters on. He was a saint to wear them.'

Jess couldn't imagine Eden in a Winnie the Pooh tie. Nor could she imagine him wanting his defunct marriage discussed in front of him. She stayed silent.

'Good thing they couldn't have kiddies. Otherwise she'd still have a hold on him now.'

The air went out of the room, as if one of Jess's gods had sucked with enormous force. She had time to see the look of pain on Eden's face, and to see it quickly smothered. 'Knott, go and do something. Anything!' he snapped as she hesitated.

Another concrete person, thought Jess.

Eden crossed his office and pulled aside one of the vertical slats that covered the window. The room was normal again. By his decree. 'Bloody Sky News. Hovering by my nick.' He turned and scowled at the paper on his desk. 'All the while, every other case sits on the back burner.'

'Anything I can help with?' Jess was peachy keen. On best behaviour. Like a child hoping her parents will let her stay up late if she doesn't cause trouble.

'Only if you want to locate a missing shih-tzu, or find whoever stole Keith Dike's van during his funeral.'

Jess bit her lip. 'Could that be relevant?'

'Not unless someone crucified him for a white transit held together with gaffer tape.' Eden looked at his watch. 'Jess, I really should—'

'I saw Pan in the town,' she said. Nonchalant.

'Where?' Eden perked up.

'Trying on clothes in the charity shop.'

Eden looked thoughtful. He had, as Mary would put it, a hard-on for Pan. Eden would never put it like that himself.

'I got in the changing cubicle with him. Had a few words.'

'You *spoke* to him?'

'Well, actually, he spoke to me.'

'*Don't* talk to suspects without my supervision. We've been through this.'

'I didn't really plan—'

'I. Don't. Care.'

Jess shrank. She hadn't bargained on such a strong rebuke. 'Sorry.' She needed to get better at this falling-into-line stuff if she wanted to stay on the case.

'Did he touch you?'

'No,' lied Jess. 'He confessed to killing Keith Dike, then said he hadn't. As if he doesn't get that this is serious.'

'I wonder if *you* get this is serious, Jess.'

'Did you pull in Unthank?'

'Mr Unthank came in to speak to me, yes.'

'And?'

'He makes a very poor impression.'

That was putting it mildly. No need for Jess to tell

Eden about her own encounter with Unthank. Not when she was still on the naughty step. 'Alibi?'

'In bed. Asleep. Alone. Trouble is, the EasySleep Inn CCTV is on the blink. No corroboration. But, before you steam ahead, no evidence he killed Gavin, either. We only have him in our sights because of the logo. I don't know why he'd want to kill his own friend.' Eden straightened his tie. Settled his shirt collar. Wiggled his shoulders in his high-street suit. 'I have to get to this PR meeting. You'd better go, Jess.'

'Yes, sir.'

'And don't call me that.'

She stood, cautiously lifting the doughnuts from the desk.

'Leave them.'

Harebell House cast a wide shadow in the setting sun.

Clutching a carrier bag, Jess hopped into Rupert's car. 'Top down, eh?'

'I thought it'd be nice,' said Rupert. 'You *do* know about nice, don't you?'

'You think you're funny.'

Rupert looked Jess's scuffed black outfit up and down. 'Good of you to dress up for the occasion.'

Jess took in Rupert's beautifully cut linen suit with, probably, almost certainly, Italian brogues. He was dressed as the Rupert he would become in twenty years. 'Thank you, Rumpole. You look lovely too.'

'Don't you ever wear make-up?'

'Do you like make-up?'

'If it's done right. Nice and subtle.'

'You should wear it, then.' Jess cocked one eyebrow. 'Accentuate your cheekbones. Narrow down that nose.' She laughed. 'Make those pretty eyes *pop*!'

'*You* think you're funny. Right, as you insisted on booking – where to?'

She directed him.

Kidbury Road.

The bridge.

The long-stay car park.

The medical centre.

The vet's.

And then the long turn into the main thoroughfare.

'I make this journey twice, three times every day,' said Jess. 'In Cambridge I could veer off in any direction. At home, it's either right or left out of the drive and then you're a hamster on a wheel. Always the same.'

'Not quite. Hamsters never get anywhere.'

'Exactly.' Castle Kidbury was a town of ruts. She enjoyed the sensation of the car speeding up as they went south-east on Cheap Street, leaving the tangle of lanes behind them.

Stuck behind a coach – 'Rustic Ripper rubberneckers,' said Rupert – they idled at a three-way crossroads. Jess knew what was behind the high wall on her right. She kept her head down. Didn't hear Rupert's chit-chat.

It was a house of mourning now.

'Shit, that's the Blakes' house,' said Rupert, as they pulled away. 'I heard Gavin's mum and dad are packing up, going away for a while after the funeral.'

It had taken two deaths for them to leave. Becky. Then Gavin. Two decades apart.

She turned her head. A small rectangle on the wall. Blurred by the speed Rupert was picking up. She didn't need to see it clearly. She knew the shape carved onto it from the dream that stalked her. A woman. *The* woman. Goddess. Water. Sky. Earth.

Paid for by muggins.

'Jess!' Rupert was cheerily indignant. 'Where have you gone? I said, is this a mystery tour?'

'What else?' said Jess.

'What are we doing here?' Rupert peered through the windscreen at the collection of tall stones that was Kidbury Henge. 'Do they have a restaurant?'

'We have a table for two,' said Jess. 'Come on. Let's get in before the sun sinks any further.'

Rupert tailed Jess up a muddy, uneven path to a wooden gate. 'It's locked.'

'Only to the public.' Jess slung a leg over the gate. 'It's always open for heathens.' She extended her hand. 'Come on, Rumpole. I assume that suit can be dry-cleaned.'

'This is *not* what I had in mind when I suggested dinner.' Rupert lifted his leg. He bent and dipped. He landed on the other side. Slapped his hands free of moss.

Jess strode ahead. This was her territory. She stopped in the centre of the ring. Turned to take in the five ancient stones. Stumpy, irregular, in the failing light they looked ready to move.

'Oh come on, haven't you even got picnic blankets?'
Rupert's public-school tones morphed into a whine.

'Sit down and shush,' said Jess, already cross-legged.
She rummaged through the carrier bag. 'On the *à la
carte* menu tonight are two pasties, two sausage rolls
and two eclairs with that funny long-life whipped
cream and jam. Lynne didn't have any scotch eggs.'

'You went to the bloody minimart?'

'Not as nice as Greggs, I admit. But the eclairs are
only just past their sell-by date.'

'Is this it? I'd have at least brought some bubbly if
I'd known.'

'Almost forgot.' Jess pulled two cans of Dr Pepper
from the bag.

Rupert gave in. He had the ability to give in without
losing face. 'If you can't beat them et cetera. Cheers!'

'My turn to ask you the question, now,' said
Jess. When Rupert glugged like that, his Adam's
apple bobbed.

'What question?'

'If you're seeing anyone.'

Rupert shook his head. Quelled a carbonated burp.
Looked horrified at himself. Recovered. 'Last proper
relationship was Pandora.'

'Pandora?' Jess found a lot wrong with the name.
Too frilly.

'Pandora Smith.'

'Same name as that model?'

Rupert tried to look modest.

'No way! Shut *up*! You went out with Pandora Smith

the model?' Jess was amazed. 'She's world-famous. Was it all red carpets, private jets?'

'I've known her, well, as long as I've known you. Our families are friends.'

'What happened? Why aren't you Mr Pandora Smith?'

'She was great. We were great. Then this big contract came up for her in New York. And I –' Rupert held up his hands – 'just didn't fancy it. New York's a blast to visit. But it's not home. And work was here. So. You know.' He seemed embarrassed. He undid the tie he'd carefully knotted for this dinner date.

'Blimey, Rupert. You gave up all that for the people of Castle Kidbury.' Jess sat back on her heels. 'I'm impressed.'

'So I have hidden depths after all?' Rupert smiled. A sideways smile. Made him look goofy. 'I'm an open book compared to you, mind. Sneaking around the country like a spy. Why'd you really leave Cambridge?'

'Like New York, it's fun to visit. A lot of history there for me.'

'I remember Stephen being jealous when you got in to study law. He and I both failed. Ended up at Edinburgh.' He riffled for and found a sausage roll. 'Loved it.'

'I'm jealous of *that*. How you manage to love things so easily.'

'You make me sound like a nitwit.'

'Nah. It's a life skill. I loathed the law. Dad insisted I apply. *The Castles are lawyers*, he kept saying. I dropped out after a year.'

'I remember. According to Stephen, it was to annoy the Judge.'

'It wasn't!' Jess wrinkled her nose. 'Well, it was a bit. I switched to history. I had a passion for the subject. Not that passion we all keep hearing about, by the way. Not like an *X Factor* wannabe who has a passion to sing but has never left their bedroom. I mean I *love* the past. I was wild to learn. This was something I could do on my own. Something my family might actually admire me for.'

'Sounds reasonable.'

'To you, maybe. Dad stopped my money. I had no grant. The old sod earned too much. He did a big number on me about letting the family down, turning my back on the sacred Castle duty to jurisprudence.' Jess noticed that Rupert was looking grave. 'I told him I was too honest to be a lawyer.'

Rupert didn't laugh. 'He actually refused to support you?' Rupert lowered his voice. 'That's bad.'

Jess shrugged. Sympathy made her want to throw up.

'How'd you manage? I'd have given up.'

'Money started appearing in my account. I've always assumed it was Mum. Dad and I barely talked after I dropped law. He expected Mum to toe the line and join the chorus of disapproval. She didn't.' Jess was only beginning to appreciate how much courage that had taken.

'Maybe your mysterious benefactor was an admirer.'

'They were thin on the ground, Rupert. After I graduated, I skedaddled to Exeter for my master's and my doctorate.'

'Yet you ended up back at Cambridge? Like *Groundhog Day*.'

Jess didn't laugh. 'A lecturing post fell into my lap.'

'No job just falls into your lap.'

Jess looked up through her fringe at Rupert. 'Want to know the truth? I was terrified. I felt like a fraud. So here I am.'

'You ran away?'

'You could call it that. My dad certainly does.' The end of a jumbo sausage roll vanished into Jess's face. 'Thought you knew all this.'

'From Stephen? I don't talk much to your brother these days. He's ...' Rupert couldn't find the word. He patted the damp grass. 'Lie here,' he said. 'Beside me.'

She resisted. A force tugged her towards him. An equal, or perhaps greater one, pulled her away. Perhaps it was the ley lines beneath them.

'Come on. I don't bite.'

With a tut, as if this was all a bit much, Jess lay down chastely beside Rupert.

The sky was flat above them. The moon had taken over from the sun. Stars just waking up. He pointed.

'See that? That's Draco. The Dragon. Do you know how far away that is? Three hundred light years. Which means we're seeing it as it was three hundred years ago. We're looking back in time. That big white star in the dragon's tail is Thuban. That used to be the polar star in Jesus's time, until the Earth's orbit changed. Amazing to think, isn't it?'

'It is,' agreed Jess. 'Except you're at least half wrong.'

207

What, she wondered, was the word for correcting a man? Womansplaining? 'The stars vary from a hundred and fifty to three hundred and sixty light years away. Thuban was the pole star when the Egyptians started building pyramids, a good two and a half thousand years before Jesus was supposed to have been born. And Thuban moved in the sky because of the tilt in the Earth's axis, not the orbit.'

'Oh.' Rupert's voice was flat. He rallied. 'You look so white in the moonlight, Jess.'

'The ancient Greeks based their calendar on the moon, not the sun. According to them, we're in the third quarter of the moon, what we call a half moon. This isn't May, it's Thargelion.'

'You really hate compliments, don't you?'

'The month builds up to Deiphon. That's an important date, when your ancient Greek pays his bills, cleans his house, offers a ritual meal to Hecate so she doesn't fuck him up with all her undead acolytes. When will Deiphon fall next? Um ...'

'I don't care.'

'Second of June!'

'I have a question.' Rupert was on his side.

Jess was still flat on her back. 'Fire away.'

'Why the sarcasm?'

'I didn't say I'd answer it.'

'It's clearly a defence mechanism.'

'Spare me the pop psychology. My defence mechanism is travelling into the past. The fighting's finished; the dying's done. That's what drew me to history. And

208

to this.' She gestured at the stone circle around them. 'It's a story, but only half told. And what *hasn't* been told, I get to tell.'

Rupert was still, his eyes fixed on Jess.

'All a bit deep, eh Rumpole?'

'That's why you like being part of the investigation. You get to tell the untold story.'

'I hadn't thought of that. Maybe you should keep up the pop psychology after all.'

Rupert flopped onto his back again. 'I've enjoyed tonight, Jess.'

'Me too.'

She felt him start, as if surprised. He said, 'And you needn't worry. No more compliments. I'll never mention how pretty your eyes are.'

'I'd appreciate that.'

'My suit's ruined.'

'Good.'

Chapter 16

ESCAPE-GOAT

Thursday 26 May

Seaweed around her ankles like green streamers.

Jess's cheeks bulge with the effort of holding her breath.

Beneath her feet are tiles of iridescent blue.

Blood in the water.

It makes a shape.

A mouth, opening wide.

Jess swims to the surface.

She shouts, I'm sorry I'm sorry.

Jess still wasn't sure what to ask of a housekeeper. She was glad to go downstairs and find that Bogna was otherwise engaged, doing something on the terrace that involved plant pots and a wheelbarrow.

At the table, the Judge turned the pages of a news-paper. 'Heard you shouting,' he said, while seemingly still engrossed in the newsprint. 'What are you sorry for?' He murmured to himself, 'Could be any one of a number of things.'

When Jess didn't answer, he said, 'The dream?'

'I don't really want to talk about it, Dad.'

'Understood.'

Outside, Bogna sang. She sang like she did everything else, with confidence.

'A Polish folk song, do we think?' suggested the Judge.

'It's Take That, Dad.'

'Take what?'

A creature barged through the back door. Clattering hooves, curved horns. It bleated and complained.

'Jesus!' Jess jumped out of its way.

'Out, Urich,' said the Judge.

The goat was a gleaming white. Handsome but peculiar, with those satanic vertical pupils. 'Naaaaaah!' he said to Jess. His tongue, meaty and pink, lolled over his teeth.

Jess flattened herself against the dresser. 'Off! Away!' She hit out ineffectually.

'U-rich!' Bogna's shout made the goat crash out backwards. She popped her head through the window. 'Don't mind him, *kochana*. He only wants to make friends.'

'Does he live here?' Jess watched the goat pick his way across the terrace, as if breaking in new shoes.

'Out by greenhouse. He nibbles his way out of pen.'

'He smells.' Jess turned to her father, who was carefully disattending. 'Doesn't he, Dad?'

'Does he?' The Judge turned another page.

'He *stinks*,' said Bogna. 'This is why I name him after husband. God rest his soul.' She looked behind her. 'No, Urich!' she shouted, and disappeared.

'Did Bogna okay the goat with you?'

'Not really.' The Judge was mild.

Jess remembered the fuss her father made when her mother brought home a stray cat. She swallowed the comparison. The fragile peace between the Castles must be mollycoddled, like a hothouse lily. 'How about lunch at the Seven Stars? My treat.'

'That sounds—' began the Judge.

'Lovely!' Bogna leant in at the window again. 'It'll save me doing bloody sandwiches. Fanks, Jess!'

'Did you book?' asked Eddie. Brawny arms. Tea towel over one shoulder. He had to shout above the buzz. 'We get news people in every day. We're already out of lasagne.'

He found them a corner table. Three of them in a space for two. Jess fussed; was her father okay, did he want to sit outside, did he want to swap seats.

'I'm *fine*,' he said, taking up the menu.

There was something about the Judge's demeanour that made people – even his daughter – dance attendance on him. As if warding off inevitable criticism. Jess took a deep breath.

'Who are they all looking at?' Bogna, her reading glasses on, peered over Jess's head.

The journalists in the bar – all instantly recognisable

by their lack of coloured corduroy and their London haircuts – were, meerkat-like, staring in one direction. While trying not to look like they were staring.

'Somebody famous, I bet.' Bogna licked her lips. 'Maybe big star like Benjamin Cucumberpatch.'

'In the Royal Seven Stars?' Jess was torn between the fajitas and the club sandwich.

'Or Katie Moss.' Bogna put her hand on the Judge's shoulder to hoist herself up. 'She loves a drink, that girlie.'

'Not in here, she doesn't,' said Jess.

Eddie took their order, advising against the fajitas. 'They look a bit … odd.' He lingered to say to the Judge, 'Hard to believe Eden dragged Squeezers in for the murders, eh? And how come that Pan bloke's still at large? He's holding court in the other bar. The journos are lapping him up.'

'Being on the bench for a decade or two taught me one thing,' said the Judge, leaning back, enjoying Eddie. 'You never know what people are capable of. It could be anybody in Castle Kidbury. It could be you, Eddie.'

'I don't have the bloody time,' laughed Eddie. He tucked away his notepad. 'It might even be you, your honour.'

'It's me.' Bogna said it so seriously that she stopped the conversation. Evidently none of them believed this to be out of the question. She cackled.

'Be right back with your bevvies.' Eddie hurried away.

Conversation seized up. Around them, the pub was

213

a mosh pit. People chatted, laughed extravagantly, as if the scent of food cooking had sent them all a little mad.

Jess people-watched for a while. She became aware that Bogna was studying something. Something close to hand.

The Judge.

His breathing was ugly. Jess saw the immense effort her father made to look normal. 'Dad?' She put a hand tentatively on his shirtsleeve.

'I'm fine.' The words creaked out.

'Jimmy?'

'Ladies, please.' A further agonising couple of minutes – both of them *long* – passed with the women staring and the Judge climbing to a plateau where he could speak again without his face losing all colour.

'Shit, Dad.'

'Language.'

'Can we talk about this?' Jess included Bogna, more naturally than she would have thought possible twelve days ago. 'What does Dr Rasmussen say? What's the treatment plan?'

'I'm weighing up my options. In the meantime, the doc's keeping me healthy. Please don't worry, Jess.'

'When people say that,' said Jess, 'they don't care whether you worry or not. They just want you to stop talking about it.'

Their drinks arrived. The Judge exploited the distraction to the full. Bogna laughed at a weak joke he made.

'Loo.' Jess stood abruptly. She left behind the table and its cargo of things unsaid. 'S'cuse me. S'cuse me.' Jess negotiated her way towards the ladies'.

A familiar voice stood out from the crowd. Jess heard Rupert's playful intonation. Then a giggle. *He giggles like a girl*, she thought, reaching up on her tiptoes to locate him.

A text from him that morning would have been nice. After their sort-of date. She recalled how she'd batted away his attempt to play nice. Perhaps the ball was in her court.

'Rupert!' She recognised the back of his head, his right shoulder. He turned, smiled. So did his companion. Their table was littered with the debris of lunch.

'Jess.' Rupert half stood, looked around for a chair.

'No, no, I'm not stopping. Just, you know, off for a waz.' She'd never used that expression before. It was jolted out of her by the extreme beauty of the woman smiling at her and holding out her hand.

'Hi, I'm Pandora,' said the woman.

'I'm Jess.' She wondered, fleetingly, if Rupert might have mentioned her to Pandora.

'Stephen's little sis,' explained Rupert.

Evidently not. 'Everybody in the pub is pretending not to look at you,' said Jess.

'Bugger, are they?' Pandora pulled her hair over her face. 'This place used to be so quiet.'

'That was before we had our very own neighbourhood psycho.' The need to visit the ladies' was now urgent, but Jess couldn't leave. She needed to take the temperature of whatever was happening between Rupert and this world-fucking-famous-fucking-supermodel. 'Did you have the fajitas?' she asked, hopefully.

'I'm vegetarian,' said Pandora. Looking at her face was like looking at the sun. 'They did me the most wonderful salad.'

'No such thing as a wonderful salad,' snorted Jess. She punched Rupert on the shoulder. Rather hard. 'Bet *you* didn't have lettuce, Rumpole.'

Jess saw Pandora's bankable eyebrows crinkle at the nickname.

'I had a strange stew thing.' Rupert sat back, observing Jess. He was interested, a touch wary, as if she was a lab rat that might bite. 'Who are you here with?' He craned his neck in the direction she'd come from.

'Not a top model, that's for sure!' Jess saw him bite his lip. 'Just Dad and Bogna.'

'Bogna?' Pandora giggled. 'Is that, like, a name?'

'It's not like a name; it *is* a name.' Jess bridled on Bogna's behalf. 'Are you in Castle Kidbury for long?'

That could have sounded rude. It did sound rude. Pandora looked at Rupert. 'Um, well, depends . . .'

Rupert had a violently casual look on his face. 'Depends . . .' he said to Jess, the dot dot dot hanging in the air.

Jess wanted to smoke with every cell in her body. She paced the cobbles outside the Royal Seven Stars. After her angry wee, she couldn't face the walk back past Rupert and Pandora.

An open-top car pulled up. It was old, and gorgeous. As was its driver.

'Iris,' said Jess. 'You're not supposed to drive.'

'Hop in, you tedious girl.'

The Judge. Bogna. Her club sandwich.

Versus Great-aunty Iris and a lipstick-red Jaguar E-Type.

No competition.

It was noisy. They had to raise their voices to chat over the growl of the engine. 'You just dumped James? You're brave, darling.'

'I'm annoyed with him. He's withholding, as usual.'

'All men of his vintage withhold. They teach it at public schools.'

'Running out on him at lunch is only what he expects me to do.'

A sideways look from behind winged sunglasses. 'If I could be bothered, I'd take you to task on that silly comment. But I managed to elude my grandson and free my beautiful car, so let's just have *fun*.'

'Josh hates you driving.'

'He hates me eating a boiled egg. He's walking some contractors around our new multimedia experience. About the history of the Castle family. Who cares about that, for heaven's sake?' Bangles danced on Iris's bony wrist as she changed gears with great authority.

Jess coveted the driving gloves. Nude-coloured kid. Soft. Expensive.

'So, Jess, what's the latest on our chum the Rustic Ripper?'

217

'It looks as though it's a serial killer. That's what DS Eden thinks, anyway.'

'You think differently?'

'Maybe. The two murders had significant differences.'

'And do you have your beady eye on anyone?'

'I don't think I'm supposed to talk about it,' answered Jess, warily.

'Tosh. It's only me. Who would *I* tell?'

'There's a suspect called Pan. The bloke with the caravans in Pitt's Field.'

'Yes, we had a run-in with him. Dancing around the grounds with a gang of naked girls. Nasty sort. Josh chased him off with a shotgun.'

'Yes, he is nasty. But there's no hard evidence to tie him to the murders. He's even got an alibi. Other than that, there's Squeezers. But he couldn't have done it.'

'You sound very sure.'

'Squeezers only commits petty crime. *Really* petty crime. He's never mentioned anything about pagan practices.'

'The poor chap's a little too cuckoo to pull off a murder.' Iris pronounced it *orf*. 'Although ...' Iris seemed to reconsider. 'These murders *are* somewhat cuckoo.'

Jess thought of her conversation with Luis Unthank. Of the prickly feeling he gave her. Her antennae had spun wildly. 'Eden's pulling in everybody who had anything to do with the victims, but so far, nothing.'

'I trust you to solve it, darling.'

'Me? I'm on the periphery of the case, Iris.'

'Piffle. You've found your calling.'

Jess had missed her great-aunt's certainty. Her belief. It wouldn't do, she knew, to thank her for it. 'I hope it's all over soon. Castle Kidbury's bent out of shape. The Seven Stars was full of journalists.' Jess closed her eyes as Iris overtook a tractor on a hairpin bend. 'Mind you, they were more interested in Rupert's bloody girlfriend than anything.' She opened her eyes. They were both still alive.

'Rupert? Your Rupert? Girlfriend?'

'He's not my— Yes, Pandora Smith. She's from round here, apparently.'

'Ah, the supermodel! The only girl I know with a sillier name than your middle one. I play bridge with her godmother. Did you know her father was convicted of fraud?'

'Really?'

'He swiped ten million from a company he chaired. Spent at least a few thousand of it on call girls and SS uniforms. Actually, Rupert defended him. I promised myself I wouldn't ask you about Rupert.'

'Ask me what about him?'

'This and that.' Iris stared out through the windscreen, and it reflected her naughty twinkle. An abrupt three-point turn. A near miss with a cow. 'Hometime, darling. Keep digging, Jess. You always were the brains of the family.'

The usual journey, but backwards, on foot.

The long turn from the main thoroughfare.

The vet's.
The medical centre.
The long-stay car park.
The bridge.
Harebell House.

A car was parked by the scenic shed Harriet had commissioned for the bins. *A mystery car*, Jess thought, instantly blaming recent bloodstained events for her hammy language. *Just because I don't know who the car belongs to doesn't mean it's a mystery.*

The door jerked open as she slid the key into the lock. The Judge stood on the welcome mat. His large feet obscured the welcome.

'You have a visitor, Jessica. From Cambridge.'

Chapter 17

POOL PARTY

Still Thursday 26 May

'This is where you want to talk?'

Jess saw the neglected pool through her visitor's eyes. 'It'll be fun,' she said, sombrely. She'd been sombre since she laid eyes on Max standing in front of the drawing room fireplace. Twenty years her senior. Smallish. Neat. Beginnings of a tum. Salt-and-pepper hair. So familiar, and so very unwelcome.

That was unfair; Max was a nice man. It was the mirror he held up to Jess's behaviour that she didn't like.

'Fun,' repeated Max, negotiating the metal ladder down into the cracked blue pool with his glass of wine.

At fifty-odd, Max couldn't sit cross-legged like Jess. He lounged against the tiled wall. He gazed around as he might at an archaeological site. 'You ought to use this pool.'

Okay, small talk first, thought Jess. She was happy

to acquiesce. 'I learnt to swim here. Stephen used to dunk me.' She hid her face in her wine. The small talk had turned out to be not so small after all. The dream claimed her for a moment, and departed.

'That's what big brothers are for.' Max savoured his wine. 'Nice of James to have me stay for dinner. There aren't many houses as comfortable as yours, Jess.'

Was that a reprimand? A suggestion that she count her blessings? 'Max, look at this.' Jess never went anywhere without the printed symbols in one of her numberless pockets. 'First, do you agree with my translation of the Ogham?' It would be a crime to have one of the country's foremost minds on the subject in her home and not exploit him.

Max scanned the page. 'Yup. "Eyes".' He looked up. 'What's this? Where's it from?'

'I'd like to tell you, but then I'd have to kill you. To do with a murder investigation.'

'Not the Rustic Ripper?'

'I'm helping the police. There are traces of mysticism to the killings. A hint of Hecate.'

Footfall along the covered path to the pool. Jess felt Max tense up; she did the same. It was only Moose, desperate to join them.

The dog slithered to the deep end, alongside his favourite woman.

'Better keep Moose away from Hecate,' laughed Max. 'You know her track record with dogs.'

'Only on Deiphon.' Jess put the giant dog in a headlock. He loved that. 'On the night of Deiphon, Moosey,

Hecate asks a lot of her followers. They have to do all the little chores they've been putting off, and they have to leave a snack out for her. Not *your* kind of snack. She prefers garlic and raw eggs and stuff. It has to be left at a crossroads or she gets proper miffed. And then they invite a stray dog into the house. They all pat it and love and snuggle it, and then they slaughter it. Because, you see, they transferred all their sins to the dog and Hecate will forgive them if the sins are disposed of.'

'She's a hard woman.'

'Hard but fair.' Jess reconsidered. 'Actually, hard but pretty unfair.'

'About time for the matriarchy to reassert itself,' said Max, looking up at the moon. 'When they were in charge of the movements of the sea and the fecundity of the earth, things were simpler. Bloody,' he added. 'But simple. When is the next Deiphon?' He counted on his fingers.

Jess let him work it out even though she knew. She'd forgotten that feeling of being with people who were as entranced by the past as she was.

'Keep Moose indoors on the second of June. In fact, keep *yourself* indoors that night. If Hecate's mixed up in this, that date might be meaningful to your killer.'

'He's not *my* killer.' Deep down, though, he was. Jess pointed to the piece of paper still in Max's grasp. 'Those other symbols, the line of shapes. Any ideas?'

'Drivel, Jess.'

'No, they *mean* something. Even if they're made up. They're based on something archaic.'

'Shouldn't you be working on your own conundrums right now?'

Here we go, thought Jess. She bowed her head.

'I'm not going to ask you what happened. I know what happened. It was one of your, what should we call them?' Max smiled. 'Your lunatic moments?'

'My life's one long lunatic moment.'

'Maybe it looks like that to you. To me, you look like a great lecturer, with a real feel for the subject. You *communicate*, Jess. You connect. That's why I wanted you in the department.'

'I was failing, Max.' Jess had stood outside Max's office, irresolute, for a long moment before she decamped the campus. As the course director, not to mention their shared history, he'd deserved some notice, a heads-up at least.

'We could've talked about it. That's part of my job. A senior lecturer's supposed to keep an eye on his people. Especially the talented ones. I might have helped. You know – you *should* know, at least – I'm on your side.'

Praise was worse than criticism. Jess groped for the right words. 'When you got me the job . . .' She held up her hand and silenced Max. 'You *did* get me the job. I know that. I was over the moon.' Jess remembered the euphoria. Repaying her mother's confidence. Hoping her father might at last take her seriously. 'Teaching Associate at St John's College, of all places. It was a fairy tale.' A Grimm fairy tale, as it turned out.

Max stroked his chin. 'Things seemed to be going well. The students obviously loved you. I sat in once or twice. I mean, you had your own style, no doubt about that, but it *worked*. Now I feel I should have seen the signs. Noticed you were struggling.' He smiled. It was a sad smile. 'Not waving but drowning, eh?'

What an apposite quote. Jess felt the oppressive waters of her dream around her. 'I never felt worthy of the job,' she admitted. 'I know I come on like a steamroller, Max, but . . .'

'Deep down you're a delicate flower?'

They both laughed at that. Max could always coax her out of a funk.

'I *am*,' she protested. 'Well, maybe a delicate *weed*.'

'You're a one-off, Jess Castle. It was my fault, really. I should've eased you in with a part-time position. Then moved things along when you found your feet.'

'Come *on*, Max! How is any of this your fault?' Jess refused to let him shoulder the blame. It was all hers, and she was hanging onto it. 'You stuck your neck out for me, and I let you down.' Shame thudded in her blood. 'Have you taken flak for it? From the faculty, I mean.'

'A bit, here and there. But, yeah, you're right. We weren't short of good applicants. One of them in particular was a bit of a star. I kept pulling the conversation back to you. So, yes, I did stick my neck out for you.'

Jess knew why. 'Perhaps that was half the problem.'

Here was the nub of it. This can of worms was never opened. It wasn't something they talked about.

'Sorry, how'd you mean?' Max squinted.

'Well, you know, what happened with us . . .'

'Happened?' Max's shrug was a question.

Was he really going to make her spell it out? 'You and me, Max. When we, when, you know …' They were two Victorian virgins, unable to use the proper nouns and verbs.

'Oh!' Max caught on. '*That!*'

Nights of talking, followed by lovemaking, in Max's book-filled Cambridge rooms. There had been a weekend away, under canvas. All pleasantly transgressive, given that at the time he was a professor and she an undergraduate. It had tapered off. But it shone bright in Jess's memory. 'Yes, *that*,' she smiled. She remembered how small that tent had been.

Max looked at her. Appraising. 'Um …' he said.

She realised. 'You forgot.' He had forgotten the talking. The tent. The lovemaking.

'It was a long time ago.'

'Not that long.' Re-evaluating at warp speed. Was Jess – oh God! – one of many? She knew Max to be kind and clever and gentle. He could be all those things and a philanderer too.

'Jess, you didn't let me finish. I was saying that, yes, I stuck my neck out for you, but there's more. *Why* did I stick my neck out? Not because of *that*. It was because I believed in you.' They both heard that past tense clang to the ground. 'You had, you *have*, all the stuff it takes to be a brilliant research fellow. You're capable of having a terrific career. Academia belongs, I hope, to people like you. That's why I wanted you to take the job. Because I believed you were the best person for it. Not because of something that happened ten years ago.'

Thirteen, actually. 'What the hell do I do now, Max?'

'How'd you mean?'

'How do I fix this?' Max's confidence emboldened her. So, yes, she was a forgettable lover, but she sounded like a hell of a lecturer. She could go back. Change the habit of a lifetime and face the music.

'Oh, Jess.' Max's face drooped. 'There's nothing to *do*. This is it.'

'What if I—'

He shook his head. 'Gordon Clarke's not ready to be persuaded.' The faculty head had never warmed to Jess. Clarke was the Judge on steroids; her anti-authoritarian schtick had gone down very badly with him. 'You can't come back, Jess.'

Her bridges were burnt. They hadn't even lit her way. 'Bet he's making life difficult for you,' she said.

'I can handle Gordon.'

She sensed his desire to console her. Her invocation of the past made him nervous to touch her. 'I'll be fine, Max. I'll find something to do.' *Murder's as good a hobby as any*, she thought.

'It's such a shame.' The sentiment was wrenched out of Max on a sigh. 'Such a terrible shame.'

Chapter 18

NEVER BE GUEST OF
HONOUR AT A FUNERAL

Friday 27 May

A modest crowd was gathered in Eddie's function room. Red flock wallpaper. Gilt chandelier. Carpet louder than the conversation.

'We need this,' said Eddie, helping Carli hand round something fizzy that wasn't champagne. 'Castle Kidbury needs to get together and mourn.'

Gavin's official funeral reception was taking place simultaneously at the Blakes' home. A last duty before they forsook the town.

'Helena,' said the Judge, as a svelte lady all in black put an empty glass back on the tray. 'Good to see you.'

'And you.'

Jess felt the extra layer in her father's greeting. The recognition that Helena's presence required fortitude.

All in a polite code that made everybody feel better without mentioning *it*, the tragedy that marked Helena out as different.

Jess hadn't seen Helena since spotting her that first day back in Castle Kidbury. All the attributes she remembered were still apparent. Elegance. Pride. A feminine lack of rough edges.

'This must be fucking hard on you,' said Jess, who was all rough edges, with none of the Judge's innate courtliness.

'It's hard for all of us.' Helena put her hand on Jess's cheek. She had been managing other people's impotent sympathy for almost twenty years. She was skilled. 'I must dash. Back to the spa.' She noticed Jess's puzzlement. 'I run the Chase Hall Spa. It's my baby. I do treatments at home, too. Bit cheaper. Come and see me for some pampering.'

'I'll do that,' said Jess, who wanted to please Helena. She would never do that; Jess hated spas more than she hated dentists. She accepted the green and pink rate card.

Richard and Doug signalled ennui by the vol-au-vents. Meera and Moyra stood by the photocopied portrait of Gavin held by magnets to a whiteboard. Dr Rasmussen, burly and unhealthy like all the best medics, drank whisky with Graham in a corner.

Jess mingled. Rupert was nowhere to be seen. He might have helped make it less sad. Less boring. There had been no texts since she'd seen him with Pandora. Which didn't matter.

Pleasantries with Kuzbari.

A sexist homophobic unfunny joke from Ryan. Carli laughed. She wore black lipstick 'out of respect'.

Susannah left to collect Baydrian and Ann. There was so much *collecting* required by children, thought Jess as she wondered what Susannah had meant when she chirped, 'See you Sunday!' over her shoulder.

There was a speech; Eddie stood up to the plate. Short. To the point. Pointless. Nobody in the room had really known Gavin.

Jess ticked off the platitudes.

Gavin was taken too soon.

He was a fine young man.

He had his whole life ahead of him.

She raised her glass with the rest of them. She felt for Gavin. The sacrificial lamb of Castle Kidbury.

Across the room, Eden watched the crowd. Every inch a policeman. Jess felt her mood lift. A kindred spirit.

Making her way around the periphery of the wake, she saw Squeezers at the book of condolence Eddie had thought to put out.

'Squeezers, Darling doesn't have to sign it.'

She helped him manhandle the whippet, its paws coated with ink, until it left a paw-shaped smudge.

'Darling insisted,' said Squeezers.

There was a yelp from the dog. Ryan had trodden on her.

'Gangway!' said Ryan cheerfully. He half carried, half guided Theresa, whose legs had given way. 'She's pissed out of her head.'

'Gavin!' Theresa could barely pronounce the two-syllable name. She sobbed. She turned her head as she passed Squeezers and vomited on him.

Ryan didn't break step.

Jess would prefer not to remember the twenty minutes she spent in the ladies' loos with Squeezers, sponging Theresa's breakfast out of his trousers.

When she rejoined the funeral, it was winding down. The crowd had thinned. Patricia Smalls, in a black trouser suit, was wagging her finger at somebody.

Jess didn't care. She scouted for Eden.

'You have no respect, young man,' Patricia was saying. 'Coming to a funeral dressed so casually.'

And suddenly Jess did care. 'Patricia,' she broke in. 'Neil's wearing a T-shirt with the name of Gavin's band on it. He's a fan. He's showing Gavin a great deal of respect.'

Neil Semple, eyes on the floor, showed no interest in the women fighting over his honour.

'Neil was at Gavin's very last gig.'

'What's a gig?' Patricia didn't wait for the answer. She sped off on oiled wider-fits.

'Hey, Neil.' Jess put a hand on his shoulder. Felt the knob of bone before he jerked his body away. 'We're not schoolkids anymore. You don't have to let Patricia Smalls talk to you like that.' She hoped his granddad fed him: Neil was skin and bone.

'Is the booze free?'

'Er, yeah.'

He sloped away to take a glass in each hand.

231

By the exit sign, duty done, was Eden. Jess got there before he could leave.

'Have you seen who's here?' She pointed. 'Unthank.' She dropped her arm. Unthank had seen her point and raised a sarcastic glass to her. 'Oh shit, he's coming over.'

'Howdy, Detective. And, no, I forget . . .'

'Jess,' said Jess.

'I thought a great friend of Gavin's like you would be at the official funeral,' said Unthank.

'Ditto,' said Jess.

'I *was*. Then I came here.'

'Back to London, are you, now you've paid your respects?'

Unthank turned to Eden. 'Is she always this nosey?'

'What *are* your plans?' asked Eden, and Jess could have kissed him for not backing up the odious Unthank.

'Not sure. Might hang around. See what's what.' He ambled off.

'You buying that?' whispered Jess. 'Unthank came to Castle Kidbury for Gavin's gig. Keith Dike's murder was . . .' Jess counted on her fingers. 'Five days before the Druid's Head. This town isn't that interesting. Particularly for a cool dude like that. Those scruffy trousers cost a fortune.'

'He's from Dalston,' said Eden. 'That's a rough area of London. Probably doesn't have much money.'

'My dear detective sergeant,' said Jess, 'you need to get up to the capital more often. A coffee'll set you back a fiver in Dalston these days. And it'll be single origin, cold press, served in an eggcup with chia seeds on the side. Nobody who wears the sort of clothes Unthank wears would stay *one night* longer than they absolutely had to in a bargain-basement hotel.'

'I agree that something doesn't add up. Doesn't make him a killer, Jess.' Eden checked his watch. 'I have to get back.'

'Are you sleeping?'

'Don't worry about me.'

'I want to,' smiled Jess.

'I'll be in touch.'

'John Eden!' Patricia swooped. Blocked his way. 'How lovely to see you out and about, socialising again. Such a pity about you and Mrs E, but here you are, on the market once more!'

'This isn't a party, Patricia.' Jess stood slightly in front of Eden. 'He's here in an official capacity at the funeral of a murder victim.'

'It's a start.' Patricia chucked Eden under the chin.

While he recoiled, she clapped her hands. 'Everybody! Quiet! I have a few words to say!'

None of the words were 'Gavin Blake'.

'I don't believe it.' Jess nudged Eden. 'She's hijacking a funeral.'

'ThinkSpace,' began Patricia, as shoulders drooped around the room, 'is a game-changing concept in the development of community centralisation. I hope – I *know* – that I'll see you all at the grand opening tomorrow night, when I'll be escorted by Castle Kidbury's most esteemed resident, his honour Judge James Castle QC.'

Jess led the applause.

Her father went pale.

'May I introduce you to the prominent broadcaster who'll cut the ribbon? Say a few words, Shane! Ladies and gentlemen, Shane Harper.'

The prominent broadcaster wiped his mouth and left his wife's side.

His second wife. Jess had heard from Bogna all about the scandal of Shane leaving his wife of many years and their four children for his personal assistant. Bogna's favourite detail from her extensive gossip column research: 'The floozy is same age as his oldest daughter!'

Skin a suspicious orange, hair highlighted and bouffant, Shane might have strayed from a Bucks Fizz tribute act. When he spoke, this Emperor of Naff had a neon mono-tooth.

'Thank you, Mayor Smalls,' said Shane, after he'd jokingly insisted that the non-existent applause stop. He cleared his throat. Peered at his notes. 'The Think Space—'

'No definite article, all one word,' hissed Patricia.

As Shane struggled to make sense of Patricia's stream of consciousness, Jess stole over to her father's side.

'... Admixture of social and commercial forms ... cross-sector integration ...'

'We've done our duty, Dad.'

They tiptoed out just as Shane half-heartedly predicted ThinkSpace franchises in London, Paris and Beijing.

The Judge had insisted they take her 'jalopy'. He and Jess drove home in a silence that befitted the aftermath of a funeral.

They weren't mourning Gavin; neither of them had known him well and the Castles weren't hypocrites. They were waiting for the other shoe to drop. For the Judge to comment on Max's visit. The silence on this subject had roared since Jess waved Max off the night before.

On the drive of Harebell House, Jess turned off the ignition.

'Come on, Dad, let's get it over with.'

The Judge paused, as though in contemplation before an historical address. 'Words fail me, Jessica.'

How she wished that was true. But no.

'You gave me your assurance – now worthless, apparently – that you were addressing your situation at Cambridge. Then, by virtue of a deeply embarrassing encounter with your superior when he presented himself at my door, I discover my faith in you has, yet again, been misplaced. The very least you could have done was give Max some sort of explanation for your desertion. Instead you hid, and you lied. For two whole bloody weeks, you skulked around the house feeling sorry for yourself, shoehorning your way into a murder enquiry that has nothing to do with you—'

'That's not fair! Eden—'

'DS Eden is a perfectly capable police officer who does *not* need the assistance of a failed history lecturer with the temperament of a child. And while we're at it, even if it weren't fair, what entitles you to justice after the disgraceful way you treat the people around you? How do you manage to crash through life believing that fairness only need run one way? You have an endless capacity for taking what you want, making demands this way and that, but the moment any pressure is applied to you, you become inert, whingeing about unreasonable expectations and—'

'Enough!' Jess threw up her hands. 'I'm not putting up with any more Jessica-bashing. Yes, I fucked up, and before you say anything, I'm giving myself permission to swear. I feel terrible about what I've done. You don't have to explain my own shortcomings to me. I feel them keenly every day. I have nightmares about the situation. I let down the department, the students, and, worst of all, Max. And you know what? Max was disappointed. And he was sad. But he *didn't* perform a character assassination on me. I'm sorry I'm not another Stephen, I'm sorry I didn't do a fucking law degree, and I'm sorry I ran away. I'm particularly sorry Mum's dead because at least I'd have someone in Harebell House who loves me even though I'm crap.' Jess's voice cracked. 'However crap I am, I'm *still* Dr Jessica Castle and not some legal secretary you get to push around. As far as these murders are concerned, Dad, I'm *useful*. Shock horror, Jess is useful for once! You're right. DS Eden is a perfectly capable police officer who happens to find my expert opinion valuable, so put that in your tweed fucking Victorian pipe and smoke it.'

Jess unbuckled and clambered out. Ready to stomp away, she stopped and turned to put her head through the open window.

'And don't worry, I'll protect you from Patricia Smalls at the grand opening tomorrow.'

The silence throbbed. The Judge said nothing.

A first.

Back in her room, Jess sat on the floor and leant against the side of her bed. She tried to enjoy the emergency Scotch egg she'd found. The doughty garage snack wasn't working its usual magic.

Everything Jess wanted was beyond her reach. She wanted Mary. She wanted to talk to Rupert. Any rapprochement with her dad was officially over. The symbols lay, inscrutable, on her bedside table.

Moose snored, taking up the bed as 'Wooden Heart' warbled on her turntable. At least she had Moose, she thought. And Elvis. The King never let her down.

But what Jess really craved was something she could never have again. What she wanted more than anything was her mother.

The normals had it in for him. They didn't know how to see, how to look. They were blind. All the care he took with the boxes and no one appreciated him. He put love into the boxes. There was no other word for it.

Love.

Sex had brought power. Made a leader out of him. He had been transformed through sex and death. This new life was exhilarating.

The dead ones were proud. They knew he'd listened and learnt. They knew he did his best. That wasn't enough for him anymore. He wanted everybody to know the amazing things he was capable of.

This time, the newspaper people would put his box on the front page where it belonged. The box would be found out in the open. He almost felt sorry for whoever found it.

Chapter 19

AN AREA OF HIGH PRESSURE

Saturday 28 May

Jess's first full shift at the charity shop began at 9 a.m. Despite the lack of payment or perks or basic respect, Doug and Richard demanded punctuality from their staff. Sleep still in her eyes, Jess left Harebell House under a cloud both literal and spiritual. The Judge had taken care not to cross her path since their frank exchange of views the evening before, and a grey mass of cotton wool cloud trembled over the peak of Gold Hill.

She didn't go back for an umbrella. She took her chances with the rain. A walk, she thought, might clear her head.

Kidbury Road.

The bridge.

The long-stay car park.

The medical centre.

The vet's.

And then the long turn into the main thoroughfare. Turned out her head was un-clearable.

A police car passed her. A yellow and blue blur. Then another. The town firmed up ahead of her. Bell Street was busy. Too busy for the hour of day.

Gossiping clusters impeded her path. Jess nodded hello to Carli, who had buttonholed Helena and Meera. She passed Graham Dickinson, hurrying towards the vet's with Shakespeare in a pet carrier. The cat farted as they passed.

Something was in the air. The excitement bit at Jess. She felt ashamed that murder was her new safe place, but it did take her mind off, well, *things*.

Crime scene tape stretched from the minimart to Rupert's chambers on the edge of the market square.

'Sorry, love.' The red-headed policeman barred her way. 'You'll have to go round.'

'Why?' Jess peered into the square. The centre was screened off with what looked like massive windbreaks. 'Is it to do with the murders?'

'Move along, now,' said Red.

Jess moved along, scurrying down an alley that let her out onto Parson's Lane. Past St Luke's. A left onto the narrow street that housed the chemist's. She peered in. Mr Kuzbari seemed lost in thought, arms wrapped around himself, staring into the middle distance.

She almost knocked. St Luke's clock chiming nine reminded her of her duties.

'You're late,' said Richard. His neckerchief was

tartan this morning. His hair, newly dyed, reminded Jess of orangeade.

'Only by two minutes.'

'Only, she says.' Richard was scandalised. 'Sort through those donation bags, missy, and less of your only.'

Plastic bags leant on one another by the counter. Jess set to. A nylon nightie. A very old bra. Three polo necks. Much of it fit only for the bin. Jess remembered her mother saying that customers mistook the charity shop for a waste disposal unit. 'Can we sell these?' She held up a pair of outsize frilled knickers that, to put it kindly, had seen better days.

'Ooh yes!' Doug swept down the stairs from the flat. All in black. Spidery. 'I have a regular customer who'll take them.' He took the panties and stowed them behind the till. 'He'll be very grateful, dear.'

'Something's going on,' said Jess as she extracted a bald Barbie and a quadriplegic Ken from a bag. 'Police everywhere. The square's cordoned off.'

'Not another murder,' sighed Richard, examining a coil of till roll.

'All these journalists clogging up lovely Castle Kidbury.' Doug tutted.

'Yet not one broadsheet reviewer bothered to turn up to *The Sound of Music*.'

Doug and Richard had cast Patricia Smalls as Mother Superior in the most recent production by the Castle Kidbury Amateur Dramatic Society. It was the casting of Doug as Maria that sunk the show, however.

'I don't feel safe walking the streets,' said Richard. 'One doesn't expect this kind of thing beyond the M25.'

The bell above the door tinkled and announced Eddie.

'What can we do you for?' said Doug. 'All our Mills and Boons are reduced.'

'I'm looking for some clothes, actually.' Eddie reached out and fingered an Aran. 'For Squeezers.'

Jess straightened up. 'You his personal stylist these days?'

'Poor old sod's on his uppers.'

'You old softie.'

'Don't tell anyone,' smiled Eddie. He didn't look the part, with his close-cropped hair and his bulldog build.

'You know everything that goes on.' Jess sidled over to him, helping him browse. 'What's with all the coppers?'

'Another body. It was me that phoned it in.'

Jess had struck gold. 'When? Where? Who?'

Sizing a hoodie against Doug, who moved huffily away, Eddie said, 'First thing. I opened my window and saw a body laid over the cross in the market square. Sort of ...' Eddie mimed the corpse's posture. Arms up and over. Head hanging down. 'Worst bit was,' he grimaced, 'the eyes were gone. Just two holes.' Eddie shuddered.

'It's him again,' breathed Jess. 'Did you recognise the victim?' This wasn't fun and games. It wasn't scuttle-butt. Somebody had lost a husband or a son.

'Nah. Too disfigured. He was well built, tall,

whoever he was. Snappily dressed. Suited and booted, you know? Poor bastard. Fat lot of good his tailoring did him.'

Jumpers and jackets went into a bag. A laughably small amount of money changed hands. Doug and Richard's prices had never been revised.

Elevenses came and went. Half a Battenberg. Dusty Springfield on the shop record player. A customer looking for a boa.

And outside, bustle. Police vans. Eddie giving a taciturn interview with no facts whatsoever to *Look West*. A dog handler asking Castle Kidbury-ites not to stroke his German shepherd.

Jess stood looking past the mannequin at the activity. Something was coalescing in her mind. *Suited and booted*.

'Just popping out for a second.'

In Jess's wake, Doug murmured, 'Her mother would never have popped out.'

'Too true,' agreed Richard.

It probably wasn't Rupert. *But then again*, thought Jess, scrolling through her contacts, *why shouldn't it be?* He wasn't immune; nobody was. His phone rang and rang. Jess began to feel hot. He answered.

'Jess, hi.'

The relief faded. Replaced, as so often with Jess, with something like annoyance. This was their first contact since she'd seen him with Pandora-fucking-Smith, as Jess now thought of the model. 'Hello.'

'So . . .' There was a question in Rupert's voice.

'So you haven't been brutally murdered and left on the war memorial with your eyes gouged out, then?'

'What?'

'Just checking you're alive. I'm calling everybody. To check they're alive.'

'Right.' Rupert sounded as if he was frowning. Or smiling. Jess wasn't sure which was worse. 'I'm not allowed into my office. It's cordoned off.'

'You're such a swot, Rumpole, working on a Saturday.' She wandered back into the shop, phone to her ear. 'So where are you?'

'I'm working from home. Well, I say working ...'

A female voice shouted, 'He's playing hookey!'

'Shush, Pandy,' laughed Rupert. 'She's terrible.'

'Yes,' said Jess. 'She is.'

'You two should meet properly,' said Rupert. 'I think you'd get on.'

Jess didn't answer. The shop door flew open, toppling a tower of Chuck Norris videos. Eden looked around wildly. He found Jess. 'Come on,' he said. 'I'm arresting Pan.'

A liveried car stood at the kerb. Doors open. Jess hurtled over the pavement, through a small, interested crowd. She spotted Neil, staring, and beside him Danny, looking perplexed. Lynne from the minimart bounced on her feet as Jess jumped into the car. 'Are you arresting her?' she shouted. 'Is Jess the murderer?'

Jess's adrenaline spiked as the car picked up speed. There is no time to fret or regret in the white centre of the action.

Chapter 20

CHILD OF THE UNIVERSE

Still Saturday 28 May

The interview room felt different this time.

Another murder had upped the stakes. The presence of DI Phillips, a carnivore from higher up the food chain, changed the air.

The detective inspector had challenged the need for Jess's presence. Eden had defended her.

'I need her,' he'd said.

Now Eden stood nonchalantly sorting through files, humming to himself.

The star of the show sat utterly still. But Jess saw how Pan's eyes tracked Eden's movements.

Jess had clocked a difference in Eden's bearing. More composed, certain. She wondered what he had on Pan. He had offered nothing in the car.

'How many more times?' said Pan. He made sure to sound bored. 'You ain't got anything on me.'

'Really?' replied Eden without looking up.

Sitting back, man-spreading, DI Phillips was older than Eden, with a long nose and the air of an undertaker. 'You have remarkable confidence for a man in your position, Mr Pan.'

'You're just wasting time, Mr Senior Pig,' said Pan. 'Your time, and the lovely Dr Castle's. Personally, time's neither here nor there to me. I'm a child of the universe.'

Eden sat. Held up an official-looking form. 'Says here you're the child of Barry and Maureen Budd from Yeovil.'

Pan's expression froze.

As if he's deciding how to be, thought Jess.

'Doesn't sound too cosy, your life at, um, let's see, twenty-eight Gainsborough Drive.' Eden looked sympathetic. 'Poor little Kevin Budd.'

'That's not my name. I changed it.' Pan tapped his foot. Fast. 'And I didn't live at Gainsborough Drive.'

'According to your social workers, you shuttled between there and your grandparents'. Very worried about you, your grandparents were. Wonder what they'd make of your record.' Eden nodded at his superior.

DI Phillips read tonelessly from a document. 'Graffiti. Petty theft. Cruelty to animals. Car theft. Arson. Actual bodily harm.' He looked up. Distaste on his face. 'An attempted rape that didn't get to court. I wonder if somebody threatened the victim.'

'My grandparents,' said Pan, 'are proud of me, as it goes.'

His foot, Jess noticed, tapped faster as he spoke.

'I deal with people every day who've had a bad start in life,' said Eden. 'Most of the time, they turn out to be useful. Compassionate. Some take the low road.' He stared at Pan and Pan stared back.

Jess sat up. This was a new Eden. Eden the enforcer.

'So sad when a parent tyrannises the home. I can imagine young Kevin getting back from school to find a drugs raid going on. Hot items being fenced in the sitting room. A couple of underage runaways in the kitchen.'

Pan yawned.

'Domestic violence is a curse.' Eden leant his chin on a cupped hand. 'If we were to look under your clothes we'd find a scar from a cigarette burn ... remind me, Detective Inspector, where it is?'

'Right thigh, John. Just below the groin.'

Pan was thinking so hard his eyes fluttered.

'It's a breach of trust when a parent beats a child.'

'Blah blah fucking blah,' said Pan. He slipped lower in his seat.

'Fathers through history have beaten their wives, Kevin, but how did it feel to watch your mum beat your dad?'

'Lawyer,' snapped Pan, sitting up. 'I want my lawyer.'

'Perhaps,' said DI Phillips, 'it made him angry, John.'

'Good point.' Eden, this new Eden, seemed to enjoy baiting Pan with this rehearsed to-and-fro. 'You might wonder if such powerlessness would mess with Kevin's developing masculinity. If it made him exert power over others in violent ways. Who knows?'

'I want my lawyer.'

'You *have* a lawyer?' asked Phillips.

'The duty solicitor, then.'

'Fair enough,' said Eden. 'I heard she's very busy today. Probably not free for about,' Eden checked his watch ostentatiously, 'an hour. Which gives us plenty of time to chat.'

'I'm not sayin' anything till the duty solicitor gets here.'

'Your prerogative, of course,' said Phillips. 'But Castle Kidbury's in uproar. Press everywhere. The death of a celebrity weatherman on my patch brings the wrong sort of attention. Our lady mayor had to be sedated. The murder *ruined* her ThinkSpace event.'

Jess resisted rolling her eyes. Surely Shane Harper was the real victim.

'Of course, you don't have to say a thing.' Eden steered the focus back to Pan. 'But I have to tell you, I'm intrigued by you.' He paused, letting the compliment land. 'You exert a powerful influence over people.'

Jess watched Pan's shoulders wiggle; flattery was his Achilles heel.

'That little harem of yours would do anything you ask.'

Pan pouted, apparently appreciating Eden's insight.

Eden located another typed list. 'You certainly manage to get by outside of society. How long is it now you've been off the radar? Fifteen years?'

'I am above society's concerns.'

'You're certainly above paying council tax,' huffed Phillips.

Jess saw a tiny gleam of annoyance in Eden's eye. *Ask him more about his mum*, she thought. *That's the way in.*

'Do you hate your mum, Kevin?'

Pan thumped the table. 'Leave my mum out of this, pig.'

'Did your dad smoke? Hmm. I think it was your mum who liked playing with cigarettes.'

'I want a solicitor now. Shut your mouth.'

'It's not your fault you turned to cutting up sheep, Kevin.'

'Don't call me Kevin!'

Jess was poised, ready to jump up. Pan was shouting now. Fizzing with dark energy. Eden had shown his claws.

'It's not nice to hurt animals, is it? Not *normal*. Started with a pet cat, didn't it? Then a neighbour's dog you murdered with a firework—'

'I want my fucking solicitor!'

'Did you kill Keith Dike, Gavin Blake and Shane Harper?'

'Shut up, pig!'

'Did you send the eyes of Keith Dike and Gavin Blake to the *Echo*?'

'What?'

'Where are Shane Harper's eyes, Kevin? The newspaper doesn't have them. We don't have them. Did you bottle it this time? Worried you'd left too much evidence? Come on, Kevin ... Pan ... you're a pro, an old hand. Don't insult my intelligence.'

'I did not fucking kill them.'

'But the sheep?'

'So I killed the sheep. Crime of the century!'

Phillips interjected. 'You previously denied the animal-cruelty charge. What's to suggest your denial of the murders isn't also false?'

'Who is this guy?' Pan jerked a thumb at Phillips.

Jess spoke. 'The ritual slaughter of animals can be a prelude to *hieros gamos*.'

'Ah,' said Pan. 'The learned Dr Castle.' He was scraping together the dregs of his usual demeanour. 'The knower of things.'

Eden folded his arms. Listened.

'*Hieros gamos* can look very like women dancing around in nighties shrieking. And everybody enjoys a good orgy.'

'You're welcome anytime.' Pan held out his arms. 'All of you.'

'But it might be an opportunity for Pan the great seducer, who is actually Kevin who hates women, to force himself on as many girls as possible.'

'No need to force anybody,' said Pan. Jess had hit a nerve. 'It's sacred sex. Look it up.'

'It's the joining of a goddess and a mortal,' said Jess. 'The man is empowered by the act.'

'How do you use your power, Pan?' Eden was quiet, intense. 'Is killing animals enough for you? Have you moved onto men?'

'If I was a killer,' said Pan, 'you'd be next.'

'Why crucifixion? Some sort of biblical fetish? Fancy

yourself as Pontius Pilate? Why the eyes? A message you want to send to the world?'

Pan threw his head back and stared at the ceiling.

'Crucifixion isn't just execution,' said Jess. 'It's about ceremony, display. A warning.'

'What are you warning us about?' asked Eden. 'To leave well alone? To respect you, perhaps?'

Pan sat, arms folded, head still back.

Eden reached for another batch of files. 'Where were you last night?'

'At the field.'

'With the women?'

'Yes.' Pan sounded teenager-bored. 'Ask any of them.'

'We did,' said Phillips. 'Some of them can't remember their names, they're so intoxicated.'

'Doesn't make for a very reliable alibi,' tutted Eden, with mock regret. 'Where were you?'

Pan's composure seemed to falter. He looked straight at Eden. 'At the field. I said.'

'You know I'm going to arrest you?'

'I know how this works, pig.'

A packet of Jaffa Cakes helped pass the time as Jess waited for Eden in his office. When she heard footsteps and butch conversation, she bundled the cardboard box back into her bag.

'*Listen*, John.' Jess's ears twitched. Phillips sounded exasperated. 'I've heard enough. The guy likes attention and he's full of hate. Plenty of motive there, for the over-done violence and the flashy telly-friendly display. The alibis are worthless. A good barrister would shoot those drug-addled women down in flames. He's strong enough, he has form and he's into all this spiritual twaddle. Ssh, John. No. Arrest him and let his lawyer make a fuss.'

Phillips stalked away.

'You heard,' said Eden as he sat at his desk.

'Couldn't help it. So you're really arresting Pan.'

'The boss is desperate for a result.'

'Aren't *you*?'

'Yes. But the right one.'

'You don't think Pan did it?' Jess remembered her eyeball-to-eyeball moment in the charity shop changing room. 'He's capable of it.'

Eden shrugged. 'He's sticking to a very simple story. That he slaughtered the sheep but not the humans.'

'I don't think he did it.'

'Why?'

'Just a feeling.' Jess snaffled another Jaffa.

'Hunches, Jess.'

'You don't like them.'

'They can be wrong. The truth is, there are many questions that if answered one way drop him in it, but if answered another way, rule him out.' Eden squared his shoulders. 'I'm going to hang on to Pan. Arrest him for possession. The boys got lucky and found some spice under his bed. We'll hold him while we look into a couple of outstanding warrants under his real name. I'm not pinning the killings on him yet. I don't want the town to relax.'

'Just in case,' said Jess.

'Just in case we've got it wrong and the killer strikes again.'

'Your bosses won't like it.'

'I'm hanging on by a thread as it is. I might as well use what time I have left.'

A volt of electricity shot through Jess. 'Eden! Unthank was wanging on about the market cross. He made a point of it. About how it was part of the furniture but signified death. Then Shane's body is left on it.' She picked up the receiver on his desk. Held it out to him. 'Call him in! Finger him, or whatever you call it.'

'I never call it that.' Eden looked perturbed. 'I'm ahead of you, Jess. DC Knott spoke to Mr Unthank about his whereabouts last night.'

'And?'

'Although you'd think Mr Unthank would have gone back to his wife and brand-new baby after the funeral, he slept alone in his bed at the EasySleep Inn.'

'Still no CCTV?'

'The manageress vouched for him. The only way out is through reception. He would have had to break a window and there was no evidence of that.'

'If he's clever enough to kill three people and leave no evidence, I'm sure he could escape from an EasySleep.'

'We'll keep an eye on him,' said Eden.

'Speaking of eyes ...' said Jess.

'I know. We need Shane Harper's eyes to come in. Nothing's been delivered to the *Echo*. I'm worried that our man – Pan, Kevin, Unthank, *Squeezers* – might be disappointed in the lack of publicity and leave them out in the open. God forbid a member of the public finds a box of eyes, or there goes our tourism award.'

Eden walked Jess out through the incident room. From every quarter came a question, an idea, an 'Oi guv!' The strip-lit square was a brain, seething with activity.

Jess peeked at screens as she passed. Earwigged on phone conversations. She greedily took in the whiteboard complete with red timelines and victim photographs and a mugshot of Pan. *Just like the telly*, she thought. *Right down to the fast-food cartons.*

As Eden bade her a distracted goodbye, Jess's hand found a card in her pocket.

Unthank's business card. Put away. Forgotten.

She looked at it. She turned to call to Eden. She decided against it. His mind was already back in the incident room.

Outside, the clouds still glowered above the police station and the broad bland sweep of Margaret Thatcher Way. Sitting in her car, Jess felt something very like a hunch.

Luis Unthank's company was called Hellcat Solutions. The card was illustrated with a freehand drawing, in hot pinks and reds, of what looked like a fidget spinner.

Hellcat, Jess knew, was a frequent historical mispronunciation of Hecate.

That fidget spinner was actually a three-headed wheel. 'Or strophalos,' said Jess to herself, enjoying the bulk of the word. 'Also known as Hecate's Wheel.'

Chapter 21

ORIENTAL HARMONY EXPERIENCE

Sunday 29 May

Water seeped through the holes in her body.

Jess was full up with water.

In it and of it, she saw a wound open up in the tiles of the pool.

She was being dragged towards it.

This time when she woke up she was only whispering the words.

I'm sorry.

If Jess lined up all the places in the world she would rather not be – including ex-lovers' beds and nosediving aircraft – this five-star spa would be near the number-one spot. The fluffy towelling robe itched. The *Plink! Plonk!* of faux-Eastern music grated.

When Susannah had picked her up an hour earlier, she'd taken in Jess's pyjamas and haystack hair. 'You've forgotten!'

It had been a wail. Jess's sister-in-law lived for spa days, marking them in red on her wall planner, checking carefully whether the price included complimentary Prosecco, carving her body into 'problem areas' to be 'targeted'.

'I didn't forget. I swear.'

Jess hadn't forgotten. She had never known. The voucher tucked into a gift bag and handed over at Sunday lunch had never been opened, and now the murders were on hold while Jess filled out a pointless form in the foyer of the Chase Hall Hotel spa.

Jess was reining in her frustration. She hated to disappoint Susannah. The two women would have disagreed about politics, about feminism, about religion, if Susannah ever gave such topics a thought. Yet Jess loved her. In a low-key, back-burner sort of way.

'Contraindications!' she grumbled.

'That means,' said Susannah helpfully, 'anything that would stop you having the treatments. Like being pregnant. You're not ...? No, I thought not. Imagine that! Or allergies, or a pacemaker.'

'I'm allergic to this music.' And the pseudoscience in the brochure. And the hush, as if they were in a cathedral and not a breeze-block hotel extension.

'We must be mindful, not flippant.' Susannah was pained by Jess's lack of piety. 'That's the whole point of the Oriental Harmony Experience.'

The attendants who whisked them off to separate treatment rooms weren't particularly oriental. Mandy told Jess, in the local twang, that she was 'dedicated to deliverin' wellness' and handed her a pair of paper knickers.

As Mandy began to scrub her – quite vigorously – with salt and oil, Jess tuned out. She disobeyed the rules of the spa. Instead of emptying her mind, she filled it with murder.

The symbols on Gavin's body travelled everywhere with her. Pan's arrest was progress. But Eden was still digging. One word bothered him. The same word that reared up in the darkened room as Mandy prepared the Yin Yang Detox Algae Body Wrap.

Why?

Jess wasn't satisfied with the motive.

Mandy left the room on whisper-soft feet once Jess was secured in some sort of foil straitjacket. The therapist had earnestly explained 'kick-starting detox-ification' and 'balancing, like, your senses and that'. As the slimy algae seeped into her skin, Jess thought about Pan. She concentrated. Hard. The way she did when she read her students' work, or contemplated the fingers of Stonehenge.

She was rewarded.

If Pan involved the women in the killings, it would bind them to him forever.

The spaced-out harem might see through Pan at some point, drift back to provincial normality. Murder, though, would shackle them together for life.

Blood had bound people together since the first drops were shed. Celtic blood brothers. Ancient Mayans. Clever leaders – and Pan *was* clever, in his shyster way – recognised the primal. Add the criminality of murder to the drama of bloodletting, and those women were hostages.

'Now if you'll just pop into the shower for me,' Mandy was back, 'we can get cracking on your mud treatment.' She lowered her voice. 'Because you are, if you don't mind me saying so, a bit dry.'

Jess *had* minded Mandy saying so. She minded quite a lot of what Mandy said. Particularly 'Are we worried about ageing at all?' and 'I can suggest something for your blackhead situation'. All in all, Jess was relieved to see the back of Mandy and meet Susannah for the all-inclusive afternoon tea in an echoing conservatory.

'Doesn't this, you know, kind of negate all the yin and yang shizzle?' Jess said, ravishing a scone.

'We deserve this.' Susannah was vehement. 'We can work off the calories in the gym.'

'*You* can. My calories are welcome to hang around.'

'I'm glad we ... it's nice to chat, just the two of us ...'

There was evidently something Susannah wanted to spit out. Jess hoped it wasn't Baydrian-related. 'How are things? With you and Stephen?'

'You've noticed?' Susannah put down her scone. 'You see it too?'

'Um ...' Jess's elementary conversational opener had been misinterpreted.

'He's behaving oddly. Not odd, exactly. No. Yes. Odd.' Susannah, unused to speaking out, was finding it tricky.

'Odd how?' Jess didn't truly want to know. Her brother's marriage was a closed book to her. Like their wedding, which had involved top hats, flower girls and the release of doves above the congregation. 'You seem so close.' Jess had overheard other women talk like this. Her brother and sister-in-law were yoked together, stoking the furnace of their large house, their gifted children, their two long-haul holidays per year. Was 'close' the right word to describe Stephen and Susannah? Jess had never put their relationship under a microscope before.

'We are, oh we *are*.' Susannah's long, slightly horsey face shone with essential oils. 'But he's been buying new clothes. Hiding them.'

'What sort of clothes?'

'Trendy.' Susannah shocked herself as well as Jess. 'I found a pair of Vans trainers. I can't help thinking ... this is silly, I mean it's *Stephen* for heaven's sake ... but, do you think, another woman?'

'Nah.' Jess shook her head. It amazed her that Stephen had managed one woman. 'He loves you, Susannah.'

'I know that.' Susannah sounded peeved. 'That doesn't guarantee anything.' Her demeanour changed abruptly. She bounced on her chair. 'Yoo-hoo!' she waved at somebody behind Jess.

Turning, Jess saw Helena coming towards them on heels that click-clacked like gunshot on the tiled floor. 'Ladies, so lovely to see you.' Helena exuded professional bonhomie as crisp as her navy pencil skirt.

There was the mandatory female badinage. Susannah insisted that Helena had lost weight. Helena made a joke about the 'naughty' afternoon tea. And then Helena was gone, leaving a wake of polite perfume.

'She's amazing,' said Susannah in a stage whisper. 'I don't know how she does it. A tragedy like that would kill me.'

Jess didn't respond.

'What do you do when you lose somebody just like that? Where does all the love go?'

Jess didn't know.

'And Helena keeps her hair so nice, too.' Susannah was in awe of such grit. 'You have no idea what love is until you have a child.' Susannah recovered enough to take the last of the jam.

'So I hear.' Jess had heard a variation on this riff many times. It never got interesting.

'It's like your heart beats outside your body,' said Susannah, her face beatific.

'Urgh,' said Jess.

'You'd know what I mean if you had a baby of your own.'

'Love is love, surely.' Jess tried not to be terse. Susannah didn't set out to imply that Jess was a withered old maid with ovaries like air-dried Parma ham.

'Ooh.' Susannah flapped her hands. 'Weren't you at Gavin's seventh birthday party, Jess?'

She had to say yes. She couldn't lie. She didn't add that most nights, when she slept, she was still there.

Chapter 22

FIELD OF DREAMS

Monday 30 May

The hand-written advertisements in the minimart window pulled Jess into another world. A world where somebody was selling a guinea pig and a toaster and would accept eight pounds or nearest offer for the pair. She heard her name being called.

Danny and Tallulah were arm in arm. She leant on him. He leant on her. They laughed. She fixed his hair. They were preposterously in love.

'They caught the killer,' said Danny. 'I told them it wasn't me.'

'Of course it wasn't you.' Tallulah was repressive. 'Don't talk about the murders, they're horrible.' She yanked at his collar. 'Look at the state of you.'

Danny beamed as she strode off.

'Come on, catch up,' shouted Tallulah over her shoulder. Danny's mother, walking behind them, looked worriedly about her as the pair hooted with laughter. She seemed nervous about them drawing attention to themselves, and she smiled anxiously at Jess, saying, 'What do you make of this?'

'I think they're a match made in heaven.' Jess was full of compassion for the worried woman who used to give her a tenner to watch Danny while she rushed out to do the weekly shop. 'Danny likes to be bossed, and, boy, does Tallulah like to boss.' Love had won and Jess was glad.

One of the hazards – or perks, if you're not Jess – of small-town life is constantly bumping into folk. A goodbye to the lovebirds and their frazzled chaperone and Jess saw Rupert and Pandora approaching. They were jaunty. Arm in arm.

'Shit,' growled Jess under her breath.

'What happened to your hair?' Rupert was amused. His amusement annoyed Jess.

'Oh this?' Jess tossed her head, insouciant. 'I had a massage yesterday. There's oil in it.'

'Right.' Rupert seemed unsure that this was adequate explanation for what was happening on Jess's head.

'I wouldn't have thought you were into pampering.' Pandora was catwalk-ready as she said this.

'No, well,' was all Jess could muster. Pandora's lustrous appearance wasn't the source of her humiliation. But it didn't help.

'And your face.' Rupert leant in to peer with horrified fascination, as if she was a bloated corpse. 'It's all blotchy.'

'That's the facial,' explained Pandora. 'Some people's skin reacts badly.' She pulled a sad face.

'Where are you two beautiful people off to?' asked Jess, wishing she could drop down a trapdoor.

'Pandora's uncle, for lunch. You've probably heard of him – Hugo Smith. He owns those vineyards in Devon. We're introducing him to Patricia Smalls.'

'At *her* request.' Pandora snorted. 'God, she's a pill, isn't she?'

Jess had something in common with her nemesis. 'She certainly is.'

'She tried to invite your father,' added Rupert, one eyebrow raised.

'I daresay,' said Jess.

'Tell you what,' said Rupert, looking at Pandora. 'Why don't you tag along, Jess? You won't have much to do now they've arrested that Pan bloke. We can watch Patricia Smalls try to seduce Uncle Hugo.'

'Do come, do!' said Pandora.

Jess paused for a moment, as if seriously considering the invitation. 'Nah. You go ahead. I'm not fit for public consumption.'

'You sure?' asked Rupert.

'So very sure,' intoned Jess disingenuously, head cocked.

'Aw, really?' Pandora seemed stricken.

'Really,' said Jess.

Rupert bobbed awkwardly on the spot. 'Right. Then we'd better be off, I suppose.'

'Right,' said Jess.

'Tatty bye then,' cooed Pandora.

Jess nodded. 'Bye then.'

'Bye Jess,' said Rupert.

'Bye Rupert,' said Jess.

'Byesy-bye,' giggled Pandora.

The two backed away, still arm in arm. Rupert's face was a question mark.

Jess pretended to look at her phone.

Arseholes, she thought.

With Pan – or Kevin – safely locked away under Eden's watch, Jess felt it was safe to visit Pitt's Field. Eden wouldn't like it, but Eden didn't have to know. It might help with unravelling the knotted mystery of the symbols.

If it took her mind off Rupert and Pandora, well, that was a bonus.

This time the camp seemed different. Less foreboding. Not so unearthly. Without their chieftain in place, the women washed clothes, prepared food, chatted. Children ran around the fire, laughing and chasing each other.

'Hello!' shouted Jess from the gate.

Two children stopped for a moment, then ran towards her. Tittering and twittering, they tugged at her skirt.

'What's going on here then?' she asked.

'We're playing horses,' said the small blond boy.

'And we're hunting for prehistorink animals,' added the older girl. 'Do you want to help us?'

'Who are we looking for?' asked Jess, down on her haunches. 'Mammoths? Sabre-toothed tigers?'

'Who are they?' asked the boy blankly.

'They're prehistorink animals.' No need to let the little girl know she'd mispronounced it. People would line up the rest of her life to tell her what she was doing wrong.

The boy took this in. 'Tell us what they look like so we can catch them and take them to our cave.'

'All right. Do you have a pencil and a piece of paper?'

The girl shook her head. 'We're not allowed them.'

'Does Pan say you're not allowed?'

The children nodded, part *Wicker Man* and part *Oliver Twist* in their dirty, oversized clothes.

'Can I help you?' The question was not polite. A string bean of a woman strode towards the gate, joint dangling between stained fingers.

'I'm looking for Caroline.'

The woman looked Jess up and down. 'You're a pig, aren't you?' She oinked and the children laughed.

'I'm an old school friend. Caroline knows me.' Jess tried to strike a blameless tone.

The string bean held Jess in her gaze. 'All right. Come with me.'

Jess followed, the children dancing behind her.

'You'll still help us hunt mammoths, though?' The girl was anxious.

'Yes, of course.' Another promise Jess wouldn't keep.

'Will that be before no-more times?' called the boy.

Jess halted in the mud. 'No-more times?'

The girl shrugged matter-of-factly, as if everyone knew. 'Yes, silly. No-more times is coming.'

Jess caught up with her guide, who was rapping at a caravan door.

Caroline emerged, bleary-eyed, into the sunlight. 'Jess?'

'That's me!' Jess hoped she sounded breezy. 'Fancy a walk?'

The other woman's glare didn't abate.

'Erm ... I don't ... we're not really—'

'Come on, Caroline. Lovely day. Sun's shining.' Jess sounded like her father. Peremptory. Little bit judgemental. 'Bring the little one out for some air.'

Caroline disappeared briefly and then re-emerged. She was putting her arms into what had probably once been a denim jacket. Her daughter, fingers in mouth, followed.

Jess linked arms with Caroline briskly. 'This-a-way!' She pointed to a far corner of the clearing.

'No pig talk,' called the string bean.

'No pig talk!' sang Jess.

Reminiscing about school didn't bring Caroline back to the real world. Nor did asking about her daughter. As they sat on a fallen tree, Jess watched the toddler potter in the mud. One thing Pitt's Field had in abundance was mud.

Up close, Caroline looked more than dirty and ill-nourished. She looked wretched. Dead eyes. Green teeth. Caroline smoked, and Jess noticed a slight tremor to her old friend's head.

'What do you *really* want?' sighed Caroline as she dragged on her roll-up.

'To see you. See how you are.'

'You're in the police's pocket, though. You want to take Pan away from us for good. Silence him.' Caroline sniffed. Loud and unselfconscious.

'I'm not with the police. I'm an academic. Until a few days ago I was working at Cambridge.'

This seemed to capture Caroline's attention. 'Wow.' She paused for a moment. As if she'd glimpsed beyond the gate of Pitt's Field and it was filled with wonder. 'What subject do you teach?'

'History. Anglo-Saxon, Norse and Celtic. All about gods and ancient tribes. You used to be into New-Age stuff at school, didn't you?'

Again, Caroline ignored the conversational lifeline. 'Do you teach astrology?'

Jess was accustomed to this question. She taught about paganism. It didn't mean she *was* a pagan. 'Well, astrology comes into it. So do sacrifices and rituals of all sorts.'

'I wish I'd studied something like that.'

'You could. You can.'

'But I'm with Pan now.' It might have been a curse or a blessing; whatever it was, it was final. 'I'm number three.'

'Number three?'

'The third chosen.'

'How long have you been with Pan?'

Caroline shrugged slightly, making circles in the earth with her mouldered trainer.

'Six months? A year?' *Please*, thought Jess, *don't let it be more*.

Caroline screwed up her face. Thinking didn't come easy. 'Three years. Yeah. More, maybe.'

'What's your daughter's name?'

'Delphi.'

Jess swallowed. 'That's a nice name. Who's Delphi's dad?'

Caroline just looked at her.

'Is she his? Is she Pan's?'

'All the children are Pan's children. Apart from Holly. And George. The ones you were talking to.' Caroline was shifty. As if there were unfriendly ears in the trees.

'What did they mean by no-more times?'

Caroline shook her head, emphatic.

'Caroline, please. This is important. Do you know who Pan really is? *I* do. His name's Kevin. He's a criminal. He's dangerous. He's hurt people in the past and he went to jail for it. He's a conman and a thug. He's under suspicion for three murders. He's not a guru.'

Caroline found her tongue. 'You want him gone because he doesn't fit the narrow pattern of capitalism. Because he teaches everything you're afraid of.'

'Why would I be afraid? Does it scare *you*?' Jess felt as if she was on to something. 'Are you afraid when you take part in *hieros gamos*, Caroline? Does it lead to something worse?'

'I'm not allowed to talk about *hieros gamos*.'

Even from his cell, Pan issued orders.

'What he teaches is made up on the spot.' Jess tried to remain rational. Hard, when she wanted to shake Caroline. 'Even he doesn't believe it. It doesn't mean anything.'

'But it *does* mean something. To us. To me.' Caroline struck her chest. She was awake now. 'Everything before Pan. *That* was made up. *That* was meaningless. School, teachers, parents, marriage. I had to get away from ...' She struggled. Waved her arms to encompass what she had escaped. '... *them*. Pan was what I needed. He understands.'

Jess saw how much Caroline's animation had taken out of her. The woman subsided. Her hands trembled and her face twitched. Gentler now, Jess asked, 'What are you taking? What does he give you?'

'We breathe from crystals.'

Jess buried her head in her hands. 'Fuck.'

'I knew you wouldn't get it.'

Jess tugged Caroline's arm. 'Meth, Caroline? Jesus Christ. We can leave now, with Delphi. You can stay at mine. DS Eden will keep you safe and social services will, I don't know, rehouse you. You're not safe here. We can go right now.' She stood up, still holding onto Caroline. 'This minute.'

Caroline shook her off. 'Pan's always right. He prophesied you'd come with your lies and try to take me away from him. He warned us there'd be no-more times. Taught us to prepare.'

'What *is* bloody no-more times?' Jess was out of patience.

'Armageddon's coming, Jess. You won't survive. Only believers will be left. Me. The others. The kids. Pan's kids, that is.'

'This is rubbish, Caroline. Pan's an unimportant speck of a man.' Jess frowned. 'Only Pan's kids? Not little Holly and George? Does that sound fair to you?'

'Look, when Pan is taken from us, no-more times begin. That's why we made sacrifices.'

'What sort of sacrifices?'

'Pan says it's not for your ears. You wouldn't understand.' Caroline swiped a hand over her face. 'The sacrifices ward off no-more times.'

'It doesn't work, does it? He's in custody.'

'He's been framed by your pig friends. He really was here with us the night that weatherman was killed. I was right beside him.'

'What night was that?' Caroline didn't answer. Jess asked, 'What day is it?'

'Doesn't matter,' said Caroline.

It would matter in court. It mattered right now. Jess couldn't believe the alibi no matter how genuinely Caroline gave it.

'It's our fault he's in prison. He warned us it would fail if we didn't believe enough.'

The circularity of Caroline's reasoning was stifling. Jess had run out of arguments. Time to beg. 'Please. For Delphi's sake. Just come with me and I'll make it all all right somehow.'

Caroline shook her twitchy head again. Unmoved by Jess's urgency.

'I can help you be old Caroline again.' Jess bent to put her arms around her friend.

Caroline nestled her head against Jess's waist. 'It's too late, Jess. It's all decided. Old Caroline's dead.'

'You heard her.' String Bean was back. She grabbed Delphi by her chubby hand. 'What's done is done. So sod off. And you,' she gestured at Caroline. 'There's pots need washing.'

One last try. 'Caroline?'

Caroline Mansfield, her sixth-form friend, the girl who'd fancied the head boy and was sick after her first shandy, didn't even look at her as she walked away.

Eden placed his briefcase on the passenger seat. Sat back. About to turn the key in the ignition, he detected movement in his rear-view mirror. He waited like a good detective.

The car park was quiet. The floodlights threw intensely bright circles on the dark ground. He'd seen something. A twig-like limb put down and withdrawn around the side of the nick.

The leg returned. Three more followed. Darling trotted into the car park.

Squeezers emerged. He slunk across the road and clung to the wall of the police station. Watching, Eden was treated to a poor man's *Bourne Identity*. Squeezers tiptoed, his finger to his lips. He stopped and bent to put his finger to the dog's lips.

Reaching the door of the station, Squeezers pulled a plastic bag from under his trench coat. He carefully placed the something on the step and minced at speed towards the car park exit.

Eden stepped out of his car. 'All right, what's going on?'

'Nothing bad, sir. Just my evening constitutional. Making sure my Darling here gets a stretch of her legs. Nothing suspicious or bad in any way, you'll find.'

'You take your constitutional in the police station car park?'

'I like the ambiance.'

'What's in the bag you just put on the step?'

'Did I put a bag? Did I? I didn't notice, sir. On the step, sir? Maybe I'm losing my marbles.' Squeezers knocked his head with his knuckles. 'I'm not getting any younger, you know.'

'None of us are.' Eden closed his car door. Gently. Squeezers was as skittish as a pigeon. 'Let's you and me go inside and see what you've delivered.'

Squeezers froze on the spot. 'I will, sir. But,' he blinked rapidly, 'I didn't do it.'

'What didn't you do, Squeezers?'

'The eyes. In the box. Horrible they are, horrible. All covered in blood and bits. I found them in the playground round the back of Conscience Lane. On the roundabout. But it wasn't me that took them out of his head, sir. I swear on my life.' He looked down at his dog, who looked trustingly back. 'On my Darling's life.'

Darling raised her ears at the mention of her name.

Eden slipped on a pair of plastic gloves he plucked from, appropriately enough, the glove compartment. Carefully, he picked up the bag and extracted a small wooden box. With a pen from his lapel pocket, he opened its lid. He frowned. With a sigh, he asked, 'Squeezers, where are the eyes?'

'Before you get angry, Mr Eden sir, in her defence, Darling was very hungry when we found them.'

'Oh God,' said Eden.

Darling licked her lips.

Chapter 23

TOO CRAZY FOR MANSON

Still Monday 30 May

'Okay Squeezers,' said Eden. 'The recorder's running. Jess is here. I'm all ears. Nice and slow. No pressure. Just explain, in your own words, how you came to find the box.'

Squeezers' voice was forty-a-day-for-forty-years raspy. 'It was a dark and stormy night. Only it was morning. This morning. Around seven a.m., I believe, sir. I was taking Darling for her morning walk round the playing field. Not another soul to be seen. Darling became restless and started pulling me towards the playground. She's an elegant lady but strong. She pulled me towards the roundabout. On the roundabout lay a box. I thought there might be jewellery in it, something I could sell, I mean, take directly to you, Detective Inspector Sergeant sir. But what I saw sent a shiver right through me, sir. I was shook to me core.'

DC Knott fingered her notes. 'Why's your dog called Darling?'

The question confused Squeezers.

Eden didn't want a confused Squeezers. 'It's just a name, Knott,' he said. 'Let's focus on the box, shall we? Squeezers, it rained overnight. Was the box wet?'

'Yes, sir. I do believe it was. Or was it? Yes. It definitely was. I think.'

Knott butted in. 'If you were so shocked when you opened the box, why'd you eat the eyes?'

Eden curled his fingers into a fist. 'Knott. He didn't eat the eyes. The dog ate the eyes.'

Knott was on a roll. A peculiar roll. 'Why were you walking your dog so early? In a children's play area to boot?'

'For God's sake, Knott. He was walking his dog like dozens of people do every day. I'll ask the questions, okay?'

Knott eyed Jess, who was careful to hide her pleasure at this exchange.

'You opened the box,' encouraged Eden. 'What did you see?'

'Two eyeballs, sir. There were straggly bits coming off them, covered in blood. Horrible it was.'

'Before Darling ate them, did you get a chance to see the colour of the eyes?'

'I think they were blue, sir. But I can't be sure.'

'Shane Harper had blue eyes,' said Jess.

'Why didn't you bring in the box immediately? Why wait, and then try to dump it on the step?'

Squeezers' face was awash with panic. 'I never done it, sir. Is that what you think? I wouldn't do something like that. I know I don't always do right, but never something to hurt a person.'

'If you were innocent, why did you wait?'

Squeezers' eyes filled up. 'I was scared. When Darling ate them, I knew I'd be in trouble. She's always getting me into trouble. I wish sometimes I'd never married her.'

Nobody commented. Nobody felt able to.

DC Knott seized her opportunity. 'Where were you on the night of Friday the twenty-seventh?'

'I wasn't nowhere, miss.'

'Help me out here, Squeezers,' said Eden. 'All you have to do is say where you were on Friday night. Druid's Head? Seven Stars?'

Squeezers hung his head.

'If you won't tell me, I can't help you.'

A knock at the door made Squeezers jump. A uniformed officer leant in.

'Sarge, you may want to have a look at this CCTV we've got.'

'Not now.' Eden was gruff.

'No, really, Sarge. I think you should.'

Eden sighed. 'Go on.'

A laptop was placed on the table. On the screen was grainy footage from a garden centre security camera. Two fuzzy individuals were easy to identify as Squeezers and his sometimes cohort Ryan. They were attempting to load barrels onto a pickup trunk. The barrels dropped. Rolled. Smashed. None made it onto the truck.

Squeezers attempted insouciance.

'Kidbury Nurseries reported a break-in on Friday night. Said several barrels of weedkiller had been disturbed,' said the officer.

'Weedkiller? What would you want with that, Squeezers?' asked Eden.

Squeezers spoke low. 'If Beefy Dave finds out I've talked to you there's no knowing what'll happen to me. I don't know what he wanted it for, sir. He never tells me.' Squeezers looked shiftily about the room. 'Says I'm better off if I don't know.'

'Look at the time stamp,' said Jess. 'The twenty-seventh, at twenty-one thirty.'

'How long were you there?' asked Eden.

The officer answered for Squeezers. 'Eight hours, Sarge. Practically till daybreak.'

'You took eight hours to *not* steal weedkiller?' asked Eden.

'We fell asleep,' sobbed Squeezers. 'Them barrels is heavy and we were knackered. Please don't nick me, sir. Beefy Dave'll kill me.'

Eden sighed. 'Squeezers, you're the weirdest petty criminal I've ever come across. You're lucky I'm busy or I'd nick you for this, but you didn't take anything, after all. In any event, what we have here is a solid alibi for the murder window. You're free to go.'

'Thank you, sir.' Squeezers stood and bowed. 'I can't tell you how much I appreciate your kindness and your exquisite—'

'Yes, all right. Off you go.' Eden shook Squeezers' hand. Looked around for something to wipe his hand on. 'One more thing. The roundabout. Was it still or moving when you found the box?'

'Moving.' Squeezers, for once, was certain.

When he'd dribbled out, Eden said to nobody in particular, 'The killer watched him take the box.'

'Yikes,' said Jess. It was a word she hadn't said since she was eight. It fitted the bill.

'Please tell me you've had a breakthrough with the symbols.'

'I'd have to lie.'

Karen made a little noise. It was a cheeky little noise. Eloquent.

'May I see this new box? The one Squeezers brought in.'

'Being processed.' Eden seemed too tired to speak in whole sentences. 'No inlays. No decoration. But it's yew. Finely made.'

'By the same person who made the first one?'

'Without a shadow of a doubt.'

'Sir,' said Karen. 'What if the gaps between the murders is a code, too?'

'Not another one.' Eden ran a hand through his hair and almost managed to untidy it. 'What was it, five days between murders one and two. Then seven between two and three. Not enough information there to help us. If it was the same amount of days, maybe.'

'Pan said anything useful?' Jess had told Eden about her conversation with Caroline.

'Pan's said nothing at all. Meditates apparently. And annoys the hell out of the custody officer.'

Karen sauntered up to Jess. Head back. 'You're so keen on your witchy woman, Hecate, but you missed something.'

'What?' Jess could see up Karen's nose.

'Shane Harper was draped over the market cross. He was in the shape of a cross. Another of your double crosses.'

'You're right,' laughed Jess. It was her cue to lay the business card on the table.

'Strophalos?' Karen had three goes before she pronounced it properly.

'It's a wheel that spins. People used to make them, not just draw them. They put a semi-precious stone in the middle and spun them. It would make a *whoop-whoop* noise. Useful, apparently, for attracting love.'

'Huh,' said Karen, whose hairstyle suggested she was above romance.

'Love wasn't a soppy romantic notion to the ancients,' said Jess. She felt a vague ache as she said, 'It was powerful. A force to be reckoned with. Majestic.' She waggled her shoulders. 'The strophalos can change the weather. Conjure a storm out of nowhere. Make it snow in July.'

'All that on a business card,' said Karen.

'I don't know about Hellcat and Hecate,' said Eden. 'These aren't hard facts, Jess.'

'I'll tell you what is a hard fact. How can the manageress vouch for Unthank never passing the main foyer when the EasySleep Inn has an automated reception desk from eleven p.m.?'

'Knott,' said Eden.

'I'm on it, sir.'

When she'd gone, Jess said, 'I keep returning to the trees on box one. They're so bold. And according to their symbolic code, they're offering clarity and wisdom.'

'Look at them from another angle,' said Eden. 'Walk round them, as it were.'

'Well, they have different names in Ogham. The ash, for instance, is . . .' She screwed up her eyes. 'Edad. It's called edad. The rowan is called luis.'

They said it together, as if it was part of a song they both knew. 'Luis Unthank.'

'The trees *are* speaking to us,' gasped Jess. Ancient history had leapt off the page and into this lamp-lit office.

'It can't be used in court, Jess. It's circumstantial at best.'

'But it's *something.*'

'It is.' Eden raised a styrofoam cup to his lips. Grimaced. Put it back down.

'I'm going to visit Caroline again. I'll keep going until she breaks and tells me what really goes on there. I can't believe she's toeing the line even though there's a murderer at large.'

'Look at Charlie Manson. He controlled that gang of his even from prison. Had a vice-like grip on their minds.' Eden paused. 'Did he die?'

'He did die,' said Jess. 'God rest his 'orrible little soul.'

'Do you remember he got engaged in prison? He was about eighty-two and she was twenty-seven.'

'Yikes.' Twice in one day that word had come in useful.

'He ditched her. Said she was crazy.'

'Typical man. It's always the woman who's nuts, even when you're Charlie Manson.' Jess had a thought. 'All the victims are men.'

'I did notice.' Eden was arch. It didn't suit him. 'Unfortunately that's about the only link. We can't rule out women victims. Statistically, serial-killer targets even out at about fifty–fifty gender wise.'

'Gender equality. So serial killers aren't all bad.'

She had a perfectly good home. Four stout walls, fitted carpets, a conservatory for heaven's sake, and yet Jess found herself walking past her car, to patrol the town, alone, in the dark.

She was, she told herself, investigating. Details mattered. *I have*, she thought, *an eye for the miniature*. Jess might notice some tiny fact that would crack the case.

She liked the thought of how much Eden would hate that phrase.

Country towns are so much darker than cities; night falls harder. There was no pastel gloaming tonight.

The high street was silent. Castle Kidbury was a creature of habit. Only the minimart and the garage kept anything like big-city hours. The other shops and services obeyed a call of the wild at around the same point of the day. Closed signs. Lights off. She had the thoroughfares to herself.

A curfew, self-imposed, kept strollers and dog walkers indoors. Nobody wanted to end up crucified. Even the press pack were invisible, presumably drinking Eddie's cellar dry at the Royal Seven Stars.

DI Phillips's advice to the community was to lay low, 'until the present situation is resolved'. Jess scoffed at such a lily-livered response to the 'situation', despite knowing that if the Judge was more welcoming, she'd be snug indoors, like her neighbours.

Crossing the market square, her Doc Martens slapped on the ancient cobbles. A roaring noise, like a dragon, turned out to be a lorry. Out of place, it hurried past her en route to the motorway.

As she patrolled Fore Street – patrolling being so much more noble than skulking – she heard a smaller noise, the silver clink of keys, from Dunch Lane.

Mr Kuzbari was shutting up shop. Jess watched, waiting for him to turn towards Fore Street. Despite her bravado, she'd welcome the company.

Rattling the door to check it was locked, Kuzbari hurried in the opposite direction, towards the dimly lit end of the lane, until he was abruptly swallowed by the night.

Jess took off after him. Why, she wasn't entirely sure. It wasn't suspicion, it was instinct. She didn't want to lose the only other human figure in the landscape.

Curiosity also played its part. There was nothing, except for back doors and bins, at the end of Dunch Lane.

Kuzbari's dim outline turned right, out of sight, and

she dashed to the corner. There he was, up ahead. It was darker here, with no kindly shopfronts lighting her way. The buildings closed in over her head; on one side the blank cliff face of a warehouse, on the other the unlovely rears of the Fore Street shops.

Rubbish bags lolled. There was a summery stink in the cooling air. Kuzbari was in a hurry.

Jess remembered to be frightened. Three people had ended up dead since her return to Castle Kidbury. The shadows might shelter a killer. She twirled, paranoid, checking behind her, and when she faced forwards once more, Kuzbari was gone. The cluster of fire escapes and grotty back entrances – such grim contrast to the polite shopfronts – offered no clue.

Jess stood still, listening hard. She heard a rustle, a squelch, the yowl of a prowling tom. Then she heard something else. A rhythmic metallic creak. The moon came out from behind a cloud and she saw a silhouette raise slightly above the roofline, then dip out of sight.

'You're a brave girl.' A voice behind Jess. She wheeled around.

'You're a brave boy,' she told Unthank, who had taken shape in the dark. She wondered if her voice shook. Her knees had certainly got the memo.

'Not bothering with the curfew?'

There was no need to answer him. Jess saved her manners for people who reciprocated. 'Do you often hang around bins?'

'I'm taking the back way.'

'From where?' asked Jess. 'To where?'

'From somewhere that's none of your business to somewhere else that's none of your business.' He took a step towards her.

Jess loathed herself for the way she jumped.

'Sorry.' He didn't sound it. 'Female friends tell me men have no idea how vulnerable women feel on the streets at night. I'll be a good boy,' he said. 'I'll keep my distance.'

Jess glanced up the alley. Padlocked doors. Not enough light. She'd lost her bearings. Was she at the back of The Buttonhole or Silver River? 'The funeral was three days ago. What keeps a hipster here? Castle Kidbury's always been boring; now it's boring and dangerous.'

'Nothing boring about danger,' said Unthank. His eyes were impossible to see in the dark. 'This place is inspirational. You're from here, so you don't get it.'

'Come on, you design groovy brands. This place is Nowheresville. Unless you're inspired by the EasySleep Inn logo.'

'You're good at sneering. The EasySleep Inn logo is a modern classic.'

'Eh?' Jess thought of the yellow, shakily drawn house on the front of all EasySleep Inns.

'It tells you what you're buying. A space out of the rain. A rest for the weary traveller.'

'The logo has a little chimney with smoke curling out of it. EasySleep Inns are more like barracks. Horrible carpet. Thin curtains. Not homely.'

Unthank pursed his lips. He seemed to feel the same

way about Jess as she felt about him; their mutual good-will would fit on the head of a pin. 'I'm walking away. Slowly. If I hear a scream, I'll come and rescue you.' He turned away. 'Or not,' he said over his shoulder.

'And if *I* hear a scream,' called Jess, 'I'll come and rescue *you*.'

The silence returned. Jess picked her way down the alley. She stopped at a rickety door with 'KEEP OUT' painted in hostile capitals.

Easing through, looking neurotically around her, Jess crossed a shadowy backyard. An iron ladder was embedded into the building. She put out a hand. Cold, slippery metal.

She looked up at where the ladder poked into the air above the roof. She knew that Mary would scale the ladder in a heartbeat, but Jess was more a creature of the mind than the body.

One foot, then another. *No looking down*, Jess counselled herself. She looked down. It made no sense to be crawling up the side of a building like a human fly. Her stomach rebelled.

Grateful to reach the top, she poked her head over the parapet. A roof, flat and bland. A tatty sofa facing away from her. Smoke scything upwards.

Weed. The smell reminded her of student lodgings, where even the mice smoke dope.

'Care to join me?' The voice came from the sagging sofa.

Jess heaved herself gracelessly onto the roof. 'I make a rubbish stalker.'

Kuzbari straightened up, turned his head. His smile had film-star glamour. His colouring suited the midnight smell of his joint. 'Come. Sit.'

It was impossible to roost on the edge of the dilapidated sofa. It absorbed Jess until she was almost lying down.

'Care for some?' Kuzbari held out the joint.

'I don't get on with dope. Makes my arms feel as if they're too long.'

He laughed, snorting smoke. 'How do you like my roof terrace?'

'Short on mod cons.' Jess looked around her at discarded planks of wood and broken flowerpots. 'But it has a certain *je ne sais quoi*.'

'It's the view that makes it special.'

Jess craned her neck. 'Hmm.' She was sceptical that the panorama of Castle Kidbury chimney pots merited the climb.

'Not that way.' Kuzbari pointed upwards. '*That* way.'

Jess gave herself up to the sky, resting her head on the back of the sofa.

'Every night, a free show.' Kuzbari's voice was a smile.

'Tonight's especially clear.' Jess thought of the last time she stargazed. With Rupert. She couldn't imagine Pandora lying on her back on wet grass.

'See over there,' said Kuzbari, his voice a low rumble. 'That bright trio of stars. They're called—'

'Vega, Altair and Deneb.'

After a slight pause, Kuzbari said, 'Sorry. Most people aren't that interested in stars.'

'I like their constancy,' murmured Jess. 'Deneb is a swan, according to the people who named the stars.'

'She swims down the Milky Way every night.'

'But never gets anywhere. Do you come here often?' Jess laughed. 'I've never actually said that before.'

'I do come here often.' Kuzbari didn't get the joke. 'Most nights, when it's temperate. I have one of these.' He held up his spliff. 'I look at the stars and I think.'

'What do you think about?' Jess pulled her knees up under her chin and half turned towards Kuzbari.

'The vastness of everything.' He settled back, his regal profile pointed at the sky. 'The smallness of me.'

Deep stuff for a tatty roof. 'Depending on your mood,' said Jess, 'that could make you feel plugged-in or deeply lonely.'

'It always has the same effect on me.' Kuzbari's voice was measured, giving no clue to which he meant. 'This sky, you see, stretches over the entire world. The moon hangs over everybody.'

Jess caught on. 'The same moon looks down on Syria and Castle Kidbury.'

He looked at her. Grateful. 'Exactly so.'

Something surged in Jess's chest. This was Kuzbari's way of communing with the people he'd left behind. His mother.

'It also shines on Peckham,' said Kuzbari, lightly, lampooning himself. 'On my wife.'

'Does it help? The moon?'

Hecate had followed Jess up the metal ladder. Goddess of the moon, she was also associated with liminal places. Thresholds. Doorways. As queen of the underworld, she stood between life and death. As an adult child returned to the family home, Jess was an expert in liminal places. In being in neither one place nor the other.

The roof was liminal, too. Between the muddy earth and the placid sky.

'I try to stare at the moon and think of nothing. To will myself to my mother's side. To tell her, somehow, that I'm coming for her.' Kuzbari reached over and pressed the joint into the tarmac. 'Which may not be true, but …'

Platitudes gave Jess hives, so she said nothing. She hoped the quality of her silence might help.

'And you, Jess? Why are you hanging around these dangerous streets on your own?'

Hardly as dangerous as the streets Kuzbari left behind. 'Home's the place where, when you have to go there, they have to let you in,' said Jess. 'But I don't want to go there. Not right now.'

'I would cut off my right hand to go home.'

'I didn't mean … That was crass.'

'No. Home *should* be taken for granted.'

'Until that's no longer possible.' Jess would have liked to take this man's hand. She didn't dare. Kuzbari was too correct for such a gesture. What's more, she distrusted her motive: his beauty had power. 'My home, well, without my mum in it, it's not like it used to be.'

'*Allah yerhama*,' said Kuzbari, with a dip of his head.

Jess recognised it as a condolence. She had a flash of

her mother in startling 3D and cleared her throat. 'Dad, well, he's not suited to solo parenting.' It struck Jess how childish it was to expect parenting at her age. But a dam had been breached; Jess's resentments tumbled through. 'He disapproves of everything I do. Or don't do. He's got some woman installed in Mum's kitchen.' Referring to Bogna as 'some woman' wasn't fair, but it popped the blister of Jess's myriad resentments; the sting felt good. 'My brother's grown up to be a stranger, and saddled me with a sister-in-law who measures out her life in spa days. And this town's gone crazy. My old school friend's waiting, *hoping*, for the apocalypse.' Rupert was next on her list of grievances, but Jess stopped short. 'Sorry, Jesus, where did all that come from?'

'I don't wish to be presumptuous . . .' started Kuzbari.

Uh-oh, thought Jess. Was he just another bossy male after all?

'Our true enemy in life is discontentment. There are troubles enough along the way, but discontentment we make ourselves. Your father, his housekeeper, they may frustrate you. But these are merely deflections. Jessica, family are not our friends. We are bonded whatever we do, whether we care to admit it or not. And you already know how it feels to lose a parent. Your father is not a well man. Allow him to be closer to you. I believe a little of your discontentment will fade.'

Jess blinked, a little ashamed.

'You are home. Your mother may not be there in person, that cannot be helped. But she will always be there in you. Your home, your father, the memory of your mother ... these are all things you should be grateful for.' He pressed his hand gently on hers. His skin was warm. 'Allow yourself to be at home, Jessica.'

The long turn into the main thoroughfare.

The vet's.

The medical centre.

The long-stay car park.

The bridge.

Kidbury Road.

Harebell House.

She was home. Kuzbari didn't realise that her house felt like a morgue much of the time. She let herself in.

Music. Whooping. Barking. Laughter she recognised.

'When did you get here?' Jess found Mary in the warm kitchen.

'About an hour ago.' Mary let Bogna out of her arms and the woman spun, dizzy, onto a chair. She was crying with laughter.

'We dance,' she managed.

At the table, Susannah sat by the Judge. They were flushed. Like children at a party.

A hug. Mary's smell of mints and faint body odour and shampoo. The radio was turned down.

'Me and Suze have been talking.' Mary ruffled Susannah's hair.

Susannah smiled, pleased with herself. Everybody was awarded a nickname around Mary.

'Why back so soon?' asked Jess.

'The rage room's kaput. Me landlord put his foot

down. A hen party booked in. Things got out of hand. There was a small fire. So I've been kicked out and now I'm staying here.'

'Dad?' Jess checked with the Judge.

'Why ask me?' he replied.

'Sure, it's all sorted,' interjected Mary. 'I can stay as long as I like. But never mind all that,' said Mary energetically, 'Susannah popped in to pick up one of the kids' toys and she's been telling me all about Stephen's shenanigans.'

'Really?' Jess knew Mary lived to meddle. 'What shenanigans?'

'You tell her, Suze.'

'It's probably nothing. Just the stuff we discussed at the spa,' started Susannah. Tears threatened. She shredded a tissue. 'He's been working very late.'

'Working late,' said Mary. Darkly.

'And he's been very grumpy.'

'Grumpy,' repeated Mary. She gave a disapproving wobble of the head.

'He won't explain all the extra work. He's still buying new clothes and hiding them.'

Mary threw her arms up. 'He won't say. He's hiding new clothes. This fella clearly has another woman on the go. I've told Susannah to leave him. Take the kids and get out. She can stay here.'

The Judge looked at the ceiling.

Jess gawped. 'You told her *what*?'

'She's got to leave him, Jess. Stephen's a total bastard.'

'I think I'll go to my study,' interjected the Judge. 'The oestrogen count's very high in here.'

291

'You can't order a woman to leave her husband.' Jess was exasperated. 'You don't know he's having an affair. All you know is he's working late, buying clothes and is in a bad mood. And that's my brother you're calling a bastard.'

'Sounds like he's being naughty boy to me,' said Bogna. She had gravitated to the sink. 'You know men. Always sneaking about, waving their little winkies around. They can't help it, isn't it?'

'I'm most certainly going to my study.' The Judge headed for the hallway. 'I need some Vivaldi to cleanse my brain.'

'Susannah,' said Jess. 'Ignore my friend. Try talking to Stephen.'

'Every time I try, he gets defensive and walks off,' sniffed Susannah.

'I can't believe I'm saying this.' Jess was about to dispense classic *Woman's Own* advice. 'Book a table for dinner at his favourite restaurant. Make yourself up. Put on a dress he likes. Then tell him how you feel over dessert. My brother has his faults, but I don't believe for one moment he's having an affair. And *you*!' Jess shot a look at Mary. 'You're nobody's idea of a relationship mentor.'

Susannah was despatched home. Bogna murmured something about killing a chicken. And Mary was sent upstairs like a naughty schoolgirl.

'Can't believe I missed a feckin' murder.' Mary stretched out with Moose on Jess's bed.

Only half listening, Jess was on the rug with a Double Decker and a book about Boudicca. 'Yeah, you really missed out, it was great.'

'Was it?'

'No, *obviously*. Someone died. You seem to have forgotten how you felt after Gavin.'

'Fair dos,' conceded Mary. She broke off from tending to Moose's ears to cross herself. 'You shagged Rupert yet?'

Jess raised her eyes from the book and returned them to the page. 'I'm not even answering that.'

'He's got *plenty* of juice in him, that one. If you don't jump him soon, some other bitch will.'

'Thankfully some other bitch *has*. His ex is all over him. Pandora Smith. She's a supermodel, or a mega-model or something.'

'*The* Pandora Smith? You're kidding. She's awesome!'

'You're too old to say awesome.'

'She's no competition, though. Poor eejit's cracked about you.'

'Pandora's welcome to him.'

Mary propped herself up. She seemed thunderstruck. 'Jaysus, Jess Castle, you're jealous.'

'I'm not. Just disappointed. I didn't think he was that shallow. I mean, fancying a *model*. That's so obvious.'

'Jealous!' Mary fell back onto the bed. '*So* jealous.'

Chapter 24

THE DEEP END

Tuesday 31 May

Jess is gasping.

Drowning.

She's fighting hard to breathe.

Swimsuits, empty swimsuits, all around.

Red. Striped. Green.

One yellow one.

She tries to keep sight of it.

Her air is used up.

This time the water is winning.

Her limbs close down.

She can't see for blood.

Jess woke up.

The dream meant business. Could you really die in a dream, or was that just an old wives' tale?

*

It was too early in the day to spot a Mary.

The house smelt good as Jess padded through it. Different to the way it smelt when Mum ran the kitchen. It felt mildly disloyal to enjoy Bogna's regime.

The empty pool was a deficit. A nought. A big hole in the ground that drew Jess to it. She sat in the deep end, Moose at her side. Both of them deep in thought.

As ever, her thoughts slid first to the boxes and the symbols on dead flesh. Those dynamic, secretive little images. Teasing her. Holding out the truth like a stripper dangles a bra. Jess knew she had the knowledge to unlock the code, but something stood in the way.

A bleat. Urich stood at the side of the pool. His strange eyes fixed on them.

Moose grunted. He didn't like the goat; the goat didn't like him.

'Want to come and join us, Urich?'

Apparently Jess spoke fluent Goat. The creature dawdled, in its knock-kneed way, towards the sloping shallow end. Hooves clicking on the tiles, horns nodding.

'Jesus, you smell,' said Jess.

Urich was difficult to insult. He nosed about, sniffing leaves. Moose watched him, his lovely brown eyes full of contempt.

Cross-legged, Jess closed her eyes and concentrated. The murders kept her mind off herself; she offered a silent prayer of contrition to the men who'd been crucified simply to give her something to do.

'Urich, what would you do if you were me?'

Urich ignored her. He was savouring a crisp packet. 'I'm a lecturer with no one to lecture. I'm verging on unemployable. Instead of some solid research, or teaching, I'm chasing hippies around campsites and standing by while an old school friend descends into addiction. As for me and Dad, we're ...' She wasn't sure of the word. Estranged was too strong. She hoped. 'We don't get on, Urich.' Kuzbari's advice was hard to put into practice. 'I can't *talk* to him. And I certainly can't talk to Mum.'

Jess slung an arm around Moose. Sturdy and blond, he was a bridge to the old days. He had known her mother. She'd been a soft touch for titbits. 'You miss her too, I bet.' She looked at the goat. 'You're right, Moose. That Urich doesn't give a toss.'

Urich, as if to emphasise the toss he didn't give, belched.

'Pan's safely put away. That's good. And yet ...'

The goat chewed. The dog panted.

'Plus there's Rupert,' Jess reminded them. 'He hasn't texted since Pandora turned up. No reason why he should, but you know, I thought we were friends.' Jess turned over her feelings the way she turned over the symbols. An outraged sense of dispossession. Disappointment. As bewildering as the boxes, Jess's attitude to Rupert changed from day to day. It was an unanswered question, one that edged nearer and nearer.

Uproar at the house. A clatter. A door slamming. Bogna racing out onto the terrace and shrieking, 'Jess! Jess! Quick!'

Up out of the pool, along the hedge corridor, up the lawn. Moose and Urich sprinted after Jess, whose pulse jumped in her throat. 'What? What is it?'

'Jimmy. He is collapsed.' Bogna followed on slippered feet as Jess dashed past her.

'Dad,' she said pointlessly as her feet squeaked on the hall parquet. 'Dad, please,' she whispered, rounding the door of his study.

'He stands up. Then he falls.' Bogna bent over the Judge. 'He is very quiet.'

'I don't like it.' Jess kneeled.

The Judge was stretched out. He'd taken a table down with him, one of the round ones her mother dotted about the house. Silver photograph frames lay face down, as did the Judge. A large vase – inherited, ugly – had smashed. Chrysanthemums lay across the back of his head, and his shirt was wet.

'Recovery position.' Jess couldn't tell if his chest was rising and falling. Her father's eyes were shut. She had the unwelcome feeling that she was at a sharp edge of her life. A hinge. 'Roll him with me, Bogna. Gently.'

'Maybe we should not touch him.' Bogna backed away.

Jess had to see his face. To check that he was still there. She took hold of him, the man she rarely touched, and turned him over.

He's so heavy, she thought. As if his thin frame was full of boulders. 'Have you called an ambulance, Bogna?' Jess had to repeat herself before Bogna answered no. 'Ring one now!' Jess's voice was a screech.

'I – is it nine nine nine?' Bogna scrabbled about ineffectually.

'Take my place. I'll do it.' It seemed vital that somebody hold onto the Judge. Tether him. His colour was bad. 'Quickly, please,' she said unnecessarily to the emergency services operator.

'He's waking up. *Dzięki Bogu*.' Bogna let out a loud breath.

'Dad. Dad!' Jess refrained from slapping his cheek. 'Are you okay?' she said, instantly regretting it. She imagined him thinking, deep in his stupefied brain, *Do I look okay?*

Between them, the women helped the Judge to a chair. He blinked. He coughed. He was confused and it was hard for Jess to witness.

'No fuss,' he said, as the ambulance arrived. 'Not the damn hospital.'

The damn hospital was where his wife had taken a long time to die. The Judge got his way. Within an hour he was beneath his own duvet, cross-faced, listening to Dr Rasmussen pontificate from the end of the bed.

'Do you hear me, James?' Rasmussen was tall, wide, and had been the same age for all of Jess's life. 'No more of these bike rides. Gentle exercise only.'

He'd fainted. That was all. Jess had liquefied with relief. The ACE inhibitors the Judge took for his aortic stenosis had lowered his blood pressure to the extent that he keeled over.

'And for God's sake, feed him properly, Bogna.'

'I keep him alive with my cooking!' Bogna rounded

298

on the doctor, who took a step back on the rug. 'Bloody cheek, mate,' she said, hotly.

'All I'm saying is—'

'You're saying I should feed him Uncle-Ben-two-minutes-ping!' Bogna's impression of a microwave made the medic jump.

'I'm saying that my patient is fully aware of the treatment options open to him. If he took advantage of them rather than cycling and eating organic this, that and the other, he might see an improvement in his health.' Dr Rasmussen clicked his bag shut, made haste to the bedroom door. 'Nobody lives forever!' he reminded them cheerfully.

'*Nobody lives forever*, isn't it.' Bogna impersonated the doctor as Jess helped her wash potatoes dug from what had been Harriet's rose garden.

The tubers were gnarly, unlovely. They'd never make the grade in a supermarket. Jess patted them with a tea towel, lovingly, as if they were toddlers fresh from the bath. Ugly toddlers.

'What does he know?' Bogna's outrage was limitless.

'Quite a lot, I should think. Especially,' ventured Jess, 'about doctoring.'

Bogna made a Polish noise of derision. 'What does he know about our Jimmy?' The sentence ended on a strangled note. Jess, who was about to say that Dr Rasmussen had been the Castle family doctor since before she was born, turned and saw tears racing lemming-like off Bogna's chin.

'Bogna,' she said tenderly. 'Hey. Come on. Dad's all right. The doc said so.'

'I worry.' Bogna's face was contorted. 'He was so sad after your mummy went. He is man who needs softness. Because he is not soft.'

'You love him, Bogna.'

'Not like boyfriend-girlfriend.' Bogna pulled a disgusted face. 'I have enough of that slop with my ex-husband. I love Jimmy like family.'

'He's grand,' said Mary, slipping out of the Judge's study. 'Roses in his cheeks again. I told him a couple of jokes, cheered him right up.'

And shocked him to the core of his being. 'Thanks, Mary.'

'Jess, maybe . . .' Mary laid a hand on Jess's arm. 'Let him have tonight before you go in all guns blazing, eh?'

'This needs to be said. Don't worry. I'll stay calm.'

'Yeah. Right.' Mary left her to it.

The Judge sat at his desk. He stopped writing when his daughter stole in. He looked abashed. 'Jess, thank you. It must have been—'

'Dad, Dr Rasmussen told me. About the . . .' she looked at a biro scrawl on her hand, 'the transcatheter aortic valve implantation you refuse to have.'

'Taking everything into account, I've decided to wait and see.'

'Wait and see what?'

'What the next few months bring, health-wise.'

'So you're the only person who gets to be consulted?'

'I do own the heart in question, Jessica.'

'Do you think you're God, Dad? Because this self-ishness is truly awe-inspiring.' Jess rushed on, allowing the Judge no opportunity to speak. 'The doc described your aortic stenosis as severe. There's only way for that to go. Untreated, it gets worse. Eventually, it leads to death.' To Hecate's underworld. 'Will you think about it?' *For me*, she wanted to add, but couldn't. 'I'll go. I didn't mean to harsh your mellow.'

'Harsh my what?'

By the jotter on his desk, something glinted red in the lamplight.

'The fox.' Jess reached out and picked up the ugly porcelain animal. It had cross eyes. 'Mum's fox,' she said. 'How did it get here?'

'No idea.' The Judge was bent over his pen again. 'Must have been Bogna moving things around. Didn't notice it there.'

'Shall I put it somewhere else?' Jess held the fox to her chest. 'I know you always hated it.'

'No need. No need.' The Judge waved his hand. 'Just leave it.'

Bogna wasn't permitted near this inner sanctum. The fox was there by the Judge's choice. Jess put it down.

'Ever heard of something called a taxi?'

Mary tutted from the passenger seat. 'Feck off, you ingrate. Don't I keep this car in good nick for you? The least you can do is give me a lift now and again.'

That was true. But Jess was depleted.

'Step on it,' said Mary. 'I want to get to the Druid's Head for happy hour.' The pub gleefully ignored the suggested curfew and was packed every night. 'It's a two for one, so if I buy six Guinnesses I'll get them for the price of three.'

'What are you, the Chancellor of the Exchequer of Drunk Land?'

'I'm a girl on a mission.'

'You're a nightmare.' Mary pushed endlessly at boundaries, but they seemed to be elastic. Jess gave her enough rope to hang herself, and Mary merrily did just that. But Jess never walked away – Mary's virtues were as blatant as her faults.

As Mary scrolled through her beloved gossip sites on her phone, pausing now and then to roar 'Cellulite!' or 'Cokehead!', Jess recalled nights when she'd rung Mary at three a.m., when she'd cried the proverbial river on Mary's shoulder, when Mary had uncoiled a rescue rope to the bottom of the deep well where Jess sat navel-gazing.

She stole a look at her friend. Short, yet with the strength of ten men, Mary was a conundrum. 'Your hair's getting a bit haywire.'

'Yeah. Needs a trim. Should have done it in Exeter. I don't think your Castle Kidbury salons can handle Afro.' Mary's mouth dropped open. 'Bastard,' she shouted at her phone.

'Why do you read those stupid sites? They only wind you up.'

'Look!' Mary held the screen in front of Jess. The car swerved. Jess swore. She pulled in.

'Don't do ... oh.' Jess took the phone from Mary and studied the thumbnail photo of Rupert. It was odd to see somebody she knew so well – *Do I?* she thought – reduced to a blurred collection of pixels in the *Daily Mail*.

'He's leaving some poncey restaurant with that Pandora.' Mary spat the name. She was no longer, it would seem, awestruck. 'Holding hands!' She was as scandalised as a Victorian spinster.

'Yeah, but, maybe he grabbed her hand to run past the paparazzi.' Jess had an urgent need to defend Rupert. To rewrite the sneering prose beneath the photo.

Mary read it out. '*Stunning Pandora Smith makes a speedy exit from a swanky W1 eatery with her old flame, provincial toff Rupert Lawson. Fellow diners said the pair looked very "cosy". "They only had eyes for each other," said a waiter.*'

'Who speaks like that?'

'They're *holding hands*.' Mary said it as if Rupert and Pandora were having sex in the street. 'And look at her. She's half naked.'

The dress *was* very low. 'It's a Stella McCartney design, according to the journalist.'

'It's not what I'd wear for an innocent dinner.'

'You always wear your combats.'

Mary treated Jess to a particularly hard stare. 'You're making excuses for him. I knew it. You *do* like him.'

'I don't, I just—'

'He's a heel, Jess. He's stringing you along.'

'He and Pandora are just friends.' Jess had insisted

the opposite until she saw proof. It was an odd moment to perform an about-face.

'Whatever.' Mary was scornful as Jess pulled away from the kerb. Usually Mary's powerful scorn was directed outwards and Jess could stand behind the searchlight. Now it was turned on her, and she was blinded. 'You can't stand posh boys. I've never met a not-posh Rupert. They simply don't make Ruperts in certain postcodes. Turns out he's riding his ex and you still defend him.'

'Rupert's not just a posh boy.' Jess braked at the lights on Fore Street. 'He's kind and he's funny and he's—'

'Leading you up the garden feckin' path.' Mary folded her arms across her sweatshirt. 'I would have bet my life savings that you and he would do the do.'

'You don't have any life savings.' Jess longed to tear away from the lights with a roar, but the Morris Traveller could only provide a polite clearing of the throat.

'Rupert's just another Hooray Henry.'

'He's not a . . .' Jess rubbed her temple. 'Can you just, you know, *shut up*, Mary?' When Mary opened her mouth, Jess shouted, 'For once! Just once, butt out!'

Mary was silent as the car trundled through the town. A baffled resentment rose off her like heat.

Outside the Druid's Head, Jess kept the motor running.

'You not coming in?' frowned Mary from the pavement.

'What's in there?' asked Jess, sullen.

'Beer. Fellas. The usual.'

'Exactly. Not in the mood.' Jess did a scrappy three-point turn as Mary watched. Jess wasn't good at being angry with Mary. She did her best, though, and didn't shout to her to call the local cabbie, or Jess herself, to get home. She neglected to even peek in the rear-view mirror until she reached the corner.

What she saw made her sit up. *Wasn't that* . . . It was. Unthank was holding the pub door open for Mary. All smiles. He inspected Mary's bottom as she passed, and then his eyes flicked to Jess's car. He gave a little wave.

She stuck her middle finger in the air.

Shit shit shit shit.

Those words helped. With the panic and the sense of failure and the disappointment of the dead.

The old ones were angry. He felt the tremors in the earth. The rumblings of their displeasure.

He had messed up. And this one was for the Goddess. Not much of an offering!

What came next? So many things could happen now, and all of them were bad.

He could still feel the crack as the box broke apart. He'd trodden it into the mud himself.

He had failed.

Chapter 25

DIRTY STOP-OUT

Wednesday 1 June

In an attempt to have her way with the LP display at the charity shop, Jess arrived early enough to have a few Richard-and-Doug free minutes. Or so she thought.

'Someone's keen.' Doug was rewinding a cassette of *Into the Woods*.

'There's hope for her yet, Doug,' said Richard.

'She'll never be Harriet,' said Doug.

'No I won't,' snapped Jess, shuffling the records into order.

'She got out of bed on the wrong side,' tutted Richard. 'Very touchy this morning.'

'Harriet was never touchy.'

'Takes after her father,' mouthed Richard, just loud enough for Jess to hear. 'You can have the first side of the Sondheim, Douglas. Then it's *La Cage*.'

'Shallow piffle,' spat Doug. 'No development. No real characterisation.'

'Can we play *GI Blues* by Elvis?' asked Jess, innocently.

'No!' It was a duet of horror.

'Heathen music,' declared Doug, fanning his face. 'All drums and hips.'

'I like heathens,' said Jess, arms full of vinyl.

The antique bell over the door chimed. Helena.

'Still on for your facial this afternoon, Richard?' she said. Bright as a button. 'You didn't confirm.'

'Sorry, petal,' replied Richard, sounding like a different person altogether. A nicer person. 'I'll be there, don't you worry.'

'Lovely. Morning Douglas, morning Jess!' Helena waved and retreated into Fore Street, trailing delicious but unsexy perfume.

Richard peered out of the window to be sure she'd gone. 'Do you know, Douglas, it still rankles with me that the parents of that boy got away scot-free.'

'It was a travesty.'

'You know, me, Doug, I never speak ill of the dead. But the boy had the gall to try and be a pop star. After everything that happened.'

'I'm bound to say the whole sorry tale would make a stunning libretto,' said Doug.

'Oh, you and your dark topics. That sort of gloom does *not* belong in musical theatre.'

'If it helps, I love *High School Musical*,' offered Jess.

'Madam, you go *too far*.' Doug made for the back office.

'See what you've done?' hissed Richard.

Jess dumped the record collection. 'Are you telling me you never bickered till I started here? You obviously both love it.'

'Well. Well. Well,' said Richard slowly. 'Now we know. Harriet would never have said such a thing.'

This time the bell above the door announced a stranger to Jess.

Richard knew her. 'Hello you!' He took the woman's elbow. She was tall. Dark. Over made-up.

A bit like a broom, thought Jess, *in a wig*.

'I need some more work blouses.' The broom moved to a rail of separates. 'EasySleep Inn are so stingy. They supply the suit but not the shirt.'

'We have a nice cotton,' said Richard. 'Sensual against the skin.'

'Steady on.' The broom had a raucous laugh. Jess warmed to her.

Placing *GI Blues* reverently in a plastic display case, Jess said, casually, 'You work at EasySleep? You must have met my mate who's staying there.'

'Probably. I'm the receptionist.' Broom studied a polyester pussy bow up close.

'He's got a memorable name. Unthank. Luis Unthank.' Jess tingled. This woman might drop some nugget she could carry, like an offering, to Eden. 'He's been at your hotel for a couple of weeks.'

'Not anymore.' Broom pulled out the blouse and held it against herself. 'Checked out a while ago. Last week sometime.' She glanced at Jess. 'Like you say, that name sticks in the mind.'

The doorbell chimed once again, this time offering up a breathless Rupert.

Jess bent quickly to her LPs.

'Jess?'

Jess was resolutely unresponsive.

'Jessica!'

'What?' As if bored of him already.

'You need to come with me,' panted Rupert.

'I'm busy.'

'This is important.'

'This is important too.'

'It's Mary.'

Jess turned fast enough to get a head spin. 'What about Mary?' She knew before he said it.

'The Ripper got her last night.'

'Fuck.' By the time she'd finished the epithet, Jess was through the door.

Richard shook his head. 'Harriet never used bad language.'

Chapter 26

A VICIOUS SPOONING

Still Wednesday 1 June

Rupert ignored the speed limit on the Richleigh road. Jess stared unseeing into the wing mirror. The news had knocked the wind out of her. Like in her dream. The one that now bled into her days. Then Rupert's assurance that Mary wasn't dead had hollowed her out completely.

'Are you going to tell me what happened or not?'

'You said you didn't want to talk.'

'*Obviously* I want to know about Mary.'

Rupert eyed her nervously, as if she was a pit bull. 'The police think she was walking back to your place from the town, the long way home by Gold Hill. They found her lying under the signpost for Castle Kidbury. The "please drive safely" one. She can't remember much, but she was going through a field and was struck on the head from behind. Whoever did it tried to get to her eyes, so she fought back with her karate or whatever it is—'

'Taekwondo,' corrected Jess.

'Yes, that. Anyway, she saw him off and managed to get away, it seems. But she's black and blue, poor thing. Eden rang me. Thought you might need somebody with you when you heard.'

'Why didn't I just go with her?'

'How'd you mean?'

'She wanted me to go to the Druid's Head with her.' A stain was growing on Jess's soul; that's how it felt. 'I was in a bad mood and drove off.'

'It's scarcely your fault, Jess. She was attacked by a maniac.'

'We had a row.'

'What about?'

'An article on the *Daily Mail* website.'

'Ah,' said Rupert.

'Yes, "ah". You looked a total arsehole.'

'I don't see why. We were just out for dinner. I can't help it if the paps were all over Pandora. Is this why you're so off with me?'

'Doesn't bother me either way, Rupert. If that's the sort of thing that floats your boat, you just carry on.'

'What sort of thing?' Rupert's sigh was loud. 'As Pandora annoys you that much, you'll be glad to know she's in the air right now, on her way to Thailand. For her wedding.'

Jess tried to conceal her interest at this revelation. 'Wedding?'

'Yes, to Baldwin Boxall.'

'The movie star? Bloody hell.' Despite herself, Jess was impressed.

'The piece in the *Mail* was just to stir up trouble. She's used to that kind of thing.'

'What was she doing back here then?'

'Seeing the family, catching up with friends. It was nice to see her, of course, but it reminded me of why we split up. She can be a bit ... obvious.'

'Yes, she can.' Jess was still cross. She just wasn't sure who to be cross with.

Jess ran ahead of Rupert at the hospital and skidded to a halt by the police officer guarding Mary's door. 'Can I go in?' she asked, out of breath.

The officer glanced cautiously at DC Knott, who lurked further down the corridor.

'Are you next of kin?' Knott relished her authority.

For fuck's sake. 'Yes, I'm her sister.'

Knott's chin sank into her neck. 'No you're not.'

'Shut up, Karen.' Jess pushed her way through the door.

'Oi!' Knott chased her in.

Mary lay on the bed. Head bandaged. Arm connected to a drip. Jess rushed to her. Embraced her.

'Jaysus, careful. I'm all broken, you know.' Mary's voice was cotton-wool-muffled.

'I shouldn't have left you.' Jess squeezed Mary's hand. 'If I hadn't been such a cow and just come into the pub with you—'

'Ah, forget about it. You're not me chauffeur. I

thought I might finish the night with a bang. But not like that.'

'No, Mary, I mean it.' Jess was broken in two with remorse. Each bandage, each scrape made it worse. As if she'd personally battered her best friend. 'I should have collected you.' There were scratches radiating from Mary's lovely dark eyes like sunrays. 'We'd have sung in the car. I'd have put you to bed. None of this would have happened if I just did the right thing.'

'I'm having a grand lie-down,' said Mary. 'The doctors are fit. Main thing is, I'm alive, Jess! You're at me bedside, not me grave, so knock it off.'

A loud bang outside the window. Like a giant tea tray being thumped.

'Where did that storm spring from?' Rupert crossed to the wide modern window. 'It's bucketing down. Bloody hell!' He took a step back as lightning crackled across the sky. They were on the top floor of Richleigh Hospital and had a ringside view of nature's circus.

'What's the betting,' said Mary, her voice weak, 'that Shane Harper didn't forecast this?'

'Careful, you're in a select club with Shane,' said Jess. She put on a horror-movie voice. 'Victims of the Rustic Ripper.' A realisation jolted her. 'If you were attacked last night and Pan is still in custody . . .'

'Pan,' said Rupert, 'is not your man.'

Jess took Mary's hand gingerly. The knuckles were bound up.

The storm ranted on outside the overheated room.

'That really came out of nowhere,' murmured Rupert.

A flash of lightning. A flash of memory. The stroph-alos on Unthank's business card. Jess didn't believe that Hecate's followers could control the weather, any more than she believed in the love potions available over the internet.

The rain pelted on the glass as if it wanted to get in. Rupert left the two women to it.

'Mary, did you meet Luis Unthank in the Druid's Head last night?'

'Luis Un-what? Don't make me laugh, Jess. It hurts.'

Jess took in the machines and gadgets hooked up to Mary. She'd never forget the way this room looked and smelt. 'He held the door for you. Leered at your bum.'

'He sounds like a man of taste. I did get chatted up by some pretentious guy with a hipster haircut.'

'That's him.'

'I gave him the elbow. Let him buy me a Guinness first, mind. He behaved as if I should be flattered that he found me worthy. Who mentions Bauhaus when you're chatting somebody up?'

The plot thickened. Jess hoped it might become clearer, but no. It simply thickened. 'What do you remember about the assault?'

'Not much. I was walking, well, staggering, by the river and then somebody just kind of *got* me with something heavy. Didn't see what. I was on the ground and he came at me again, so I let him have it with a son kal chigi. That bested him, so I got up and went to run, but he jumped me again. Trying to gouge me eyes out, the

315

mad sod. I let rip with a naeryeo chagi. That floored him, so I ran. I must have passed out, further on, under the sign, because that's where a rambler found me this morning.' Mary frowned. 'What the feck *is* a rambler, anyway? They're always finding bodies, aren't they? Somebody should check out those rambler dudes.'

'You didn't see the guy? You can't even guess who it was?'

'I've told yer man Eden as much as I can remember. It's not easy to get a good look at someone when they're trying to gouge out yer eyes with a spoon.'

Jess laughed. While she laughed, she started to cry. It was noisy.

'Exactly. A spoon, I ask you.'

'How's your head, Mare?'

'I've got a bit of concussion but it's quite chill, to tell you the truth. A bit like top-quality ganja.'

'I was so frightened when Rupert came for me.'

'I'm fine. Forty winks and a cup of tea'll sort me out.' Mary half smiled. 'So the toff fetched you? Maybe he's not so bad after all.'

'Your poor eyes.'

Eden appeared. He acknowledged Jess, then spoke to Mary. 'I think we've got everything we need from you, Ms Spillane. Forensics have finished, so you're free to ... um ... wash. Call me if you remember anything. Even if it seems trivial.'

'I will, Detective Sergeant,' replied Mary. She batted what was left of her eyelashes.

Eden went a little pink.

Jess said, 'Unthank was in the pub. He knows Mary's my friend and he knows I don't like him. Besides, she knocked him back. Male anger equals male violence far too much of the time.'

'We're talking to everybody who was in the Druid's Head.'

'Plus, according to the EasySleep receptionist, he checked out days ago.'

'That's not what he's telling us.' Eden's brow puckered.

Jess didn't mention the storm. It didn't count as a hard fact.

'Hang on.' Jess's thoughts dodged here and there. She wasn't accustomed to worrying about Mary. 'How do we even know Mary was attacked by the serial killer?'

'We found a box at the scene,' said Eden. 'Splintered and smashed, but handmade, just like Shane Harper's. No markings.'

Mary was peeved. 'Not good enough for a fancy box like Keith Dike, am I?'

No doubt about it. It wasn't a random mugging. Mary was supposed to die. Jess felt the vice of her conscience tighten. She might easily have been responsible for a second death.

'Find out whether Pan made any calls from custody.'

'You do know he's a copper, Jess?' Mary sounded washed out. 'He knows what to do.'

Eden gestured to the door. Jess followed him to the corridor.

'Let's keep things calm for Mary. She's putting on a front, but shock will set in soon enough. We let Pan go

317

yesterday evening. Don't look at me like that, Jess. His lawyers wangled bail on the drugs charges. We couldn't make anything else stick.'

'You let your prime suspect go and hey presto, Mary's on her back having her eyes scratched out.'

'You're preaching to the choir, Jess, but Mary described someone near enough her own height. Pan's six feet tall. During the struggle, she grabbed his face and she's certain the assailant was male and had no beard.'

'Can we take the word of a drunk person?'

'I heard that,' called Mary. 'Nothing sobers you up faster than being attacked from behind with a spoon.'

Eden and Jess moved further down the corridor.

'Theresa,' said Jess. 'We said, remember, that she was more likely to kill Mary than Gavin.'

'She crossed my mind, but she's a slip of a thing. Plus whoever attacked Mary carried out the murders, remember.'

'Could it be someone else from Pitt's Field?'

'Pan's the only male there.'

'Can't you pull him in again? Please.'

'Jess, I know you're shaken up about your friend. Let me do things my way. Our killer has broken his chain of male victims. Nobody's safe. No sniffing around on your own. Got it?'

'Got it.' Jess, her shock receding, saw the purple splashes beneath Eden's eyes. The shabbiness of his shirt collar. 'When did you last go home and get some shut-eye, Detective Sergeant?'

'I slept in my office last night.' Eden yawned. 'I'm packing up the house. To sell. So ...'

The guard had slipped. Exhaustion will do that to a man. Jess imagined the ex-marital home being packed away into boxes. She just knew he'd label them all carefully.

'Looks like that storm cleared up as quickly as it appeared. Sit with Mary for a bit,' suggested Eden. He whistled up Knott and they left.

Jess peeped through the glass at Mary. A black eye starting to blossom.

I shouldn't have driven off.

Chapter 27

THINKSPACE

Still Wednesday 1 June

'Welcome back. Dust the Pyrex,' ordered Doug, before Jess had got fully through the charity shop door.

Nobody passed the window display of plastic shoes. News of the fourth Ripper abomination had got round. Castle Kidbury was a ghost town. That was, until Carli trotted up, looking for 'something sparkly'.

'Would Richard do?' As Doug bent double at his own joke, Carli explained that she wanted to surprise her boyfriend.

'Ryan's so good to me,' she cooed, whipping through the rails with the focus of a velociraptor. 'I thought, maybe a boob tube?'

'Boob?' repeated Richard uncertainly. 'Tube?'

'My Ryan's such a diamond.' Carli homed in on sequins and bugle beads.

'Hmm,' said Jess.

'You know what?' Nobody knew what, so Carli carried on. 'Since these stupid murders started, Ryan collects me after my shift at the Seven Stars and walks me home. Every. Single. Night.'

'He's a white knight,' murmured Doug.

'Except for last night.'

Doug and Richard side-eyed each other.

'Don't worry,' laughed Carli. She held a glittering vest to her torso. 'My Ryan's not the Rustic Ripper. He was helping his mate to move house.'

'At night?' Richard pursed his lips. Hard.

As Jess stood outside the changing room and gave a running commentary on Carli's choices – 'Yeah, nice, no, too big, a bit I-shag-footballers' – she fretted that eventually everybody in town would fall under suspicion.

Was it possible they'd never find the murderer? Castle Kidbury needed Eden to clinch this case.

Eddie was at the door. 'Carli in here?'

'She's trying on our worst tops,' said Doug as Carli emerged in a rhinestone bustier.

'Bleedin' hell,' said Eddie, averting his eyes. 'The cops have imposed an official curfew, love. Nine p.m. I like to cooperate, so I'm shutting up the Seven Stars early.'

A tremor travelled through the shop. Curfews were for war-torn streets on the television news. Jess remembered Kuzbari and wondered what memories this might trigger.

'I find meself eyeing up every punter who orders a pint,' said Eddie.

'Lovely day like this.' Richard gestured out at the bright street. 'Should be people out strolling, chatting.'

They all looked out at Fore Street. Its unnatural tranquillity underlined the hard core of fear they all carried nowadays.

Richard broke the silence. 'Eddie, I have the perfect tuxedo for you.'

'I'm not really a tuxedo man ...' Eddie was already half into the jacket; Doug had his ways.

Eddie's eyes appealed for help like a rescue pup in an RSPCA poster.

On the grounds of *It's funny*, Jess declined to rescue him.

'Don't you look swish!' Richard was riffling around for 'a jaunty neckerchief' when Patricia Smalls appeared among them. She, too, had her ways: materialising from the ether was one of them.

'Duty calls!' she said. 'I need you all at ThinkSpace.' When nobody moved, she clapped her hands. 'Chop-chop!'

'Don't you chop-chop me, Patricia Smalls,' said Richard. 'I have a business to run.'

'Do you though?' Patricia put her head on one side. 'Is it actually a business? Isn't it more of a hobby?'

Jess laid a hand on Richard's arm. He was a Vesuvius of elderly homosexual rage.

Meera came to the door. Her abrupt about-turn didn't save her. Patricia pulled her inside by the elbow.

'You'll come, won't you, Meera dear?'

'Come where? I was just popping in to see if the boys

had any salt and pepper sets. Squeezers keeps stealing ours from the cafe.'

Richard shook off Jess. 'This shop, madam,' he said to Patricia, 'is a vital part of Castle Kidbury. Hobby indeed.'

'And so is ThinkSpace. The difference is, Richard, you're the past and ThinkSpace is the future.'

Meera put up a fight. 'I have to get back to The Spinning Jenny. We're having a run on toasties and I—'

'Meera, there are no customers today.' Patricia dealt with her feeble parry. 'I've gone to great lengths to pull together another grand opening for ThinkSpace after Shane went and got himself crucified. By pulling various strings, I've managed to procure the services of Carl Apthorpe.' She looked from face to face. 'Are you really telling me you've never heard of Carl Apthorpe? The youngest Area Manager Morrisons supermarkets have ever appointed?'

'Quite a coup,' murmured Doug.

Patricia turned sheepdog and herded them out of the shop. 'Out! Out!' There was no withstanding such self-assurance. Generations of Smallses had spanked footmen with the same gusto Patricia brought to mayoring.

Browbeaten on the pavement, the sheep gave themselves up to their fate. Jess saw a figure she knew in the passenger seat of Patricia's car. Leaning down, she whispered, 'Dad?'

She read his expression. *Yes, she got me too.*

*

'All aboard the good ship ThinkSpace!' Patricia, scattering exclamation marks, led the charge through the empty lobby of the old library. 'No definite article, all one word!'

No more felt-and-tin-tack noticeboards, thought Jess. No more handwritten signs asking for silence and the disposal of chewing gum. She missed the leaflets for after-school clubs and local charity events and bake sales.

'First floor.' Patricia strode ahead up a stone staircase. 'And this, people, *this*, is ThinkSpace.'

This isn't anything, thought Jess. The old reading room was a bland shell. Strips of power outlets and ethernet ports circled the walls. They'd usurped the shelves Jess remembered so fondly. Two blank flipcharts bookended the grand room, replete with unopened packets of marker pens. Air conditioning hummed. A4 sheets dotted around the walls suggested, in silly handwriting fonts, that those present do what they were presumably doing already: 'be', proposed one; 'live', 'breathe', 'choose', offered others. Beanbags in Google colours dotted the new vinyl floor.

Patricia's hostages greeted the ones already installed. Rupert was there. Graham Dickinson. Mr Kuzbari was edging towards the exit.

Good luck with that, thought Jess wryly as Patricia intercepted him.

'I'm scared,' said Rupert, joining Jess and the Judge. 'What's happening?'

A makeshift curtain concealed one end of the room.

'That,' said Eddie, who knew everything about everything, 'will be whisked back to reveal a commemorative plaque. Squeezers was asleep behind it earlier.' He waved at somebody behind Jess. 'Speak of the devil!'

'I've been evicted,' said Squeezers, with miserable dignity. 'It was cosy behind that curtain.'

'Where will you go now?' asked Jess.

'Home to Mother.'

'That's nice.' Jess tried and failed to imagine what the mother of Squeezers might look like.

As Squeezers meandered away, Eddie said, 'He means Mother Nature.'

'Eh?' Jess's mind, so full of Hecate, flew to that many-named goddess.

'He sleeps rough, Jess,' said Rupert. He bent to look into her face. 'Don't go trying to fix him, Jess. You can't save the world.'

'At least I want to try,' said Jess. Her heart was inside out since Mary's assault.

There was milling. And mingling. A desire to be elsewhere. The townspeople defined the term 'captive audience'. While Rupert was drawn into a conversation about the proposed one-way system by Lynne of Minimart fame, Jess attempted to engage her father.

'You were in Syria, Dad, weren't you?'

'How'd you know?' The Judge's surprise softened his face.

'There's a framed photo on the wall of your study.' A younger James Castle in khakis, with a row of stuffy-looking men straight from a British Empire production line. Squinting into desert sun, their noses peeling. 'It says "Damascus 1975" under it.'

'Fancy you noticing that.'

You don't know the first thing about me, thought Jess. She noticed everything.

'I was part of a Foreign Office team. We were sent over in the aftermath of the Syria–Israel conflict.' The Judge looked back through the years and was sobered. 'Hell of a mess. Wonderful people. Such a political predicament. One could have wept for them.'

There was a hidden hinterland to the Judge's life that Jess could only guess at. 'Let me introduce you to a real live Syrian.' As she guided him over to Mr Kuzbari – without taking his arm; they were still at odds, after all – Jess gave him a potted history of Castle Kidbury's new pharmacist. 'Ask him,' she said, 'about his mother.'

She left them together. It was a mistake to stand on her own. Patricia Smalls was on her like a lioness on a wounded gnu. 'There you are! Have you seen the MeetZone yet?'

'I have to speak urgently with DS Eden about, um, urgent matters.' Jess prised the mayor's fingers off her arm and sought sanctuary with Eden.

She followed his line of sight.

'How does he have the nerve to show his face?' growled Jess.

Pan lay on one of the beanbags. Hands clasped across his tummy, he was serene, at ease. Alongside him, lolling awkwardly, was Caroline. She watched him constantly, taking her cue from him. When he made a joke, she laughed. When he pontificated, she listened earnestly.

'A few of his ladies peeled away while he was locked up,' said Eden. 'Might be the start of a rebellion. We've reached out to see if they want to rescind their alibis, but no dice yet.'

'They want to put some clear water between themselves and Pan. Probably snuggling back into their nice ordinary lives.'

'I'm a patient man, I can wait. But I don't want another murder before I solve this case.'

Wandering past them, Theresa didn't acknowledge the police officer and his consultant. She was with Ryan, the pair of them deep in conversation.

'She'd better not let Carli see her getting so pally with Ryan,' said Jess. She knew how small-town women were about their men. Many a time she'd seen a hank of hair pulled out at a house party.

'I checked out her alibi for Mary. Just in case. In A&E at Richleigh all night with unexplained stomach pains. Poor girl doesn't have much luck.'

'Hmm.' The mention of Mary disturbed Jess. She needed her at stultifying dos like this. She would visit her bedside later, Jess decided. Expiate her sins by the ritual offering of magazines and grapes.

In lieu of Mary, Eden did nicely. Not as lively, but reliable. He didn't wander off. He didn't expect small talk. He gave Jess time to practise her mysterious new skill. She found that she knew, without trying, where Rupert was in the room.

Now he was talking to Squeezers. Something changed hands. A tenner.

You lovely old hypocrite, thought Jess, as Squeezers folded the tenner into a complex origami shape and stashed it down his trousers.

Eden nudged her. 'Friend of ours,' he said discreetly, as Unthank wandered past.

His nose in the air, the Londoner semaphored he was above this gathering. When Jess hailed him, he ambled over a touch too slowly.

'Hear you got knocked back last night!' said Jess cheerfully.

'Sorry. Don't understand.'

'My mate Mary. You chatted her up at the pub. Those wedding vows you made must be pretty flexible.'

'It's got nothing to do with you,' said Unthank. He tacked on an artificial giggle for good measure.

'Perhaps not, it's got something to do with *him*, though.' Jess jerked her thumb at Eden.

'Look, I've been dragged off the street to this ersatz dump and I'm not in the mood to chat, okay?'

The way Eden disregarded Unthank's entitlement delighted Jess.

'I have some questions, sir,' he said. 'For you and the manageress of the EasySleep. Seems you both misled me about the duration of your stay.' He placed a hand on Unthank's arm.

The look of outrage Unthank gave Eden's hand was

ignored. Eden spirited him away with such authority that even Patricia Smalls stood back to let them leave.

Untethered, Jess looked around for Rupert. She found Pan. Or rather, he found her. He had a way of standing just a smidgeon too close, so Jess couldn't see around him. She was in the mood to fight fire with fire.

'Something special about your spunk, is there?'

'Dr Jessica Castle, you wash that mouth out.' He was amused. That wasn't Jess's aim.

Why, she wondered, was this creep the only person who called her by her proper title? 'I had a lesson in no-more times. Apparently only the children you father get to survive Armageddon. You don't truly believe that bollocks you feed your followers, do you?'

'Belief. Truth. All phantasms, m'dear. We all believe in something. You, for instance, believe that you're doing *good*.' Pan sketched quotation marks in the air. 'You think you're going to catch the naughty killer. When all you're doing is running around town in your toy car getting on people's nerves.'

'Oh shut up.' It wasn't Jess's most Wildean comeback.

'At least I look after my people. I keep my kiddies near. I feed them. Clothe them. I instruct them in the *real* ways of the world.'

'The women under your spell collect child benefit.' Eden had estimated an 'income' of £30,000 a year from what he termed 'child farming'. 'Not bad for lying around pontificating all day.'

'Did you see your dad much when you were ickle?'

'What's that got to do with—'

'Did you curl up and sleep at his feet? Did you have a network of loving women looking out for you? Was your dad always there, always on hand? That's how my children live.'

'Why don't you write a handbook? Pan's Guide to Parenting.'

'Maybe, my dear little blinkered clever clogs, traditional families aren't all they're cracked up to be. There you are, blundering through your life, daddy issues written in neon across your forehead, begging for love and turning it away in the same breath.'

There was that sensation again, of being watched. Of being a frog pinned to a table while Pan slit her open.

Pan could talk an avalanche. 'I'm pure. I talk to my kids. I listen. I don't tell them they have to study this or be like that. They own themselves.'

Jess butted in. She was forceful, too, when riled. And she was very riled. 'Spare me, Pan. Those children are let down every day. They're cold and hungry and they don't go to school and you spend their benefits on crack to keep their mothers in line. You're the Manson family, not the fucking Waltons.'

Their mutual hate fest was interrupted by a strange smell. They sniffed.

'Sage?' said Jess.

A Native American – from Taunton – was performing a purification rite. He wafted a burning wad of sage leaves.

Meera coughed until she cried.

Doug shouted something about health and safety.

Undeterred, Patricia thanked Big Chief Low Eagle – who Jess recognised from the petrol station – and stepped to a lectern. She fiddled with the Tandy microphone.

'We're honoured to see you all here today.'

'So you should be,' said Richard. '*Emmerdale*'s on.'

'We are honoured,' repeated the mayor, 'to action the first example of a forward-thinking community paradigm.' Hurtling manfully on, Patricia took a run at her script. 'Here is a place where community excellence, cross-creativity and trans-development can be achieved through extraordinary local reach-out and interdisciplinary relations.' She drew a grateful breath.

'Sounds positively indecent,' said Doug. 'Interdisciplinary relations?'

'I'm barring anyone who's into *that*!' called Eddie.

'Sounds like fun!' shouted Carli.

'Shush, please,' urged the Judge. 'Let's allow the lady to speak.'

'*Thank* you, James,' simpered the mayor.

Jess's phone vibrated in her pocket.

Fancy coming over to mine for dinner
tomorrow? R x

Jess leant to look at Rupert, a few feet away, between Meera and Moyra, phone in hand. He ignored her stare.

Go on then. Any chance of kebabs?

Rupert's phone pinged. Jess saw the smile he smothered as he read her text.

Head respectfully down, *à la* Martin Luther King making his 'I Have a Dream' speech, the mayor said, 'Please allow me the privilege of introducing Mister. Carl. Apthorpe.'

Patricia hadn't managed to poach the national photographers from the Seven Stars. One lone local snapper captured 'Mister. Carl. Apthorpe.' run through the crowd. He punched the air. He asked them if they were all right and when they murmured that they were, he asked them to say it louder.

'I love this town!' shouted Carl.

'It's all right if you like that sort of thing,' said Graham.

'Who are you?' asked Danny from a beanbag he shared with Tallulah.

'I'm glad you asked, young man.' Carl lifted both arms. His shirt was stained with sweat. 'I'm from the land of *yes*. I'm from where *completely* happens.'

'I thought he was from Morrisons,' said Moyra.

'Why don't you say "yes",' asked Eddie, enjoying himself, 'when I ask you to open more checkouts on a Saturday morning?'

'And why is all the hummus gone by twelve?' demanded Doug. This was an old gripe.

That's a date then. x

Specifically, thought Jess, reading the text, *it was the second of June*. Deiphon. Hecate's big night.

'People of Castle Kidbury,' bellowed Carl. 'I am buzzed to declare ThinkSpace well and truly open!'

Moderate applause.

Patricia yanked on a tasselled cord.

Carl punched the air again.

The curtain flew back.

The residents of Castle Kidbury stared.

Beneath the plaque was a fat, glistening turd.

Doug vomited. Tallulah gasped. The photographer clicked away.

Patricia's cries could be heard as far as Richleigh bypass.

'Bring me Squeezers!'

Chapter 28

DANCING ON HER OWN

Thursday 2 June

The water is blood.

Then the water is yellow.

She can taste it in her mouth.

It tastes metallic as Jess relaxes and lets herself spiral down to the bottom of the pool.

It tastes like shame.

Brushing her teeth with extra gusto, Jess tried to shake her head clear of the dream. How to exorcise herself of it? How to escape its insistence that she was as guilty as the killer?

Eden wasn't picking up. Karen wouldn't help. Jess had no idea what had transpired with Unthank – *Luis* Unthank – in the interview room.

She had hours to kill before dinner with Rupert. Not for Jess a grooming regime of waxing and contouring and trying on every item of clothing she owned. Rupert would take her as he found her. And he would find her all in black with untidy hair.

She roamed the house. She missed Mary. She missed Bogna, too; that was a first. Bogna was visiting Mary at the hospital. Buns had been made.

Stopping at the threshold of the master bedroom, Jess saw the Judge checking himself out in a cheval mirror. He tweaked the lapels of his pale linen suit. He met Jess's eye in her reflection.

'Never in nor out, are you?' he said.

'Liminal, that's me.' *Me and Hecate*; Jess was reminded of the date. Deiphon. If she were an Ancient Greek she'd be sweeping the floors and looking for a stray mongrel to sacrifice. 'Where are you off to all dolled up?'

For an answer, he held out a gold cufflink. 'Would you?'

He used to ask her mother that same question in that same voice. *For a year*, thought Jess, *he's had nobody to help him with his cufflinks*.

'Best cufflinks, eh? Do you have a date?'

Again he didn't answer and Jess's heart raced. *Ye Gods*, to use one of his expressions, *it couldn't be true, could it? Both of them off on dates?*

If going to Rupert's constituted a date.

'Kuzbari seems a good man, Jessica. A gentleman, in fact.'

It wasn't a word that sprang to Jess's twenty-first-century lips. But it described Kuzbari perfectly.

When she'd settled both his cuffs, the Judge took her hand.

She couldn't remember when he'd last done that. Her fingers folded around his.

'Don't worry too much about your Syrian friend, Jess. Sometimes the answer turns up just when it's needed.'

Answers were what she needed most. But all she could think was, *He called me Jess.*

Opening hours were posted on the gilded gates of Kidbury Manor. Instructions for coach parties to use the rear car park. A cheerful reminder that the Gifte Shoppe was having a sale of jams.

Jess ignored them all and trudged round to a discreet door in the ancient, venerable wall. Ignoring the laminated exhortations to keep off the grass, she crossed the lawn. Also ancient, also venerable. Her ancestors hadn't done things by halves. The house was wide, a warm stone outline in the dying light. Gables and mullions and a gargoyle or two.

Jess found it hard to be proud of the old place. She saw past the design and felt the sweat. Each brick handmade and placed just so by somebody who lived and died an unrecorded life. As a child, she could recite the name of each and every Lord Kidbury, right back to the family's ennoblement in 1691.

Like a breeze on her face, the memory owned her for a moment. Jess used to think of her heritage as romantic. Dashing. Then she had woken up.

Radicalised as a teen, proclaiming her Everywoman

credentials with punky eyeliner and her first Doc Martens, she saw only privilege hanging from her family tree. Unearned wealth. An inbred cousin with one toe too many.

Past arrows pointing towards toilets and the rose garden and the Kidbury Kafé, Jess slipped into a court-yard. The cobbles were new; her cousin had recreated something that had never existed in the first place. One of many things Jess held against Josh was his blithe ability to spell cafe with a K.

A small door glowed yellow in the ivy. 'Private', warned a plaque.

'Darling, *what* a surprise!' Great-aunty Iris's voice oozed from the intercom. And then Jess was indoors, glass in hand, lump in throat – from the nicotine fog, not sentiment – bum on velvet chair, watching Iris jive on a priceless rug.

The record was scratched. Jess watched Iris defy her years in a floaty dress that seemed to have no seams and was the colour of twilight.

'Dancing,' said Iris, tapping her ash in the direction of a small sleeping dog who was little more than a collection of tumours, 'is better than yoga for one's core.'

'Who is this?' The music was sophisticated. Knowing. Ablaze with rhythm. 'His voice is amazing.'

'Louis Jordan.' Iris folded herself into an armchair. 'Marvellous singer. Real twinkle in his eye. There are those who say he was the father of rock and roll.'

'Surely that's Elvis.' Jess was ready to scrap.

'Elvis, child, is the *king*.' Iris crossed long legs that had once nabbed her a lord. 'How's our wild Mary?'

'Refusing to admit she needs to take time to recover.' Jess had apologised again. Mary had told her to shut up. Again. 'When I think of what could have happened ...'

'Crucially, it didn't happen, so let's move on.' There was empathy, not chill, in Iris's advice. She knew about her niece's soft core.

The living room of Iris's flat above the stables told a story. African artefacts. Fringed lampshades. Dusty books on Kenya and Nairobi in particular overpopulated the shelves. There was even a ventriloquist's dummy parked on one of the window seats, threatening to mutter something evil. Iris's was not a life half lived.

'Oh God,' she muttered, as heavy feet sounded on the stairs. 'Here comes my only grandchild to tell me about the day's takings. When will he accept I don't bloody care?'

'Jessica Castle, as I live and breathe!' Red jumbo cords to match his cheeks, Josh had nothing of his grandmother in his design. Bumbling, gosh-darn cheery, his curling hair peppered with leaves, he'd been 'helping' the manor's maintenance team cut down a diseased oak.

The current Lord Kidbury loved helping; he believed that nobody noticed his title, that he was simply one of the guys. He was oblivious to the fact that the 'guys' tended to schedule big practical tasks when his lordship was elsewhere.

'Joshy,' said Jess, surprised by the childhood nickname springing so eagerly to her lips.

'What's all this I hear about you getting mixed up in our spooky murders? I suppose all those qualifications on witchcraft and druids had to find an outlet somewhere.'

'Jessica has a PhD, which is more than you have, Josh, darling.' Raining on Castle women's parades was a Castle men's habit: Iris would have none of it.

'I confess, I can't see how you make money in your line of work.' Josh asked the kind of guileless questions children do. *Why are you fat? Is that a wig?* He didn't mean to offend his cousin when he pressed her, saying, 'Is there? Any money in it, old girl?'

'None whatsoever,' answered Jess, happily.

'Shame. Those university fees cost James a pretty penny.' Josh picked up his grandmother's mail and began to look through it.

'You know full well Dad didn't—'

'You have a one-track mind, Josh,' interjected Iris, briskly. 'You're interested only in the bottom line.'

'Quite right. Take the manor for example, Grandma. Far too big for you on your own. Now, the public gets a bit of heritage. We get some dosh. Thank God for Yanks, I say, and their deep pockets. They go potty for a title.'

'I had an American lover once.' Iris's cheekbones were dangerous in the lamplight. 'Before your grandfather, of course. He, I seem to remember, went potty for *me*.'

Josh moved briskly on. 'Takings are down again,' he

said, as Jess wondered why men of her caste, so keen on being 'male' and 'blokey', wore scarlet corduroys.

'I don't care, darling,' said Iris. 'You know I don't care. It's time we gave away this pile of rubble.'

'Grandma, you're so cute,' said Josh.

Iris gave him a look that was anything but cute.

'Did you get my email about the fun day?' asked Josh.

'Probably,' murmured Iris.

'Do you think the clown's a good idea?'

Jess said, 'Clowns are never a good idea.'

Josh, whose geniality was Teflon-coated, refused to believe her. 'Kiddies love a red nose and a silly suit.'

'In that case, why not send the little darlings to the House of Commons?' Jess was rewarded by a snort from Iris and bemusement from Josh.

'No, no, Jess. It's a *fun day*. Hay rides. A donkey, possibly. You can help out, if you like. Staff costs are *killing* me.'

Jess squirrelled that away to tell Rupert later; *Me! Helping out at a bloody fun day!*

Running a hand through his regulation public-school quiff, Josh said, 'I can cope with bad weather and a one star on TripAdvisor, but a psycho on the loose is bloody bad for business.'

'People no longer think of chocolate-box views when they hear the name Castle Kidbury,' lamented Iris. 'They think of crucifixions.'

'Hey ho.' Josh really did speak like that. 'I must run, Grandma. Bills to pay!'

'Well,' said Jess, 'it *is* Deiphon.'

'It's *what*?' Josh's big baby face was puzzled.

'The dark moon. End of the lunar month.'

'Oh, thought it was something real,' said Josh amiably.

As the evening drew closer, Jess found she couldn't shake off Hecate.

'He visits me each and every evening, to tell me about the damn takings.' Iris poured herself a whisky when Josh left. 'Josh is a good boy. A kind boy. But when will he notice that I don't care even a little bit about the business?'

'Does it ever make you sad that strangers are tramping all over the lovely house you and Uncle Seb lived in?'

'It is indeed a lovely house.' Iris looked out at the cobbles. There was no view of the manor from her windows. 'But we were more than happy in Kenya. I wouldn't have married Seb if I'd known a dreary old *title* came with.'

Only Iris could make being an aristocrat sound like a chore. 'Yes you would.' Jess's great-uncle was a dim childhood memory. She recalled the smell of tweed. A gruff laugh. A voice shot through with kindness. Weak, though, according to Jess's father. *But then*, thought Jess, *we're all weaklings compared to his honour Judge Castle, the man who's facing down aortic stenosis all on his own.* 'You loved Uncle Seb.'

'So I did. But, Jess, he was just a man. We're all just people, when it comes down to it. Please don't expect so much from anyone, this Rupert for example, that he has no option but to disappoint.'

There was a story there. Jess could smell it. 'What did Uncle Seb—'

'Like I say, child, he was just a man.' Iris drew the curtains and closed the subject.

For now. Jess would return to it, always susceptible to the lure of a mystery.

'*Families*, darling.' Iris patted her lap and the small dog – a hate figure around the manor – leapt up. 'If only one could choose them.'

'You can.' Jess refused to say '*One* can'. 'They're called friends.'

'True.' Iris pressed the dog flat. It began to snore. 'I could live on a desert island with my girlfriends, but if I wasn't related to Josh, I wouldn't talk to him at a cocktail party.'

There was a silence, filled on Jess's side with thoughts of Josh's father, Iris's only child. If David Castle hadn't been killed in a hunting accident – *possibly*, thought Jess, *the poshest way to go* – things might be very different at Kidbury Manor.

'What about me? Would you talk to me at this cocktail party of yours?' Jess was smug. Sure of the response.

'You, young lady, are my favourite, as you well know. Cornetto?'

'God yes.' It occurred to Jess that, as she was en route to dinner with Rupert, she should save her appetite. *Ha!* She accepted the ice cream with happy avarice.

'If I ever get married,' said Jess, 'and I won't, but if I ever did, I'd have Cornettoes at my reception.'

'We had foie gras,' said Iris. 'Poor geese. Stuffed with food day after day.'

'There are worse ways to go.'

Iris watched Jess chomp stolidly on. 'You and your father, sharing a house, without Harriet. Can't be easy.'

'We're good.' Jess relented under that blue laser stare. 'Most of the time.'

'Families don't have to get on. Once you realise that it's most liberating.' Iris was the sarcastic version of Kuzbari. 'Did I ever tell you I cut off my stepsister's hair in her sleep? No? Another time, darling. However one feels about one's rellies, we're imprinted on one another. They're the portraits in the hallways of one's mind.'

'He's so frosty about me helping out with the murder investigation.'

'Couldn't *possibly* be because he's worried about his only daughter, could it, now?' Iris pushed her bangles up her arm. 'Perfect though you are, Jess, some of the friction with James is down to you. You're angry with him for getting old.'

'We all get old.' Jess gave Iris a speaking look. 'Well, most of us.'

'Compliment accepted. And denied.' Iris moved her chin, moved out of the light she'd carefully stage-managed, and aged a decade. 'You taste the end when you reach my age. We catch the ones we love checking us over when they don't know we're looking.'

Jess hung her head. 'Guilty.'

Iris had a little trick she often used. She would say nothing. Stare at her companion. The silence would swell. It would take on meaning. She pulled that trick now, saying eventually, 'You're angry with your father because you smell death in the air. Not today. Not tomorrow. But not on some distant unimaginable date either. It makes you feel insecure, because daddies are meant to be always there. He can't help growing older.'

'He can control seeking help for his health,' said Jess. Very fast. Very cross.

'Insisting on doing it his own way, and refusing good advice. Whoever does that remind me of? Jess, he's scared. Death is no longer abstract when you're James's age. Remember the hours he spent in hospitals when your mother was ill.'

Jess remembered only too well. She'd passed the ward where Harriet had died on her way to visit Mary. She'd had to catch her breath.

'You know,' said Iris, 'that I hate morbid talk, but try and keep things tidy with James.' She reached out and laid a forefinger on a large photograph of Seb, framed in silver. Beside it stood a colour snap of her son in a cot, his features still baby-soft. 'Losing a loved one without a gentle goodbye haunts one forever. Deny yourself a proper leave-taking and you'll be bent out of shape. You'll do the strangest things.'

Jess felt like a child again. Perplexed by the grown-ups and the way they hinted at deeper, darker truths.

Iris rallied. They talked of this, they talked of that. Jess left her suddenly.

She was late for Rupert.

Chapter 29

MUCH DEPENDS ON DINNER

Still Thursday 2 June

There was a lift at the Old Mill apartments. Jess hummed to the muzak as she ascended to the fourth floor.

The refurbishment was sleek and metallic, in contrast to the bold utility of the original mill building. Jess knew which she preferred; she was sniffy about developments that despoiled honest working architecture to create allegedly luxurious apartments. She foresaw some good clean fun teasing Rupert about his by-numbers bachelor pad.

Shit, thought Jess when Rupert answered the door. He was dressed up. Just a white shirt and grey cords, but they were an upgrade. Jess heard her Doc Martens slap on the porcelain floor and hoped the rip in her camo jacket wasn't too obvious.

'Brought you this.' Jess pushed a bottle of own-brand plonk at her host.

345

'Right. Good. Great.'

The white shirt was carefully undone to tastefully allude to luxuriant chest hair, which distracted Jess.

'You okay?' frowned Rupert. He held out his hand for her jacket. When she handed it to him, their fingers grazed.

Skin on skin.

A warm shiver.

Jess accepted a glass of tap water along with his *You're a cheap date* comment and tried to sit on the sofa that bisected the open-plan flat.

White, leather, over-designed, it was more of a bench. Jess perched. 'Nice windows,' she said. And they were. Floor to ceiling, they made a mural of Castle Kidbury.

'Almost a blank panel tonight,' said Rupert. 'The moon's a no-show.'

Deiphon. The dark moon. 'I—' she began, just as Rupert spoke. 'No, you go first,' she laughed.

'How was your day?' Rupert was hovering.

'You what?' Jess looked him up and down. Rupert was never banal. Not with her. 'It was, you know, day-ish. Sit down, Rupert. You look as if you're on your way out.'

Rupert sat abruptly. As if he was Moose. 'Hope you like risotto.'

'Depends what's in it.' Jess took a sip of her water. She rebooted her manners. 'I *love* risotto.' Middlebrow jazz, the kind Jess abhorred in bars, sputtered in the background of their silence. 'Takes a lot of stirring.'

'It's all about the rice,' said Rupert.

'Yeah,' said Jess, slowly. She laughed. 'Jesus, Rupert, what's wrong with us? We're playing at grown-ups.'

'I know, right?' Rupert looked relieved. 'It's not like we've just met.'

'Perhaps we only work in public.'

'I hope not.'

The dim lighting, the jazz, the newly discovered and rather nice chest hair turned each of Rupert's utterances to code. Jess hadn't had much luck with symbols lately.

Things loosened up a little. Jess was enlisted to chop tomatoes. The tiny shiny kitchen was a medley of high-end finishes. 'You live in a Nespresso advert, Rumpole.'

'I hardly ever get to cook at home.' He turned from his stirring. 'So this is nice. You here, I mean. Cooking for you.'

'I'll cook for you one evening.' The tomato was as plump and bloody as a heart. Jess hesitated, the knife in mid-air. She saw gore where she should have seen salad. The murders had seeped into her imagination. 'I haven't cooked in ages,' she said quietly.

As they took their platefuls to the table, the flat didn't seem so polished to Jess. It was calm. Safe. The candles on the table, although possibly part of that code she mistrusted, would be kind to the hollows beneath her eyes.

'Tell me stuff,' said Rupert. He had a fleck of chive on his chin.

'Like what?'

'Stuff like ...' Rupert did not convince with his pretence at deep thought. 'Your last relationship.'

'It was fun. Then it wasn't. Bit of a mess.'

'I tend to have long relationships. Not much good at flings. I like, you know, continuity.'

'I *don't*,' said Jess. 'I'm restless.' She remembered, a little too late, that there's no need to tell the whole truth in every situation. She felt like she was at a job interview and had just answered the question 'What's your worst fault?' with 'I'm a thief' instead of 'I'm a perfectionist'.

'Whereas I sit at the same table in The Spinning Jenny every time I go in.'

'I'm sort of crazy,' said Jess. 'I sometimes sit in the window. Sometimes I hang about the counter. Wild shit like that.'

'You don't like talking about yourself.'

'I'm just not that interesting.'

'I disagree.'

Both of them ate in silence for a while, thrilled and scared by the line in the sand Rupert had just hopped over.

Rupert said, 'Do you like apple pie?'

Jess, who loathed apple pie, said, 'Adore it.'

She loathed it so much she asked for seconds, out of guilt. 'Did you make it?'

'I'm a metrosexual, Jess, not an actual woman. It's from Waitrose.'

'Now you mention it, I can taste the middle-class-ness.'

'Coffee?'

'Nah. I'll be up all night widdling.' Jess was impressed by her own ability to destroy atmosphere;

even candlelight couldn't prettify that mental image.

Rupert was unfazed. He rooted out some mint teabags. They sat side by side, primly apart, on the uncompromising sofa.

He generated heat. She *felt* his nearness. Jess wondered if she had the same effect on him.

'I'm bad at this, Rumpole.'

'At what?'

'Low lights. Lingering looks.' Something had become clear to Jess. She needed this man. His friendship was important to her.

'I'm not what you'd call a professional.' Rupert smiled.

'Hang on, weren't you engaged at one point?' Jess put her hand to her mouth. 'I remember Stephen telling me. Years ago.'

'Don't remind me.' Rupert closed his eyes. 'I bought her a ring and everything. We were so young. We were practically toddlers. Well, we were twenty.'

'She had a posh name . . .'

'Saffron.'

'What happened? Why aren't you married?' That thought, of Rupert ringfenced by A. N. Other, caused a sharp pain in Jess's ribs.

'She was a lovely person. It just wasn't right.' Rupert pouted. 'You jealous?'

She hesitated. 'A bit.'

'Good.'

On the coffee table, Jess's phone vibrated. She leant forward. 'Eden,' she said. 'I'd better take it.'

'Can't you have a night off?' Rupert was peeved. He

retired to the kitchen and opened and closed cupboards.

Eden's voice was tinny. He was out there somewhere in the big dark blank beyond the Old Mill's picture window. Jess regretted allowing him in, but he had news and she was soon caught up in it.

'Unthank,' he said. 'Not our guy. The manageress lied because Unthank was in *her* bed on the nights of the murders. They met at the Baldur gig, and their affair has been going on ever since.'

'What about the wife in Dalston?'

'I can't arrest him for adultery. Unfortunately.'

'So he's in the clear?'

'Completely. There are timestamped selfies and movies.'

Jess assimilated the news. 'I really thought ... The Hellcat angle, the strophalos.'

'They aren't hard clues, Jess. Hecate won't solve this case.'

'You can say I told you so if you like.'

'I'll just say goodnight.'

She debriefed Rupert, who interrupted her halfway through. 'Let's not talk about the case, eh?'

'Sorry. I'm a one-note samba.'

'It's all murder murder murder with you.' Rupert made her laugh and that made *him* laugh. 'I still worry, Jess. Violent crime investigations can be dangerous if you go in too deep.'

He could have been talking about relationships. There was magnetism in the air and they were two helpless iron filings. She could kiss Rupert now. He wouldn't pull away. He would press her against him.

The quickest way to burn a friendship is to turn it into romance.

'Murder's off the menu,' said Rupert. 'Let's enjoy the bright lights of Castle Kidbury laid out at our feet.'

'It's hardly LA.'

'No. It's better.'

They both stared out at the sleeping town. The traffic lights winking on Fore Street. A stammering streetlamp on the Keep.

'Have you ever had a girlfriend who *didn't* have a mythical name?' Jess edged a little closer. 'I mean, there's Pandora and her famous box. Saffron is mentioned a lot in old works. Hecate is sometimes referred to as the saffron-cloaked empress of the sea, the sky and the underworld.'

'*You* can talk.' Rupert deliberated. He went for it. 'Jessica Guinevere Castle.'

'No!' Jess was outraged. It was a family taboo to say her middle name out loud, and he knew it. She roared with scandalised laughter and flew at him.

Rupert grabbed her wrist as she hit at his chest.

He held it. They struggled playfully. They stopped laughing.

Rupert's landline rang.

He tutted.

She groaned. She moved as if to untangle herself.

'Let's leave it,' he said. He said it like a dare.

Jess always took dares.

They stared at each other as the phone clicked off.

Please don't leave a message, whoever you are, thought Jess.

A disembodied voice filled the room.

Squeezers was saying, high-pitched, nervous, *'Hello Mr Rupert. I'm having a bit of bother.'*

'You're Squeezers' lawyer?' Jess gaped.

'Hardly. I help the poor bugger out now and then.' Rupert gritted his teeth. 'Go. Away. Squeezers.'

Squeezers rambled on. *'I'm a bit worried, Mr Rupert. I've been slightly silly.'*

Jess removed her hand. 'Go,' she said. 'Squeezers has nobody.'

'Promise you'll be here when I get back?' Rupert walked away backwards, picking up his coat and his keys.

Jess had never known a man so comfortable with eye contact. 'I promise.'

Alone, tingling, she threw herself back on the sofa with a groan of lust. She congratulated herself on wearing one of her more presentable bras.

The window drew her with an unearthly force. She wanted to be rooted tonight; she wanted to wait for Rupert and ignore Deiphon. This was her night off.

Deliberately, she turned away from the glass.

A framed artwork was on the floor, facing the wall. Jess saw the nail it had hung on.

She turned the frame around. It was a black and white shot of Pandora. Jess recognised it, an advert from early in the model's career. She was naked – naturally – in black and white, holding a camera against what Jess was pleased to note were very small breasts.

Had Rupert taken the print down because Jess was coming round? Was that good? Or bad?

This, she thought, *is why I don't have relationships*. The second-guessing. The jumping to conclusions. Her sheer wrongness about Unthank had unnerved her.

The camera was an Olympus.

Another little nudge from the ancients. A brand name borrowed from the home of the gods. Jess had been to the modern-day Mount Olympus; no gods there now, just souvenir shops.

The unscientific side of Jess's brain, the part she didn't encourage, kept trying to catch her attention. Jess knew mythology was a code. An enduring one. It was no surprise to see its echoes everywhere; her last lecture had been on that very topic.

'Crossing Over', she'd called it. The overlap of the modern and the antiquated. Like Hecate, she'd said to her students. Crossing between worlds, myths refuse to die, they simply retell themselves.

Like her dream.

It refused to know its place. It threw shards of memory in her path for her to cut herself. Jess felt its insistence. If she, just this once, stood still and listened, then maybe the dream would find a voice.

An image firmed up. Landed – *plop!* – in her consciousness. She'd been reaching and reaching and now suddenly it was easy.

A plaque.

Wooden. Made with care and craftsmanship.

A three-headed goddess, surrounded by carved waves, with a carved moon above her.

And inlaid along the bottom, a series of dots and dashes that seven-year-old Jess hadn't known how to read. Adult Jess read the ogham with ease.

'Hecate', it said.

And muggins here paid for it.

Chapter 30

MANNERS COST NOTHING

Still Thursday 2 June

Jess had the roads to herself.

She was high as a kite on her new certainty. She had begun to dial Eden's number, only to drop the phone back into her bag. This was a hunch; he didn't like hunches. How to explain to a creature of reason that she had decided to trust a dream?

She drove fast. Like an arrow shot from a bow. Jess had sufficient self-awareness to know that part of her reluctance to involve Eden was so she could have the glory of breaking the infamous Rustic Ripper case.

The road was narrow, little more than a lane, when she left the beaten path. The route was new, the turning remembered from childhood outings when her parents would point it out. Don't go down there, they'd say. Only one house down there and you wouldn't want to visit it.

I can always whistle up support later, she thought.

*

She got out. Closed the Morris Traveller's door quietly.

Jess was only a mile from Castle Kidbury, but the soft dip of the valley meant she saw only unscrolling black fields. The lonely house was abruptly white, like a tooth. One window was lit. Out in the front yard, it was silent and dark and she shivered.

Her phone ruptured the silence.

Mary's voice was tinny. Barely there, and breaking up. 'How's ... going ... you and Rupert?'

'I left. Long story.'

Mary's surprise was evident even though the reception was poor. Knowing she was safe in her hospital bed subverted the eerie landscape for Jess. A little.

'I thought ... tonight ... Rupert ...'

Jess tried to fill in the hissing blanks. She remembered the scribbled note she'd left on his fridge. 'Sorry.' So abrupt. Another regret to add to her collection.

As Mary prattled, Jess edged forward. She saw a shed. *Cue horror-movie music*, she thought as she pushed the door and it creaked in pain.

A tool shed. Woodworking equipment. All of it kept beautifully clean and in mint condition, in contrast to the near-derelict surroundings.

'Shit,' said Jess. She felt her aloneness.

'Shit what? What shit?' squawked Mary.

A voice behind Jess asked, not unreasonably, 'What are you doing in my shed?'

Jess jumped. 'You frightened me!' Buying time, she put her phone to her ear, but the connection was severed. 'Listen, Mary, I'll call you back. I just ran into an old friend.'

Neil Semple looked as if he might dispute that title.

'What am I doing here?' Jess hadn't rehearsed a reason. 'I was passing and I saw your light and I thought, hey, why not catch up?'

'Catch up?' Neil's lips were a lifeless blue. 'Why?' He was puzzled. Inhospitable. The mistrustful runt of the litter. 'Nobody visits.'

'Until now!' Jess was toothy. 'Can I come in? I could murder a cup of tea.'

Later, she thought, *I'll tell Mary I said that.*

Indoors was only marginally more domestic than the yard.

In a cave-dark room, furniture loomed, tall and ugly. A dresser. A table. Hard chairs standing at angles to each other. All like doll's house pieces plonked down anyhow by a giant hand.

'Do you want to sit down?' Neil's offer was half-hearted. 'Nana used to ask people if they wanted to sit down.' He looked as if he didn't understand all this sitting-down business. Physically, he was obviously about Jess's age, but he had the mannerisms of a child. Shy. Mulish. Wanting to be elsewhere. 'You could sit there.' He pointed to a leather armchair, brown and stained.

'I'd love to.' Jess kept it light. 'Shall we put a lamp on? I can't even see your face!'

'No leccy.' Neil took a step and disappeared

completely in the blackout. 'I got this, though.' A burst of cold light made Jess cower. Neil had powered up a battery-driven lamp, the kind campers use. It cast a frosty pall over the room. Like snow.

'I would have tidied a bit,' said Neil. 'If I'd known you were coming, like.'

The cottage was beyond tidying. It needed to be bulldozed and started over.

'Tea,' said Neil. 'Tea,' he repeated. 'I don't have none.'

'Glass of water?'

'Okay.' Neil didn't move.

A grinning face was picked out in the barren light.

Propped among cracked crockery on the dresser was a carved wooden disc. Jess took it down. She felt Neil tense, but she held it with reverence and he didn't stop her.

She knew the face. Broad features. From the eyebrows, leaves sprouted. More greenery gushed from the open mouth.

'Did you make this, Neil?'

'Granddad did. We like to talk about the Green Man.'

'Me too. There are so many theories and stories about him.'

'He looks after the woods. He cares about trees and plants and little animals and that.'

'The Christians adopted him. There's usually a representation of the Green Man among the gargoyles on old churches. But he's pagan through and through. He has more in common with Cernunnos than Jesus.'

'Who's that?'

'A shape-shifter.' Jess drew him in. 'Guardian of the

forest. He had horns, though, so the church wasn't keen on him. Horns mean, you know, *him*.' Jess motioned to the floor.

'Old Nick,' said Neil. He was warming up slightly. A warmed-up cadaver.

'Exactly. Christians are scaredy-cats. They say that the wood of the cross was grown from seeds placed under Adam's tongue as he died.'

Neil didn't respond beyond a faint shrug.

Which was odd, in a town suffering a plague of crucifixions. 'Sorry, Neil. I go on a bit, don't I?'

'S'all right. You're like the radio.'

'This carving is amazing. Are those your granddad's tools out in the shed?'

'Yeah. I don't use them. I could never be as good as him. He's a genius.'

Jess had heard her father talk about Neil's grandfather. He hadn't called him a genius. He'd said the old man was cruel. Puritanical.

'You and your granddad, you like to talk about the old ways.'

'They're not old,' said Neil. He was taken aback. 'They're all around us.'

If she lived outside of society in this godforsaken house, Jess could believe that too. She felt the isolation. She realised her mistake in going it alone. She glanced at the phone in her hand.

Neil, seemingly so inattentive, saw the look. 'The Green Man clogs the airwaves. That phone's just a lump of metal here.'

'It was sad about Gavin, wasn't it?'

'S'pose.' Neil didn't jump at the name. 'Never liked him.'

No faux respect for the dead here.

'Remember his seventh birthday party?' she asked.

'Yeah.'

'I still have nightmares about it.'

Neil looked vaguely surprised. 'Why?'

'Because, well ...' It hardly needed explaining. 'We were in the water when Becky drowned.'

'She wasn't the only one hurt that day.'

'Well, yes, somebody else cut their leg.' Jess swallowed. Steadied herself. She was at the red-hot heart of the murders, reliving a brutal fragment of the past that they both shared. He was unmoved. By Becky's little body in its sunshine-yellow swimsuit. By the people he'd crucified. 'They lived to tell the tale, though.'

'It was a rubbish party. I was only there 'cos Granddad used to work as Mr Blake's handyman. Mrs Blake didn't want me there.'

'Mrs Blake was a right old cow.' The truth was exhilarating. Jess could easily imagine Gavin's pretentious mother rubbing the scruffy kid's nose in it, implying he was lucky to be invited. 'Your granddad carved that lovely sign for the pool, didn't he?'

'Mr Blake didn't understand what granddad did. He didn't even know the lady on the sign was Hecate.'

Here I am again, whispered the goddess.

The oblivious Blakes with their new cars and their new pool and their new values had no notion of what

Granddad Semple had made for them. 'Hecate's a powerful protectress.'

'Don't get on the wrong side of her, though.'

'She'll be out there tonight,' said Jess. 'As it's Deiphon.'

When Neil lied it was obvious. 'What's that?' he said. A handful of tics gave him away.

'I bet your granddad knows. How's he keeping these days?'

'He's dead.'

'Oh, God, I'm so sorry, Neil.'

He looked insulted. As if everybody should know. 'Look.' He took down an obituary torn from the *Kidbury Echo*. 'He passed over last January.'

A scowling photograph above a paragraph or two. Jess read out his name. 'Eric Yeats Ernest Semple.'

Her backbone shivered like mercury. E. Y. E. S.

The box was being frank the whole time. Hiding the truth in plain sight.

She forgot to be subtle. 'Where do you keep your van, Neil? I didn't see it out front.'

'Don't have one.' He slammed his fist against his forehead.

Jess jumped back.

'Water,' he said. 'You wanted water.'

'It doesn't matter.'

'Things like that *do* matter. I'll get you a glass of water.' He added, 'On a tray, and everything,' as the murk of the kitchenette claimed him.

There was much banging of cupboards. 'Will a cup do?'

Jess was on her feet, flying around the room. Prying. 'Yeah, 'course.' She was looking for something. Anything. She darted looks at the kitchen as she took in a small delicate chisel lying on a mouldy Mills and Boon. Somebody had drawn a moustache on the swooning heroine. A tattered teddy bear sat on a ream of photocopier paper. A vase held plastic flowers, their colour long leached away. A blister pack of antihistamines leant on a ball of twine.

'Must get lonely out here on your own,' she called. If he spoke she could gauge where he was. Finish her snooping before he returned. 'Do you miss your grandparents?'

'I talk to them all the time.' Neil ran a tap.

'That's sweet.' It wasn't. Jess opened a drawer. Found only ballpoint pens and receipts.

'I look after the house for them.' A crack. A cup dropping and breaking. A smothered curse. 'They love this place.'

'Hmm.' A naked doll stared at Jess from inside a Tesco bag.

'That's why they're buried here.'

'Do you visit them in the churchyard?'

'No. They're buried *here*.' In the kitchen, Neil stamped his foot.

Jess looked down at the floorboards.

'Under ...? Don't you need special permission for something like that?'

'It was Granddad's idea. When he knew he was going, like.' Neil was almost – almost – bright as he sought out another cup; Jess heard him scrabbling in a cupboard. 'He told me to bury a coffin-load of bricks in the graveyard, but to put him and Nana under the house. So I did. I always do what they tell me.'

'May they rest in peace.' Jess couldn't think of anything to say that didn't end in a scream, so she reached for a handy platitude. She turned her attention to a dusty sewing box. Needles. Pinking shears.

'You won't snitch on me, will you?'

''Course not.' Jess imagined them, decaying, ghostwhite and miserable as sin, below her Doc Martens.

Neil returned with a tray. He looked at the chair, seeming puzzled that it didn't contain Jess, then found her. 'What you doing?'

She'd stopped, unable to move on. Transfixed by what she had found below a tangle of embroidery silks in the sewing box.

'You looking at my photos?' Neil put down the tray. The cup fell over. 'Them's private.'

Jess was red-handed. Red-faced.

Neil came over, took the Polaroids out of her hands. 'Have you had sex?' he said.

Jess didn't answer for a moment. Too busy panicking. 'You shouldn't really ask people that.'

'That means you haven't. I have. *Loads*.' He waved the snaps. The glossy squares were a discordant modern note in the primitive room. 'See?'

On closer inspection, the abstract swirl of colour coalesced into pornography. Close-ups of interlocking genitals. Like a manual, a how-to. Not sexy. Repulsive.

'These are private, Neil. I don't want to look at them.'

'Sex is holy.'

'Maybe. But these pictures aren't.' Jess grimaced, and she saw him flinch. His face hardened. Not a Dickensian urchin anymore; more a Dickensian thug.

'*Hieros gamos*,' he said. He was insistent. His sap was rising. 'Look. Look at me.'

She took the Polaroids. She had to. The naked flesh looked like a butcher's window. She saw glistening pubic hair. A mauve blur of genitals. A scar. A curved scar near the groin that smiled at her.

'I really should get back,' Jess said. 'DS Eden's expecting a call from me.'

He was unreadable. Neil might have believed her. *Does it make any difference when his blood's up and Hecate is about and his itch needs scratching?*

She left the house. He left with her. Matching her step for step. They passed the shed. They reached her car. She got in. Every movement deliberate. Tensed for him to shape-shift.

Please please start first time. The aqua-blue Morris Traveller behaved impeccably.

Neil knocked on the window. Jess rolled it down.

'Goodbye,' he said, like a good boy. 'Thanks for coming.'

She drove. The wheels moved. The lane met the road. She picked up speed.

Behind her, headlights.

A large vehicle in her rear mirror. Gaining on her.

She put her foot down. The speed limit was irrelevant.

The van could outpace the old car.

It came upon her like a dragon. Neil's face in her mirror.

He overtook.

He sped away.

Jess grappled with her phone. One hand on the wheel. She was going too fast. 'Rupert!' she shouted when his voicemail kicked in. 'I know you're annoyed with me but pick up. I worked it all out. The dream kept poking me. It's obvious. It's all about the pool.'

The road curved. She threw down the phone. Fought to keep control of the car.

The curved scar, like a mouth, had spoken to her.

There would be blood spilled for Hecate tonight.

Chapter 31

CHIVALRY IS NOT DEAD

Still Thursday 2nd June

Karen Knott was sleepy. She worried about her mother, and her mother's legs. Karen spent little time at home since the Rustic Ripper started his nonsense. 'It's quiet out there, guv,' she said, peeking through the slatted blind.

'Good,' said Eden. He was photocopying pages of close type. Karen's job, really.

'Not a soul about. Except for that daft woman at the bus stop.'

'On her own? During a curfew?'

'Asking for trouble, boss.' Karen squinted. 'It's that Theresa.'

'She shouldn't be out alone. Not now our man's developed a taste for women. Nip out and tell her so, Knott. Bring her in here and we'll organise a car for her.'

'I'll give her a piece of my mind while I'm at it, sir.'

'Actually, Knott, I'll do it.'

Eden's mobile rang the moment he left. Karen answered it. She was distracted, watching her superior jog along Margaret Thatcher Way. 'Eden's phone.'

'Karen? It's Jess Castle. Put Eden on. It's urgent.'

'You're breaking up. Who is this?'

'Jess! It's Jess! Eden, please. Now.'

'He's otherwise engaged.'

Across the road, Theresa was shaking her head. Pointing to the bus timetable. Wrenching away her arm when Eden tried to take it. 'Little madam,' murmured Karen. 'What hunch are you working on now, Jess?'

'It's not a hunch. Neil Semple is the killer.'

'What? You're breaking up.' Karen breathed on the window and drew her initials on it.

'He's in his van. He's going to kill someone tonight. Take down this number plate.'

'Say again?'

'B D five O K H.'

'You don't have to ring in just to say you're okay.'

'Tell Eden!'

'*Somebody's* very bossy tonight. Don't you worry, Jess. We're looking after Castle Kidbury as per. Eden's checking that Theresa's safe. Oh, hang on. Aw, isn't that lovely? Chivalry isn't dead. That daft Neil Semple's pulled up and given her a lift.'

The line cut out.

*

367

In her layby, Jess screamed at her phone.

Foot down, she flew into town.

She got lost. In her home town. She wouldn't have believed it possible, but a new development of mews houses between Gold Hill and the Keep had sprung up in her absence.

A pretty green and pink card was propped up on the dashboard. It was creased after a long sojourn at the bottom of Jess's bag.

She found the cul-de-sac she wanted. A van tore out of it, passing her at speed. Jess had a glimpse of Neil in the cab.

Her newfound certainty faltered. She hadn't expected to see the death vehicle there.

On foot, she sped past double-locked doors and windows that showed only slits of light through drawn curtains. The residents of this new street of narrow houses imagined themselves safe.

The lantern above number eight, the end house, was dead. Jess rang the bell before realising the front door was open.

'Hello?' Jess had watched countless detectives do this on television. She'd always hissed, *Don't go in, you idiot!* She understood now. Faced with an unlocked door and a dark house, there is only one way to proceed.

Nerves screeching, Jess nosed through the dark kitchen. It was at the front, in the modern style. Her eyes got with the programme and blobs firmed up into objects. Everything in its place. Kettle. Toaster. A dining table for two that pierced her heart.

'Anyone home?'

The sitting room answered her question. A lamp was shattered on the cream carpet. A cup lay on its side beneath a caved-in coffee table. Framed photographs and ornaments had leapt to their deaths from a shelving unit.

A wrecking ball had bounced through the room. Nothing was in the right place. Disorder ruled.

The lady of the house had been taken. One low-heeled shoe dropped in the struggle. Blood had been spilled on the rug. Jess stumbled in her haste to get out of there, to get after Neil's van. The crunch of glass beneath her feet disguised the gentle *thunk* of her phone landing on the floor.

A framed photograph lay under her foot.

A line of children along the side of an indoor pool. Different ages, but none more than eight. Some tiddlers in the front row.

Squinting in the sunshine. Gappy teeth.

There's me, thought Jess. *Long hair. Scowl. Itchy bikini.*

And Gavin, already handsome. Theresa next to him. Still freckled, and possibly already in love. Caroline in heart-shaped sunglasses. All of them blemish-free, almost new.

At the back, Neil was a scruffy outsider with knock knees. He didn't look evil. He looked sad.

'Hello Becky.' The smallest of them all. Only four. The black and white photo rendered her swimsuit grey, but Jess knew it was yellow.

Everybody alive. Everybody more or less okay. As soon as the photo was taken, Gavin's mother had grabbed the nearest kid to her.

Me.

Jess remembers it with the seven-year-old viewpoint of her dream. She feels the grip on her arm. Slightly too tight. She looks up at Mrs Blake. She wonders why the lady is speaking funny. Kind of loose. Her lipstick's smeared.

She's saying something about the lifeguard having to go away for a minute. 'Look after the little ones for a while, love.'

Jess is annoyed. Her fun is spoiled. There is no sense of responsibility in this memory. The little ones are fine. Playing boring baby games in the their smaller, shallow, circular pool.

There's a scream. A loud splash at the deep end. A girl has slipped on a piece of glass.

'Urgh! Blood!' shouts Gavin. He points at the red smoky shape in the pool. The girl is crying, doggy-paddling.

Jess panics. Is she supposed to do something? Is she in charge of the older children as well as the smaller ones? She lowers herself into the water.

Adults appear. The water froths as they jump in. Shouting. Screaming. Caroline is crying, but that's nothing new.

Jess is in the thick of it. She was told to keep an eye. She shunts the bleeding girl onto the tiles.

She feels pretty good. She's a bit of a heroine. She can feel the relief all around her.

The drama subsides until there's another scream and they're all looking at the small body in a yellow swim-suit. Face down. In the big pool.

Jess looked at what must be the last photo ever taken of Becky. 'I'm sorry,' she said.

Jess had been feeding her subconscious and now it roared. She listened. Obeyed. She turned and tripped, entangled in the spilled innards of an ironing basket.

On the other side of the room, her phone buzzed unheard. Rupert's caller ID.

Jess scrambled to her feet. A jumper had its woolly arms around her ankles. A penny finally dropped. 'Dry-clean only,' she shouted to the empty house. 'No bleach!'

Another photograph hung by the front door. Becky, her face close to her mother's. Jess made it a promise.

'I'm coming to get you, Helena.'

Everything was moving so fast. Small suns flew at him in the dark.

He tasted the salt on his lips and was ashamed. Tears were for babies.

It had gone too far. He could see that now. It had made such beautiful sense at first.

He couldn't think straight with all those lights.

He had let down the dead.

He had let down the goddess.

Chapter 32

What we do in The Dark

Still Thursday 2 June

Jess parked by the high wall that separated the Blakes' house from the road.

Not one car had passed her on the way. The omnipresent media shone their light elsewhere, and the old adage about there never being a policeman around when you needed one proved to be true.

Night had crept into Jess's car. She saw the plaque, by the wooden door that stood ajar. The family had finally moved out, after two tragedies. That door should be locked.

Shit, she thought. *I'm right.*

Time to put her money where her mouth was.

Panic had bit when she couldn't find her phone. There would be no cavalry for Jess. *I'm Helena's cavalry*, she thought, and stepped out of the car.

It was deathly quiet. As still as a snapshot. The

house, its sloping roof just visible above the wall, stood by the meeting of three roads.

Not a traditional crossroads, but the rarer three-way crossing, as preferred by Hecate. The meeting of the roads was where the goddess appeared at Deiphon, to collect her ritual meal.

Jess pretended to be brave, and it got her across the road. Under a signpost that pointed back to town, she could see a dim white circle. It was a paper plate. Jess stole closer. She saw a bulb of garlic and an egg still in its shell.

Myths had stayed on the page before now. Jess was looking at a ritual offering to the saffron-cloaked empress. Neil was celebrating Deiphon.

Jess hurried towards the door in the wall. She knew the story. She knew that if you looked back at the meal, Hecate became visible. Her followers, the vengeful dead, would swarm from her side and claim you as their own.

As a twenty-first-century academic, Jess studied superstition; she didn't believe it. She had to turn around and look at the plate.

Jess turned her neck. Her shoulder followed suit. But only so far.

She couldn't turn around.

The Morris Traveller waited. Jess decided to speed back to the cop shop and return mob-handed.

She heard a scream. Muffled. Female. She was through the door in the wall like a shadow.

The lawn tilted. The house was impressive. Many chimneys. Bristling with mod cons.

Beyond the house, the pool was housed in a glass box that had seemed immense to Jess as a child. A spectral half-light seeped from within. Jess climbed the lawn in a crouch.

The silence had reasserted itself, but Jess filled it with imagined kiddie shrieks and splashes. All her senses told her to run. Her feet ignored the advice. She was drawn to the glass house by duty. Compassion. A need to confront her own ghosts.

The eerie light had a banal explanation. The under-water lights were on in the pool. Jess bent lower still. She couldn't see anybody around the pool, but she clung to the safety of the shadows. This side of the glass structure included a seamless sliding door that was pulled open a few feet.

Jess scrambled sideways on the grass, so that she could squat opposite that gap and *think*. A tree reared out of the darkness. Jess knocked into it so hard she fell back. Her shoulder was sore. She looked up and saw no branches. It was a crucifix.

The cross's arms reached out. They were empty. Jess's heart began to salsa.

She saw figures in the pool house.

A woman lay in a puddle of water, as if she'd been dunked like a witch. It could only be Helena. Theresa knelt over her, hair falling over her face.

Above them stood Neil. Legs apart, he looked almost heroic. Then he aimed a glancing kick, as if trying to score a goal. The football was Helena's head.

Jess dashed through the glass gap, slithered on

the slick floor and shouted the first thing that came into her head.

'Oi!'

It worked. Neil stared. Theresa stood. Helena was up like a gazelle unexpectedly spared by a lion. She staggered though and was easily caught. Neil pulled back his fist and caught her on the side of the head with a piston punch.

The woman fell as if she had no bones. She fell against Theresa. The knife Theresa held fell too. It made a silver noise on the tiles.

A pool separated Jess from the action, both too wide to cross and not wide enough to protect her.

This was it. The red-hot centre of it all.

Chapter 33

HIEROS GAMOS

Still Thursday 2 June

'I've been expecting you,' said Theresa.

'That's a corny line, and no you haven't.' The knife by Theresa's foot seemed to glow like kryptonite. 'There're two of you, then?' She looked from Theresa to Neil and back again. 'Two psycho dipsticks for the price of one. Lucky old Castle Kidbury.'

The muted slapping of the disturbed water was a wormhole straight to Jess's nightmares. The shallow round pool was still there. So were the pearly tiles. The changing room. Why hadn't this place been knocked down?

'Little Miss Know-it-all. Or is it Ms? You look the kind who'd be bothered.'

'Call me what you want,' said Jess. 'As long as you call me.' One eye on Helena. The woman was a damp, motionless shape in the shifting light show made by the water. A dark flower blossomed on the tiles around her fair head. Jess had been guilty at times of putting the puzzle before the people; that mustn't happen here. 'Why involve Neil, Theresa? I'm assuming this was all your idea.'

Neil looked from one woman to the other, then down at Helena.

'Of course it was my idea,' said Theresa. 'Neil doesn't think. I rescued him. This town has done nothing for him. Or me. There are two Castle Kidburys. Our one doesn't have window boxes and indoor swimming pools. We don't matter. Until suddenly ...' Theresa took a bow. 'We do.'

'She's Hecate.' Neil blurted it out. 'She knows everything and she sees everything. She caused that storm after we done Shane Harper. Tonight we're going to really, you know, do it, *hieros gamos*, and I'll be a king.'

'So she controls you with the promise of sex,' said Jess. She was inching around the pool towards Neil. Despite the tough talk, his body language was reticent. As if he wanted to be elsewhere. Away from this glimmering glass tank with the shadow of a cross against the back wall.

'Poor Neil was untouched by human hand until he met me.'

'She saved me,' said Neil. When he looked at Theresa, there was something pure. In amongst the craziness and the violence and the mind games, Neil had managed to fall in love.

'It was the end of market day in the square,' said

378

Theresa. 'Kids were pelting him with rotten food. That scene never makes it into the tourism brochures, does it?'

'She took me down the woods,' said Neil. 'She kissed me. It was right lovely.'

'Don't forget the blow job,' cackled Theresa. 'I blew his mind while he burbled on about little green men.'

'The Green Man,' mumbled Neil.

'Hey, you, bitch face!' yelled Theresa. 'Get back where you was! Keep an eye on her, Neil. Do I have to do everything?'

'I recognised you in Neil's Polaroids.' If Jess could keep Theresa talking, if she could undermine Neil ... If. If. If.

'Liar. I never let him get my face in them.'

'I saw your scar, Theresa. A little crescent shape from when you slipped on broken glass at Gavin's seventh birthday party and fell into the water. I saved you.'

'Don't flatter yourself. I wasn't in that much trouble, and besides, all the grown-ups came running. It was Becky you should have saved.'

'Shut up!' That was torn out of Jess.

'We're all killers here,' laughed Theresa.

'I hated that party,' said Neil.

'I was only there because my mum cleaned for the Blakes,' said Theresa. 'As you kindly reminded me at Gavin's last concert, Jess. I fell in love with Gavin that day.'

Over a four-year-old's dead body, thought Jess. She began her slow progress again. Edging towards Helena.

'Neil!' Theresa's voice was a lash. 'Can't you see that whore trying to get to Helena?'

'Less of the whore, if you don't mind. I am, in fact, a modern female in charge of my sexuality.'

The crucifix loomed in the corner of Jess's eye.

Neil gave a whimper. 'It's all gone wrong, goddess. What do we do now?'

'Think, Neil,' said Jess. If she could get Neil onside, he might help her when it came to the crunch. 'You can get back from this.'

'Neil's mine,' snapped Theresa.

'Hear that, Neil? She reckons she owns you.'

'Tell her,' said Theresa. 'I own you, body and soul. What do we *do*, stupid? That's obvious. We make two martyrs instead of one.'

'Theresa's no goddess. It's you, Neil, who has the knowledge and the sensitivity, who respects the old ways.'

'Don't talk about her like that.'

'You do her dirty work,' said Jess. 'You drive the van. You make the crosses in your grandfather's workshop. You supplied the boxes. They're works of art, Neil.'

'Yada yada yada,' said Theresa.

'Theresa makes out she's the brains of the operation, but it's you who knows the real traditions. It's you who listens to your grandparents. You added all those little tributes to Hecate. Attacking Mary by the signpost. The crucifix at the crossroads. The market cross. Those boxes have a voice, Neil, but Theresa can't hear them. Your granddad made those boxes with such care. She didn't know his initials were on that first one, did she? Wouldn't Hecate be able to read Ogham?' She felt the weight of all the death. She felt the sadness of it all. 'Come with me, now, and we'll stop all this.'

'Why would he go with you?' said Theresa. 'What can Castle Kidbury offer him?'

Jess was stymied. She couldn't say respect; Neil had been bullied from childhood. Neither could she say a normal life; he was, she feared, beyond one. 'Neil,' she said, calm and flat, 'you have a choice to make. Make the right one.'

He wouldn't look at her.

'I could just leave.' Jess motioned behind her. 'You couldn't catch me, Neil.' She lifted a foot. 'Doc Martens. Nothing better for running away in.'

Theresa swatted that away. 'But you won't run away, will you, you bleeding heart? The moment you leave, we crucify this hedge-pig.' She poked Helena with the tip of her boot. Something about Jess's reaction must have pleased her, because she did it again. Harder.

'Bodies. Mutilation. Fear. Why?' asked Jess. 'Seriously, why?'

'Because it's time somebody stopped the straight white men,' yelled Theresa. 'They're allowed to be shit at their jobs, be mean to everybody and still have all the money and all the power. They think they run the world.'

'Keith Dike didn't run the world,' said Jess.

"No, but he stole the parish Christmas Club fund and spent it on scratch cards. The whole town turned a blind eye. Instead of putting him in jail, they put him in the paper. They *rewarded* him.'

'Are you referring to his prize marrow in the Castle Kidbury show?'

'He took up half a page! Look at Shane Harper. Left his wife and his kids and ran off with somebody half his age. Said it would rain for the last royal wedding. Wrong. Said it would snow on Christmas Day. Wrong. But he gets to be on telly every weekend.'

'You really do need to get out more, Theresa.' Jess would have laughed at the parochial nature of the men's sins if they hadn't died for them. 'Helena isn't a straight white male.'

'This one's personal,' said Theresa.

'And Mary?'

'Your tarty friend wasn't my idea. Believe me, she'd be dead if I'd been involved. Ask him.'

Neil looked ashamed. 'I did it on my own, for Hecate, because Mary stole Gavin from her.'

'Jesus, Neil, you tried to murder Mary because the woman you love was jealous of her getting off with the man *she* loved.' Layer upon layer of dysfunction; the pair were an onion of ugliness.

'But you couldn't finish the job,' said Theresa. 'Idiot.'

It was time to close the space between them. Jess began to move with purpose. One foot in front of the other. A confrontation was unavoidable. She had to gamble that Neil would help her – or at least hold back – when the moment came.

'It was an offering to you, goddess.' Neil was close

to tears. He turned to Jess. 'She *is* Hecate.' He began to shout. Shake. 'She talks to my grandparents. They tell her they're proud of me. She caused that thunderstorm.'

'Did she tell you she was going to make a storm, Neil? Or did she simply claim it afterwards?'

'She . . .' Neil's mouth quivered. 'Don't ruin it, please. This is sacred. This is important!'

'Neil, it's just murder.'

'It's Deiphon. We're going to have *hieros gamos* and I'm going to be different and—'

'Theresa has no idea what Deiphon is. Do you think she's going to stop killing? Where does it all end?'

'It ends in destruction,' said Theresa.

'Neil, you don't look happy about that.'

Theresa sighed. As if nobody *got* it. 'Neil has no need of happiness. His reason for living is to do my bidding.'

'So, let's say you kill everybody in Castle Kidbury.' Jess addressed them both. 'Then what? Do you blow up the world one picturesque market town at a time? This can only end badly for you, Neil. She'll throw you under the bus when the time comes.'

'Neil,' said Theresa imperiously, 'would follow me into the gaping jaws of Hell.'

'Why *should he* follow you into the gaping jaws of Hell?' Jess took a step along the edge of the pool. Helena had been motionless for too long.

'Theresa loves me.' Neil managed defiance.

'Jesus, Neil, wake up! Theresa doesn't love anybody. She gets her kicks putting hate into people.'

'She's a goddess!'

'She works in Poundland, but let's not quibble. Humour me, Theresa.' Jess gabbled as she drew closer to Helena. 'Why the band logo on Keith's body?'

'Don't you know love and hate are married, Jess?'

'I prefer to think of them as estranged.'

'My love for Gavin was the mirror of my hatred for everybody else. The logo was pure.'

'Like the rest of this, that logo meant nothing.'

'I'm going to enjoy crucifying you.'

Jess was six feet from Neil.

Incongruously clad in soft grey pyjamas, Helena could almost be asleep. Jess was now near enough for Theresa to fly at her. 'Why kill Helena, or me, for that matter? It's over, Theresa.'

A slow shake of the head from Theresa. She was enjoying herself.

'Theresa, I called Eden from my car. He's on his way.'

'You didn't call anybody.' Theresa was composed. 'They'd be here by now.'

'Okay, say you do kill us both,' said Jess. 'You're rumbled, anyway. I solved the puzzle on the box. The trees spoke to me.' That was true. The truth had floated to the surface. Now came a lie. 'It's all written down for the police to find.' In fact, the revelation was only in Jess's mind. A mind that might soon be making a pattern on the tiles.

Theresa twitched, staccato, like a pigeon. 'The boxes can't lead the police to me.'

'Not you, maybe.'

Theresa's shoulders came up to her ears. 'What the fuck did you do, Neil?'

Jess answered for him. 'His name is on them.'

'No, no, she's lying.' Neil backtracked. Literally. Putting space between himself and his goddess.

'It was subtle. Took me forever to work it out.' Jess burnt with the exhilaration of cracking the code. 'The trees, Neil. I've been focusing on their meanings, but I forgot that the Ogham alphabet is based on trees.' She ticked them off on her fingers. 'First was the ash, which is nion, or N, in Ogham. Then the poplar, which translates as edad. That gives us an E. The yew is idad, and lastly, we get an L from the rowan tree which, in Ogham, is luis. The trees spell out a name. Neil.'

He gaped at her.

'You want to be caught, Neil.' Jess understood at last. 'You want to be stopped.'

The silence was bulky. Theresa filled the pool room with her animus.

'Hecate, I'm sorry,' managed Neil.

'Show me how sorry you are. Kill them both.'

Neil didn't move.

'Looks like your boyfriend has finally—'

Theresa launched herself at Jess like a cat.

The heaviness of Theresa's body landing on her own was an affront that Jess felt in every inch of her. Sharp joints found soft parts. Fingernails found skin.

Having only ever fought with words, Jess wasn't prepared for the all-consuming nature of physical combat.

The floor that met her back was hard. Her skull filled

with pain. Beneath Theresa, Jess became pure instinct. A palm under Theresa's chin kept her at bay. A knee thrust upwards found Theresa's groin.

Their scrap was frantic.

Jess learnt fast. She tried to hurt, after a lifetime of trying to do the opposite. A bang on the side of her head blinded her for a moment. A punch to her stomach, although smothered by their closeness, brought vomit to her lips.

'The knife, Neil!' yelled Theresa.

He was looking into the water. Motionless as a daguerreotype.

Jess called, 'Help me.' She wondered if she'd actually spoken. All of her was intent on the struggle. Theresa was as heavy as a bag of cement. A bag of cement that squirmed and jumped.

Until there was no heaviness.

Theresa was off her, and scrambling towards the knife.

Jess made an unforced error. One she regretted in the split second she made it. Instead of scuttling away, she got to her feet and followed Theresa.

The edge of the pool was slick. Jess came down on her knee. No time for the pain to register because Theresa was upon her again. Her speed seemed diabolical.

Squatting on Jess's chest, Theresa was alive with dirty electricity.

Theresa was, Jess realised, enjoying herself.

'Did you ever wonder whether we took out the eyes before the sacrificial lambs died or after? Congratulations, Prof, you're about to find out.'

Jess exploited the time Theresa took to gloat by shooting out both hands to grab her wrist.

With no idea where such strength came from, Jess was holding back the knife. It wavered close to her face. 'Neil! Please!'

The knife a blurred silvery point above her eyeball. Sweat.

Blood rushing through her like a bullet.

Then Jess felt it. The inevitable falling away of her stamina.

Theresa felt it too. She was plugged into Jess, their battle every bit as intimate as sex. A curdled pleasure spread over her face. Jess read her own death sentence in Theresa's eyes.

The shadow of the cross disappeared. The back wall of the pool flashed blue. The expected stab didn't come.

Alert, ears pricked, Theresa sat back on her heels.

Absurdly, Jess heard Rupert. He was shouting. 'Theresa! Put the knife down!'

Shrinking, fearful of the blade, Jess turned her head. He was on the far side of the swimming pool.

A hand moved to Jess's throat. The hand closed.

'Rupert,' gasped Jess.

'The police are here, Theresa.' Rupert held both his gloved hands out in front of him. 'Be sensible, Theresa. Drop—'

A splash. A shout. Female, this time.

'Jaysus! Shut up, Rupert.'

Through failing vision, Jess saw a figure hurtle

past Rupert, knock him into the water and keep coming. At speed.

Jess could breathe. The hand had gone. She could move. The knee on her chest was gone.

A blur beside her. Mary on top. Theresa on top. Mary with her fists raised. Theresa's fingers finding Mary's eyes.

The knife was by Jess. With revulsion, she shoved it into the water.

On hands and knees she was groggy, able only to watch. Mary had skill; Theresa had fanaticism. It was an even match. Jess regretted drowning the knife.

A shape in the pool like a huge bat. The bat spoke. 'I'm coming, Mary!'

Rupert pulled himself out of the water. The bat wings were revealed to be his coat, which now clung to him, sopping wet.

He staggered.

Mary threw Theresa face down onto the tiles with such force that Jess felt the impact in her own bones.

Panting, Mary sat astride Theresa. She pulled her opponent's arms back, holding her fists like a posy.

The clatter of police. Eden's face, concerned, focused. He was as glorious as Zeus. Or Jupiter. Or Amen-Ra.

Behind him, Knott fell on her arse in a puddle.

Jess's throat burnt. Her brain teemed. Rupert's face appeared as he got down on his knees in front of her. His ebullient hair was smarmed down. He stank of chlorine. He didn't seem able to speak.

So Jess spoke instead.

'You took your bloody time.'

Chapter 34

TIT FOR TAT

Friday 3 June

Deiphon was over. The sun would rise soon, exposing and cleaning every dark nook and cranny of Castle Kidbury.

The drugs could only do so much. Jess limped, her bad knee singing, down the hospital corridor. Her head was sore. The cast on her wrist chafed already.

Hospitals never sleep. Even though it was the uncertain hour before dawn, Jess heard the clink of trolley wheels and the squeak of soft-soled shoes. She slipped into a small room. One survivor visiting another.

'Helena?' she asked softly.

'Yes. Come.' Helena was groggy. Even propped up against stiff crackling pillows, she exuded a talcum femininity which transformed the practical private room into a boudoir.

'How're you doing?' Jess sat on the side of the bed. 'I

hear they're keeping you in for observation. You were out cold for fifteen minutes or so.'

'I can never thank you enough for what you did.' Helena tried to sit up a little more.

'Stay, stay. No need to thank me.'

'But you saved my life. You risked your own.'

'You can do the same for me sometime.' Jess heard herself. This was no time for flippancy. She shut her mouth and let the woman thank her. At length.

'Three lives lost,' said Helena, finally. Her lips thinned to nothing. Her nostrils flared.

Jess recognised a kindred soul; Helena didn't want to cry in front of her. 'Neil got away. Just vanished in the scrum.' For once his cellophane demeanour had worked in his favour.

'He's not dangerous without *her.*'

Theresa had become an evil too fearsome to name. Jess hoped Karen Knott triple-checked the lock on the holding cell. 'Neil was a mash-up of victim and perpetrator,' said Jess.

'Poor confused man-child,' murmured Helena.

Jess thought of the clues nobody had picked up on. The antihistamines at Neil's godforsaken house; the wheezing monster on the hill had suffered from hay fever, not asthma. The reinternment of his grandparents beneath the kitchen floor. The pristine workshop. All there in plain sight, for the world to see. *People in pain*, thought Jess, *are the most dangerous of all.* 'Did you wonder,' said Jess, 'why I turned up at your house last night?'

Helena didn't meet her eye. 'Are you going to tell me?'

'I had no idea you were in danger. It was serendipity that I got there so soon after Theresa and Neil dragged you away. I knew it had to be them who'd taken you. I knew they were killers.'

Helena fiddled with the neck of her NHS gown.

'Still no questions, Helena? Like how did I know Theresa and Neil abducted you? Here's another one – how did I know where they'd taken you?'

'Jess, it's so late. Or is it early?' Helena managed a tired laugh. 'I need to rest, and so do you.'

'This needs to be said, Helena.' The room grew smaller. Dawn is a time for secrets. 'It wasn't a random attack. Your murder was going to be different to the others. Theresa was taking revenge on you.'

'On me? Our paths never crossed.'

'Just once they did, Helena. You murdered the love of her life.'

It was a statement, not a question, but Helena nodded. Her face found a paler colour, somehow.

'I went to your house to encourage you to confess to the murder of Gavin Blake.'

A comment of Iris's had set dominoes falling. They clicked and they clacked until the last one down had sparked a revelation.

Losing a loved one without a gentle goodbye haunts one forever.

Jess set off carefully down a thorny path. 'I remember you dropping Becky off at Gavin's party that afternoon.' Seven-year-old Jess had been hopping about in the hallway, looking for the loo, when Mrs Blake opened the door to Helena and her daughter, Becky. 'Becky was upset.'

'I never used to tell her off,' said Helena. She'd given up trying to look innocent. She surrendered to the memory. 'Never needed to. But I was tetchy that day, and Becky was moody. I'd had a huge row with my husband.' She glanced at Jess. 'Out of Becky's earshot, of course.'

That 'of course' was a sticking plaster, thought Jess. Helena would never know if her daughter heard the shouting or not.

'It was one thing after another, when usually we were so calm. She didn't want to wear her yellow cossie. She didn't want her hair combed.'

'Sounds run-of-the-mill to me,' said Jess. 'I used to hide under my bed when I saw my mum get out the hairbrush.'

'I snapped at her,' said Helena. Abrupt. As if confessing to, well, murder. She put her face in her hands. Her voice was muffled. 'I pulled her hair while I did her plaits and ... I was *glad*.'

When Helena couldn't go on, Jess digressed a little. 'I was three years above Becky at school. I remember a teacher, Miss Lee, asked Becky's class to draw their hero, and the paintings were put up in the assembly hall. There was a Postman Pat and a Spider-Man or two.' She drew down Helena's fingers from her wet face. 'Becky drew you.'

The other children noticed how close Becky was to

392

her mother. Jess had asked Harriet, 'Why can't you arrange my dinner in a smiley face like Becky's mummy does?' Harriet had suggested that perhaps Jess should go and live with this Becky's mummy if she was so wonderful.

'I dumped her at the party like a package.'

Jess didn't remember it that way, and said so. Iris had been on the money; Helena's recollection was poisoned with guilt.

'All afternoon I missed her little face. I planned our evening, how I'd make it up to her. I went to pick her up at three. That's what it said on the invite. Three.' Helena faltered again. 'I could have stayed when I dropped her off,' she said. The words were thick in her mouth. 'Gavin's mother asked did I want to hang about and have "wineypoos" with the other mums. I didn't fit in with her and her friends. They weren't my type. So I left Becky there and went home.'

Jess could hardly bear to listen. Expecting wet hair and a party bag, Helena had returned to an oddly febrile atmosphere. An ambulance. The awed, not-quite-comprehending quiet of the children gathered together like lambs by a clutch of adults. A mummi-fied shape in a blanket being brought out through the sliding glass door of the pool house. The kernel of the bad dream already knitting itself together in Jess's young head. She'd drowned many times over in her childhood bed. Its return had been a bony finger prod-ding her to remember. 'You never got to say goodbye.'

'With sickness I would have had a grace period. A

chance to hold her little body to me. Tell her I loved her.' Helena tried to describe the scope of her pain. She stuttered, made half sentences. Her arms were suddenly empty, she said. Becky's room became a museum. All the little shepherd's pies – with extra vegetables smuggled into the recipe – sat uneaten in the freezer.

Gathering herself, Helena said, 'It was hard to make sense of Becky's death. I needed, desperately, to know what happened. The Blakes . . .' After decades, it still stung. She closed her eyes. 'They wouldn't take my calls. I hammered on their door. Nothing. Other parents told me they'd drank heavily at the party, that the teenaged boy hired to keep watch on the pool was nowhere to be seen, that the kids jumped in and out unsupervised. I didn't want to blame them, Jess. It was about *knowing*. It was about Becky. About her death having meaning.'

'I heard they did all they could to avoid responsibility.'

'The inquest was obscene.' The word didn't suit Helena. 'They wriggled and told half-truths. *She* sobbed. As if she was the one who . . .' Another pause. 'I listened to Gavin's mother say how nobody would ever understand the toll it had taken on her. As if I should apologise for my daughter's rudeness in dying in their pool.'

'They broke your heart twice over.'

Helena stared. 'No, Jess. There was nothing left to break. I saw my girl reduced to a debating topic. Nobody mentioned the gap in her teeth, or the way her hair, this bit,' Helena patted the top of her head, 'would never lie flat.'

The silence allowed both women to take a deep breath.

'The verdict was misadventure. The Blakes opened champagne outside the court.'

Jess imagined the solid hate that began to calcify inside Helena as she heard the corks pop.

'I watched Gavin grow from a boy to a teen to a man. I couldn't shake the feeling that he was growing up *instead* of my Becky. Yet her death didn't touch him or his family.' Helena turned an urgent face to Jess. 'Am I wrong about that? Did my grief colour my judgement?'

Jess considered. This was a time for truth, after all, and she said, finally, 'You're not entirely wrong. Gavin never spoke about the drowning. He was shallow, unthinking, spoiled.' Speaking ill of the dead left a bad taste in Jess's mouth. 'That doesn't mean the tragedy didn't affect the family, though.'

'He was wasting a life that Becky would have grabbed with both hands.' Helena seethed, two livid points of red on her cheeks. 'That stupid band. His witless songs. Drugs. Going around as if he was a celebrity.' Her hands went to her face again. 'I do hear myself, Jess. I know how I sound. It wasn't Gavin's fault. He was seven when it happened. He was as innocent as Becky.'

'Grief does horrible things to people. My sister-in-law asked me where all your love could have gone when it didn't have Becky.'

'Tell her when it has nowhere to settle, it turns

into rage. I couldn't even *look* at my husband. I saw Becky in his face. Then I had to watch him leave and remarry, and replace our daughter with twin boys.' Helena steeled herself, sitting taller in her papery gown. 'Killing Gavin wasn't about Gavin. It was about his parents. To put them through what I went through.'

Jess understood the motive. She understood the timing; the Rustic Ripper murders were the perfect cover to bereave the Blakes and get away with it. The *how* was more tricky. 'How did you manage the murder on your own? You're so petite.'

'You know those urban myths about mothers lifting parked cars when their child is trapped? They're not myths. I read about a woman who faced down a polar bear. Some lady in Texas bit off a dog's ear to get it away from her toddler. The truth?' Helena shrugged. 'It was easy.'

She followed Gavin after the Baldur gig at the Druid's Head. 'To your house, Jess.' A vigil in her car was rewarded with Gavin dawdling out some hours later. 'I jumped out, opened the bonnet, peered into it. Gavin wandered over. Still tipsy. Post-coital smugness on his face. Asked me if I'd broken down.'

'Surely he recognised you?'

'Not a flicker. I relied on his self-absorption and he didn't let me down.' Gavin hadn't seen the tragic mother. He saw a middle-aged woman, unfuckable and therefore unworthy of his interest. 'He didn't even notice I was wearing a workman's boiler suit. I burnt that later, in the spa incinerator.'

The car was easily mended and Gavin accepted her offer of a lift.

'He made it easy for me by falling fast asleep in the passenger seat. Didn't even need to use the sedatives I'd had such trouble getting hold of. I parked up in the churchyard and popped on my latex gloves.' Helena looked at her hands. 'The same ones I use for colonic irrigation.'

Nice, thought Jess.

'He didn't know a thing.' Helena was firm; this sounded important. 'Never opened his eyes.' She'd practised stabbing, she told Jess, with a Waitrose chicken. 'It wasn't the same.'

'You put him on St Agatha's crucifix because you couldn't build a cross yourself.'

'I can't even hang a picture, never mind make a cross. It took hours to manoeuvre his dead weight up there. It felt so blasphemous, posing him over Jesus like that.' Helena described the macabre dance. Pressed indecently close to the cadaver. Huffing and panting. 'I kind of propped him against Our Lord, then wound the rope around his neck, pulled it tight, then held on to him while I reached out to lasso his hands. It was touch-and-go, but I had to finish what I started.'

'And the eyes?'

'That was the worst part.' Helena surprised Jess by imitating the *schlurp!* the eyes made as they popped out. 'I almost threw up, but I held it in. The DNA would have implicated me.'

'How did you know about the eyes in the first place?

Eden was rabid about keeping details from the public.'

'I have Paul Chappell to thank for that.' Helena, who'd lived alone, carefully tidy and self-sufficient since Becky's drowning, had stuck a toe in the dating waters. 'A silly website matched me with the editor of the *Echo*. I had lunch with him two days after the first murder.'

Jess imagined the scene. Paul Chappell must've thought all his birthdays had come at once. A comb-over and a terrible suit sitting at a bistro table with a fragrant, carefully accessorised beautician.

'Paul's a lovely chap, but we had nothing in common. I could tell he'd made an effort, poor man.' In a last-ditch effort to impress, Paul had boasted that he knew 'official secrets' about the case on everybody's lips. 'He reckoned there'd be more murders. I was only politely interested, but he told me about the eyes. The engraved box. Something clicked. An idea. How I could use this for cover and finally put into practice the fantasy that had been sustaining me for years.'

Jess imagined the making of excuses, the lunch cut short. Paul deflated and alone and paying the bill.

'Trying to decide which symbol to use flummoxed me. What do I know about pagan whatnots? I just used the first emblem I saw. A plain little circle.'

They said it together.

'Dry-clean only.'

Jess saw that symbol every single day on her clothes and yet hadn't made the connection.

'That looked vaguely supernatural. So I just carried

on, you know, *carving* them. No steam iron. Dry-clean on low heat. Do not wring.'

'Did it help? Did killing Gavin ease your pain?'

'Not even a little bit.' Helena tipped her head back. Jess saw her eyes fill with tears she wouldn't allow to fall. 'It was cruel. He was their only child. You should have let Theresa crucify me.'

'Never. Becky would never have forgiven me.'

'Do you think,' said Helena, 'that you'd be friends?'

When Jess thought of Becky, it was of a cipher; the name equalled death. It was time to lie. And lie well. 'I *know* we would.'

Jess held Helena. Daylight had claimed the room. This moment was over. 'There's somebody here to see you.'

Helena settled her hair. Sat back. Laced her fingers in her lap.

Jess let Eden in and left them to it.

Out in the corridor her legs wobbled. Her wrist itched. Tears threatened.

Lift doors opened. Rupert stepped out.

'Drive you home, miss?'

$$\text{IIII} \quad \perp \quad \text{IIIII} \quad \text{IIII}$$

I don't want to be bad.

Chapter 35

TOWARDS AN ENDING

Saturday 4 June

A kitchen should be busy. It's the engine of the house. In Harriet's day – her name was already a byword for an era, like the Georgians, or the Tudors – Harebell House's kitchen had whirred and ticked.

Today, it approached Harrietian standards.

Bogna was making sausages. Jess couldn't bear to look. Moose patiently pimped his cracked tennis ball to Kuzbari, who was accepting a coffee from the Judge. Josh was whistling cheerfully to himself, sitting back and manspreading on a wooden chair. Iris smoked in the doorway. Liminal. Hecate-like.

There was no curfew on the soft evening drifting through the garden beyond the windows. No eyes were being gouged out. No crucifixes sprouted in the green green grass of home.

Jess stroked the grain of the table and listened to Kuzbari as he leant against a cabinet.

'Now that it's finally happening, things are moving fast.' When the Judge had asked Jess to help with his cufflinks, he'd been on his way to talk to some old friends at the Foreign Office. 'If all goes well, my mother will be here, safe and sound, by the end of next week.' This prospect had worked like a facelift on Kuzbari. His skin shone. A burdened, sad look that Jess had thought inherent was gone from his eyes.

Bogna budged both men out of her way and piled a string of fat bangers into a plastic bucket. She waved a sausage in the Judge's direction. 'He pulls strings, isn't it?' She loved to show off her slang. 'All these high-up men. Old boys' network. Nudge nudge wank wank.'

'However you managed it, whatever strings you pulled, James,' said Kuzbari, '*Shokram*, my friend. *Shokram* from the bottom of my heart.'

Gratitude made her father fidget, so Jess said, 'I can't wait to meet your mum.'

'She is ... interesting,' said Mr Kuzbari.

The diplomacy made Jess even more keen. 'And your wife? Will she come and join you at some point?'

'We'll see.' More careful diplomacy.

The pointed look Bogna threw Jess over the sausages was ignored. The pharmacist's looks and demeanour had been commented on by the housekeeper. More than once.

Almost tripping over Moose's ball, Kuzbari approached Jess. 'May I?' He flourished a pen.

She held up her left forearm, its plaster sleeve already dingy. Jess angled it so he couldn't read Mary's 'Get

402

well soon you old slag!!!' He signed with a flourish below the neat 'Rupert J. Lawson QC'.

'We'll miss you, Jess,' said Kuzbari, dotting the i.

'You won't,' said Jess. 'Your mother will keep you busy.'

'Where are you going?'

'Don't ask!' advised Bogna. 'Some mad little plan in that big brain, eh?' She tapped Jess on the fringe with a sausage.

'I have to set my life going again. Like a gold watch,' said Jess.

Iris regarded Jess through a haze of violet smoke. 'Wherever you go, Jess, you take yourself with you.'

'I haven't thanked you for helping me discover that Helena murdered Gavin.'

'Little old me?' drawled Iris. She was wearing a linen shift that would look like a bin bag on Jess.

'You and Susannah. Comments you made about love and loss. I must thank her too.'

'Don't expect her to understand what you mean. Mark my words, as James would say, the next drama in this family is that marriage.'

'I won't be around to watch,' said Jess. While there was a puzzle to solve, she'd been useful. 'I can't stand by and watch the triumphant return of Pan. They're saying he won't even do jail time for the drugs.'

'The papers,' said the Judge, 'are calling him a martyr for the way the police fingered him for the murders.'

'I wouldn't worry about Pan,' said Iris. 'A prominent member of the Women's Institute owns Pitt's Field.

She'll have him evicted and the rest of the WI will run him out of town. They're more ruthless than the SS.'

'Let's not talk about him.' Jess felt tainted by her runins with Pan. 'It'll be good to put some miles between him and me.'

'And Rupert?' Iris spoke quietly, drawing her in.

'I can do without him,' said Jess. 'We've only known each other for a few weeks, after all.'

'Lives change in the blink of an eye.' Iris was watching her great-niece closely.

Pretending not to notice, Jess stared out at the line of trees that marked the edge of the Judge's fiefdom. She recognised a poplar. 'I spent days agonising about the meaning of the trees on the first box,' she said. 'In the end they were being absolutely straightforward and I was meeting them with complexity.'

'You've lost me, darling. Is it a metaphor for you and Rupert?'

'Maybe.'

Bogna dropped a sausage on the floor.

'Leave it!' called Jess. 'It belongs to Hecate now.'

'No, it belongs to Moose now,' said the Judge. 'Not like you to be superstitious, Jessica.'

'Superstitions evolved to help people. It would be dangerous in less hygienic times to eat something that had fallen on the ground.'

Bogna was steely. 'Are you saying my floors aren't clean?' She pointed at Josh, who jumped. 'In front of a lord?'

A voice from the garden curdled all the blood in the

room. Even Moose jumped at Patricia Smalls' cry of 'Yoo-hoo! Only me!'

The Judge had time to say, 'Sometimes one misses the curfew,' before the mayoress was among them.

'You don't mind me coming round the side and letting myself in? I'm practically family, after all. Mmm! What's that lovely smell.'

'I make sausage,' shouted Bogna, slamming the larder door.

'Oh.' Patricia, who held a small dense cake on a footed plate, revived her expression. 'How charming!' She noticed Josh and curtsied. Her knees cracked as she got up, and Josh's already red cheeks turned a deeper hue. 'Lord Kidbury, I daresay you're here to celebrate James's news. I dashed here the moment I heard.'

'Dad's news?' Jess looked to her father.

'I don't have any,' said the Judge.

'You're going to have an operation, dear. I heard it from my ex-cleaner's brother's sister's girl who works at the health centre.'

'Oh. *That*,' said the Judge. 'Wouldn't call that news.'

'I made this humble offering to mark the occasion.' Patricia held up the cake reverently with both hands.

Bogna got there first. 'This does not mean he can stuff face with sugary shit.' With one deft movement she slid the fruit cake into the bin and handed back the plate.

Jess longed to applaud. Kuzbari, who had better manners, asked the fuming Patricia what was going on at the old library. 'I see the think space is boarded up.'

'No definite article, all one word,' said Patricia. 'I'm

glad you asked. I'm planning something that will make the Castle Kidbury brand shine even more brightly. A soft play centre.'

'Aw,' said Bogna, indulgent. 'Nice for the kiddiewinks, isn't it?'

'That's just it!' Patricia Smalls was triumphant. 'It's soft play for adults.'

Jess imagined it. It sounded like a lot of fun. It also sounded like the trumpet that heralds the end of life as we know it.

'There's a real proper celebrity lined up to open it this time. Nic Lasco.'

'The chef?' Jess was genuinely impressed. 'The one with his own show where he teaches regular schmucks to cook? He's sex on legs.'

'I prefer a Nigel Havers type myself,' said Patricia. 'Mr Lasco will be here to film some dreadful reality show, but I'll exploit him for all he's worth. You'll come, James, won't you, to the soft play? We can have a good bounce together!'

The Judge had no answer to that. Kuzbari, hiding a snigger, jumped as Patricia poked him. 'And you! You can chase me down the padded slide!'

The back door opened and gave them Mary.

'Does nobody,' murmured the Judge, 'use the front door anymore?'

Warm. Radiant. Slightly drunk. Mary complimented Bogna's sausages and told Patricia Smalls she was looking 'hot'. 'You the lord?' she asked Josh. 'Fair play to you, Joshy boy.' As Moose lifted his paws to her shoulders, Mary lifted her chin in Jess's direction. Her black eye was in full pomp, and she'd done up the other eye to match its peacock colours. 'Ready?'

'Just about.' Jess stood and herded up her phone and her keys and her bag. 'We're meeting Eden at the Seven Stars, Dad,' she explained. 'For what he tells me is the traditional lock-in whenever they wrap a case.'

'Eddie will be in his element. Give him my best.'

'Will do, Dad.'

'Before you dash off, do you have a moment?'

She did.

Jess followed the Judge to his study. He sat behind his desk, then seemed to reconsider and perched on the edge. 'You didn't have that dream this morning, Jessica.'

'No. Do you mind if we don't talk about this, Dad?'

'We must talk about it.'

'You don't know what happened at that party.' Jess hadn't answered Helena's confession with one of her own.

'I do. I was there.'

'I don't remember you being there.'

'You were seven, Jess. You saw what a child sees. I think it might require some interpretation for you. The Blakes had a horrible marriage. Drank far too much, the pair of them. Especially her. So keen to impress. By the time we got there, there was plenty of booze sloshing around. Didn't feel like a kiddy party at all. Mrs Blake was dancing on a table, her make-up sliding all over her face.'

'Like a clown,' said Jess.

'That's what a child would think, yes. The lifeguard had been hand-picked by her. No experience, just a muscly teen from Richleigh. One of the mums saw what happened. Mrs Blake was, how can I put this, *kissing* him rather enthusiastically. Then she shoved him into the changing room, set down her empty glass and grabbed the nearest child. You, Jess, were the nearest child.'

Jess remembered the fingers around her skinny arm. The odd looseness of Gavin's mum's face and voice and the wobbly head. It had scared her then; now she'd recognise drunkenness.

'We heard screams. We saw blood on the tiles. We saw long hair streaming. I thought ... Mum sent me off for a whisky to calm me.'

'You thought I'd fallen in?'

'When in fact you saved the day.'

'You freaked out because you thought I'd fallen in?' Jess didn't want to skim over that.

'Is that so unbelievable?'

Jess and her father regarded one another.

'Listen to me,' he said. 'Jessica, when that woman asked you to look after the others, she was in the wrong. She had no right to load that responsibility onto your narrow little shoulders. The duty of care was hers. Just because you happened to be standing in the wrong place at the wrong time does not make you responsible for Becky's death. The pool was full of people. Nobody noticed the poor girl. We all share regrets, but nobody would blame a seven-year-old child.' The Judge patted Jess's arm. Awkwardly.

She tingled at his touch. She wanted to cry. 'Except me, Dad. I blame myself.'

'Am I a clever man, Jessica? Have I made many difficult decisions in my career and influenced many lives?'

'Um, yeah.'

'My word carries weight. My judgement on that frightful day is this; you are absolved.'

'I'll visit, Dad, when you've had the operation.'

'Don't make promises you might not keep.'

'Dad,' she said as they both stood, 'thanks.'

The lack of guilt was like a new coat; Jess would have to get used to it. She was a little dazed when they returned to the kitchen. She would have welcomed the chance to cry; she would have liked to cry into her father's shirt.

She noticed him blowing his nose energetically. They'd had a moment. She would treasure it. There might not be another.

'Judge, what plans do you have for that auld barn out the back?' Mary asked.

'Plans? Only some vague notion of using it to bath Moose. Why?'

'I'd be happy to tart it up for you. A lick of paint. Connect the electrics. Put in a bog, et cetera et cetera.'

'It's been neglected for years.' The Judge's brows drew together. 'Spiders. Damp. Full of junk.'

A model of disingenuousness, Mary said, 'I'll manage. You can pay me back by letting me live in it, if you like.'

Blindsided, Jess stood with her bag over her shoulder. Why did Mary want to stay in this backwater?

When the Judge spoke it was in a voice higher than his usual thoughtful baritone. It was the only voice he had to talk about his wife. 'Harriet used to daydream about doing something with the barn. Making it pretty. Didn't she, Jess?'

There was a question beneath the question. Jess recalled his pooh-poohing of her mother's whimsies. Doing up the barn. Turning a vintage caravan into a sewing room. Taking in exchange students. Jess readily translated her father's code. He was acknowledging that he had stifled Harriet with his disapproval.

Jess smiled a reprieve. 'What my dad's too polite to say, Mary, is that you can't barge in and claim the barn as your own without even—'

'Splendid idea, Mary.' The Judge was over-adamant. 'Do us all good to have some youthful enthusiasm about the place. Do what you like with the draughty old place. I give you carte blanche.'

Jess stared.

Mary leapt. The Judge's arms stayed stuck to his sides as she smothered him.

'You're a diamond, Jimmy boy!' She put her hand to her mouth. 'Shit. I forgot.' Her expression darkened. 'I ran into Eden.'

'And?'

'It's Neil.'

'What's Neil?' Jess was impatient.

'He's dead. Hanged himself.'

Jess froze. Another death. Patricia Smalls rolled her eyes. Bogna shook her head.

'There was a note.' Mary was subdued, with the Irish respect for bad news. 'Eden didn't tell me what it said, but apparently it was only six words long.'

Kidbury Road.

The bridge.

The long-stay car park.

The medical centre.

The vet's.

And then the long turn into the main thoroughfare.

The last journey.

The sameness of the route didn't irritate Jess anymore. It was comforting. A nice little furrow she could follow without thinking too hard. From now on she would travel without a map.

A Seven Stars lock-in. Late. Loose. Castle Kidbury unlaced its corset after weeks of fear. Laughter slightly too loud. The fairy lights over the bar fuzzy and bright.

Rupert was back to his groomed self. He smelt of Penhaligon aftershave, not chlorine. 'Cheers!' He clinked his glass of definitely-not-house-white with Jess's Coke.

'Cheers yourself, Rumpole. Gotta wee.' Jess stood up.

'Ever the lady.'

In the toilet, Jess encountered Mary. And Moose.

'Jaysus, the lack of talent in this pub should be punishable by law.' Mary hoicked up her combat trousers and checked her teeth in the mirror.

'What about Squeezers?' Jess competed with the whine of the hand dryer. Moose looked at it, weighing up whether it was a threat to his women. 'He'd be a tender, inventive lover.'

They both laughed. And then they both felt bad. They both said, at once, 'Poor Squeezers.'

Jess had bugged Eden once more, earlier that day, about the police harassment of Squeezers. She might as well, she'd thought; she'd soon be gone and her stock was high on the back of the arrests. 'Get Beefy Dave off Squeezers' back,' she'd said, hotly.

Eden had lowered his voice, drawn her into his office. 'Beefy Dave doesn't exist.'

'He does,' Jess had insisted.

'Have you ever seen him?'

'No, but that doesn't mean anything.'

'Squeezers isn't just some dotty little fellow who adds colour to Castle Kidbury. The poor man has serious mental health issues. I've spoken to social services on his behalf, but they can't help him if he won't cooperate. If I arrest him regularly he gets a night in a warm cell and a square meal.'

Jess had been chastened. 'I've been accusing you about him since I got back.'

'Like I said, Jess. It's all under control.'

It was good to know.

As they braved the bar together, Mary whispered, 'You look at Rupert's mouth when he talks. That's a dead giveaway, sister.'

A corner table came to life. 'Here she is!' Doug half-stood. 'Our amateur sleuth!' His bow tie had come undone. 'Brava, Jess!'

Richard raised his glass. Graham, his nose red and his expression petulant, had to be nudged to do the same.

'We saw you being interviewed on Sky News,' said Richard.

'Oh God, did you?' Jess had been accosted as she left the hospital. 'Did I make any sense?' She hadn't mustered the courage to watch her performance.

'You made perfect sense, my darling,' said Doug.

'Looked awful, though,' slurred Richard. 'I said to you, Doug, didn't I, poor cow looks *dreadful.*'

An arm squeezed Jess's shoulder. She was pulled against a capacious and warm bosom. Meera said, 'Hey, be nice to this lady. She might have saved your lives.'

Jess leant her head on Meera's shoulder. It was that sort of shoulder.

Graham said, 'Who'd bother killing Richard?'

'Me!' said Doug. 'If it meant I didn't have to listen to Lloyd Webber ever again.' He narrowed his eyes at Jess. 'You didn't come in for your shift yesterday.'

'Doug!' Meera was sharp. 'She fended off two serial killers. Give the girl a break.'

'Harriet,' said Richard, 'wouldn't let a little thing like mass murder get in the way of her loyalty to the shop, that's all I'm saying.'

Meera gave Jess a friendly shove. 'Go, love. Leave these idiots to their crème de menthe.'

It felt like a boozy last supper. This time, Jess could leave Castle Kidbury knowing she'd done something worthwhile.

Rupert seemed a long way away. The Seven Stars was a quicksand of people reaching out to say congratulations, or well done, or God you looked knackered on Sky News.

In full WAG armour, eyebrows like mouse skins and foundation the colour of the sun, Carli was wrapped around Ryan. 'Hey, Jess,' said Ryan. 'Top bird.'

Turning from the bar, a glass in each hand, Luis Unthank said, 'Happy now? I've been dumped. We were in love and now it's over because of the police dragging me in all the time.'

'Dumped? But you're married.'

'She knew. She understood. It's complicated.'

Mary said, 'I heard she didn't know about the baby. That's what got you dumped, mate.'

'Tell me,' said Jess as Luis downed his beer in one, 'why Hellcat?'

'That's my wife's nickname for me.' Unthank smirked. 'In bed.'

Yuk. 'And the strophalos?'

'The what? On my card? Just a striking image I nicked from the internet.'

There I go again, thought Jess. *Joining dots that aren't even there.*

Somebody jostled her and apologised. It was Tallulah, dragging Danny along in her wake.

'You caught the murderer,' said Danny, as he passed.

'I kind of did,' agreed Jess.

Rupert had guarded her seat. 'You're a celeb.'

'You were in the paper too, Rumpole,' said Jess.

'They didn't print my picture because I'm not a pretty laydee.'

'Did I ever thank you for rescuing me?' asked Jess.

'I wouldn't call it rescuing—' Rupert stopped short. 'Actually, I would. I *did* rescue you and, *no*, you haven't thanked me.' He sat back. Waiting.

'Is that . . .? It bloody well is!' Jess jumped up. 'How has Pan got the nerve to show his face?'

'Hey, hey, easy!' Eddie lifted a tray of empties over his head as Jess barged past. 'What's that look on your face, Jess? No trouble tonight, not at a lock-in.'

'I need to tell Pan he's not wanted.'

'I get it,' smiled Eddie to the back of her head. 'You come back and you solve *all* Castle Kidbury's problems? Be careful, Jess.'

'S'cuse me, Squeezers.' Jess pushed past him. At their feet, Moose bumped noses with Darling.

'You haven't seen me.' Squeezers tapped the side of his nose.

'Well, I *have*.'

'I'm on a secret mission. No, don't give me the third degree!'

'I'm not interest—'

'All right I'll squeal! Beefy Dave wants me to kidnap a member of the royal family.' Squeezers shrank back, his dingy colouring a perfect camouflage in the wood-heavy pub.

Over by the quiz machine, it was business as usual for Pan. In a T-shirt bearing the slogan '#1 SUSPECT', he commanded the attention of two long-haired, crop-topped, prettier-than-they-knew teenage girls. As Jess drew closer, she heard his self-righteous drone.

'The state, you see, can't handle my realness. I'm, like, on this level.' Pan held his hand above his head. 'They're, like, down here.' He bent down, touching the floor. 'You damsels, you vessels of light, you're way more clever than the so-called leaders.'

The girls tee-hee'd. Hair was flicked.

'I'm a bad boy, you see.' Pan's eyes had stars in them. Dark stars.

'That's true.' Jess barged in, a black exclamation mark among the sugary girls. 'This boy's so bad he has herpes.'

The girls looked at each other and melted into the crowd.

'Don't you know when you're not wanted, Pan?'

'I *am* wanted, petal. By you, if you'd stop fighting it.' Pan's grin was a scythe. 'Give in. Undo that chastity belt.'

'Where are your followers?' Jess made a play of looking high and low. 'Oh gosh. They've all gone. Seen through you and scarpered. Without them you're just a man who's slightly too old for his tight black trousers.'

'There are plenty more where they came from, my sexy little sleuth. Always a rich crop of fucked-up middle-class girls to harvest. I'm doing a public service. I should be available on the NHS.' He leant down, almost nose to nose with Jess. 'You know how it goes, Jess. I take up the slack for all the stern daddies and their struggling little girls who grow up not sure if they're loved or not.'

She drew back. 'I hear you're being evicted at last. No-more times has arrived, just like you said.'

'You heard wrong. I bought the lease to Pitt's Field. Here to stay, my deario.'

'What did you buy it with? Magic beans?'

'My last loyal and faithful disciple sorted out all the sordid money stuff. Here she comes now.'

Caroline didn't make eye contact with Jess as she handed Pan a pint.

'You're *joking*, Caro. You bought the field?' Jess persisted until her old friend gave in and looked at her.

'You don't understand.' Caroline was sullen.

'You're right, I don't. Where's Delphi?'

'There.' Caroline gestured downwards. Delphi, nose runny, clothes jumble-sale, was curled up on the pub carpet. Caroline lowered her chin. 'I'm number one, now. Not number three.'

'Only because numbers one and two had the good sense to get the hell out. Caro, please!'

'Don't call her that. You're not friends anymore.' Pan pulled Caroline to him. 'I'm all she needs. We're rebuilding. We are conduits to the supernatural, the pagan.'

Jess said, 'Actually, come to think of it, it's weird that we should have this conversation on the feast day of Sala.'

'Just what I was thinking,' said Pan.

'Sala, the Wolf of Love. Offspring of Viggo and Serkis.'

'The Wolf of Love!' Pan threw back his head and

417

howled. Heads swivelled. Eddie popped up above the crowd, alert for trouble. 'I celebrate his feast day every year.'

'Caroline,' said Jess, leaning in. 'Sala, Viggo and Serkis are three of the actors in *Lord of the Rings*.'

'Bitch.' The word struck Jess as she turned away.

A glass was pressed into her hand.

'On the house.' Eddie winked as he passed. 'Only Coke. It should be champagne. Good work, love.'

Eddie never gave anybody a drink on the house.

Except me, thought Jess. She swam back towards Rupert. Towards the back of his head. It was distinctive, with its chipper hair.

'See you tomorrow?' Moyra's flushed face was in Jess's. 'For your usual? A nice hot chocolate and a natter.'

'No, Moyra.' Jess thought of her one pathetic bag, sitting packed on the rug by her bed.

Concerned, Moyra opened her mouth to say something. The women locked eyes. She thought better of it. Patted Jess's arm instead.

As the throng finally parted and delivered Jess to Rupert, Mary sprang up from his lap. 'Here you go. Just keeping him warm for you. Me and Moose are off to the Druid's Head. Better class of bloke there, by which I mean worse, if you see what I mean.'

Jess did, and wished she didn't. 'Mary.' She followed her to the door. 'Why are you staying in Castle Kidbury? I don't get it.'

'You don't, do you, you eejit. This place is gas now

the serial killers are gone. People travel the world to find a town like this, and it's your home. You do what you like, but I'm staying put.' She took Jess's chin in her hand. 'I do love you, you wassock,' she said, and kissed her on the forehead. Moose barked. Mary whooped. They were gone.

'Over here!' The designated coppers' table was by the door.

'Here she is!'

'Cheers, Miss Marple!'

It was the fag end of the evening. They were all past their sell-by date. Except for Detective Constable Karen Knott. Crisp in chain-store jeans. Sipping a sherry. A daring dot of lipstick. 'You broke every rule in the book,' she said. 'Next time you might not be so lucky.'

'There won't be a next time.' The Morris Traveller was filled up with petrol. A note to the Judge had been written, with a PS for Bogna.

'I still think Squeezers had something to do with—'

'Shush, Knott!' Eden stood up. He was tipsy. Just a touch; his tie was undone. This was tantamount to a state of undress.

Jess perceived a distance between John Eden and the rest of the boys in blue. He wasn't one of the guys.

'Helena's been refused bail,' he said.

'Shit. Why? She's hardly a threat to the community.'

'You say that, Jess, but she crucified a neighbour.' Eden rubbed the back of his head. The hair fluffed up. This would not happen if beer had not been taken. 'I wish there was something I could do for her, but my part's over.'

'A tragedy twenty years in the making. Four lives ended.'

'And many more ruined. A murder,' said Eden, swaying slightly, 'is a pebble dropped in a puddle. The ripples last forever.' He seemed as surprised as Jess at this foray into philosophy. He downed a squat glass of something yellowish. 'Time to reintroduce myself to my house.'

'I can't imagine you at home.' Jess tried. Armchair. TV. Nest of tables. Nope. 'You're a copper through and through.' She smiled. She would miss him. 'A *good* copper.'

'Maybe.' The whites of Eden's eyes were pink. He slurred slightly when he said, into her ear, 'But you're the real deal, Jess.' He pulled away, brushing her arm with his hand. 'You read people. You *get* stuff.' He paused to sigh. 'You have solid-gold instincts.'

'What happened to Mr Procedure? Isn't policing about science and footwork and putting the hours in?'

'Police work, yeah.' A sober Eden would never say 'yeah'. 'Mysteries, though, need intuition. Don't quote me, but you're a natural, Jess Castle.'

He said goodnight. He left.

Jess pushed people out of her way and grabbed Rupert by the arm. He spilled his drink. She dragged him outside.

Chapter 36

THE HANDS ON THE CLOCK
GO ROUND AND ROUND

Early hours of Sunday 5 June

If the stone circle was a clock, Jess and Rupert were the hands. They lay at a slight angle to each other. Quarter past two, their bodies said.

Which was about the correct time.

On the car journey to the sacred spot, Jess had realised that Rupert was drunker than she'd thought. A non-drinker, she was used to the strange acceleration in a companion's intoxication. At some point in an evening out, she would diverge from them. They would laugh at bad jokes. Lust after unpicturesque strangers. Sing.

Rupert wasn't quite at that stage. He was soft-eyed. Merry. Likely to say more than he should.

'So,' he said, as they looked up, their gaze penetrating

421

millions of light years into the navy sky. 'Sooooo ...'
Rupert drew out the word until it sounded absurd.
They both laughed. 'So,' he repeated, keeping it short.
'Mary's decided to hang around.'

'No accounting for what Mary does.'

'Yeah, so, well.' Rupert swallowed audibly. 'I
s'pose ... I mean ...'

'Are you this eloquent in court?'

'Do you ... us ... is this ...'

'Spit it out, Rumpole.'

'You sure you want me to? Do you really want me
to spit it out, Jess?'

'Up to you.'

There was no sound except the rustles and whispers
of the night closing in on itself.

Could Rupert feel the charge in the earth? Jess's
body hummed. She had read many theories about stone
circles. Most concerned energy. The ancients believed
the circles harnessed it, that the stones bounced it back
and forth. Growing. Redoubling.

Jess could only look sideways at the possibility that
the electric charge was one she and Rupert brought
with them. That their silence fed it.

Finally, Rupert spoke. 'Moose did a poo right by the
billiard table.'

Jess was relieved at the change of subject. She was
also insanely disappointed. 'He knows better than that,
the naughty boy.'

They talked of Moose's manners. Of the chances –
high, they agreed – that Mary had pulled by now. Of

the amazing-ness of the moon. Rupert didn't return to the train of thought that had run off the rails.

The energy waned.

'Are you damp?' Rupert tutted. Stood up. Swatted at his backside. 'I'm damp. Sodding grass. We should make a move, Jess.'

She stayed put. Stretched out. Hands behind head. Eyes closed. Moonbathing. 'Maybe I should stick around for a bit. For Dad. Work out what's up with Stephen. Help Mary with the stupid barn.'

Somehow, she could hear Rupert's grin.

He lay back down. He whistled 'Wooden Heart'.

The energy began to thrum again.

Jess smiled up at the moon. *I'm a natural*, she thought. *I'm a bloody natural.*

Acknowledgements

So many people are involved in the creation of a book. We want especially to thank Jo Dickinson, for leaping on the idea and asking only, 'How fast can you give me three chapters?' Jo, you are the epitome of an editor and you are appreciated in these particular writers' garret.

Sara-Jade Virtue, you're the best. No, shut up. You are.

Writers know what other writers need when it comes to encouragement and support and commiseration, and we get all those from Kate Furnivall, Chris Manby, Penny Parkes, and Lucy Dillon. Civilians who figure high in our List of Gratitude include Kate Haldane, Bogna Rasmussen, Sonia Lopez-Freire, Steve and Jozette Lee, and Tim Payne.

And you. The reader. Without whom this would all be for nothing. Thank you.